The Difference Between Us

An Opposites Attract Novel

Rachel Higginson

The Difference Between Us
An Opposites Attract Novel

Rachel Higginson

Copy Editing by Amy Donnelly of Alchemy and Words
Cover Design by Caedus Design Co.

Other Romances by Rachel Higginson

The Five Stages of Falling in Love (Adult Second Chance Romance)

Every Wrong Reason (Adult Second Chance Romance)

Bet on Us (NA Contemporary Romance)
Bet on Me (NA Contemporary Romance)

The Opposite of You (Opposites Attract)

To Katie,
Without whom I would have lost my mind.
Here's to Jazzercise, future communes,
and the Big F'er!

Single, single, double for life.

Chapter One

I walked into the meeting fifteen minutes late.

That's when the murders began...

Just kidding!

Nobody was murdered. Nobody did any murdering for that matter. It was only our weekly planning meeting, held every Monday at four o'clock, rain or shine, blizzard or earthquake, or zombie apocalypse. Because that was how my dinosaur of a boss rolled.

Every Monday at the same time, the entire staff of SixTwentySix Marketing gathered together in the sleek conference room eight stories above downtown Durham and went to war. Or that was what it felt like. My boss, Mr. Tucker, or Mother Tucker as I liked to call him, presided over the meeting at the head of the table. His firm fist pounded like a gavel as my colleagues and I battled over coveted accounts and lead positions while skillfully dodging less lucrative projects.

Because I was a minnow in a sea of sharks, guess who always ended up with the dud accounts?

A family insurance firm is in need of a new logo? Something updated and eye-catching, but also a straight-up replica of the same one they've used for eighteen years? I'm your girl.

A family dental office hoping to pull in new customers with some flashy social media graphics? Yep, I'm all over it.

A dinky Baptist church that basically needed someone to explain PowerPoint to them? Watch out world, I can explain the hell out of PowerPoint.

Which was basically what the pastor had asked me to do. "Please get Satan out of this program so we can use it on Sunday mornings."

I was pretty much the go-to girl for all things boring and uninspired. But it paid the bills, and I had high hopes of moving up one day. For now, I was ~~somewhat~~ happy to pay my dues. I'd start with logos and promo pics, so that tomorrow I could move up to six-figure social media campaigns and citywide advertisements.

It was all in my five-year plan. Along with being on time to a meeting every once in a while.

My boss glared at me from his ~~self-appointed throne~~ chair, tracking my every step as I quietly tiptoed around the room in three-inch heels. So basically, not tiptoeing at all. I clunked clumsily on the bamboo floor, causing every set of eyes to turn my way.

Waving meekly from behind my planner, I ignored the smirks from my smug coworkers. They thought they were big deals because they had things like job security and savings accounts. I was just grateful to have a seat at the table.

I was the youngest designer at twenty-seven working at a cutthroat graphic design company and didn't have a ton of perks. My coworkers resented me, my clients underestimated me, and my boss barely remembered that I wasn't his secretary.

I kept waiting for the call into the corner office. Mr. Tucker would raise one bushy eyebrow and say, "We appreciate all you've done for us, Holly, but we're going in a different, more punctual direction."

Squeezing between two swiveling, leather chairs to take the only available seat, I set my planner on the table, hid my phone on my lap, and pulled a pen from hair. I crossed my legs at the ankles and leaned forward attentively—the consummate professional.

"So nice of you to join us, Mitchell," he grunted.

My last name was Maverick. And my first name—Molly. But for some reason I'd never found the courage to correct him. It was borderline ridiculous at this point, but I'd let him get away with it for nearly three years now, so mentioning it to him after all this time seemed ~~humiliating~~ awkward.

Every time I got paid, I breathed a sigh of relief that at least human resources knew my name.

I flashed him a closed-lip smile and waited till he turned away before I brushed my bangs out of my eyes. Slumping just barely in my seat, I clicked on my pen and pretended to start taking notes in the margin of my planner.

To the Mother Tucker, it looked like I was an excellent listener. To my Erin Condren organizer it looked like Fourth of July at nighttime—a horizon full of exploding fireworks that were all shapes and sizes; metaphors for the current status of my spiraling career.

And I didn't mean because of the celebratory sky. I was referring to the gunpowder and fiery explosions part.

Mr. Tucker began going over standing accounts. Different designers gave updates and reports for forty-five minutes. I focused on the details of my drawing so I didn't embarrass myself further by falling asleep.

Finally, after so much ass-kissing from my coworkers that my own lips felt chapped, Mr. Tucker pulled out his ivory cardstock stationary. For as many modern advances as SixTwentySix Marketing had made in the last several years, Mr. Tucker was as old school as they came.

His idea of marketing revolved around magazine advertisements and call-based surveys. I wasn't even sure he had an email account set up in his name. He'd started STS sometime shortly after Alexander the Great tried to invade India, and then named the company after his anniversary date so he would never forget.

Romantic, right?

I'm sure the first Mrs. Tucker felt honored. I wasn't so sure how Mrs. Tuckers two, three and four felt about it.

"We have some new bids today." He grinned at us as though he were holding the winning lotto numbers and one of us was going to be lucky enough to win them. "And they're good ones." He turned to his son and heir of the company, Henry Tucker, or as I liked to call him ever since he propositioned me at the Christmas part three-fourths of a bottle of Jack Daniels deep, The Little Tucker, and winked. Henry beamed under his father's approval, basking in the recognition he didn't deserve.

Henry spent more time chasing girls around the office than he did growing his dad's business. And he knew as much about modern marketing as my shoe. Luckily for both Tucker men, part of our paycheck was commission based.

Monetary incentive drove this company to succeed. Well, money and coffee. And a fair amount of Thai takeout from the restaurant across the street.

Also, and maybe this was just me, but Swedish Fish had been a big part of the small success I'd had.

How else was I supposed to stay awake during projects? I was designing dental logos, remember?

11

There were only so many fonts that could simulate a smile with words.

Mr. Tucker started going through his list, assigning each item to different designers based on seemingly zero information about either the client or his employee. From hours of observing him during these meetings, my best guess was that he picked whomever he noticed first. But other factors I was considering were names he could remember quickly, favorite colors by shirts, favorite colors by ties and Morse code by way of rapidly blinking eyelids.

There was no rhyme or reason to his madness. The same designers that were picked to be Art Directors were chosen to be Brand Identity Developers the next week. He grouped talent together as meticulously as a pig playing the violin. And somehow, we still managed to be the lead marketing firm in the city.

The only good thing that came from the Mother Tucker's management style is that we had all been forced to diversify. I had joined the company excited to specialize in social media marketing, but thanks to my random assignments, I was also awesome with logos, branding and websites.

"That leads us to our biggest client of the year yet." Mr. Tucker paused dramatically, priming the room for what we'd all been waiting for. It was only the middle of February, so it wasn't like he had many clients to compare, but rumors had been floating around the office, making this an already coveted account.

"We're going to need at least three leads on this one," Henry Tucker said, dangling the carrot. "So be prepared to share the commission." He grinned smugly. "With me."

I wrinkled my nose at the slimy way the words fell out of his mouth. This account was about more than money and commission, there would be a reputation that came with it. This was a way to move up in the ranks and demand respect and become an STS legend.

Sure, money was a thing I would always need, but my aspirations were bigger than the size of my paycheck. If I secured this account, I could be picky about future accounts. I might even capture Mr. Tucker's attention long enough to get him to remember my name.

"That's right," Mr. Tucker crowed, breathing heavily as if it was a concerted effort to sit in his comfortable leather chair. "Black Soul Productions has asked us to revamp their entire platform. They want a new logo, and a new advertising campaign. They want a social media plan. And more. This account could mean very big things for us in the future. Black Soul has an extensive client list of their own. If we do a good job with this one, we could see residual accounts for years to come. Obviously, I've asked Henry to take the lead on this one. I trust his vision and leadership to handle such an important account." Father and son shared an allied smile. "Why don't you round out your team, Son? Nothing but the best for this one."

Black Soul Productions was a local record label that had recently signed some breakout artists. When rumors had started surfacing that they wanted to update their look and expand their presence, I had done my research. They had a strong list of B-list clients and with their latest signings had the potential to become a nationally respected brand. Their social media presence would be everything. If I could get on that team and create a sustainable social strategy, they would be unstoppable. It was definitely a big task, but so worth the effort.

"Thanks, Dad. And don't you worry about this account. I'll take care of everything." Henry's eyes scanned the room, jumping from one designer to the next, all the way around the table. I held back a squeak of anticipation. At least I could trust Tucker Senior to pick at random, thereby freeing me of disappointment when I wasn't chosen. Junior was a different story.

For some unsubstantiated reason, Henry thought of himself as a ladies' man, and therefore acted as though he were God's greatest gift to women. To my knowledge he didn't succeed very often, but his lack of success did nothing to dampen his confidence. Which was saying something since he was the second highest paid employee and set to one day take over the marketing empire his dad had built for him.

He wasn't even terrible looking. He used more hair product than I would have encouraged, giving him a slightly greasy appearance. And the gold chain necklace tucked beneath his performance polo wasn't exactly the height of men's fashion. But his teeth were decent, and he worked out.

There was just something about him that wasn't appealing. I couldn't put my finger on exactly what it was, but I knew enough to duck under his arm and slip out the back staircase when he'd drunkenly cornered me at our office Christmas party. And I wasn't exactly in a position to turn down men. My last date had been four waxes ago.

Henry's gaze lingered on Catherine Dawes, a drop-dead gorgeous blonde with Photoshop-like curves and *Madmen* vintage style to accentuate them. He stared appreciatively at her for a long time, before deciding better of it.

She was by far the prettiest woman in the office. But she was also a ballbuster, and I doubted she'd put up with any shit from Henry, no matter how special his dad said he was.

The tension in the room heightened, twisting and pulling, threatening to snap at any second. We all wanted to be chosen. We all wanted it badly.

There wasn't a person in this room that wouldn't fight tooth and nail to be on this team, even if we did have to work with Junior.

"Ethan," Henry decided, surprising us all. Ethan Baker was at least ten years older than me and had a wife and a couple kids. The entire room jolted in surprise. It wasn't that Ethan was a bad designer, he was probably the best in the office at brand development, but we were all surprised Henry had been able to ignore the temptation to surround himself with hot girls. "I want you to take point on branding. Are you up for the task?"

Ethan smiled confidently at him. "Absolutely." He cleared his throat and leaned forward in his chair. "I actually heard a rumor about this account earlier in the week and I've been playing around with ideas if you'd like to see what I've come up wi—"

Cutting Ethan off abruptly, Henry smiled, flashing unnaturally white teeth, and said, "I would. Later."

Henry's gaze moved back to the conference table, enjoying every second of lording his power over us.

I held my breath and waited to be passed over. I vaguely realized I'd started to click my pen obnoxiously thanks to the nervous anticipation coursing through my blood like a rabid rabbit.

I forced myself to smile serenely and look as grown-up as possible. I wanted this account more than anything. I had been secretly preparing for it since I first heard the rumor that it was a possibility. This project was exactly up my alley of expertise. Black Soul would need someone with a strong social media game. They would need someone that could identify with a younger crowd and bring them into the tech-savvy internet world. They needed someone that understood filters, and search engines. And the seven seconds window of time people devoted to new information.

I didn't know if Henry realized that too, or if by sheer power of the mind I'd willed him to pay attention to me. But either way, he turned his creepy, tractor beam smile my direction. "What do you think, Maverick?"

My cheeks instantly flushed when the attention of the room turned to me. I hated being the center of attention. I hated that everyone in the room was now staring at me, judging me, weighing my worth. It didn't matter that I knew I was right for the job or that I had the chops to tackle this project. With everyone watching me, I felt completely unqualified. But not unqualified enough to give it up. "Y-yes. Of course." I set my pen down on the table and then pushed it away so I wouldn't be tempted to click it again. "I'd love the opportunity to work on this project."

"It's a lot of hours," Henry reminded me. "A lot of late nights."

Out of the corner of my eye, I saw Catherine's face flinch in disgust. Her reaction only added to my nerves. *What was that about?* "I can handle it," I said firmly.

There were only a handful of other designers in the office that could juggle both the graphics and vision side of this project. Sure, they were more experienced, more professional, and more cutthroat. But I was on my way to being all of those things.

Kind of.

Someday.

My confident smile wobbled. Okay, cutthroat wasn't really my thing. But it could be. Black Soul could make it be.

"Good," Tucker Senior announced from the head of the table after Henry had picked a few more designers for support staff. "That's settled. As usual, if you have questions or concerns, don't bother me with them."

My coworkers and I laughed our obligatory response that we gave every time he made that joke and began to gather our things. Meeting officially over. Thirty minutes late. But over all the same.

I glanced down at my phone. Three missed texts and two more missed phone calls.

Where are you???

Shit. I had to go.

By the time I stood up, the room was abuzz with excitement over the Black Soul project. For the Durham area, SixTwentySix was the best marketing firm around. But this project could build our reputation to national acclaim. And the commission wouldn't be bad either.

I tried to slink out quietly, but I didn't make it far. "Black Soul, huh?" Brian, one of the few designers that was under thirty years old, asked. He was a total hipster with too-tight pants and a man bun. Basically, he was an adorable hotdog.

"Exciting, right?" I tried to squeeze past him, but Daria from sales stepped in front of me.

"Do you think you'll meet anyone famous?" she asked.

"I, uh, no?" I spin-moved to the right and managed to take two steps closer to the door. Henry moved in front of me, a shit-eating grin plastered on his spray-tanned face.

"Do you have a minute, Molly? I wanted to personally welcome you to the team."

Checking my phone as discreetly as I could, I tried not to flinch and bit back the truth. "Yeah, sure. I have a minute." Quite literally, one minute.

He stepped over to the corner of the conference room, and I breathed a sigh of relief that he hadn't taken me back to his office. This would be much easier to get out of.

Henry's hand landed on my forearm, just above my bent elbow. He squeezed gently and kept his hand there.

Suddenly, all concerns of being late, and feelings of glee for being chosen for the team vanished, and an uncomfortable feeling of ickiness washed through me. Oh, no, was Henry Tucker hitting on me?

I glanced down at his hand where it sat too warm and sticky against my bare skin. He didn't remove it. So I shifted the things in my arms, and took a subtle step back.

He followed me.

Ugh.

"I'm expecting a lot from you, Molly," he said in a smooth, deep voice.

Fear of being too inexperienced for the job I was just assigned pooled in my gut. Like a swamp. With fifteen-foot alligators. I smiled widely to distract attention from the green tinge of my skin. "I know. This is a big job. I'm really thrilled to be part of the team."

Henry's expression softened. "I believe in you, Maverick. I think you have exactly what I need."

I licked dry lips and tried not to notice when Henry glanced down at my chest. Gross.

Shifting my planner in front of my body, I cursed myself for not buttoning my sleeveless blouse up to my chin. "Thanks, Henry. I'm looking forward to working with you and Ethan on this." Lie. Total, complete lie. But one that needed to be said.

Henry leaned forward, bringing us uncomfortably close together. "But mostly me, right?" He winked.

He actually winked at me.

Letting out a nervous laugh, I nodded and said, "You got it."

He finally released my arm, and I sucked in a deep breath to regain my personal bubble. "We don't have a meeting with Black Soul until March. They want to see the full package before they approve anything, so we'll need to work hard to put together a stellar presentation. We'll start planning tomorrow. I'll email you the details later tonight."

"I'll look for them," I promised.

He caught me looking at my phone again. "Are you in a hurry to be out of here today? I figured you'd want to stick around and gloat."

My smile had frozen in place a long time ago, and now wasn't the time to drop it. "Gloating's not really my thing," I told him. "Plus, I'm late for another meeting."

"Oh, really? Work related?"

I shook my head, "It's definitely work, but not STS. I'm planning my best friend's engagement party, and I was supposed to meet the caterer forty-five minutes ago."

Henry stepped back, and I relished the additional six inches of separation. I wasn't normally one of those people that hated being touched, but Henry had zero regard for space. I'd been at STS for three years. During that time, I'd never been able to warm up to the Little Tucker, even though he'd always been nice to me. And he could remember my name, unlike his father.

Slipping out of the conference room in a surge of other employees anxious to get home for the day, I hurried to my desk to grab my purse. Emily, my one true friend at STS, stopped by my desk. She leaned her weight on her hands and kicked up her legs. "Congratulations!"

I smiled at her, and it was real and genuine. It felt so freaking good. "Thank you! I feel like pinching myself. I can't believe I got picked."

"I can," she said sincerely. "You have the best eye for detail here." She leaned forward, cupping her mouth with her hand. "And the best taste. Black Soul is going to fall in love with you."

"I'm just hoping they don't fire me."

She rolled her eyes. "Enough with the modesty, Molly. You deserve this. We should definitely celebrate. Drinks? Dinner? Strip club?"

My shoulders slumped, knocking my purse strap loose. "I wish. A strip club is obviously in order." I hoped she knew I was joking about that. Sometimes I couldn't tell if she was being serious. Although with her lavender hair and septum piercing it was hard to picture her surrounded by oiled up, half-naked men thrusting their crotches in her face. I shook my head, ridding my imagination of that terrifying mental picture. "But I'm supposed to go over the menu for Vera's engagement party. Wyatt's going to kill me."

"Oh, that's better!" She waggled her eyebrows. "Celebrate with Wyatt. Celebrate real hard."

I threw my planner into my purse and snorted. "What is wrong with you?"

Her eyebrows jumped to her hairline. "What is wrong with *you*? Have you not seen Wyatt?" She fanned her face, being dramatic like usual. "He's a hottie with a body. And you could use a body if you know what I mean."

17

Shaking my head, I reminded her for the umpteenth time, "We're just friends, Em. Seriously, just friends."

Her mouth turned down in a frown. "Such a disappointment. Hot men are always wasted on you."

I hitched my purse up again and ignored the heat of embarrassment painting my cheeks. "Yeah, well, we can't all be you with your perfect boyfriend, perfect relationship, and perfect three-bedroom house."

"And perfect dog," she added. "You forgot the perfect dog."

I stuck my tongue out at her. "And the perfect dog. In my limited experience, all the hot men that have been interested in me were also douchebags. I'd rather have someone nice than hot."

"Hmmm…" she mused, considering her long-term boyfriend. "Alex is both of those things. But so is Wyatt."

"And yet we're only friends."

She rolled her eyes, but didn't push the topic. "Congratulations again! Happy hour tomorrow to celebrate?"

"Obvs."

She blew me a kiss. I waved goodbye, and then practically sprinted to my car. My phone buzzed again, signaling an incoming text.

I hate you.

Wyatt really was just a friend. The *I hate you* text confirmed it. Or he had been prior to my making him wait for over an hour.

Chapter Two

I parked at Cycle Life, the bike shop my best friend's brother, Vann, owned. I'd stupidly worn heels today and my feet ached as I hurried across the street to Lilou, one of the hippest restaurants in the city. It was the perfect spot for an engagement party for two of my very favorite people.

Especially since Vera and Killian had met there. Or technically, in the parking space where I'd just left my car. Basically, this area was very significant to their relationship and future wedded bliss.

Vera and Killian had hated each other at first. He'd been an arrogant asshole, and she'd been scared to trust anybody after her scumbag of an ex had spent years abusing her. My heart squeezed thinking about that time. Vera was so content now. She'd found a happily ever after that would last forever. But I couldn't help but feel sympathy for her every time I thought about her and Derrek together.

She still wore the scars from her relationship with him. Even if Killian was amazing and thoughtful and kind. I sometimes wondered if she would ever be completely over that time in her life. It was my goal to help her wholly move on. I was the biggest advocate for her happiness.

Which was why I'd volunteered to head up her surprise engagement party. Volunteering to oversee was not one of my brighter moments, but I wasn't going to leave it in Vann's hands. Her ultra-healthy brother would have hosted it on some mountain biking trail and served granola bars for appetizers.

Not that I was any better at food than him. Vera and Killian were the master chefs. I told people I loved burnt toast because I was physically incapable of making it any other way.

And that's why I enlisted our other good friend Wyatt to help me out with the menu. Plus, he'd somehow convinced his scary boss to let us host the event at Lilou, but only because the cranky restaurateur, Ezra Baptiste, was also Killian's best friend.

Once I'd made it to the side door of Lilou, I typed out a quick text to Wyatt.

I'm here.

Then I paced back and forth for five minutes while I waited for him to open the door. My feet ached from wearing heels all day and a headache had formed around the base of my skull. Despite my Black Soul victory, I needed today to be over.

I thought about my earlier conversation with Emily. She loved to go out to celebrate work wins. But honestly, success stressed me out. I did not feel like the competent graphic designer I pretended to be. There was too much pressure to do whatever it took to get the best jobs. And then there was always that feeling of my work not stacking up to my coworkers. I had to prove myself in every single task and I couldn't escape the pressure to always be interesting and innovative and unique.

I preferred to celebrate alone, with a bubble bath and bottle of wine. Or paintbrush in hand, in front of a blank canvas. The last thing I wanted to do was go out to a crowded bar and talk about all the ways I got lucky enough not to crash and burn. I'd much rather enjoy the excitement by bringing it to life in vibrant colors and paint-covered portraits and artistic expression.

The side door swung open and Kaya poked her blue-haired head out. "He's so pissed at you."

I ignored Wyatt's edgy sous chef and her gloating. Her favorite thing in life was pissing off Wyatt, so me showing up an hour and a half late and right in the middle of hectic dinner service was probably the highlight of her day.

Stepping inside Lilou's kitchen was like walking into a tornado. People were everywhere, working on prepping, cooking and plating all at once. Stainless steel surfaces were covered with dishes, and perfectly executed food, and oh so sharp knives. Wyatt stood in the middle of the flurry, tall chef hat covering his buzzed head, tattoos peeking up over the collar of his pristine chef's jacket.

20

He had changed a lot in the last few months. When Vera and I first met him, he'd been more relaxed, way more laid back. He would always come visit us at Vera's food truck that used to park at Cycle Life and together we'd gang up on Vera, always teasing her about Killian.

But since Killian had left Lilou to open a restaurant with Vera, Wyatt had stepped up as executive chef and lost his ability to chill. He was all drive, meticulous precision and serious career mode now.

To be fair, he basically worked every second of every day, so work mode was also life and survival mode. But I missed my friend that liked to joke around and steal food when Vera wasn't looking.

"Wash your hands," Wyatt barked at me.

I realized I was breaking a few health code rules by hanging out in a kitchen I did not belong in, so I decided not to argue with him. Or ask him to say please.

"I'm so sorry," I said instead. "My meeting ran late."

Drying my hands on a paper towel, I turned around and faced him. He was leaned over a drool-worthy dish inspecting it closely. With one finger wrapped in a hand towel, he swiped at the edges of the plate, removing a rogue drop of sauce. He passed it to a stoic waitress and nodded. She grabbed the plate and disappeared into the dining room.

Wyatt turned his handsome face to me. "And? Did you get the big, life-changing job?"

I loosed a smile. "I did!"

His lips twitched with a proud smirk. "Atta girl."

I beamed at him, thankful for his confidence in me. We had been talking through texts more than usual to plan Vera and Killian's party.

Wyatt's head jerked in the direction of a counter near the coolers. He was back in super serious mode again. "Everything's cold now, but that's what I've come up with so far. You're welcome to taste what's there and let me know what you think Vera will like best."

"She'll like whatever you make, Wyatt. She's not picky."

He made a sound in the back of his throat. "I'm not going to make just *whatever* for Killian Quinn and Vera Delane. They're beyond picky. Their entire life's work is based on being picky."

I rolled my eyes at the obvious hero worship Wyatt still had for Killian. "All right, all right. I'll be picky too."

"I appreciate that."

Wyatt went back to work and I walked over to the spread he'd laid out on the counter. Different entrees on varying plates, bowls and platters covered the stainless-steel countertop. Everything was cooked to perfection and visually appealing. Wyatt had taken a menu and turned it into a stunning piece of art.

I loved to paint and draw. I mean, really loved it. My favorite thing in the world was to take a blank canvas and bring it to life, to make it something more than it was. I saw the world in vibrant colors and interesting angles. I saw people in expressions I wanted to make immortal, and poses that could be painted. I wasn't an artist, not really. But creating something with my hands gave me a deep sense of purpose and meaning.

That was how I felt about Wyatt's food. And Killian's and Vera's, and all of these friends of mine in the food industry. They didn't just cook something. They created something—something inspiring and lasting. They didn't just add spices; they built flavor profiles that would never be forgotten. They didn't just throw together ingredients; they painstakingly crafted the most perfect dining experience possible. Each dish possessed the perfect bite.

They were artists. And I respected them deeply for what they did.

I picked up a skewer with a hunk of meat, a roasted tomato, and slice of cucumber drizzled in a white sauce that seemed familiar. Shoving the entire thing into my mouth, I moaned into my hand. "Is this *the* sauce?" I asked around the too-big bite.

"Yeah," Wyatt called over his shoulder, knowing what I was talking about without having to look.

"These for sure then." I moved on to mini wedge salads with bacon and blue cheese crumbles, and fresh mozzarella balls wrapped in prosciutto and basil with a tomato puree for dipping. There were meatloaf meatballs, and buffalo chicken smothered French fries. There were even house made sausages wrapped in some crispy dough and sliced to bite-size that basically tasted like *more please*.

I stared at the spread again, shocked and overjoyed and near tears. "Oh, my gosh, did you make all of her dishes?"

Wyatt sounded distracted when he answered, "The ones I could remember. I did some of Killian's too." He glanced at me over his shoulder. "With my own spin of course."

"Wyatt, this is amazing. And so much more than I was hoping for. You're a genius!"

"It's not a big deal."

"Are you kidding? They're going to love everything. Every single thing."

He ignored my compliments. "So how many people are you thinking?"

"I'm not sure. Vera only has like ten people on her side. Killian is the popular one."

22

Wyatt's staff laughed like I'd told a joke. But it was the truth. Maybe Vera was a generally more pleasant person than Killian, but she'd never had a wide circle of friends. And I was pretty much her only remaining friend since Derrek had spent so much time isolating her. For as grizzly as Killian could be, he knew a ton of people. Sure, most of them were in his industry, but they were still the kind of acquaintances that got invites to an engagement party.

Wyatt laughed at one of the jokes another chef made about Killian's popularity and how the only reason he had so many friends was because they were too scared of him to decline. Then he said, "Well, let me know when you have a final number so I can shop for enough ingredients."

I picked up a tiny dessert cup. *Yum! Chocolate mousse.* "I sent out like fifty invitations to Killian's people. Do you think they'll all come?"

Wyatt's head bobbled back and forth as he thought about it. "I'll plan for that many. Someone will take home leftovers."

I licked the remaining chocolate off my lips. "I volunteer as tribute. Also, when you're done grocery shopping let me know what the total is and I'll pay you back."

He waved me off. "Don't worry about it."

This wasn't the first time we'd had this conversation. He had decided to be obnoxiously stubborn. "Seriously, Wyatt, you're already making the food. At least let me pay for it."

"Not happening," he murmured.

"I'm paying you anyway. Even if I have to guess the total."

Wyatt turned around, his eyes twinkling and a grin pulling at his lips. "What's your guess?"

"My guess?"

"Guess the total."

I looked at the food on the counter and calculated it times fifty and then considered my own personal grocery bill. "One hundred dollars." The kitchen staff laughed again. "Uh, two hundred dollars?" They kept laughing. "Ten thousand dollars!" I really hoped not because I would need to hit up those paycheck advance places if that was the case.

Four more dishes passed Wyatt's inspection and then left the kitchen in a flurry of waiters dressed in black and swinging doors. "How are you going to get them here and keep it a secret?"

Just then, the pass-through door opened and Ezra Baptiste stepped into the kitchen. His cold gaze scanned the space quickly before landing on me.

"Busted," I whispered to myself.

23

His stare turned glacial as recognition hit him. It was safe to say he wasn't expecting to find me invading his place of business. His jaw flexed once... twice. But as mad as he was he seemed frozen in place, unable to decide what to do next.

"Hey, boss," Wyatt greeted him. He sounded more confident than I knew he felt, but I also knew it was because he wanted Ezra to take him seriously, respect him as master of his domain.

Good luck, Wyatt. Ezra barely seemed capable of having a soul most days, let alone the ability to show human emotions like respect and trust. Wyatt had his work cut out for him.

On the other hand, I didn't need Ezra's admiration or for him to take me seriously. I didn't have to work for him, and other than the engagement party, I never wanted to work with him either. Mostly I just wanted him to forget I existed altogether.

Ezra looked at Wyatt as though he was surprised to find him where he was supposed to be. In fact, he seemed a little more discombobulated than usual. Clearing his throat, he said, "I came in here to talk to you about... it can wait." He turned his attention back to me and I felt like dropping to the ground and army crawling to freedom. "Molly, why are you here?"

Somehow, I managed to stay on my feet and brave him, even though every instinct screamed to run. "Taste testing," I heard myself say.

His broad shoulders shifted and rolled. He struggled to collect his patience before he said, "Excuse me?"

I waved a hand at the cluttered counter. "For the engagement party. Wyatt wanted me to taste test."

Ezra's eyes narrowed. "I'm positive Wyatt is capable of choosing the menu on his own. You're not allowed in my kitchen during business hours, Molly. You don't work here. I need you to leave."

Shame and embarrassment attacked in unison, spiraling through me until I wanted to call off the entire party. Or at the very least, host it someplace else.

Anywhere else.

Like a bowling alley.

Or the moon.

That would teach him a lesson.

I cleared my throat and managed a weak, "Sure thing."

Picking up my purse from the floor I tried to calmly leave through the side door again, back the way I came.

"Not that way," Ezra clipped out through the very, very quiet kitchen.

The entire staff had stilled, watching in horrified amusement as their scary boss attacked poor, helpless, little old me. And okay, maybe I broke the rules and Ezra had every right to toss me out on my ass, but didn't one of them want to stick up for a damsel in distress?

Where was my knight in shining armor?

My rebel without a cause?

I looked at Wyatt for help, but the best he could do was shoot me an apologetic frown. *Traitor.*

My eyes slammed shut and I decided I would be okay with an alien abduction right about now. Or a marauding band of pirates? How about Godzilla? Could I at least get a good, old-fashioned Godzilla attack? Anything to save me from Ezra's judgment.

Spinning around on my heel, I held my chin high, even though all I wanted to do was hang my head like a shamed child. I walked across the kitchen with all the poise I could muster in feet that were over high heels three hours ago. Needless to say, it wasn't my most graceful moment.

Ezra Baptiste was one of the most intolerable men I had ever met. Arrogant, condescending, offensively good looking, he had all the qualities of a human I tried to avoid. Not only that, he'd once attacked my professional taste and that was something I would never forgive him for.

We were forced to interact with each other thanks to our mutual friends, but in the last few months I'd gotten really good at avoiding him. Not that it was hard. He owned three successful restaurants in Durham and co-owned a fourth. He was wealthy and busy, and it was weird that we knew the same people.

He was all cool, important businessman. Most days, I felt like I was playing dress-up as an adult. I paid bills, went to work, and lived alone. Yet nothing about my life fit well, like when I was a little girl and would try on my mom's dresses.

Ezra was a man that knew who he was and what he wanted in life. I was just a girl trying to figure out how to check my own oil.

He led me through the kitchen and around the corner to his office. I thought about bolting out the front doors. Would he chase after me? No. He was too composed for that. Sue me for being a public nuisance? Maybe. Was it worth it though?

I sucked in my bottom lip and decided that yes, yes it was. But then I remembered I needed to talk to him about the party. The party he was hosting at his restaurant. So I reluctantly faced my fears and followed him inside the small, but organized office space.

He turned around and propped his hands on his hips. He looked so elegant in his suit, even with the jacket discarded over the back of his

25

chair and his tie loosened around his neck. I had the strangest urge to run my thumb over his cheekbone.

I shivered, shaking off that oddly sympathetic instinct.

Needing to remind myself of who this man was, I spoke before he could. "I'm sorry, Ezra. It won't happen again."

He stared at me. "I hope you understand that I can't have non-employees hanging out in my kitchen during business hours. The health inspector would love to catch you in there just to shut me down."

Guilt mingled with shame and my heart pinched with regret. I held my hands up. "I get it. Really."

Looking out the door, then back at me, he let out a slow breath. "So are you ready for Friday? Do you need anything else from me?"

It had been Wyatt's idea to host the party at Lilou and he'd been the one to approach Ezra about it. I had kicked myself every day for letting him talk me into it. Sure, it would be extra special to Vera and Killian, but what about me? All I got out of it was an awkward conversation with this guy, and a whole helping of guilt for how much more Wyatt and Ezra were contributing.

I mean, it was my party, and so far, I'd sent out invitations and found a cute new dress on clearance.

"I think we're ready. I'll be here Friday afternoon to set up decorations as long as that works for you?" He nodded. "Are you sure it's not a problem to close Lilou for an entire night? I feel awful."

He expression relaxed, softened. "I'm happy to help."

I wanted to argue with him, but I held my tongue. He had been the one to offer the date. He'd picked Friday night, not me.

Steeling my courage, I asked one more favor of him. "There is just one more thing," I started. His dark eyes narrowed and his lips thinned. "I'm not exactly sure how to get them here. I'm wondering if you would make up an excuse and invite them over? Or call them with some big, fake emergency that you can't handle without them?"

Ezra Baptiste was the very definition of tall, dark and handsome. His hair was always trimmed neatly and combed in a way that screamed important. His jaw was always cleanly shaven, and his clothes always perfectly tailored and expertly pressed. He was basically the exact opposite of his best friend Killian.

But right now he looked utterly bewildered, erasing all of that sophisticated aloofness he worked so hard to pull off. "You want me to call them?"

"Or text," I offered. "Whatever way works best for you. Just make up a foolproof reason for them to hurry over here."

"You should probably do it," he argued. "That seems like something you'd be good at."

What did he mean by that? That I was good at lying? "What excuse could I possibly have for them to meet me at Lilou?"

His jaw ticked. "I don't like lying to my friends."

I cleared my throat, hating the way he made me feel guilty for trying to surprise our friends with an awesome party. I was doing a good thing, I reminded myself. It wasn't even really lying. "Then don't lie. Tell them you have a surprise for them. It will be the truth."

"That will ruin the night."

I placed my hands on my hips, mimicking his stand-offish pose. "Forget I asked. I'll figure it out."

"Now you're mad," he accused.

"I'm not mad." I was totally pissed. "There's nothing to be mad about." Except that he was being unnecessarily difficult when all I wanted him to do was shoot Killian a text that said, *hey come over here for a minute*. "I thought it would make more sense coming from you, but it's not a big deal."

He stared at me for a long moment before he said, "Do you have a coat?"

"What?"

"A coat," he repeated. "Did you leave it in the kitchen?"

"Er, no." Trying to recover from conversational whiplash, I explained, "I didn't wear one. I came straight from work." I also hated coats. Sure, it was frigid outside and my car would be an icebox by the time I left, but coats always got in my way. I had a long, cashmere duster on over my rosy pink blouse and gray trousers, and that was enough for me. Plus, my office was hot as Hades in the winter and even if I wore a sweater to work, I usually shed it before lunchtime.

Ezra scowled at me but didn't press the coat issue.

"So we're good for Friday?" I asked, hoping to wrap this up. I had an exciting night of eating supper alone and washing my hair ahead of me that I was anxious to start.

"What decorations are you going to use?"

Another topic shift and I felt dizzy trying to keep up with him. I just wanted to go home, heat up a cup of soup, and binge watch bad reality TV. "Nothing too extravagant," I told him. "Lilou is pretty enough. But I wanted to grab some flowers for the tables, and I have some pictures and stuff I want to display."

"I have a florist," he volunteered. "You don't need to worry about flowers unless you want to."

"Oh, it's not a big—"

"She's used to the space," he continued. "I'll call her now."

Translation: Don't bring your crappy carnations into my pristine sanctuary.

"I don't want to add to your plate," I offered weakly.

He moved around to the back of his desk. Picking up his cell, he started scrolling through his contacts. "Did you have a specific flower in mind?"

"Vera loves peonies," I heard myself say. "But it's February so I was going to see what was available."

He nodded, absorbing the information. "Color scheme?"

"Red," I told him. "I found these vintage spice racks that are flat with slots in them. I was going to use them as centerpieces."

"Here, write down your email address and I'll send you the florist's info. You can drop off the spice racks before Friday and she'll handle all the details."

I numbly picked up the white pad of paper and scrawled my email address for him. I should have stood up to him more, and told him I had the flowers and the decorations covered. But I was intimidated.

Severely intimidated.

He took the notepad back and inspected my email address as though I'd given him a fraud. He looked up at me and I could see wheels spinning in his head. He had something to say and it was anybody's guess what that was.

"There's one more thing," he said.

A nervous flutter trembled in my stomach. "What is that?"

He opened his mouth to answer just as the cellphone in his hand went off. He glared down at the screen and let out an impatient sigh. "I have to take this," he murmured.

I could recognize a brush off when it was aimed directly at me. "No problem. I'll see you Friday. You have my email if you need anything else."

I turned to look at him as I walked away. He glanced up at me from across the room and I was once again hit with how attractive this man was. Usually, personality meant more to me than looks, but Ezra apparently didn't need a sparkling temperament for me to find him striking. I wanted to paint him. I wanted to capture that consternated expression on his face by immortalizing it on canvas.

His thumb swiped over his phone, answering the call before I'd left the office. "Bye, Ezra," I whispered to his stoic face. He didn't respond.

Turning around at the door to his office I fled Lilou, his part of town, and this whole entire day.

Chapter Three

I grabbed a bottle of wine on the way home and uncorked it as soon as I walked in the door. My sixth-floor apartment on the edge of downtown was cute, mostly affordable, and close to work. I had moved in two years ago when I finally trusted that my salary at STS wasn't going to suddenly disappear.

It was supposed to be this big landmark of adulthood. I had a full-time job and my own place, yay! Except mostly it felt lonely. And I wasn't one of those girls that needed people around me all the time. I liked space. I liked privacy. But there was something about living alone that had started to feel... isolated. Like it wasn't my choice anymore.

I was thinking about getting a cat.

After my promised cup of soup, I tried watching something on Netflix, but I couldn't settle on any one show. I set down the remote when I'd spent forty-five minutes scrolling through the endlessly mediocre options. There were only so many times a girl could binge watch *The Office* without demanding her very own Jim Halpert from the universe. And nobody wanted bitter Pam walking around in real life.

My afternoon played on repeat in my head, until I'd poured myself another glass of wine and given up trying to dissect why getting the project I wanted badly felt so very empty. Black Soul would be a huge step forward for my career. I'd already spent weeks mentally devising an advertising plan that was both relevant and original.

This was the thing that was going to solidify my place at SixTwentySix, gain respect from my coworkers and make Mr. Tucker finally remember my name. But now that it was go time, I second guessed my life goals. Was this really living the dream? Could I really spend the rest of my life making social media packets for people that didn't understand the proper use of hashtags?

Sidenote: #iateasaladforlunch is a useless hashtag.

Second sidenote: #hashtag— also useless.

But you try explaining the term "searchable content" to anyone not carrying a millennial card. And yet I always got stuck with outdated clients that refused to grow their business with the "pound sign."

I gnawed on my bottom lip while I moved my glass and cell phone to my office. Well, office-ish space. I'd intended to set up the second bedroom with a desk, bookshelves, and if I was feeling frisky, a fern. Instead, I kept my laptop on my coffee table, my work odds and ends in a drawer in the kitchen and my books in waist-high stacks next to my bed.

In this room I'd covered the floor with old sheets and propped an easel perpendicular to the windows. The small walk-in closet was filled with canvases of every size—some fresh, some finished, a few were somewhere in between.

I had moved a folding table in here that I'd snagged at a garage sale in my parents' neighborhood. I'd covered it in another sheet and used it to organize my paints, brushes and other odds and ends. The adjoining bathroom had been turned into a drying room—more cleaned brushes were laid out on every available surface.

Vera called it my studio. But for me, it felt more like a guilty pleasure. An embarrassing hobby that sometimes cured boredom, sometimes became an outlet for frustration and disappointment, and sometimes was more important to me than breathing.

But it wasn't anything more than that. Once upon a time, I'd had an adolescent dream of becoming a world-famous painter, spending my days hovering over canvas, wielding a paintbrush and my soul as inspiration. But that was before I'd come to terms with necessary evils like bill-paying, car-owning, and meal-planning. I was a real grown-up now with a real, grown-up job. A job that I sometimes even liked. The whole starving-artist thing just wasn't practical.

I'd indulged my creative side throughout high school, and then done what most other artists did after graduation. I found a job in a loosely creative field and walked away from all of the other impractical daydreams that wouldn't offer stability or consistent paychecks or a 401k.

30

But on days like today, when I was reminded of how bad adulthood tasted and how desperately I wished I could run back to my younger years when I didn't have to pay bills or live alone or wonder what men like Ezra Baptiste were really thinking, I quietly escaped to this sacred place and poured out all of these irrational, conflicting thoughts onto stark, white, glorious canvas. In essence, I stopped thinking altogether.

My landlord had tried to sell me on a roommate when I first moved in, but the thought of dealing with another person day in and day out sounded exhausting. And when I'd leased this place, Vera had still been in Charlotte. She was the only human I could imagine sharing a living space with for longer than three days.

But now she had Killian for that.

Their relationship was another current event that turned funny in my gut. I was so happy for my friend. Like beyond happy. Like maxed out with happiness. Vera deserved every single second of bliss and marriage and happily ever after. She had been through absolute hell with Derrek, and Killian was so perfect for her in every way. They were #relationshipgoals to the extreme. *See that proper use of a hashtag? Suck it Green City Mowing.*

So why did I feel left behind?

I pulled a hair tie off my wrist and piled my long mane of nearly black hair onto the top of my head. Fiddling with my bangs until they were out of my way, I stripped out of work clothes and threw on the over-sized t-shirt a past boyfriend from college had never claimed. Not that I'd offered to give it back.

There were zero lingering feelings for Brady... Brady... Brady-something. But his high school football t-shirt was large and super comfortable and something I was unwilling to part with.

I went about preparing my paints and setting up a fresh canvas on the easel, replacing the latest portrait I'd been working on. I had been in the middle of a winter sunset. Pinks, oranges, and deep purples streaked across a sky filled with thin gray clouds. The sun was an orange globe over a downtown Durham dusted with layers of white snow that had never actually fallen this year. Windows glowed in yellow light and the streets below were... still a work in progress.

I had plans to finish the piece, adding people and vehicles and all the little details I loved about my city. My fingers itched to deepen the sun, blur the edges and streak the pastels with richer color. But I didn't have a sunset in me tonight. It was cold outside, but there was no snow and my thoughts were wild and disorganized and I didn't want to paint something beautiful.

31

I needed raw and vulnerable and confused.

I needed to unleash these erratic emotions and turn them into something I could see, fix, and then abandon.

My fingers trembled as I picked up my brush, so I gripped it harder, digging the end of it into my palm. Sitting down on the very edge of my stool, I gave up fighting internal battles and turned them over to the canvas. It was more than cathartic. It was healing and thinking and soothing all at the same time.

I threw myself into the art of creating something without even having a fully conceptualized idea of what I was going to paint. I just let the day press in on me, crushing me beneath the weight of everything I was so unsure about until it came oozing out my fingers, spilling onto the canvas in purposeful brush strokes and arcs of color.

When I was forced to sit up straight again to give my aching neck and shoulders a break, I realized two and a half hours had passed. With the creative spell broken, I stared hard at my work, startled as if seeing it for the very first time.

Angular lines made a strong, stoic jaw. Full lips pressed into a frown. There was a sharp slash of a nose. Two chocolate eyes stared back from beneath determined brows. His hair was pushed back, unkempt in a way he would never really allow. It matched his loose tie and the perplexed scowl he wore—figments of my imagination, characteristics I'd given him in this fictional version that he'd never tolerate in real life.

Staring at my handiwork, I saw that I hadn't really captured Ezra at all though. My lines were too hard. My colors not exactly right. His eyes were too shallow. His jawline... his cheekbones... his defined edges were too hard and too wrong, and I hated that I hadn't done them justice. That I'd failed. And I couldn't shake the nagging feeling that I was missing something.

This wasn't Ezra. This was very clearly a picture of someone trying to paint Ezra.

I slumped on my stool, rolling my stiff neck back and forth. "Ugh, why am I even trying with you?" I asked the canvas. I stared at the eyes that weren't Ezra's at all. "I still don't like you."

My phone buzzed in the other room, so I left Ezra to go grab it. It turned out I had four missed texts, but this one was the first I'd heard. All from Vera.

7:03: Are you a famous rock star yet?

7:48: Are you at least the famous graphic designer for rock stars yet?

8:56: Does the silent treatment mean bad news? Want me to go down to your office and raise hell? Whose ass do I need to kick?

8:59: In other news, I'm heading to spin class at five-thirty tomorrow morning and I need a friend. Please please please? Don't make me get into wedding shape alone!!!!

Ick, spin class. Nothing like having a bike seat up your bum first thing in the morning.

Me: Sorry, my phone was in the other room. Obviously I'm famous. But only because my sex tape is such a crowd pleaser. And spin class? Isn't there prenatal yoga? Hot yoga? Any kind of yoga?

Vera: Last time we did early morning yoga you fell asleep in Child's Pose.

Me: So did you!

Vera: Which is why we're doing spin class!

Vera and I had joined a gym together shortly after her engagement. She'd decided to lose fifteen pounds before her wedding and wanted me to go through the pain and suffering too. She was one of those girls that carried her weight like a Kardashian. No, she wasn't the skinniest girl ever. But damn... *dat ass*.

I didn't have an ass. Or thighs. Or muscles of any kind. I was like the female version of Gumby. If Gumby had decent-sized boobs and hipster bangs.

Me: Vera don't make me.

Vera: This is for your own good. I'm torturing you because I love you.

Me. I don't love you.

Vera: Liar liar pants on fire.

Me: You're buying me coffee after. And an Egg McMuffin. And also, I demand hash browns.

Vera: What's the point of working out if I buy you McDonald's after? Also, HELLO! Chef here! We're not going to McDonalds.

Me: We'll see.

Vera: 5:30. Don't be late!

I realized I'd been tricked, but chances were Vera would have always talked me into it. But she better not hold back the McDonald's. On that point, I was very serious.

My phone buzzed again, but this time it was an email. Choosing to ignore it for a while, I set to work cleaning my brushes and tidying up my workspace. After I'd dropped my wine glass off next to my sink, I double checked the locks on the front door and balcony. I didn't really think someone would scale six stories just to steal my costume jewelry and hand-me-down furniture, but I just knew that the one night I didn't check it would be the one night I had to deal with a serial killer. A Spiderman-impersonating serial killer.

After brushing my teeth, washing my face, and changing from the oversized t-shirt I used for painting to the oversized t-shirt I used for sleeping, I crawled into bed and wiggled my toes under the sheets. It wasn't very late, but if I was seriously going to meet Vera at the crack of dawn in the morning, an early bedtime was in order.

Checking my phone one last time before I plugged it in for the night, I saw the email I'd ignored earlier. My heart jumped in my chest and a large horde of butterflies suddenly took flight in my belly, dipping, diving, and flapping giant wings.

Ezra.baptiste@yahoo.com

A strange panic stirred the already fidgety nerves inside me. I wondered how he'd gotten my email address until I belatedly realized I'd been the one to give it to him. For his florist.

Because he had a florist.

The man had a florist!

Could we all just take a minute to roll our eyes in unison? Please and thank you.

My finger hovered over the email, but I couldn't make myself open it. What did he want? Why had he emailed me? Why did I care so much?

I thought about the half-finished painting of him in my office and decided to burn it. All evidence that I'd contemplated the shape of his eyes and curve of his jaw must be destroyed ASAP.

Ugh, it was stupid, but the truth was hard to face. I wanted to hate Ezra. Or maybe not hate him, but at the very least be unaffected by him. And I still couldn't make myself not care.

He was too cool, successful, and larger-than-life. I couldn't help but be mildly fascinated by him. I wanted to know how late he worked every day, and how early he got up. I wanted to know how he took his coffee, and which of the four restaurants he owned was his favorite? I wanted to know if the rumors were true that he really named his restaurants after his ex-girlfriends. I wanted to know so many things that I shouldn't want to know.

Seeing his name in my email inbox did funny things to my resolve to ignore him. He'd made a terrible first impression on me, but if he wasn't so wholly intimidating, I might have given him a second chance. Instead, it wasn't just that a business owner had insulted my sense of design... it was that *Ezra Baptiste* had belittled me.

Another email came in while I stared at Ezra's. The email was from my boss, Henry the Little Tucker, and had Ethan Baker cc'd. I opened it with a touch of my finger and zero fear or uncertainty.

I scanned the work details, noting our meeting time tomorrow. Henry sent a second email before I'd finished the first one. When I opened it, I had to pause at the oddity of it. He was apparently back to being inappropriate. I deleted it as soon as I finished reading, *Really looking forward to working with you on this, sweetheart. Let's kick some Black Soul ass.*

Wrinkling my nose, I somehow found it easier to open Ezra's email after reading Henry's. Although it took me a second to see the words. It was hard to shake off the creepy feeling Henry managed to vibe my way through email.

It was probably nothing. He just wanted this account to do well. So did Ethan and me. There wasn't anything to read into. I decided to forget it ever happened and never bring it up again. There. Done.

Denial was a sign of maturity, right?

I blinked and Ezra's concise and unexpected email came into focus.

To: mollythemaverick@gmail.com
From: ezra.baptiste@yahoo.com
Date: February 20, 2017 19:48:22 EST
Subject: Friday Night Confirmation
Molly,
I never confirmed that I would get Killian and Vera to the restaurant. I've got it covered so don't worry about it.
I also reached out to my florist and she will be in touch with you tomorrow.
What are your thoughts on wine? Would you like to look over my cellar? I have time this week, but I'll need to schedule in advance.
Let me know,
Ezra
P.S. The temperature isn't supposed to get above thirty tomorrow. Wear a coat.

I read the email three more times. And then another three times for good measure.

Was he serious?

I rolled over and contemplated forwarding the email to Vera. This situation seemed like it needed a second opinion. But then Vera was all in love right now and she might not see everything with clear eyes.

Her vision was currently clouded with hearts and wedding bells.

And it would ruin the surprise of her surprise engagement party.

Wear a coat.

Ezra Baptiste. Businessman, restaurateur, weatherman.

After twenty more minutes of staring at my phone until the battery icon turned red and I had to plug it in, I decided on my reply.

To: ezra.baptiste@yahoo.com
From: mollythemaverick@gmail.com
Date: February 20, 2017 21:58:52 EST
Subject: Friday Night Affirmation
~~Dear Ezra...~~
~~Dear Mr. Baptiste...~~
~~Jerkface...~~
~~To whom it may concern...~~
Ezra,
Thanks for getting the happy couple to Lilou. I really appreciate everything you're doing for the party. I'm sure your florist knows exactly what she's doing. She can just do her thing. If she's taking it over, I don't think I need to be involved with that part. As for the wine, I have zero thoughts. I'll defer to your expertise. Unless you don't have time. Then we can just make Wyatt do it.
See you Friday.
MM.
Also, in case you're interested, I'm wearing a blouse tomorrow. And a pencil skirt. But no plans for a coat so far.

I pressed send before I could overthink it. Although in hindsight, I probably could have come up with something way wittier had I given it a few more minutes.

Refusing to dwell on it, I turned off my phone and shut off my lamp. Of course, it took me another hour and a half to fall asleep. And when I finally did, I dreamed of a strong jaw and a better brush that would get the arc of his eyebrows right and the curve of his barely there smile. I dreamed of dark, dark eyes and a weird fascination with my coat.

I woke up regretting my late-night email and wishing I cared about wine, and flowers, and Black Soul Records.

I also woke to a simple, concise, infuriating email.

To: mollythemaverick@gmail.com
From: ezra.baptiste@yahoo.com
Date: February 21, 2017 01:19:38 EST
Subject: Re: Friday Night Affirmation
Stubborn woman.

Chapter Four

"You're officially dead to me."

Vera collapsed against the wall gasping for breath. "I'm officially dead," she panted.

I wiped my sweaty forehead with the back of my hand and glared at her. "I can't feel my legs."

"I can't feel my butt," she countered.

"I can feel mine way too much. After what I just went through I'm pretty sure that machine owes me dinner."

Vera giggled, but it was weak and breathless. We'd walked out of spin class like pros, high-fiving random strangers on the way, and sipping from our water bottles like we could care less about hydration.

But once we'd turned the corner, we'd let our true colors shine. I couldn't suck down my water fast enough, and someone had crawled inside my body and lit my lungs on fire. *Owie*.

"Maybe spin class was a bad idea," Vera relented. "We should have at least started in the beginner's class."

My eyes bulged. "That wasn't the beginner's class?"

"Does that make it better or worse?"

I glared at her. "Vera, I can't move my body. My muscles have gone on strike." Demonstrating my point, I waved my foot around weakly before dropping it back to the ground. "You could have at least warned me that I was facing an expert level class."

"What would that have mattered?" she laughed.

I lifted my chin stubbornly. "Because then I could have prepared."

"By getting in shape in less than twelve hours?"

"By running away to Mexico where you couldn't find me."

She rolled her eyes, grabbed my hand and tugged me toward the locker room. "Come on, lazy bones. I'll buy you breakfast off the dollar menu to make up for it."

Vera's promise of McDonald's was the extra burst of energy I needed to survive the walk to the showers. I stood under the hot stream for longer than I should have, and still my motor skills were jerky at best when I emerged and tried valiantly to get dressed. Thank goodness the workout we'd survived was all legs because my makeup could have ended in disaster if my arms were as tired as my trembling thighs.

"Did you even go to sleep last night?" I asked Vera as she leaned forward with an open mouth to apply her mascara.

She moved the wand away from her face so she could yawn. "For a couple hours. I thought opening a food truck was a lot of work. It's nothing compared to the restaurant."

"Have you and Killian decided on a name yet?"

She snorted. "Nope. Right now, we're bouncing between Verian, which is our two names squished together, and The Blue Table, which has no significance whatsoever, but it sounds cool."

"I like both of them," I told her. "Verian is clever."

"Cheesy," she corrected. "It's super cheesy. But I don't mind the sound of it."

I smiled at my reflection while I applied lip stain. "You know what you should name it, right?"

Turning her head, she looked at me. "What's that?"

"Salt," I told her, referring to one of Killian's very first interactions with her cooking. "Just call it Salt." Expecting her to laugh with me, I was surprised when she didn't. "I'm just kidding," I added quickly.

She slammed her palm against my shoulder like she was high-fiving my clavicle. My poor, abused legs wobbled, but miraculously didn't give out. "Molly, you're a freaking genius!"

"Huh?"

"Salt. It's brilliant. Fucking brilliant! I can't believe we didn't think of it sooner."

"Are you serious?"

Her head bobbed wildly. "So serious. It's simple and memorable and so meaningful to us. It's seriously the best name I've ever heard."

My lips lifted in a proud smile. Having worked in marketing for so long, I knew she was right. Salt sounded cool. It broadcasted like the trendy new restaurant taking the city by storm that it was. Of course, with Killian and Vera at the helm, that was always the restaurant's destiny, but a stellar name would give it that extra something special that would keep people talking about it.

She had already pulled out her phone and called Killian before I could say another word. "He's probably sleeping," she muttered distractedly.

It was only seven-thirty in the morning. Which for them was practically the middle of the night. Killian and Vera were basically nocturnal. They started work when most of us got off, and stayed well into the early morning hours to clean up and shut down.

Currently, they were working to open a gorgeous new space where they would cook side by side, leading the city to new heights of culinary genius. For now, before they officially opened, their lives had somewhat balanced out. But understandably, after so many years working in busy kitchens night after night, neither one of them could really give up the late-night life.

"Salt!" Vera practically shouted into the phone as soon as she heard Killian's sleep-roughened voice.

I heard him grunt out a confused, "Wha?"

"Salt," she squealed. "For the restaurant. Let's call it Salt!"

The next time he spoke, his voice sounded much more alert. Vera began prattling off how it was my idea, but also how it was perfect. She moved to the side of the locker room for some privacy. And some space. She always used her hands to talk. When she was this excited she was bound to give someone a black eye if she wasn't careful.

I finished my makeup and gave my bangs a little extra TLC. I'd pulled the rest of my long hair into a bun at the nape of my neck, hoping to look professional for my first day on the Black Soul project. I'd also gone with the exact outfit I'd described to Ezra in my email last night.

My plum pencil skirt hit just below my knees and molded to my body over thighs and a butt that still burned. I'd paired it with a gray long-sleeve, ruffled blouse and matching gray pumps. And because it was winter and cold outside, I'd even worn pantyhose. The kind with the seam running up the back of the leg because, obviously, I needed extra incentive to get myself into pantyhose.

I added some jewelry, and checked the lines of my tucked in shirt making sure the frills lay nicely and hadn't been waywardly placed. Staring at myself in the locker room mirror under terrible lighting and with not enough sleep, I wondered what was missing. Because something wasn't totally right.

My makeup was on point, and my style trendy enough to get by. My hair was tamed today, and my nails had been recently manicured. I looked how I was supposed to look for the job I was supposed to have.

Sure, there were things that I would change about myself if I could. I'd always thought my nose was too upturned and my eyes too big beneath my small forehead—which was why I did the whole bang thing. I definitely wouldn't have complained about bigger boobs or hips that had some flare. There was a scar on my collarbone that I liked to keep hidden. It was from when Vera and I were kids and Vann thought he was a ninja. Vann still apologized for the throwing star incident to this day.

Anyway, there were definitely things about me that I would change. But this *missing something* was hard to pinpoint. It didn't feel physical to me. It was deeper than that. Trickier than that.

My chest ached as I examined myself and nibbled on my bottom lip, hoping to figure out why I couldn't just be happy with where my life was. Why couldn't I just be happy for my best friend without having this existential crisis in which I questioned every single life choice I'd ever made?

I looked over at Vera where she stood leaning against the wall. Her free hand tugged on her wild hair that was still drying, and she smiled into the phone with googly eyes and imaginary hearts floating around her head. She had never been so in love. She had never been this happy before.

And I *was* happy for her. I was. But her happiness only spotlighted my unhappiness. Her bliss only shed light on my misery. Her joy revealed my lack of. Her contentment exaggerated my restlessness.

I couldn't figure out why. It wasn't really about Killian or her engagement and not-so-distant wedding. It wasn't about Vera finding her soul mate, true love, and Disney-esque fairy tale.

Honestly, I had never really been all that into the happily ever after. Even as a little girl, when I pictured being a grown-up, it was the job I dreamed of, not the man. It was the career, not the house in the suburbs with two-point-five kids and a matching poodle that I wished for. Plus, there was no one in my immediate circle that I would even consider dating.

Except maybe Chris Pratt. Obviously, I considered the entire cast of *Guardians of the Galaxy* in my immediate circle.

So why the gaping hole in my chest where there should be nothing but spastic enthusiasm for my best friend?

40

She hung up the phone and did a little dance of glee. "He loves it!" she squealed. "He's calling our business manager now."

"Business manager? You're so fancy I can't even handle it."

She wrinkled her nose. "Not even close. But this guy is a lifesaver. He handles the million phone calls and deals with the contractors when they're idiots. He is basically doing all the jobs I don't want to do."

"How did you find him?"

"Ezra," she replied casually. Like it was easy to say his name, and talk about him, and throw him into conversations. Like he wasn't the most successful person we both knew. "He has all the connections."

"I still can't believe he's so cool with Killian opening a restaurant. You're going to be his competition now. Isn't he at least mildly pissed?"

She shook her head. "Not even a little bit. But I also don't think he looks at us like competition. Ezra is a lot like Killian in that they're hard to get to know, but once they trust you, their loyalty is pretty much unbreakable. Ezra is really happy for Killian."

I made a humming noise in lieu of a verbal response.

"You should give him another chance, Molls," Vera suggested. "He's not that bad when you get to know him."

Grabbing my toiletries from around me, I threw them into my makeup case and walked over to my gym bag. The locker room had started to fill up with the before-work crowd, and it was getting steamy and uncomfortably warm.

"I'm sure he is," I agreed with her. "He's all rainbows, sunshine, and no judgment."

Vera snickered. "No, he's none of those things. But he somehow grows on you anyway."

My stomach growled loudly and I took the opportunity to change the subject. "I'm starving, Vere. Feed me."

She grabbed her gym bag and made a sour face. "I would like to feed you. Real food. What we're about to do is basically defiling the food industry. I just want you to be aware of that."

I narrowed my eyes in thought. "I think I'm going to get a breakfast burrito too. I deserve it after what you put me through."

"Blasphemy!"

Grinning at her, I held the locker room door open. "You only have yourself to blame."

She batted her eyelashes at me on her way out. "Should we try Crossfit next time? Whole30? Your mom's old Cindy Crawford tapes?"

We laughed all the way to our cars. And then all the way through our short breakfast. And then when we said goodbye in the parking lot to go our separate ways.

The crazy thing was, I would try any stupid workout or diet or doomsday cult Vera came up with because I loved her too much to tell her no. And because I'd hated it when she lived in Charlotte. And I'd really hated it when she'd been with Derrek.

Vera had been through hell before she came back to Durham a year ago. Whatever emotional turmoil I was going through now couldn't compare to what my best friend had faced. Honestly, the good outweighed the bad anyway. My joyful feelings for my friend were so much larger than my own, selfish, pity-party ones. My pride in who she'd become and how hard she'd worked to get where she was now would always outshine my personal feelings of self-doubt and insecurity.

Because she was closer to me than any other human. Because we'd been through good times and bad times, and really good times, and really, really bad times, and that's what friends did. We put each other first. We stepped outside of ourselves and our issues to cheer each other on and root for each other's happiness.

Vera had found her soulmate and that gave me hope. Maybe I didn't have an exact idea of what my perfect ending looked like, but that didn't mean I wouldn't find it.

****

Thanks to traffic I probably should have anticipated, I walked into the office twenty minutes later than I had planned. I was flustered and sore and unexplainably out of breath because I rationalized that I should be in ultra-shape now after my psychotic spin class this morning.

I had just enough time to say hi to Emily, drop my purse at my desk, and grab my notebook and laptop for my morning briefing with Ethan and Henry.

"They're already waiting for you," Emily murmured while I searched for my favorite pen.

"I'm not even late!" I protested.

"Yeah, well, good luck convincing them of that."

I growled something profane at her, and then scurried to Henry's office. Emily was right. They were there and already talking about the account.

Scooting behind Ethan's chair, I took a seat and held my shoulders back, even though I felt like curling into a ball and apologizing for who I was as a human.

"Molly," Henry greeted. "So nice of you to join us."

"Sorry," I blurted. "I thought the meeting started at nine-thirty."

Neither man confirmed my statement. Instead, Henry passed me a packet of papers about Black Soul, including a marketing plan that he'd already devised. My heart sank to my stomach. I'd wanted to be a part of this process, not delegated tasks he didn't want to deal with.

"As creative director, I want you to know my door is always open. I'm here to go over every minute detail and help guide you in the right direction," Henry explained. "Ethan already has some great ideas for an updated logo. We've gone over his vision and I'm confident he's off to a good start." My heart sank further. I had some cool ideas for their new logo. There was so much to do with a name like Black Soul. "Molly, I'm going to work side-by-side with you on the social media packet. I want my hands on every part of this project."

Avoiding Henry's awkward stare, I nodded and made notes in the margins of my planner as if this wasn't exactly what I'd expected. Sure, I had hoped for more. Or I'd at least expected to be part of a conversation that I could have petitioned for more. But the majority of my career so far had been in social media.

On one hand, I already knew I would excel because that was where I felt comfortable. On the other hand, it came with zero respect. The older designers in my office had no idea how valuable a strong social media presence could be. There was so much to do in the way of advertising on the numerous different platforms, and unlimited potential to be innovative and unique.

And yet, the people I worked with were still bidding on expensive print spots and TV commercials. They were single-handedly keeping magazine publishers in business. Because it obviously wasn't the missing throngs of subscribers. And don't even get me started on commercials.

Besides the elderly, who had the patience to watch anything on live TV?

"Are you good to make some graphics that coincide with the logo Ethan develops?" The Little Tucker asked.

"Yep," I answered, working hard to swallow bitter disappointment. To Ethan I said, "Send me all of the mockups you are going to take to them and I can develop a coinciding online plan. As long as you give me enough time to put something together, we can give them the whole picture of what their campaign will look like."

43

Ethan marked something in his notes. "That's a great idea, Molly."

I breathed a subtle sigh of relief. This wasn't the first time I had pitched an approach like this. Usually I got polite nods and hums of resigned acceptance only to be totally forgotten about until the morning of the pitch. I was good at my job, but even I needed more than thirty minutes to put together an entire campaign.

I'd even confronted designers that I worked with often, trying in vain to explain why I would want to pitch the advertising campaign along with the new logo, but I could never get the good old boys to see the big picture.

And some of them weren't even boys! In the beginning, I'd assumed I'd be able to count on females to fight battles with me. Because girl power! And solidarity. And a strong, mutual hatred of our periods. But it turned out women in the workplace could be just as vicious, if not more so, than men.

Where men brushed me aside and ignored my requests, talents and opinions, women strapped on armor and waged war. Men barely acknowledged my efforts. Women assumed I was trying to destroy their career by furthering mine.

Unfortunately, Henry wasn't nearly as forward thinking as Ethan. "You're going to create an entire ad campaign for each logo pitch? That seems like an excessive amount of work on your end. I think your efforts are better served on price points and potential reach."

"It won't be an entire campaign for each logo. More like simple mockups featuring the logo in several different capacities. I'd like to have a graphic for desktop and mobile, website versus social platforms. It will give the client a bigger picture of how the logo will look during the campaign."

Henry pinched his nose with his thumb and forefinger, thinking over my idea.

"It will benefit the logo," Ethan added. "And help the client pick the best one. I think Molly is on to something."

Henry stared at my legs until I wished I'd worn something more practical. Like sackcloth. Or a giant tarp. "We'll see," he finally sighed. "I still need everything else from you though, sweets. Just 'cause you're getting sidetracked with this, doesn't mean you can slack off with my stuff."

I swallowed back annoyance at the nickname and accusation. "I won't," I promised. "I'm on top of this."

He leaned forward, resting his elbows on his desk and smiled back. But then he kept smiling and staring, looking at me long enough that I started

44

to feel uncomfortable beneath his warm gaze. I crossed my legs nervously and he tracked the movement with hungry eyes. "I'll bet."

Clearing my throat, I looked down at my notes again and pretended to write something. In reality, it was a tiny drawing of an eyeball. I needed an outlet for this nervous energy. The Little Tucker was such a skeez. Was it so much to ask that he restrain his dirty-old-man tendencies while at work?

Henry turned back to Ethan while I added an arrogantly arched eyebrow and thick eyelashes that didn't belong on the man in my doodle. The eyeball stared at me from the flat page of my notebook, judging me, dissecting me… seeing parts of me I wanted to remain hidden.

Ezra.

He'd followed me to work. I thought about his email this morning. *Stubborn woman.*

A sultry wisp of heat curled in my core. Most days I felt like a tiara-wearing toddler playing dress up with my mom's heels and checkbook. I was in a grown-up life I didn't know what to do with. And yet, that email had made me feel like anything but a little girl.

I added lines around the pupil, making it appear bloodshot. Then I sketched some shadows on the bottom lid, darkening the corner, spreading a bruise beneath. In a few seconds, I'd transformed something mysterious and beguiling into a grotesque version of itself.

I took a deep breath. That felt better.

By the time Henry wrapped up the meeting, I was in desperate need of another cup of coffee. McDonald's didn't have the worst brew in the world, but the overdose of sugar and carbs from that excursion pulsed at my temples with the beginnings of a headache.

"Stay a sec, honey," Henry ordered as Ethan gathered his things.

I nibbled my bottom lip and hugged my notebook against my chest so he couldn't see the Eye of ~~Sauron~~ Ezra I'd distorted.

"I'll start sending mockups as soon as I finish them, Molly," Ethan added with his belongings in hand, already halfway out the door. "If you have notes on anything, feel free to share them. I'd love some feedback."

My mouth lifted in a genuine smile. "Will do. Thanks, Ethan. I'll send you what I come up with too."

He tipped his head. "Sounds good."

Ethan walked out of the office, but before he could get out of hearing range, Henry bit out a gross accusation. "He's married."

My throat dried out and all the moisture in my body evaporated. If I could have shriveled into a Molly raisin, I would have gladly welcomed it. "Excuse me?"

"Ethan is married, Molly. I thought you had more class than that."

My heart jumped in my chest, trying to climb up my throat and throw itself out of my mouth. I eyed the window behind Henry, loosely debating the impulse to jump out of it. "I don't know what you're insinuating."

Henry's annoyed expression turned patronizing. He let out a patient sigh and stood up. His fingers trailed over the desk as he came to stand in front of me.

His office was the second biggest, inferior only to his dad's. There was plenty of space to spread out, but I'd moved my chair closer to his desk during the meeting so I could see everything on his computer and appear interested. Which turned out to be a huge mistake.

Now that he'd stopped right in front of me, he leaned back, balancing his butt on the edge of his desk and stretching his long legs toward me. They settled on either side of my own, brushing against my almost-bare calves.

I pushed back with my toes, greedily putting space between us. Unfortunately, my chair legs got caught in the carpet. His ankle pressed against mine causing my mind to spin with anxiety. How did I get out of this situation without making it even more awkward than it already was?

Was it totally out of line to fake a heart attack?

Or what was less sexy than a heart attack?

How about diarrhea?

If Henry was coming on to me again, diarrhea was sure to shut that shit down.

Literally.

Imagined or otherwise.

But could I live with the whole office knowing I had to flee Little Tucker's office because of a bout with dysentery?

No. No, I could not.

Inappropriate or not, I'd rather face Henry than that reputation. Besides, between this and the Christmas party incident, I was starting to wonder if maybe Henry Tucker just didn't consider personal space? His love language was obviously physical touch and making everyone around him uncomfortable with his overreaching, inappropriate behavior.

Instead of making an excuse to leave, I tucked my legs beneath my seat and looked up expectantly at my boss. He might not know how to be a professional, but I did. He could learn a thing or two from me and my gigantic personal bubble.

"He's married," Henry repeated. "I didn't peg you for the kind of girl that shits where she eats. But I guess I was wrong."

His comment reminded me of pretend diarrhea and I wrinkled my nose in disgust. "I'm not interested in Ethan," I said firmly, needing him to get this immediately. And also to stop talking so loud. "Even if he wasn't married, he's not my type."

Henry's lips lifted in a sly smirk. "Oh, really? What is your type?"

"Men that aren't married," I bit out, trying desperately to stay polite.

"So me then?" He grinned.

I noted a coffee stain on his lapel. "Excuse me?" I heard myself say for the second time. This could not be happening. He could not seriously be hitting on me! Even three shots of tequila deep, I'd been super clear at Christmas. My name was no. My sign was no. My number was *hell no*.

"You said you're interested in men that aren't married. I'm not married. You must be interested in me." His grin stretched, greedy and wolfish.

Swallowing down nerves, fear of losing my job, and a hefty dose of awkward, I admitted gently, "Actually I have a long list of criteria. Which is why I'm still single."

"Thank the good Lord for that," Henry muttered. His eyes took another trip down my body, slowly caressing every inch of me from the open neckline of my blouse to the pantyhose I had been so set on wearing today.

A sick feeling crept over me everywhere his gaze lingered. I resisted the urge to clutch my collar together and slap him.

He was my boss. Maybe he was being inappropriate and obnoxious, but he was still my boss.

And the reason I was on this account to begin with.

"Do you need anything else, Henry? Or am I free to go?"

I regretted my wording as soon as the question left my lips. I couldn't have told you exactly what I'd said, but whatever it was seemed to encourage him. His expression lit with interest and he leaned toward me, bringing our bodies closer together. He smelled like cheese and cheap cologne.

"For now, Molly. You're free to go for now."

I scurried out of his office like a scared church mouse, but by the time I'd gotten back to my desk, I had almost convinced myself there was nothing wrong with his behavior.

Henry Tucker was an ass, but he was still my boss. And the son of the CEO, set to inherit this entire office. He wouldn't mess that up by overstepping with his minions.

Still, it wasn't hard to consider passing off this account to someone else, to someone more qualified and not nearly as grossed out by the

Little Tucker. Maybe there would be an equally glorifying account in the future. Maybe I could make progress at the company without a big account, without drawing attention to myself.

Maybe a long lost aunt would die and I would inherit a huge sum of money making me independently wealthy.

I dismissed the idea as quickly as it had come. Quitting now would set me back light years. I hustled my ass off to get this account, putting in hours and hours with local skating rinks and putt-putt golf. Finally, my hard work was going to pay off with a national campaign and a big, fat commission. I wouldn't screw this up, not even to get away from Junior.

Maybe he was creepy and touchy and crass, but as long as he kept his hands—and legs, face, and all other body parts—to himself, I could put up with him until the end of the project. Black Soul would do more good for my career than Henry could ever do bad. And STS was the lead media company to work for in this area.

I fell into my desk chair and threw my notebook down on my keyboard. A chill settled on the back of my neck, forcing a shiver down my spine.

You can do this, I told myself. *He's just a flirt. It's not you, specifically. It's how he is with every girl.*

I believed that was true. It didn't make me feel any less dirty.

Chapter Five

Molly,

Meg is asking for the spice racks you mentioned. Are you able to drop them by Lilou this afternoon? I can send someone to pick them up if it's too much of a hassle. I am also wondering what time you will be coming to set up tomorrow. I want to make sure someone is available to let you in.

Ezra.

P.S. It's going to be in the fifties tomorrow. You'll want to wear your bikini to the party, I'm sure.

I glared at Ezra's latest email with my mouse hovering over the delete button. I had heard that successful people were often eccentric weirdos beneath all of their glamor and money. That had to be the reason Ezra was obsessed with the weather.

And my outerwear.

Emily rolled into the aisle separating our desks. "Is it the Little Tucker again?"

"Ha!" Tearing my eyes from Ezra's unexpected email, I turned to my friend. "No, not this time. But give him five minutes, I'm sure he'll chime in any second."

Since our meeting Tuesday morning, Henry Tucker had been a constant thorn in my side. There was micromanaging. And then there was Junior's super-mega-micro-managing that made me want to stab him with my stapler. He was either emailing me at all hours of the night and day or calling me during those same hours. And when I was at work, he had taken to sneaking up on me whenever I was alone—in the breakroom, outside the restroom, in the parking garage. I swore he wore slippers to work since I never heard him coming.

He was so in my business that I never actually had time to devote to my projects. He wanted to know every single, minute detail of what I was working on and then he wanted me to explain the how and why of each so he could be sure it was worth my effort.

And the entire time he was in my business, he couldn't seem to remember my name. I was starting to wonder if dementia ran in his family. First Mother Tucker never called me by my name, and now his son seemed only capable of referring to me in a series of awful pet names. Darling. Sweets. Babe. Pretty girl. Honey. And ~~the one that made me feel especially stabby~~ my favorite—sweet cheeks.

I shuddered in disgust just thinking about it. When I realized his degrading terms of endearment weren't going to end, I'd thought about going straight to Tucker Senior. Surely this was harassment of some kind? But then I'd heard him call Catherine Dawes doll, and she hadn't done anything more than ignore him. If she could suck it up, so could I.

Besides, we'd only just begun the Black Soul account. I didn't want to make things tense with Henry when I'd have to work with him for months.

Yes, his pet names were obnoxious. And outdated. And beyond tacky. But, they weren't hurting me in a physical or emotional sense.

They were just annoying.

So, I put up with him, reminding him of my real name whenever I got the chance.

"So if it's not HT, why are you glaring at your computer?" Emily asked.

I raised my eyebrows, smoothing out the scowl I hadn't realized I'd been flashing. "It's that engagement party I'm throwing," I told her. "I'm being forced to work with my friend's fiancé's friend and he's difficult."

"The chef?"

"The owner," I clarified. "Ezra. He's a know-it-all. And he's apparently detail-oriented because he wants me to sign off on every little thing. There's only so much I can agree to before I'm just like, dude, whatever napkins you think are best, just go with those." I smiled at her so she could see I was partly joking.

She laughed. "Well, he didn't get where he is today by skipping over the details."

I puffed out a short breath. "You're probably right about that." Glancing at the clock again I contemplated skipping out of work early so I could run home and grab the spice racks. If I left now I wouldn't have to deal with traffic on the way to Lilou.

There were still a few things I wanted to pick up before tomorrow night, and I didn't want to fight bumper-to-bumper traffic as I hopped around town.

Emily scooted closer and dropped her voice so our nosey coworkers couldn't hear. "Hey, a few of us are heading to happy hour after work. Are you in?"

I watched my mouse click reply and shook my head at my own weakness. "I wish," I mumbled. "This account is going to give me a drinking problem." She shot me a sympathetic look. "But I can't," I went on. "I have to deal with last minute party details. Maybe next week?"

Emily rolled her chair back behind her desk. "I can't believe everything you're doing for this party."

I shrugged, feeling shy. "Vera deserves this," I told her simply. "I'm happy to organize. Besides, I'm not really doing a whole lot. Wyatt and Ezra seem to have everything covered. I'm just showing up."

"You're a good friend," Emily decided.

I rolled my eyes at the computer. "You don't even know. Vera and I go way back. All the way back. I wouldn't be who I am today without her."

"Ah, she's one of those friends."

I smiled at a framed picture of us on my desk. It was one of my favorites, taken when we were both in college—before Derrek. We were at her dad's house, goofing around in the kitchen. She was holding a whisk and I was holding a paintbrush. We had been making cupcakes for Vann and the grand opening of Cycle Life. Vera had the brilliant idea to try to make them into little bicycles. She'd made perfect cupcakes and enlisted me to paint the frosting. By the end of the day we were covered in flour and sugar, and sick from eating so much batter and laughing too hard. Her dad had snapped the picture. She had powdered sugar on her cheek and I had a stripe of black frosting down my nose.

It was only seven years ago, but it felt like a lifetime. So much had happened since then.

"We raised each other," I told Emily. "It's weird that she's getting married."

Not hearing the catch in my voice or noticing the wateriness of my eyes, Emily said, "So what you're saying is you'd like me to set you up with Adam's friend?"

I shot her a look. "Ugh. No. That is not at all what I'm saying. That is the last kind of complication I need right now." I bit my lip to hide my grimace. Because was it really? I acted busy and overwhelmed, but what did I really have going on right now? I was maybe facing an early mid-life crisis and secretly googling good apartment cats. I had started to worry about the amount of Diet Coke I drank and whether it was too early to start using an anti-aging serum. But other than that, Vera's wedding was the most exciting thing I had going on currently. And it wasn't even my thing.

How pathetic was that?

Emily's phone rang, diverting her attention long enough for me to respond to Ezra's email.

To: ezra.baptiste@yahoo.com
From: mollythemaverick@gmail.com
Date: February 23, 2017 16:27:33 EST
Subject: Final Destination
Ezra,
I'll swing by my apartment and grab the spice racks after work. I can drop them off at Lilou in an hour? I only have four of them. Wyatt was planning to let me in tomorrow. Is that okay?
MM.
Also, bikini it is! I'm changing the theme to tropical. Is it too late to cancel the peonies? We could do orchids instead. And leis. We'll definitely need some tiki torches. Wyatt should roast a pig! How do you feel about a parrot or two? Three? You're pure genius, Baptiste. Pure genius.

"Do you have the graphics for the new logo?"

I jumped, letting out a startled squeak. Henry Tucker hovered over my shoulder, his face too close to mine. I rolled back in my chair, forcing it over a random cord that acted like a speed bump in my hurry to get away from his coffee breath and invasion of my space.

He laughed at my expense. "Did I scare you?"

You always scare me sat on the tip of my tongue, but I wrestled it back. "I wasn't paying attention. Sorry."

His smile turned into a leer. "The graphics?" he pressed again. "Am I going to see them before the end of the day?"

I nodded. "I was just about to send them over. I have a few finishing touches and then I'll upload them to our shared file."

Henry usually emailed everything directly to Ethan or me. He said he liked personalized interactions and it was easier for him to keep track of our individual progress. I refused to communicate through email with him. After Tuesday, I'd asked him to move to our shared file with Ethan.

It was silly. And way over the top since we were talking about email. But I felt safer with Ethan involved. Henry didn't use pet names in there.

"See that you do, doll face," Henry said. "Will you be around later if I have notes on them?"

Something uneasy slid through me making my stomach clench. It left a trail of slime in its wake. It was a legitimate question. Only it reeked of fishing. I was suddenly grateful for Ezra's email. "Actually, tonight I have a thing. Sorry. And tomorrow I'm only here in the morning. But save your notes in the shared file. I can work on it over the weekend."

Henry's smile turned thin and forced. "I should make you come in on Saturday to make up for all the time you're missing, yeah? This is an important account."

I shifted in my chair, crossing my arms over my chest and rolled back further. "We haven't even met with the client yet."

He barked out a laugh. "I'm just kidding, honey. Enjoy your weekend. We'll hit it hard again on Monday."

I tried to smile, but it wobbled and fell flat. "Sounds good."

He winked at me. "But I want those graphics before you leave today. Can you handle that?"

Nodding confidently if for no other reason than to just get him out of here, I said, "Absolutely. Seriously, they just need finishing touches."

He straightened, pointed a finger gun at me and said, "You're a gem, Molly."

I breathed out at the use of my actual name. It was refreshing to hear it after a week of honeys and doll faces and every other sickly-sweet moniker used only on females.

And I just wanted to make a note that I was not the kind of feminist that saw a man and ripped off her bra so she could burn it in effigy. I was more the laid back, equality means equal kind of twenty-first century girl. Hell yes, there should be equal pay. But I also acknowledged that lots of women chose not to enter the workplace at all because they'd rather raise a family. Good for them. We lived in a society where both kinds of women were celebrated and cherished and supported. And it was beautiful.

However, could we all just take a second to acknowledge the kind of backlash I would get if the next time Henry Tucker asked me to do something, I winked at him and declared, "You got it, champ." Or "Bucko." Or maybe, possibly, affectionately, "Dickhead."

I glanced at Tucker Senior's door and imagined him calling security to escort me out of the building for picking on his number one son.

My computer dinged and another email from Ezra popped up.

To: mollythemaverick@gmail.com
From ezra.baptiste@yahoo.com
Date: February 23, 2017 16:49:44 EST
Subject: You're hilarious...
If you even think about bringing a bird into Lilou, so help me God, Maverick...

I found myself smiling at the computer screen. I pictured his eyebrows furrowed with fear, his mouth pressed into a firm frown. I imagined his long, elegant fingers tapping out a furious reply.

I might not like Ezra Baptiste as a human, but I seriously liked messing with him.

Dismissing the idea of sending another return email, I got to work on the graphics I promised Henry. I waited to send them until I had all of my things packed up for the day. I put my purse on my shoulder, sent the file, shut down my computer, and then bolted from the office without even saying goodbye to Emily.

I didn't want to risk running into Henry again. I was officially off the clock.

Swinging by my apartment to grab the four centerpieces took longer than I wanted it to, but eventually I made it to Lilou and was able to balance all four of them in a precarious stack from cradled forearms to perched chin.

The hostess hurried to open the door for me and I squeezed between her and the frame, just barely managing to hold on to the spice racks.

"Can I help you?" the college-age girl dressed all in black asked.

"I just need to drop these off," I told her. "They're for a party tomorrow night."

She stared at me blankly. "Is someone expecting you?"

"Yes," I told her while eying the host stand and wishing Ezra had given me more explicit instructions.

"Who?" the hostess with the most-ess asked bluntly.

"Ezra, Wyatt, most of your kitchen staff."

Her eyebrows lifted in surprise. "I'll find Mr. Baptiste," she offered.

"No, that's okay—" But she was already gone. Belatedly, I realized I should have asked for the floor manager. Now I would have to deal with Ezra.

So help me God, Maverick...

I shivered and it had nothing to do with the cold weather.

A manager walked over a few seconds later and asked if I was making a delivery. I explained that the hostess had gone to find Ezra. He stood next to me and waited to find out if I was telling the truth or not. Because in my wide-leg trousers and cold-shoulder sweater, I apparently looked like a dangerous criminal.

Ezra arrived thirty seconds later, mouth already turned down, eyes already laser focused.

"Molly," he greeted in his usual way. "Let me get those." He shot a glare at his floor manager and scooped up the centerpieces before I could object.

"Uh, thanks."

He tilted his head toward his office. "Walk with me."

Not waiting for my reply, he turned around and headed back the way he came. I glanced nervously at the snooty floor manager and clueless hostess.

Neither offered any comfort or help.

Ezra paused just before he reached the dining area and noticed I wasn't directly behind him. "Molly," he clipped out.

His terse order got my feet moving and I reluctantly followed him around the outer edges of the restaurant toward his office.

Nerves jumped and buzzed in my stomach, my fingers tingled and I tried to build my case quickly against this man I didn't know what to think about anymore.

It was the way he said my name, I decided. That was how he kept getting me to do his bidding.

I'd always disliked my name. Even as a child I had realized it sounded like a child's name. Now as a grown-up it was the farthest thing from mature. It was on the opposite side of the spectrum from sexy and sophisticated.

Molly.

It sounded like a toddler's name. Or your best friend's name. Or the eccentric cat lady that never left her apartment.

No wonder I'd been friend-zoned so often. No guy could imagine themselves married to a plain, boring Molly.

55

Except when Ezra said it, Molly didn't sound boring or plain or friendly. He said my name like a command. He glided over the consonants and caressed the vowels. When Ezra said my name, I was anything but the crazy cat lady. I was bold, beautiful, and everything defiantly female.

I responded to Ezra because he said my name how I had wanted to hear it my entire life.

"Shut the door," he ordered as he set the spice racks down on the center of his desk.

"Am I in trouble?" I asked archly.

His back was to me, but I heard him clearly when he said, "Only if you've brought tropical birds with you."

"They're in my car. I'm telling you, it's a world-class menagerie." When Ezra didn't laugh at my reference, I tried to help him out. "*Aladdin*? You know the Disney movie?"

He turned around and planted his hands on his hips. "I've never seen it."

"Are you serious? It's like a staple of my childhood. Vera and I would constantly fight over who got to be Jasmine."

He shrugged. "I didn't have a Disney movie kind of childhood."

Instantly, I regretted every word I'd spoken in the last two minutes. I wanted to snatch them out of the air and shove them back in my mouth. Instead, they buzzed around the small office like biting flies. I knew he'd had a tragic past. I knew his mom had died when he was a kid and he lived out the rest of his childhood in foster care. I knew he hadn't known his dad until he was almost dead. But I only knew any of that because Vera had told me. So it wasn't exactly like I could bring it all up now.

I settled on a weak and pathetic, "Huh..."

His gaze moved over me, noting my fitted sweater and the cutouts over my shoulders and biceps. A smile tugged at his lips but he refused to loose it. "Thank you for bringing these by. I'm sorry Meg didn't reach out to you directly. She can be spacey."

"It's not a problem," I told him. "Don't you think they'll be cute?"

He lifted the top one up by the corner. "They are symbolic."

I couldn't tell if that was a compliment or an insult so I chose to move on. *Oh, did I say move on? I meant, poke the bear.* "Picture them bursting with peonies."

He looked up at me and where I was expecting to find a battle in his eyes, I found only amusement. "I'm not sure I even know what a peony looks like."

I couldn't help but smile. "Cute," I repeated. "It looks cute."

The corners of his mouth lifted in a devastating smile that reached all the way to his rich, chocolate eyes. My breath whooshed out of me in a surprised exhale. I had expected him to argue with me, to challenge my taste. I did not expect him to soften and warm, and *look like that.*

I bit down on my bottom lip, schooling my expression and filling up with irritation. I wanted him to pick a fight with me. I wanted him to dismiss me for an important call or forget I even existed. I did not need him smiling at me and giving me all of his focus and talking about Aladdin—which everybody knew was the hottest of the Disney princes.

I blamed the Hammer pants and cartoon abs.

"So, what's the final head count?" he asked.

Happy to have something to focus on, I answered quickly. "Fifty-ish I think? I'm not totally sure because a lot of Killian's friends were maybes. Or they were planning on coming late, after they closed their kitchens."

Ezra chuckled a low, throaty sound. "That's why I picked a Friday night," he confessed. "I was hoping they would all have to work."

"Are you serious?" I asked because I couldn't tell. "Won't that make Killian mad?"

"I did it *for* Killian. Honestly, he could care less if anyone from the industry showed. He has Vera. That's what matters to him."

I wondered if Ezra understood the point of an engagement party at all. The plan was to invite all of the happy couples' friends so they could bring gifts or money, or simply show up and shower them with love. It was all about support and camaraderie. It had nothing to do with making Killian and Vera feel comfortable. Obviously.

"So does fifty-ish include your date?" Ezra asked casually.

I waved off any idea of him flirting with me because that was basically insane. "I think Steph mentioned setting me up with someone? But I can't remember his name."

Ezra's smile disappeared in favor of his usual frown. "Steph that works for me?"

"Yeah."

"How do you know Steph?"

"Wyatt," I explained. Then I canted my head to the side, wondering how aloof this man really was. "Wyatt and I are friends."

"Is that who Steph is setting you up with?"

"God, no," I laughed. "No, this guy is from a different restaurant I think. And not a head chef. Steph was very adamant that I don't want to date a chef."

"You don't," Ezra agreed. He must have seen confusion all over my face because he quickly added. "I currently employ several of them and they're not dating material. They're the worst."

"Even Killian?" I teased.

"Especially Killian. Although he doesn't work for me anymore."

"Well, this guy is a server somewhere? Or bartender? I can't remember the details. Honestly, I'm the token single friend at this point. I'm set up so often I've stopped bothering to remember their names, let alone their professions."

Ezra's smile returned and with it my heart fluttered and unwanted butterflies took flight. He opened his mouth to say something more, but we were interrupted by a hard knock on the door and Wyatt's head popping in. "Oh, sorry," Wyatt mumbled barely sounding apologetic. "Karen Savoy is here. She wants to have a word with you. And me, apparently."

Ezra's pleasant expression disappeared and he was once again all business, completely serious. "I'll be out in a moment." To me he said, "Thanks again, Molly. I'll see you tomorrow."

I smiled pleasantly and said goodbye to Wyatt and Ezra so they could deal with Karen Savoy—whoever that was. Deciding to forget about my almost normal conversation with Ezra, I ran the rest of my errands and picked up Chinese takeout on the way home. I spent the remainder of the night watching a documentary on an unsolved murder and freaking myself way out, even though all I wanted to do was paint.

But when I finally fell asleep, after at least twenty minutes of hysteric worrying, I was proud of myself for leaving my paints alone. And the memories of Ezra's smiling mouth. And his crinkled eyes. The way he gentled and heated and became something else entirely.

When I woke up in the morning, I checked my email and fought the urge to paint all of him over again.

To: mollythemaverick@gmail.com
From: ezra.baptiste@yahoo.com
Date: February 24, 2017 02:39:01 EST
Subject: World-Class Menagerie
I watched Aladdin. You should have always been Jasmine. Every single time.

Chapter Six

I clutched the cool glass in my hand and slipped to a corner of the room where I could hide from the potential date Steph had introduced me to. Steph was one of Wyatt's friends that I'd gotten to know through hanging out with him. She was sweet and energetic and had terrible taste in men. She'd sworn up and down that her friend Trent would be perfect for me.

Trent was a bartender from Greenlight, one of the cool, late night venues in the plaza. Once she'd introduced us, I realized I knew who he was and didn't hate looking at him, so I'd spent the first third of the night trying to talk to him.

At first, he seemed nice enough, although I never felt the flicker of chemistry or intrigue that was usually a good sign. He was taller than me and obviously worked out more than the occasional spin class. He had a nice smile and sturdy teeth. His laugh wasn't obnoxious and I knew he had a job. My internal checklist would have been complete if I'd been able to hold his attention for longer than three seconds at a time.

From my brief time hanging out with people in the food industry, I knew two things about bartenders. 1. They got a lot of action. 2. They expected a lot of action.

Bonus point. 3. They enjoyed attention. But it didn't really matter to them who they got it from.

Or at least the ones I'd met so far. So I'd put in some time with Trent while he continued to scan the room for potentials just in case I didn't work out. I'd ducked away at the first possible opportunity.

I'd already decided to make it my mission to avoid him for the rest of the night. Plus, the party seemed to be a success and I wanted to check out my handiwork.

Well, it wasn't totally my handiwork.

Actually, barely any of it was my handiwork.

I'd brought some centerpieces and recruited part of the team, but really Wyatt and Ezra deserved all the credit.

Also, credit was due to Meg, Ezra's florist, who wasn't even a florist. Her email signature had referenced one of the premier interior design firms in the city. I'd googled her, expecting a middle-aged plastic blonde. Instead, I'd gotten a chic redhead that couldn't have been much older than me.

I hated her immediately.

No, that wasn't true. I'd disliked her immediately. I hadn't hated her until I'd walked into Lilou three hours ago and seen what she'd done to the place.

Lilou was usually a stunning sight, but tonight I'd actually lost my breath when I walked inside the door. She'd taken my vintage spice racks and filled them with vibrant red peonies in overflowing bouquets that added magic to Lilou's already enchanting decor.

She'd draped more peonies over the iron bars on the windows and hung them in glass lanterns from the ceiling. She'd tented sheer fabric and layered the ceiling, transforming Lilou from trendy restaurant to epic event hot spot. Then she draped twinkling lights all over because clearly we needed more charm.

She'd strategically placed food stations around the room and grouped Wyatt's Vera-inspired menu from back in her short-lived food truck days in perfectly edible harmonies. And she'd somehow convinced Ezra to move tables out of the way so she could set up a dance floor that was currently crowded.

This was the party I hadn't been brave enough to hope for. Getting Lilou as the venue had been a big enough deal. What Meg had accomplished was... next level brilliance. And I had Ezra to thank.

Speaking of Ezra, the man didn't disappoint. He'd called Killian earlier in the day and asked him to bring Vera by the restaurant to try the tasting menu of a new executive chef he was considering for Bianca, one of his other restaurants. Killian and Vera had jumped at the chance to check out the new blood.

60

The surprise was only sort of ruined when they walked in the side door to the kitchen instead of the front door. The guests hadn't been expecting Killian and Vera to sneak up on them from behind.

Still, a surprise was a surprise. Vera had burst into tears and Killian had wrapped his arms around her and kissed the top of her head. The photographer Meg had enlisted snapped away, capturing the beautiful moment forever.

Now, well into the party, I was three champagne cocktails deep and working on my fourth. Vera danced with Killian in the middle of the floor, arms wrapped tightly around his neck, cheek pressed against his chest.

My heart kicked at the sight of them and I took another drink of champagne. I scanned the room, noting Ezra smiling at Meg, no doubt congratulating her on a job well done. My job well done. I took another drink of champagne.

"Where can I get one of those?" A pretty blonde pointed at the drink in my hand.

She had to be from Ezra's list of invites since I didn't recognize her. She was stunning in a white shift dress that showed off one elegant shoulder and a whole lot of leg. I wondered if Ezra bugged her about wearing a coat.

I took another sip.

"Just stand here for a minute," I told her through numb lips. I pointed at a seemingly floating tray of drinks making its way through the crowd. "Careful though. They're the kind of good that's dangerous."

"Yeah, Aidan is the best." She referenced the bartender while adjusting the strap of her dangerously high stiletto. "But then again my brother only hires the best."

Her words bounced around in my champagne infused brain. "Your brother?"

She nodded across the room. "Ezra," she clarified.

Her answer only confused me more. "Ezra is your brother?"

"Half-brother," she clarified. "Mostly though he's a pain in the ass." She suddenly smiled wide, throwing her head back and laughing like a lunatic. When she righted herself again, she whispered, "Pretend like we're having a really good time. If he thinks I'm sulking he'll come over and make a big deal about it."

My eyes sought him before I gave them official permission to do so. Sure enough, he was staring over at us, watching his sister intently. Belatedly, I loosed a smile and laughed at her non-existent joke.

She laughed again, only this time it seemed genuine. "Thanks," she said. "I'm Dillon by the way. Ezra's younger, wiser, more attractive sister."

I smiled at her. "I'm Molly. Vera's younger, wiser, more attractive best friend."

We shared another laugh. Mine was louder than usual, fueled by stress and alcohol.

"You're the mastermind behind tonight, aren't you? Ezra said this was all you."

I squinted at her, trying to decide if I'd heard her right. The dance music was loud, but not that loud. "Oh, you mean the party? Yeah, I guess it was. Ezra should really get the credit though. Or his florist, Meg. She did all the..." I waved in the general direction of some flowers. "Décor."

Dillon snorted. "I figured. It has her flare."

"Gorgeous, isn't it?"

Dillon wrinkled her nose. "I was going to say it smells like a funeral home, but we can go with your answer. It's nicer."

I laughed again, instantly liking the pretty blonde that was nothing like her brother. They didn't even look alike. It was hard to reconcile them as siblings, and my muddled thoughts questioned if maybe she was lying.

"Are you sure you're Ezra's sister?" I asked, speaking my mind before I could think better of it. "You're so much more—"

"Pale?" she filled in.

"I was going to say pleasant."

"Ha! Well, that too, I suppose."

I looked back and forth between Dillon and Ezra again. He had dark hair and eyes, and olive skin. She really was paler. Her blonde hair just a few shades darker than her bright white dress, and her big blue eyes were inviting and sweet, unmarked by the heaviness in Ezra's.

"You really don't look anything alike though," I heard myself say. "He's so..." I trailed off before I could finish the sentence with stupid adjectives like hot, sexy or drool-worthy.

"He favors our dad," she explained. "Where I'm like my mom. She was all Viking."

"Sorry," I added quickly, realizing belatedly that I was asking a perfect stranger bizarre questions about her sibling. I opened my mouth to ask another stupid question like how Ezra knew Meg, or how often does Meg do Ezra's flowers, or is florist code for something else? Like hooker? But Dillon cut me off, saving us both from the disaster brewing inside my mouth.

"Oh, shit," she mumbled. "He's coming over here. If he asks, tell him we were discussing mature adult things like politics or nuclear physics. Or the weather."

I didn't have time to process her request before Ezra approached us. He went straight for his sister, pulling her into a brief hug. "Dillon," he greeted in that way of his that wasn't a greeting at all. . Never "hello" or "hi" or "hey girl." Just first names and broody looks. "Glad you made it."

"I wouldn't miss it," she told him. "Killian's family."

"You'll love Vera too," he told her. "When they're done dancing, I'll introduce you."

"I've already met the best friend," Dillon nodded to me. "Molly's been keeping me company."

Realizing it was odd that Dillon knew who I was, I was slow to reply. "Politics," I finally blurted. "We were just discussing politics."

Ezra's eyes narrowed on me, then dropped to the empty champagne flute in my hands. "Dillon is always discussing politics," he confirmed. "When I'm not around that is."

She gave him an innocent smile. "That's because you're such a know-it-all. I prefer people with open minds."

"And you think that Molly is one of those people?"

"Hey!" I protested.

He reached forward and grabbed the glass from my hands, dropping it on a tray as a waiter walked by us. The move was so smooth and effortless my mouth unhinged and I bristled. *I could have done that myself!*

Or okay, I probably wouldn't have noticed that waiter. He was moving too fast and he kind of blended in with everyone around him. But I would have caught the next one.

"Molly *is* one of those people," Dillon insisted. "And she agrees with me about Meg's design taste. You have to stop using her."

Ezra's shoulders lifted and dropped with an impatient sigh. "Don't be petty," he warned. "She did a fantastic job. Besides, this was very last minute. I didn't give her much time."

Dillon rolled her eyes. "Time has nothing to do with it. She's over the top. I told you that last time. I don't know why you don't listen to me."

Feeling out of place while the siblings bickered over flowers I took a small step to the side. "I'll just… I'm going over… somewhere else." I pointed across the room.

Ezra's hand fell to my forearm, stilling me. "I'll find you in a minute."

"Why?" The question popped out of my mouth before I could think better of it.

His dark eyes turned to me and he gave me his full, undivided attention. I sucked in a sharp breath at the intensity in his look, the utter power barely restrained beneath his cool expression. He was all sleek

63

lines tonight in a white dress shirt, tailored gray trousers and thin black tie. His hand on my arm was hot and firm, freezing me in place like it had magical powers.

"I'd like to talk to you," he explained.

I struggled to swallow through the new lump in my throat. "About what?"

He lifted his hand from my arm and I scooted another step away from him. "I'll find you," he promised. Then he turned back to Dillon and I instantly felt dismissed.

Noting the exit locations I contemplated escaping, but in the end, I settled for dropping by one of the food stations. I hadn't eaten anything yet and the alcohol was clearly catching up to me. Wyatt had done a spectacular job with the spread and I decided I should tell him that.

Chicken and waffle slider in one hand and a refilled champagne cocktail in the other, I made my way to the kitchen. I briefly remembered Ezra's warning about setting foot in there the other night, but just as quickly dismissed it. He wasn't technically open for business and so I wasn't technically breaking his rules.

I found Wyatt in the center of his kitchen, king of his newly claimed kingdom, leaning over a tray of appetizers. He was all focus and serious vibes, meticulously inspecting them for any faults. Without lifting his head he yelled at someone behind him about double checking temperatures. His hands never wavered from where he worked to perfectly drizzle sauce on top of a skewered meatball.

"Wyatt, please just acknowledge that everyone is drunk by now!" a woman yelled from by the coolers. "This isn't fucking *Top Chef*!"

Wyatt spread his hands wide on the stainless steel table, gripping the edges in an effort to keep his cool. He dropped his head and roared, "Goddamnit, Kaya, if the mousse isn't perfect I'm going to fucking fire you!"

I watched Kaya grin at his back, pleased that she'd gotten to him. "I'm here on a volunteer basis tonight, asshole! You can't fire me for helping you out." The rest of his cooks ducked their heads and focused intently on staying out of his way.

"And I thought Killian was scary," I said loud enough to catch Wyatt's attention.

His head snapped up and I had the pleasure of watching his cheeks turn red. "Killian had *me* for a sous chef," he growled, throwing a murderous glance to the back of his kitchen. "And I didn't run my mouth constantly."

Kaya dropped a tray of chocolate mousse cups next to Wyatt. "That's because you were too busy using it to kiss his ass." She walked away making smooching noises.

Wyatt glared at the desserts. "So help me God, if these aren't perfectly fucking executed."

"I should put a cuss jar back here," I told him. "I'd be rich."

"You're trying to push me over the edge, aren't you?" Wyatt snarled at me. "You've joined forces with Satan's mistress and the two of you are in cahoots to give me an aneurism."

"Who's Satan's mistress?"

Kaya raised her hand. "That would be me. It's our esteemed chef's affectionate pet name for me. Along with Madam Satan, She Devil, the Antichrist's Baby Mama, and Mrs. Bin Laden."

Mrs. Bin Laden?

I swallowed a laugh since it was obvious Kaya didn't appreciate her nicknames. "Quite the hostile work environment you're fostering, Wyatt."

He grumbled more curse words beneath his breath, but overall chose to ignore my comment. "What can I help you with, Molls?"

I shrugged and took a nervous sip of my champagne. "Just stopped by to see how you were doing. I was hoping you would be done by now and could come hang out with me."

Wyatt reached up to tug at his tall chef's toque. "Wish I could, but I have to finish up desserts. I'll be out as soon as we clean up."

"So in like three hours?"

"Sorry." He frowned. "You hired me to work. I'm still working."

I didn't really hire him. He volunteered. But I understood that he still had a job to do, and I didn't want to get in the way. "Find me later?"

His expression softened and his eyes warmed, transforming his looks completely. Wyatt was a total bad ass. At only thirty years old, he already commanded one of the best kitchens in the state. He'd inherited Lilou from Killian, taking over to fill giant shoes. But Wyatt hadn't faltered for a second. From what Vera had told me, Ezra was seriously impressed with how Wyatt was able to handle the kitchen, the menu, and the staff.

Wyatt wasn't hard to look at either. He was tall and lean, his corded muscles like taut ropes against bone. High cheekbones, a square jaw, perfectly shaped ears, on top of a rock-hard body, and kick ass kitchen skills? Yes, please.

Also, I only noted his ears because his shaved head drew attention to them. I didn't have like an ear fetish or anything weird.

But what put Wyatt at an entirely different level than most of the good-looking men I knew, was his bad boy attitude complete with facial

65

piercings and tattoos. All the tattoos. From his wrists they snaked upward, over sinewy forearms and cut biceps, ducking beneath his clothes and reappearing around his neck, all the way up to those strangely attractive ears. Wyatt was the kind of guy that made butterflies leap, and dance, and dive—and panties melt right off your body.

The first time I met Wyatt I thought for sure I was going to combust from sheer nerves. Because he wasn't just pretty to look at, he was also one of the coolest people I'd ever known.

Unfortunately for me, we'd gotten to be too good of friends. For like a hot second I thought there would be something between us. But now he fit firmly in the friend zone. And I knew I was the same for him.

It was a bummer I would never get to know what it was like to make out with him, because I knew, *I just knew* Wyatt would be the best kisser ever. Instead, I had to settle for a good friend that I could actually rely on.

It was the worst.

Also, in case of a flat tire or if I ever needed help moving, it was the best.

He smiled at me and my heart warmed with platonic affection. "Save me a dance?" he asked gently.

"Only if you promise not to kill your sous chef," I countered.

His eyes hardened again just thinking about Kaya. "We'll see."

I left the kitchen only to run straight into a brick wall. Thankfully, I saved my champagne before the delicate flute smashed against Ezra Baptiste's six pack of steel abs. I landed my free hand on his chest that seemed to be made out of the same super-human muscle metal.

I let my hand linger as I pretended I needed help balancing—okay, maybe I really needed help. Apparently I'd had more to drink than I realized. I looked up at his angry expression and tried not to cringe. "Oops."

He glanced over my shoulder. "Were you in my kitchen again?"

I shook my head quickly. "No?"

Ezra let out a huffy sigh. "Molly."

"Not all the way in," I amended. "More like on the fringes. Just the edge. The door barely closed behind me."

His jaw ticked. "Why?"

I tilted my head to the side, trying to make sense of his question. "Why what?"

"Why were you in there," he clarified. "What do you need?"

My stomach dipped at his question, like I'd been unexpectedly thrown in the front car of a rollercoaster. "N-nothing," I told him. "I was just looking for Wyatt."

66

If possible, Ezra's eyes darkened even further and an angry cloud took up residence over his head. He was always too handsome to look directly at, but like this, with his eyebrows scrunched together over his nose and his jaw hard and firm and so angular, he looked like a god, like a marble statue that had been expertly carved. I had the strongest urge to run my fingers over his nose, to memorize the exact curve of his jaw and trail my finger through the wrinkles next to his eyes so that next time I painted him I would get every single detail right.

"You need Wyatt?" Ezra asked.

"To dance."

"To dance?"

I nibbled the corner of my lip and tried to collect my thoughts. "He's busy so he can't dance with me."

Something changed in Ezra. His demeanor shifted, moved, and then settled. It was hard to explain how I noticed it because it wasn't something physical. If I was painting him right now, it wouldn't have been something I could have marked with physical features. And yet it was there, in his aura, in his being. I would have had to throw away the painting altogether and start over from scratch, trying to capture the essence of this mysterious man.

"I'll dance with you," he said.

He couldn't have surprised me more if he would have told me he was about to fly to the moon. "You don't have to—"

His hand covered mine that still happened to be on his chest. "Come on," he said, cutting me off. Then he stalked off toward the dance floor, tugging me after him.

I just managed to set my champagne on a table we passed before I was swept up on the dance floor with him and all of the other guests. I caught Vera's dad's eye as he sat at a table with a few other people his age. He waved at me and smiled. I think I managed to look panicked in return.

Ezra's free hand settled on my waist and he stepped into me so that our chests brushed. I felt the press of his muscular thighs against my bare legs thanks to my mini dress. He towered over me, making me feel small, delicate… feminine.

One of the corners of his mouth lifted in a confident smile and I realized there was no running away without making a ridiculous scene. I was trapped.

I was stuck dancing with one of the world's crankiest, hottest, most difficult men.

Chapter Seven

Surreal.

That's how I felt. Wrapped in Ezra's strong arms—the softness of his clothing a distinct contrast to the muscles beneath—was absolutely surreal.

All around us the music pulsed and the atmosphere bewitched, friends laughed and dishes clinked, and I stood there frozen with confusion. I blamed the champagne.

Henceforth, I would avoid expensive, delicious, hypnotizing drinks and stick to the cheap grocery store bargains I was used to.

Goodbye, Dom Perignon.

Hello, Martini and Rossi, my old friend.

Because obviously the better brands got me into trouble!

To be honest, I could hold my own on the dance floor. I'd even been on enough blind dates to navigate any enthusiastic fondle with ease. But this was an entirely new level of stressful firsts.

I stood, stiff as a board, in Ezra's arms. And he wasn't any better. We swayed back and forth like thirteen-year-old strangers forced together by well-meaning teachers at a middle school dance. I half expected my seventh grade science teacher to lay her hand on my shoulder while she measured the distance between Ezra and me with a ruler.

Except there was also this air of adult awareness that made things bizarrely and sexually intriguing. Ezra's thighs brushing mine. His hand pressed against my lower back. The occasional resting of his jaw against the top of my head. I felt every single inch of him and not one part felt lacking or less than. Ezra was completely, wholly, utterly man. He made every other past dance partner and blind date feel like the junior high cesspool I'd ridiculously compared us to.

He wasn't a thirteen-year-old boy enslaved to hormones and braces. Ezra Baptiste was smooth, successful and so freaking sexy I felt jittery with anticipation. He didn't jolt me back and forth or step on my toes. He moved me around the dance floor with grace and skill, wowing me, charming me... seducing me.

Even if his seduction was accidental.

He cleared his throat and I fixated on the long, slender column of his neck. I was constantly, and possibly weirdly obsessively, trying to figure out how to paint his face. Trying to figure out how to get his expressions just right and bring out that something invisible I couldn't explain. And yet he had so many other parts and pieces I hadn't even begun to dissect yet.

Like his throat. Or the width of his shoulders and the alluring way his clothes hung off them. I glanced at our entwined hands and tried to memorize the way mine looked so delicate and small compared to his. I wanted to draw the way his tie cinched around his collar or laid against his solid chest. I wanted to measure the width of his shoulders so I could recreate them on paper, canvas or a bathroom stall.

I felt like throwing back my head and screaming at the top of my lungs, *Fine, I'm attracted to him! Are you happy now?*

It was yet to be determined exactly who I would be yelling at. The universe? God? Cupid? It didn't matter. Whoever they were, they were to blame for this inconvenient attraction to one of the world's tersest men.

Yep. Tersest.

"Are you okay?" he asked with that smooth, even voice that could not be ruffled or perturbed.

Ever so elegantly, I pulled myself from my tangled thoughts and replied, "Huh?"

"You seem tense," he added.

Champagne forced the truth from my lips. "You make me nervous."

His concentrated gaze found mine. "Why?"

Oh, how to answer that loaded question. I tilted my head to the side, my long hair fell over my shoulder and I confessed, "Probably because the first time we met, you told me my style was juvenile at best."

His eyebrows drew down. "I didn't say that."

70

The truth strengthened my courage and I added, "You also said that your clientele was too wealthy for my cheap taste, and that if I ever wanted to make it in this city I was going to have to try harder."

His eyebrows dipped further. "That doesn't sound like something I would say."

I laughed. I couldn't help it. He looked so… affronted! "Are you serious? That sounds exactly like something you would say!" I felt myself loosen up in his arms. His hand pressed tighter against my back, drawing me closer to him. "*You* asked *me* for advice and then hated everything I had to say."

"That's not at all how I remember it," he countered, referencing the first time we'd met. Vera and I had made reservations at Lilou and then waited six weeks to get in. When we finally did, Killian had given us the five-star treatment, but Ezra had stopped by our table for all of five minutes. Just long enough to insult me. He continued, "I distinctly remember you calling me an old man with dated taste and a tacky dinosaur of a website."

I was positive my expression was a mirror image of his, insulted, outraged and maybe, possibly a little ashamed. "I wouldn't say those things," I countered. "I'm not that bold."

His laugh was hard, bit out with the barest amount of real amusement. "Molly, every single thing about you says otherwise."

Stepping back, I pulled my hand from his and dropped my voice. "What is that supposed to mean?"

He didn't tolerate the space between us, lunging forward and crowding me once again. "That you're not only bold, you're also a snobby know-it-all."

My chin trembled once, betraying me. I took another step back and willed my spine to straighten and my nerves to steady. It wasn't that his insult had wounded me so severely or that I really cared all that much what Ezra thought of me. But I had never been great at conflict. Actually, I was kind of the worst at it.

Regardless of how right I felt or how zingy my insults were, the few confrontations I'd braved in my life had always ended in tears—my tears.

It had been an issue all my life. Oh, how I desperately wanted to be tough, to stand up for myself with steely grit and relentless mettle. I would watch movies about girl fighters or women overcoming immense odds, and would pep-talk myself into believing I could be one of them. I would practice imaginary conversations in the shower, coming up with the best comebacks.

But then something like this would happen and instead of evolving into the empowered, tenacious, take-on-the-world boss-bitch I knew that I was, this wimpy, pathetic version of myself would emerge instead.

The tears were just the icing on the tragic cake.

"You don't know me," I whispered, not caring if he could hear me or not over the loud music and celebrating crowd. I took another step back, anxious to flee before the tears came and Ezra lost whatever remaining shreds of respect he had for me. Feeling a punch of misplaced courage, I added, "And you don't know the first thing about web design."

His teeth slammed together making his jaw jump from the impact. I took two more steps backward and he didn't follow this time. I nearly stumbled when I ran into a body behind me and when I turned around and saw that it was Vann, I threw my arms around his neck and hugged him tightly.

"Are you okay?" he asked in my ear.

"Now I am," I told him.

Vann's arms wrapped around me in a rare hug and he squeezed me tightly. He was the older brother I'd never had and even though we were rarely touchy with each other, I could tell his protective instincts were already on high alert.

I tried to pull back, but Vann held me close. "Seriously, are you okay, Molls?"

Nodding against his shoulder, I confessed, "Seriously, now I am."

He absorbed my words without asking me to explain. "Want to dance?" he asked after we'd been hugging and swaying for long enough that people around us probably already assumed that's what we were doing—even though the music wasn't slow, and I was wrapped around him more like a boa constrictor trying to swallow him whole than a girl trying to get with him.

"Yes, please," I told him, unable to hold back a single sniffle.

We started dancing, albeit in a subdued, careful kind of way. Vann wasn't a big dancer and I was suddenly very tired. He smiled gently at me. "I was coming to rescue you," he said. "You looked pissed, and I know Ezra can be an asshole."

"He is an asshole," I snarled. *You're a snobby know-it-all.* I might have even growled.

Vann grinned. "Maybe. But it looked like you were handling yourself just fine."

I never handled myself just fine, but I didn't need to remind Vann of that. "Where's your date?"

"Subject change much?" he asked me with two raised eyebrows. Still he said, "I don't bring dates to family events. There's too much commitment implied."

Restraining an eye roll, I wondered if Vann would ever be ready to settle down. "We can be old maids together," I told him. "Eventually, we'll move to a house in the suburbs where you can have a garage full of bikes and there would be room for my thirteen cats. You do the cooking. I'll do the laundry."

Vann stared at me in horror before it turned into something more... perverted. "Plus, then we could get laid whenever we want."

Bleck! Sleeping with someone I considered family was basically the grossest possible future. I made a gesture at his crotch region. "I don't want or need any of what is happening down there. I'm positive it needs to be tested, Mr. Afraid of Commitment."

"You're one to talk, cat lady!"

We laughed at our lack of prospects, and then spent the next hour having a great time and drinking more champagne cocktails. Or maybe the champagne was just me?

I forgot all about Ezra and the crappy way he made me feel, and also the guilt that I knew I didn't deserve. I hadn't initiated anything. I'd only been defending myself. So why did slinging insults make me feel so bad?

Eventually the kitchen staff filtered out, stripped down to t-shirts and black work pants. They greeted the other industry people they knew and grabbed drinks in an effort to catch up to all the fun.

That's really when the party really started. Wyatt grabbed me from Vann's care and forced celebratory shots on Vera, Killian and me. Then we moved back to the dance floor and tried to groove off our buzz. Until Wyatt shouted shots again and back we went. Rinse and repeat.

Basically, it was a fabulous night of laughter, love, and so much alcohol. I even danced with Trent until he got overly touchy and started suggesting lewd ways to end the night. I pawned him off on Steph who didn't seem to mind his grabby hands at all.

By two, the guests had mostly left, my head was light, and my blood buzzed beneath my skin. I stared down at my bare feet and wondered where my shoes had gone.

Vera's arms wrapped around my neck from behind and she squealed, "You're the beeeessst best friend everrrrr!!!"

"I know!"

"And this was the beeessst night everrrr!!"

I grinned like an idiot and whirled around to face her. "I know!"

73

"Thank you for this party," she told me, glassy eyed but sincere. "It was so unexpected."

Even inebriated, I knew I couldn't take all the credit. "Wyatt and the antichrist did most of the grunt work," I told her. "I'm just the mastermind. It's no big deal."

Vera giggled. "Antichrist?"

"Ezra," I clarified.

Her forehead wrinkled as she scanned the dance floor. "Where is Ezra anyway? I should thank him too."

"He probably had a panda to sacrifice or children to terrorize."

Vera snorted. "A panda?"

I shrugged. "He's just that mean."

She shook her head at me. "Be nice, Molls. At the very least he throws a good party."

Linking her arm in mine, she tugged me toward the side of the dance floor. "Did your dad leave?"

"Oh yeah. A long time ago. So did Vann, I think."

"He didn't stay long," I said.

She yawned into her hand. "Well, he doesn't drink or dance or eat, so there probably wasn't a whole lot for him to do."

"He danced with me," I laughed. "Not well. But he did dance."

I squinted at a table that had been all but ransacked. Stripped toothpicks lay in dry heaps like picked at bones from a battlefield surrounded by smears of wasabi aioli and Sriracha ketchup. One lone cheeseburger slider sat in the middle of a plate, abandoned.

Squatting down, I searched for my shoes underneath the table. I lifted the tablecloth and lost my balance, falling ~~clumsily~~ gracefully to my knees. "Ouch."

Vera's laughter taunted me from overhead. "What are you doing?"

"Looking for my shoes," I mumbled.

"I can see your underwear," she cackled. "Or where underwear should be."

I made a squeaking sound and bolted upright, smoothing my lacy minidress over my bum. It was a bold choice for someone that preferred to blend into the background, but I'd felt pretty in the sheer, cut out long sleeves. Plus, it was semi-backless and I had a moment of arrogant glee, when my back hadn't looked totally chubby in it.

But all night long, it had been a constant effort to remember not to bend over at the wrong angle or sit spread eagle in a chair. Mainly, I pretended I was in a three-legged race with myself and my ankles had been invisibly tied together.

74

You can see now why I ditched the shoes almost as soon as I'd stepped on the dance floor.

I spun around, using my toes like rudders, unsure of how I was going to stand up without exposing myself more. "I should have worn pants! Why didn't I wear pants?"

Vera bent over, giggling so hard she stopped making sound.

"Help me!" I demanded. "I can't get up without flashing all of your friends my girly bits!"

She wheezed in and out as she struggled to breathe through her laughter.

I sat back on my heels, tugging at my skirt so the angle didn't betray me. "Fine. I'll just sleep here. Sitting up. Don't worry about me."

Killian cast a shadow over me as he stepped up to his fiancée. "Molly, why are you on the floor?"

"Because she's not wearing underwear!" Vera exclaimed.

My face flushed red, cadmium red to be exact, and I said a little prayer for a six point earthquake. I didn't want one strong enough for like a bunch of fatalities. Just one intense enough so that the floor would open up and swallow me whole.

When that didn't happen, I calmly explained to Killian, "I'm wearing underwear."

He blinked at me. "I believe you."

Vera only laughed harder.

Wyatt stepped to Killian's side, followed by a few of the kitchen staff I knew. "Why are you on the floor?" he asked.

Now how was I supposed to get up? There were too many witnesses and I didn't have the kind of street cred I needed for a crotch shot!

I wasn't even cool enough for a nip slip at this point.

Although why my alcohol-soaked brain thought those were markers of celebrity right now was beyond my very limited grasp.

"I've decided to live here," I told Wyatt. Patting the ground next to me, I added, "This is my new home."

Vera leaned heavily on Killian and explained, "She's stuck."

I let out a huff that tossed my bangs in the air. At least she hadn't brought up my underwear again.

A hand stretched out in front of me. I looked up at Ezra's disappointed expression and cringed. "So by all means just stare at her," he deadpanned.

My cheeks flamed a brighter red. But I wasn't the only one sporting a fierce blush after his admonishment.

I put my hand in his just to make this moment end, and he tugged me to standing. To be honest, it wasn't my most graceful rise from the ashes moment, but I was happy to be on my bare feet once again.

Pulling my hand from Ezra's as soon as I could—ignoring the heat, strength and perfection of his hand completely—I forced myself to mumble a quick, "Thank you."

He raised his ~~stupid~~ eyebrows. "How did you end up on the floor?"

"I was looking for my shoes."

Without flinching or acknowledging the weirdness of his words, he said, "I put them in my office so they wouldn't get lost."

Raising my chin to keep from dropping my mouth open, I accepted his words with my very best poker face.

Vera was less smooth. "That was so nice of you, Ezra! You are the nicest ever! Molly, wasn't Ezra so nice to do that for you?"

Killian and I stared at Vera in horror. I called Ezra Killian's BFF, but only because there wasn't an easier way to explain their relationship. From everything that Vera had told me, things were always strained between the two. She said the bromance was of the die-for-you variety, but neither of them really liked the other one.

Vera and I were also a Bryan Adam's song. But we were all about the love.

"You don't have to answer that, Molly," Killian offered. "My drunk girlfriend doesn't know what she's asking you."

Ezra shot Killian a murderous look and I heard myself snort a laugh. "I think after tonight she's officially your drunk fiancée," I told him, ignoring the Ezra bunny trail altogether. "But she's definitely drunk. You should probably get her home before she starts singing."

"Singing?" Wyatt asked.

"When Vera drinks too much she starts acting like she's in a musical. She starts singing everything."

Killian nodded somberly. "It's true. And terrifying."

Wyatt barked a laugh. "I'd like to see that."

This time the murderous glare came from Killian. "That's all right. I'll get her home before we get to that part."

It was my turn to cackle. "He's only saying that because after the singing comes the stripping!"

Wyatt tossed his head back, his whole body shaking from laughter. Killian put his arm around Vera just in case she jumped the gun. "Thank you all for a fantastic night," he said sincerely. "You guys are the best."

I grinned with pride, but before I could say anything, Vera belted out a loud, sing-songy, "Thank youuuuuuuu!"

Killian shook his head at her, but his expression was complete adoration. "And that's our cue to leave."

"Mine too." I hid a yawn behind my hand. "Although I should help you guys clean up."

"Don't let him make you," Killian warned. "He has people for that."

"Yeah, people like me," Wyatt grumbled.

Ezra looked at him. "Since when have I made you clean up front of house?"

Wyatt swiped his hand over his mouth and I suspected it was to hide a smile. "Tonight?"

Ezra made an exasperated face. "No, not tonight. Killian's right. I do pay people for this." He placed his hands on his hips and looked around at the mess. "Although I suspect they're going to charge me double this time."

Killian made a sound. "At least."

I shuffled over to the table I'd just been peering under, horrified that Ezra was going to have to put more money into this party that was all my idea. "I don't mind helping. Really."

Wyatt beat me to it, clearing the plates. "Don't touch those," he ordered. "They're mine."

I let him stack serving dishes and gather cutlery, waiting for the linens I had no idea what to do with. "I'll call you tomorrow, Molls!" Vera shouted behind me.

"Not till after lunch," I called back. Watching Killian guide Vera out of the restaurant did something funny to my insides. My heart swelled at the same time my stomach wobbled and pitched.

Vera was so comfortable with Killian. In a way I had never seen her before. I hadn't gotten to know Derrek very well while she'd dated him, but the little bits I had seen were unsettling and worrisome. With Killian, she was herself. She laughed loudly and smiled all the time, she was obsessive over her craft and their restaurant, and honest with her weird sense of humor. She didn't put up with Killian's shit, but in this totally adorably infatuated way gave it right back. She was in love—totally, completely, healthily in love.

And I hated that I was jealous of her.

Dancing with Trent tonight had reinforced my staying single policy. He'd been obnoxiously over the top in his efforts to seduce me and yet I found all of them tacky and easy to decline. It had been nice of Steph to think of me, but I was over being the single friend everybody wanted to set up.

Next time somebody came at me with a blind date, I was going to point them in the direction of Wyatt or Vann. They were just as single as me.

Hopefully.

At least I liked to think they were.

Chapter Eight

"*L*eave them," a rumbly voice ordered.

If I hadn't been so inebriated, I would have jumped. Ezra had snuck up on me and I didn't even notice him standing to my right. "It's fine," I told him. "I want to help."

He dangled my strappy stilettos from his fingertips. Pointing at the tablecloth I was wadding up from the tabletop, he said, "Tell me where they go and I'll let you handle them, but right now you're more of a menace than anything else."

Glaring at him, I continued to ball the tablecloth in my hands. "Obviously they go in the hamper." It was the first thing that came to mind and I realized how idiotic it sounded. The hamper? Because Lilou also had a laundry room?

"So wrong," he murmured. "So very wrong. Besides it's a trick question. When the cleaning crew comes in, they'll take the linens with them. It would be helpful though if you left them where they are instead of making the nice, hourly-waged people hunt them down."

Throwing the linens back on the table, I reached for my shoes. He pulled them out of reach and I swayed trying to right my drunken self. "If you're not going to let me help, then you might as well let me go home and go to bed."

"How are you getting home?" he asked while holding my shoes in the air where I could not reach them.

I looked up at my shoes, debating on how badly I needed them. It didn't matter how cold it had gotten outside or that I was pretty sure it was illegal to drive without shoes on in North Carolina.

Just to be difficult, I crossed my arms over my chest and said, "Are you hitting on me, Baptiste? Because holding my shoes captive is a tactic I've never seen before. Or maybe it's old school? Is this how people your age get dates?"

His eyes widened in surprise. He wasn't expecting snark. "People my age and everyone else that doesn't want you to die on the way home tonight. I'll give you a ride."

"I was going to call an Uber," I admitted.

He turned around, taking my shoes with him. "I'm cheaper."

You're also an asshole. But I didn't say that out loud. "Seriously, it's no big deal!" I hollered after him. "I have the app!"

Only, judging by his Lilou website, he probably didn't even know what an app was. Great. Now I was going to have to explain all of modern technology to him. This night was never going to end.

"I also have your phone," Ezra shot back. When Wyatt stepped out of the kitchen, Ezra paused to ask him to lock up.

Shoes were one thing, but my phone was vitally important to every aspect of my life. It was basically my soul locked up in gadget form. If he confiscated my baby, he'd have access to allllll of my life—including my very secret, very private Candy Crush obsession.

Ezra disappeared into the kitchen and I hurried after him.

"Is he really giving you a ride home?" Wyatt asked as I zipped by.

"He's holding my accessories hostage," I told him.

Wyatt stared at me agape, but I didn't have time to explain before I disappeared into the kitchen. All the lights were on while Wyatt's skeleton staff cleaned the remaining dishes and put away food. Ezra waited for me by the side door, holding my shoes and my purse.

"I've already cleaned out your bank accounts," he said when I finally caught up to him. "And destroyed your credit."

I stilled. "Was that a joke?"

He lifted one shoulder in a barely-there shrug. "I guess we'll find out."

"It makes sense," I told him. "Your restaurants aren't named after ex-girlfriends. They're stolen identities."

His lips twitched once, but he held back his smile. My drunken brain convinced me that I needed to see it. That I needed to witness it one more time just to prove that it was real. I tried smiling at him, hoping to coax something out of him. But he only stared at me and then finally thrust my shoes out like he couldn't stand the idea of holding them for a second longer.

"I presume you didn't wear a coat tonight," he said as way of getting my ass out the door.

With one hand poised against the wall to keep my balance, I bent over just enough to slide each one on. "My weatherman told me it was supposed to be warm this weekend and I stupidly believed him."

"Your weatherman said it was going to be *warmer* this weekend and it is."

Losing control of my motor functions, I reached out and brushed my knuckle over the wrinkled space between Ezra's consternated eyebrows. "You're always so serious," I told him.

He didn't say anything for a long time, choosing instead to examine my face, and my dress, and the shoes that had already started pinching my toes again.

Imagining what he probably thought of me made me shrink back. I wasn't like the girls he normally dated. Not that I knew what kind of girls he normally dated. But I had to be so different than what he was used to. With names like Lilou, Bianca, and Sarita, they sounded exotic, interesting. I imagined long-legged pinup models with perfectly coiffed hair and million dollar smiles. They would tie scarves around their heads when Ezra took them for Sunday drives in his red convertible, and smoke cigarettes out of cigarette holders.

He was basically a Cary Grant movie. And I was so different than anything he was used to. My cheeks flushed for the hundredth time tonight, and I contemplated moving out of Durham and North Carolina, and possibly the entire continent of North America.

"If I drive, can you give me directions to your house?" he asked, pulling me from my spiraling thoughts. His voice had pitched low, going extra deep and rumbly in the silence of the empty kitchen.

"Yes. But you can also put me in the back of an Uber and I can give them directions too. I'm very good at giving directions. I can give them to almost anybody. It's just one of my many talents."

"You're drunk," he said as way of argument. "I'm not handing you off to a stranger."

He was driving me home for my own protection? I stared at him, trying to make sense of his harsh words on the dance floor and his thoughtfulness in the kitchen. "Okay." Again, I tried to reconcile his generosity. And failed. "Thank you."

Holding his elbow out to me, he led me through the big steel door and toward his waiting sleek, sporty, super-expensive black car parked in the alley directly next to Lilou. It sat beneath a rough garage-like structure covered in ivy.

"This is your car?" I asked, dumbfounded. There was obviously no way I could ride in it. It looked more expensive than my entire life. And I didn't mean that in an accumulated-assets kind of way. I meant on like a physical, existential, me-plus-my-assets-plus-every-other-thing-about-me-past-present-and-future-plus-potential-cats kind of way. This car was insane.

"Pretty, isn't she?"

I could only nod dumbly.

"She's an Alfa Romeo," he told me. "She's new."

Holding back a sigh, I said, "Of course she is." *That's Alfa Ro-may-o for those of you reading it like Romeo and Juliet. Because this isn't that kind of story, yo.*

Ezra held the door open for me and I sobered a little as I slid onto buttery leather. He climbed in a second later and handed me my purse.

"Sorry," he murmured. "I don't know why I'm still holding onto it."

"Clearly you want a restaurant called Molly," I teased. "You're trying to steal my identity after all."

He stared at me, his eyes shrewd and investigative. I stared back, brave with liquid courage and unafraid of what he would find. Although I didn't know what he was looking for or why he was suddenly being nice to me.

"It does have a nice ring to it." Just one side of his mouth lifted. "Or maybe I would call it MM. M's? Maverick? The thing about you is that there are just so many possibilities."

Sliding my tongue over my dry bottom lip, I didn't know what to make of this sudden sense of humor. "Maverick sounds like a sports bar and that doesn't really seem like your type."

"You say that, but you don't really know what my type is, do you?" Before I could respond, he turned back to his new car.

The car purred to life, rumbling and growling, and making all kinds of sounds I'd never heard a car make before. He expertly reversed out of the alley and then went forward into the flow of traffic. For a few minutes, I just listened to the hum of the engine and wondered if I would henceforth compare all other cars to this one—which was clearly setting me up for a very disappointing life.

Or a future as a stripper.

He glanced at me out of the corner of his eye. "I don't know where I'm going."

I gave him directions to my apartment complex and settled back into the comfort of the passenger seat. The radio hummed very softly with

82

music I didn't recognize and could barely hear. Mostly the car was filled with the sound of the engine zipping through traffic or purring at stoplights.

I should have been spitting fire at this man that had so completely insulted everything about me earlier tonight. But alcohol and my friend's future wedded bliss had made me soft and culpable. So instead of wrapping Ezra in my deadly web and then biting his head off for a midnight snack, I closed my eyes and let myself feel gratitude.

"Thanks again, Ezra," I said sincerely. "The party was a major success. Lilou was perfect. Meg is a genius. And you already know that Wyatt is the best. You did a pretty great job of swooping in to save the day."

Of course he picked up on my change in attitude right away. "Are you being nice?"

I tilted my face toward him and frowned at his profile. "I blame the alcohol."

His lips twitched but I couldn't be sure if it was because of an almost smile or if he'd developed a facial tick. There was a good possibility he was about to have a stroke. "Me too," he said.

Not knowing what else to say after that, we both fell silent. I turned in my seat so I could stare out the window, but the streetlights cast a glare and I ended up staring at Ezra's reflection instead.

From where I sat I could see the faint stubble that had appeared along his jaw, equally as black as the hair on his head. His sharp nose that looked like cut marble in the window reflection. His high cheekbones and long throat. Those masculine shoulders that were so ferociously broad before his torso thinned to a tapered waist. He could have so easily been a model in a different life. Or maybe even this one still. Depending on how the restaurant biz turned out for him.

He drove with pure confidence, weaving in and out of late night traffic like he moonlighted for NASCAR. He commanded the car in the same way I imagined he handled all things in life—with total control and determination. And he never once lost his concentration to look at me.

He didn't just do things. He conquered things.

All the things.

He was too much for me. Too sure of himself. Too successful. Too self-possessed.

Too manly.

Too way, way, way out of my league.

By the time he pulled up in front of my apartment complex, I had stopped breathing altogether. Nerves ran in panicked circles inside my chest, forever bumping into each other as they tried and failed to settle. I pictured them with their hands in the air and their mouths wide in desperate concern. *Abort, abort!* They screamed. *Run for the hills!*

As if I could just jump out of Ezra's car, ninja-roll into the bushes and live the rest of my life foraging in the Appalachians. Pretty sure that was a future *60 Minutes* cautionary tale in the making.

Ezra put the car in park and hovered his hand around the ignition. "Can I walk you inside?"

"Please don't!" Waving him off, I said, "I got this. I'm just up…" I pointed in the general direction of the sky.

"Do you have everything?" he asked.

I wiggled my feet and tapped my purse in my lap. "Yep." My hand slid over the door until I found the handle.

"Molly," Ezra stalled me with just that one word—with just the way he used it.

I half turned to face him. For the first time in our entire acquaintance, I saw hesitation and maybe even uncertainty.

"What you said about my website… I'm just wondering… Maybe if you have time… I would be willing to pay you if you would take a look at it again."

My pulse skipped as I stared at him in an effort to decipher if he was serious or not. Even if I didn't have the Black Soul project right now, who would want to work with a restaurant owner that had no misgivings about calling you names and insulting your taste? No thanks. That initial five minute interaction pretty much ruined any and all future work-related collaborations between the two of us.

And hopefully all the non-work-related collaborations as well.

This was what happened when I was nice. I should know better than to be nice.

I prepared a professional excuse in my head, something about a new project and not having the focus for him. But what came out was unfiltered truth instead. "Ezra, that's a terrible idea."

"It's not," he insisted, not even phased with my answer, almost like he'd anticipated it. "I'm surrounded by 'yes' people. Save for Killian and Dillon, I have nobody willing to tell me the truth. They're all afraid of me."

I shouldn't have laughed. Really. He was being open and honest and… open and honest. But the look on his face was like the businessman equivalent to a three year old's pout.

After I laughed, he looked less adorable. It was more like the businessman's equivalent of a murderer.

"Molly."

84

He said my name and I shivered. I blamed the weather, the leather seats, and the full moon. "*I'm* afraid of you," I told him. "Just not tonight because of, you know, the champagne." He opened his mouth and I quickly added, "And getting me drunk every time I have to work with you is not an option. This isn't normal for me. I'm usually very responsible."

"Two Advil, two Tylenol."

"What?"

He tapped his fingers on the steering wheel. "And an Alka-Seltzer a half hour after you wake up." His gaze found mine. "For your hangover tomorrow."

I pressed my lips together to keep from smiling. Tomorrow I would be thankful for his home remedy, but tonight I couldn't help but analyze him. "You're always so…" I struggled with the right word to describe him. Thoughtful was the easy choice, but he wasn't really thoughtful. That implied he was being generous with the information for the other person's benefit. And Ezra was definitely not looking out for me for the sake of me. No, it was something more like… "Practical."

Avoiding my eyes again, he looked forward and if it was any other man I would have sworn his cheeks flushed. "I'll email you the details of what I'm looking for. You can decide for yourself what you think about the project."

"You're crazy."

His smile was short-lived and filled with self-confidence. "I'm used to getting what I want."

I felt my sigh all the way down to my toes. "Now that I believe."

His phone buzzed in the cup holder as if accentuating his point at three in the morning. Which meant it was time for me to end our temporary truce and go to bed.

"That's my cue to leave," I mumbled more to myself than Ezra.

"That's not what you think—"

"You don't have to explain it to me," I said quickly.

But apparently he felt like he did. "It's my sister."

I talked over him, knowing it didn't matter who it was because it wasn't my business. "I'll see you around, Ezra."

I hurried from the car, partly because it was a chilly night and partly because I couldn't wait to get away from him. He had been nice. I could admit that.

But I also had to acknowledge that I wasn't myself around him. Under normal circumstances, I was polite and kind. I listened attentively and responded considerately. I was all the adverbs that were nice, and reserved, and mature.

85

Something about Ezra made me lose my cool. I became a snarky, nagging shrew with bite. The filter over my mouth and mind dissolved completely and I was left with only raw truth and rough edges. And I had no problem telling the man no. Which was crazy for me, since I was a ride or die people pleaser.

Deciding to forget about Ezra completely and only remember the non-Ezra parts of the evening, I made my way up to my apartment, totally ignoring the Alfa Romeo that waited to drive away until I was safely inside my building. I started stripping as soon as I'd dead bolted my door. Purse on the kitchen counter. Shoes trailing behind me. Dress off. Bra off. Hair up.

I grabbed an oversized t-shirt, then headed to the bathroom to brush my teeth and deal with the excessive process of taking off my party makeup. Why, oh, why was waterproof eyeliner such a vindictive biotch?

I settled for good enough and headed for my bedroom.

That's when things went off track.

I stared at my bed for a long time. I had made it this morning so it was nice and inviting with the covers turned down at one corner. My phone was on the brink of dying, so I needed to charge it. And then I needed to go to sleep. I was still buzzed and I had things to do tomorrow, and a million other reasons I had to go to bed that I couldn't exactly remember off the top of my head.

So that's what I did.

Just kidding. I turned on the hallway light and headed to my studio where I spent the next three hours trying my best to make domineering shoulders and a jawline that could cut glass. I obsessed over eyes that were nothing but endless mystery. And a mouth that could be so inviting and open, and then cruel and closed off in the span of three seconds.

The moon went to bed before I did. And when I finally released myself from my painting prison, I was no closer to getting the lines, angles, and colors right than I had been a week ago.

When I went to bed it was out of pure frustration and defiance. And when I closed my eyes it was his that taunted me from my dreams. His eyes stared at me, daring me to try harder, be better, to give up this fight with my lust, and give in to my tiny, insignificant crush on him.

Chapter Nine

*B*uzz.

Buzzzzz.

Buzz. Buzz. Buzz.

I rolled over and slapped my open palm on the nightstand. Then I slapped it again, hoping to find my cell phone. Fumbling around like a blind zombie for a few seconds, I finally grappled the thing into my possession and squinted at the time.

Noon.

Ugh.

I flopped on my back with the unanswered phone still in hand. I'd had six hours of sleep. Or something like that. Clearly, not enough.

For a second, I stared at my bedroom door and remembered why it had been so ~~late~~ early when I finally fell asleep.

~~Ezra.~~

Vera. It was Vera's engagement party and I had celebrated in excess. And everybody knows that when you drink too much you're wired for hours afterward.

Full of energy.

Unable to fall asleep.

Ugh, again.

Despite my sleepy state, urgency to destroy last night's ~~evidence~~ paintings pounded through me. Like a herd of elephants rampaging on roller skates.

Or maybe that was my head?

Either way, I knew I had a mess to clean up—literally and figuratively.

My cell started to buzz again, and I cursed at the ceiling fan slowly spinning overhead. Instead of bringing the phone to my face, I rolled over and planted my face on the phone—after I'd swiped answer of course.

"Hello?" a man said—*just kidding, that was me*. I said hello with a man voice because that's what I sounded like first thing in the morning.

"Molly," my mom sighed into the phone. "I thought you'd been trafficked."

I rubbed my eye with my fist. "Huh?"

"Sex trafficked," my mom clarified. "When you didn't answer the first time."

"I, uh, wha?"

"Molly Nichole are you just now waking up? It's noon!"

My mother was as hardworking as they got. She had been a public school lunch lady for thirty plus years, so that meant she was used to being up at hours that I still considered the middle of the night. She spent her day managing rowdy kids for both breakfast and lunch, and then she went home and managed my dad who was just as bad. She never took sick days or slept in on weekends. She didn't have hobbies or shows that she liked, and didn't really know how to have fun in any capacity. She worked, and she worked, and she worked.

And she expected me to do the same.

"It's Saturday," I croaked. "My one day to sleep in."

"Why do you need to sleep in?" she demanded, her voice hardening with concern. When my mother got nervous she didn't flutter around like a butterfly afraid to land, she tromped through the situation like a dangerous predator that had been threatened with extinction. My mom was not a dainty flower. She was a Tyrannosaurus Rex—lethal except for the tiny arms.

"I threw Vera an engagement party last night, Mom. It ended late. I'm tired today."

"Hungover you mean." Well, she wasn't wrong. "But that was nice of you. Vera's a good friend."

My mom loved Vera. She loved the entire Delane family. We'd been neighbors growing up. Well, my parents and Hank were still neighbors. It was only Vera, Vann and me that had moved on.

For her—someone that valued a hard work ethic— Vera's dad, Hank Delane, was everything a man should be. He loved his dead wife fiercely and honored her memory by sticking around and doing right by their kids. He worked as hard as possible to provide a good life for them and see that they were well taken care of.

Because of him, Vera and Vann had also learned to work hard. My mom saw them owning their own businesses and doing well for themselves as a tribute to the father that raised them. As a kid, she'd encouraged me to spend as much time over at their house as possible. And now as a grown-up, she pushed me to be as much like Vera and Vann as possible.

And if you hadn't picked up on it by now, she did not think I was doing a very good job of emulating them. Something she blamed on my dad.

It didn't matter how many times I told her that I worked for a great company or that I could pay all my bills or even that I had a benefits package—which, by the way, was more than Vera could say until recently.

She took my interest in painting as a sign that I was two days away from giving my life over to the bottle and quitting everything I'd worked so hard to achieve.

Art was just an outlet for the lazy deadbeat in me.

Because obviously there was a lazy deadbeat living inside me, listlessly scratching at my interior walls in a half-hearted attempt to slump its way out. "Get out of my way, Work Ethic!" it would yell from the couch of my heart, throwing empty two liters of Diet Coke at my brain all while scratching its hairy butt. "I can't see the TV, Retirement Plan!"

Then it would yawn, revealing Dorito-stained teeth and grumble, "Okay, fine. I give up," before it's head dropped back and it started snoring loudly.

Thank you ladies and gentlemen, I'll be here all week.

"Molly," my mom snapped.

"I'm listening," I answered quickly, half wondering if my daydreaming hadn't accidentally turned into real dreaming. There was a line of drool down my chin. A good indication that I might have fallen asleep for a second.

"Your father wants to know when you're coming home for dinner."

I shoved my face into the pillow and breathed until my pillowcase was hot and smelled like morning breath. I loved my parents. I really did. And they loved me. At least I hoped they did. But family dinners were always stressful.

Deciding it would be better to get it over with rather than drag it out for the next month or ten years or whatever, I said, "I'm free this weekend."

"Tomorrow then." My mom turned her head from the speaker to cough. When she returned she sounded older than she had before. I knew she was tired, but this version of her first thing on a Saturday made her sound worn out. "I'll make your favorite."

My heart softened with her gesture. She could be sharp-tongued and impatient, but she was gold on the inside. Pure gold.

"Thank you, Mama."

She chuckled at my endearment. I only called her mama when I wanted something so it had become a kind of joke to us. "All right, Molly. You're awake now, so go make the most out of today."

"Love you."

There was a slight hesitation because she grappled with expressing emotion. Finally, she admitted, "Love you, too."

I hung up the phone with her and flopped back on my pillow. My mother was the person I loved most in this world. She was also the person that had messed me up the most.

I tried to console myself by believing that was the norm. Most moms meant well. That didn't mean their children weren't loaded with baggage that they had to carry for the rest of their lives.

Right?

Was I crazy to think that maybe, just possibly, my mom had overburdened me?

I'd tried to talk to Vera about this before, but she hadn't had a mom growing up. She looked at my family the same way I looked at hers—with longing and subtle feelings of wishful what ifs.

Sure, through her eyes, I had two parents and family dinners every night. She saw my mom take me shopping and help me sort through drama at school. She had been there for my first period and given me the most awkward sex talk in the history of sex talks. She'd gotten her nails done with me once in awhile, if it was summer and she didn't have to work in the lunchroom.

But from my first-hand perspective, I also knew family dinners came with a price. And I often wondered if it would be better with only one parent if that meant you didn't have to listen to two parents fighting all the time. She took me shopping, but only bought me outfits she deemed appropriate and mature enough. She'd spent many nights talking to me about friends from school, as in which ones to hang out with, which ones had potential, and which ones I should avoid at any cost lest I end up catching their dead-beat tendencies. She'd handed me a box of tampons and told me that I could now get pregnant. And that if I ever came home knocked up, she would never speak to me again. And yes, I'd sat through the sex talk with her, but I walked away feeling more confused than ever.

I was also fairly confident that my parents had only had sex the one time and that I was magically conceived in the accidental process.

Getting our nails done now was mainly me forcing her to do it in a desperate effort to get my mother to relax. Because I was terrified she was going to give herself a heart attack, or an ulcer, or a wart on the tip of her nose or something.

One of the great things about Vera being my best friend was that she was a constant reminder of how grateful I should be to have a mom. And I was. But there were parts to my mother that drove me absolutely crazy.

I already knew family dinner tomorrow night would be one of those things.

Stretching my fingers, I ignored the urge to head to my studio to paint. My mother's voice still lingered in the air and I didn't want to taint my sacred space by inviting her negative energy. I would likely lose some fingers as they sporadically fell off my body thanks to her intense hatred for all things creative.

No, instead, I abandoned my bed and my phone and did the honorable, mature thing. I took a shower and scrubbed all the booze bleeding from my pores.

God, I smelled like tequila.

I blamed Wyatt, the shot master.

When I got out of the shower, my phone was alight with notifications. It was like a buzzing Christmas tree. I sprawled on my bed again, wrapped in a towel, my still drying hair dripping onto my shoulders and the comforter.

I checked all my socials first, liking the silly pictures from last night that I had been tagged in and smiling at the fun that had been had. Then I switched over to my emails, deleting shopping coupons and car maintenance ads in favor of checking in on work just to prove my mother wrong.

After responding to two emails from Henry, one about the Black Soul project and another vague one about hearing about an exciting opportunity for me on Monday, I declared my mother *officially* wrong. I'd taken advantage of Saturday afternoon and managed to respond to not just one, but two work emails. Booya.

That's when I noticed the email that I should have seen first. I had been so curious to find out what Henry's "secret project" was, and then ultimately so disappointed to discover he hadn't actually told me that I'd skimmed right over email from the *ezra.baptiste@yahoo.com*.

Now that I looked at it, there was a string of three of them grouped together on my Gmail app.

The first one read,

Subject: You know you want to…
Take the job, Maverick. I'll make it worth your while.
~EFB
P.S. I promise to stay out of your way.

I pondered what the F could possibly stand for while my stubborn will fought career-obsessed butterflies in a battle for power.

Francis?

Frederick?

Fitzgerald?

Ferret?

Ezra Fucking Baptiste? I wouldn't put it past him.

Moving onto the second email, I opened it with more trepidation.

Subject: About last night.
Molly,
Forgive my late email. I was wired after the party and couldn't sleep. The truth is, I've looked up your profile on your company website, and while I'm impressed with your work, you're still green. I'm offering you a job that I believe will build your portfolio and credibility. Working for me will help you land better clients. And, you should know that I'm willing to pay whatever your fees are. This is a win-win for both of us.
~EFB
One more thought. I see that you are drawn to grey and yellow, but I'd rather not.

Was he serious?

Grey and yellow?!

What did he know about design? Nothing! Nada!!! Zilch! He should stick to what he was good at— being an asshole—and leave me and ~~my favorite~~ the trending colors alone.

And. AND! He'd spelled grey with an E when everybody knew that gray with an A was the American-English spelling.

And it was romantic.

It was the romantic way to spell gray.

92

I mean for that reason alone it was obvious this man was a sociopath. Or worse. A realist.

Gross!

Fury convinced me to open the third email. Well, fury and morbid curiosity.

Subject: This will be good for you.
I'll see you Monday. We can discuss the details then.
~EFB
Also, I don't know if I said it already, but I just wanted to thank you again for your work on the engagement party. I appreciate all that you did.
One final thought, since she's a pain in my ass and reading over my shoulder, I'm forced to tell you that Dillon says hello. And that she enjoyed meeting you.
That's all, Molly. Talk to you soon.

For half a second, I pondered all of his post scripts and how he seemed to say more at the end of his emails than at the beginning. But then I pushed away that ~~adorable~~ weird quirk to make room for the justifiable outrage boiling in my blood.

He'd insulted me on so many different levels. It was hard to decide which one should be the most upsetting.

From assuming I was more interested in money than integrity to insulting my design style *again* to assuming I would take the job simply because he demanded it. The man was intolerable.

He clearly wasn't used to hearing the word "no." Or "no, thank you." Or "not a chance in hell, buddy."

I had the strongest urge to paint again, but only so I could create something vaguely in his image and then turn it into a dart board.

Sitting cross-legged in the middle of my bed, I repressed the flattered preening of my ego. Okay, for like a hot second I could admit that it was nice to be considered for Ezra's website revamp. And not just considered, but aggressively sought after.

I had no doubt he would pay well. And somehow I knew that if I demanded more money, he would pay that too.

Not that I would. I wasn't totally greedy.

But not for one second did I really believe that he would keep his nose out of my business. In fact, for hardly knowing him or seeing him or wanting anything to do with him, he was perpetually in my business.

I held my phone with both hands and tapped out the quickest reply I could. There was no reason to prolong whatever was happening here. The emails needed to stop. The unsolicited advice needed to end. And Ezra Baptiste just needed to disappear from my life altogether.

Subject: Let me stop you right there.

~~Dear Ezra Franklin Baptiste...~~

~~Hello, Ezra Fenwick Baptiste...~~

~~What up EFB...~~

Ezra,

There's no need to call me Monday since we'll have nothing to discuss. I apologize that you're so set on the idea of us working together when I am super set on us not working together. If you're really that interested in SixTwentySix though, I'm happy to refer you to another designer that I trust.

Best,

MM.

P.S. Tell, Dillon I say hello back and that I enjoyed meeting her too. And that she's hands down my favorite Baptiste.

I pressed send with a feeling of complete satisfaction. I'd remained professional, polite and persistent. All the right P's. Now he would get the message loud and clear and move on.

He was a successful business owner with restaurants to run and empires to build. His attention span was probably the equivalent to a chipmunk on crack. Monday would come and go and so would his thoughts about me or what I could do for his business or my penchant toward gray and yellow and all things *green*.

And I would be more vigilant to avoid Ezra as often as possible. Now that the engagement party was over, I wouldn't need to seek him out again, and the chances of me ever running into him on accident were very slim.

It wasn't like we ran in the same circles or shopped at the same organic, uppity grocery stores or vacationed on the same private tropical islands. I would stay on my side of the city and he could stay on his.

There was only Vera's wedding to worry about, but we would be back to being strangers by then. Like divorced strangers. We could share joint custody of Vera and Killian, alternating weekends and Wednesdays.

We would pass each other coming and going or at the occasional party hosted by our mutual friends, but he had his world and I had mine and ne'er would they ever meet.

94

I stared at my phone, refusing to close my eyes and conjure his eyes, his nose, or the breadth of his strong hands. I ignored the tingle in my fingers begging me to paint and draw and create something that could capture that unnamed thing in him I found so obnoxiously fascinating. As I finished my hair and put my makeup on, I stubbornly refused to head back to my studio and examine what I'd done the night before.

As I made lunch and took two Tylenol, two Advil and an Alka-Seltzer, I chose to forget about the advice Ezra had given last night and the way he'd focused so intently on me.

And then I proceeded to erase from my mind the three emails today, the emails from before that, and every interactions I'd had with him since I met him.

He had his life. And I had mine. And everything about us was too different to even consider working together or near each other or in a general vicinity of each other. We were too different and too set in our own ways.

Good luck, Ezra Fezziwig Baptiste. Godspeed.

Chapter Ten

Nobody had turned the porch light on at my parents' house. It looked foreboding from the street, like the house you wanted to avoid when you went trick-or-treating as a kid because you knew they would hand out pennies instead of candy.

That basically summed up my childhood. Always pennies. Never anything sweet.

The front room was dark as I stepped inside, even though the still winter sun had started to set an hour ago. Typical. My mom wasn't concerned with making me feel welcome. She'd already invited me over for supper, so her obligation had been fulfilled.

Light from the kitchen situated at the back of the house glowed burnished orange on the dated carpet, spreading a long rectangle to the edge of a scuffed coffee table. I could hear my mom knocking around in the kitchen, putting the final touches on supper. Pots clinked and water boiled, drawers opened and spoons stirred, but no radio or TV could be heard. Just her huffing at our supper and my dad's distant cough from their bedroom.

I stood there for a minute, invisible and unnoticed. Taking a deep breath, I inhaled a bouquet of memories and emotions. My chest tightened and I couldn't tell if it was from regret for agreeing to this or nostalgic longing for when I was a kid and hadn't had any responsibilities. Whatever the feeling that settled so heavily on my heart, it made me want to purge it from my body, get it out of me and eternalize it on something else. I wanted to paint this exact moment, somehow move it from reality to canvas.

I would focus on that stretched rectangle of light, make it the very center of the portrait. The carpet would need to be just the right, faded shade of brown. I would need to spend hours detailing the grains of wood from the coffee table. The doorway would need to be the right proportion.

And then in the background I would add my mom at the stove, her peppered black hair pulled in a low ponytail. I would bow her head over her pot, taking care to detail her curled fingers around a wooden spoon and the black sweatpants and t-shirt she would no doubt be wearing. But I would leave her face hidden, unseen.

Somehow I would bring in the master bedroom. Maybe just a sliver of the doorway with the corner of a bed and a pair of large socked feet hanging off the edge.

I would put it all together in grays and blacks and woodsy browns. I would reserve all the color for that one window of light. And then I would let the viewer read into the story whatever they wished. I would let them look at this secret picture of my family and infer whatever story it told them.

Because it would depend on them, on their view of the world. This could be a story of resilience and loyalty, of people sticking it out no matter what, a happily ever after. Or this could very easily be a tragedy. I still hadn't made up my mind.

I jingled my keys and cleared my throat. Dropping my purse on the recliner near the window, I made as much noise as possible and headed toward the kitchen.

"I'm here!" I called so everyone in the house would know I arrived.

My mother turned from her spot at the counter and looked over me in her hawk-like way. She never wore makeup so her eyes had a beady quality that was unsettling when they were critical. "Hi," she said.

"Hi." The pressure in my chest tightened. I subtly worried over my choice of clothes and shoes and every single life choice I'd ever made.

She turned back to supper and tilted her head. "I need you to set the table. I asked your father to, but he has a very important obligation in the other room."

"By that, you mean taking a nap," I teased. "No worries, Mama. What's the point of coming home if I don't get to do chores?"

Without turning around or acknowledging my upbeat candor, she snorted at her simmering dishes. "He's had a very rough day of napping.

His afternoon nap apparently wasn't enough. And you know, I interrupted him with the vacuuming, so he had to start over once I was finished. The man has no stamina."

"He has stamina, Mom. He's been married to you for over thirty years." I had long since stopped trying to stay out of things between my parents. That might sound crazy to the normal, non-confrontational person, but for me, I'd learned my lesson the hard way too many times. If I stayed out of it, it never ended. If I jumped in and started reminding my parents of how much they loved each other, they stopped just to get me to stop.

It was how I kept the peace.

One might think that this would make me brave enough to jump into any kind of conflict or throw myself into volatile situations or maybe, even simply stand up for myself. But the truth was, having to handle my parents all of my life made any kind of conflict extremely uncomfortable for me.

I even congratulated myself for the great relationship Vann and Vera had. I took full responsibility for them loving each other so much.

I couldn't stand them fighting when we were kids. I burst into hysterical tears the minute they started after each other. It wasn't so much that Vann cared so very deeply for me, rather he has always hated when girls cried. It's one of his biggest fears—weepy females. So he would do anything to get me to stop—even get along with his annoying kid sister.

As we got older, Vann started treating me less like a girl and more like a sister which meant my tears had less and less effect on him. So, during our teenage years, I stopped crying and resorted to simply leaving. We could have been in the middle of a homework assignment or a Vera-inspired cooking experiment, but if the atmosphere felt even slightly tense, I would pack up my things and leave.

Not for their sake, but for mine.

Fighting drove me crazy. And after having listened to a pretty constant soundtrack of it for my entire life at home, I had gotten decently good at stopping it, fixing it, or running away from it.

"He can't afford the divorce," my mom grumbled.

"Mom, he knows I'll set the table for you. I always do. And I always will."

She snarled something under her breath and threw potholders at the table like Frisbees. My mom was this interesting mix of plucky, tell-it-like-it-is ballbuster, and pearl-clutching church lady. In one breath, she'd give my dad hell or toss potholders at the table like she was a frolfing superstar, and the next she'd lecture me for complaining about my boss or putting my elbows on the table.

When the potholders were set, she spun back to her stove and mumbled angrily about my dad's grotesque use of his napping privileges. I already knew what kind of night it was going to be before my dad ever made an appearance. If my dad was on his second nap today, there was a reason.

Because in this house, if Mama ain't happy, ain't nobody gonna be happy until the very, very end of time. Like the way end. Like after the epilogue and acknowledgments and sequel preview.

I picked up three napkins and started folding them into origami cranes, placing each one in the center of our ancient Corel plates. The eat-in kitchen was small and dated, but it did something to ease the aching in my hollow chest.

My parents were difficult and angry and deeply bitter, but they also cared about me above everything else. And I knew they loved each other. Even if they had a hard time admitting it. But it always made my memories an interesting mix of longing and loved, of bad memories mingled with great ones.

"You know he lost his job again," my mother said in a harsh whisper. "*Again*, Molly."

I stared at my mom's back and lost the ability to form words. Her stiff shoulders and robotic movements said words she would never say out loud. *What are we going to do now?*

She never asked that question aloud, because she'd always had the answer. She would figure it out. On her own. Without help and without my dad. She would scrimp enough money to get by and continue to do whatever it took to pay the bills and put food on the table. She would do what she always did—clean up my dad's mess.

My dad had never been able to keep a steady job. Which was kind of funny considering how many times he had been hired. That was the thing about my dad, he had no trouble finding work. He just couldn't keep it. People loved him. His bosses always started out loving him. *I* loved him. He was boisterous and charming and completely irresponsible.

And he was a salesman. When I was very little, he sold cars. And knives, and cookware, and even life insurance policies at one point. In middle school, he'd moved to canvassing neighborhoods to sell roofs and then fences and finally gutters. When I got to high school, he had a steady job of selling medical equipment out of an office.

My mom and I had sincerely hoped that the office job would be a turning point for him. He even wore a tie to work and came home every day whistling.

But whatever it was that afflicted my dad when it came to finally pulling it together, had reared its ugly head and come back with a vengeance. When he lost the office job, he didn't find another one until after I'd graduated and left the house.

In recent years, he'd had sporadic part time work with a tree service, but he wasn't exactly a spry twenty-something-year-old. Manual labor was hard for him at his age. So he'd given that up, to try his hand at selling boats.

He'd managed that for eight months.

My heart dropped to my toes like it was made of stone. I grasped at my chest where there was only a gaping hole now. "He'll find another job, Mom," I assured her in an insistent whisper. "He always does."

She didn't turn around. She didn't even flinch. "At least you're not here anymore," she said.

I focused on the napkins again. I didn't know what she meant by that. Maybe she was happy I didn't have to carry these burdens anymore, that I didn't have to watch my dad spiral into depression as he tortured himself for not being able to keep work like most other people. Or maybe she was happy she didn't have another mouth to feed and body to take care of. Maybe she was just glad she had one less thing to worry about now.

"If you need help, Mom, I can—"

Her hand snapped up cutting my words off, stiff as a board. "No, we don't need help. Especially not from our daughter. You got your bills to pay, and that new car of yours, so don't you even think about us. This is your father's mess. Let him figure out what we're going to do."

The hole in my chest widened, cracking my body cavity with dense fissures that spread like disease all the way to my toes. "Well, just let me know if I can help," I said stubbornly. "You've taken care of me my entire life, it's important for me to be able to help you."

"Molly Nichole, it's *my* job to take care of *you*."

And there it was, the confusion that always bit at my skin, like little stinging gnats. Was that all I was to her? An obligation? Another job where she had to pick up all of my dad's slack?

I accidentally bent the neck of my crane napkin. I tried to fix it, but the napkin wasn't stiff enough and I only made it worse.

My dad's heavy footsteps could be heard ambling down the hallway. Without verbally discussing it, Mom and I shut down our job conversation and focused on our individual tasks.

"Patty, have you seen my green t-shirt?" my dad started talking before he'd even reached the kitchen.

"It's in the laundry room," my mother answered, still staring at her ham balls. "It's dirty."

"Son of a bitch," my dad grumbled in return. He turned the corner to the kitchen and stopped in his tracks, surprised to see me standing over his table. "Well, now, if it isn't the most beautiful girl in North Carolina."

I looked up from my task and grinned at this man I wanted so desperately to be the hero instead of the villain in my life story. He was thin and gangly, but for his round belly stretched by his six-foot three-inch frame, made it an awkward effort for him to stay standing. He leaned against the doorframe and smiled back.

"Hi, Daddy."

"Hey, kitten. Missed you."

I left the table to wrap my arms around his middle. "I missed you, too."

He kissed the top of my head and said the same thing he always said to me. "You know, I didn't think this growing up thing all the way through. I didn't think you'd move away and stay away. You were supposed to come back, Molly Monster."

I sniffled against him, feeling frustrated tears prick at the corners of my eyes. I would not let them fall, but the pain in my chest had become a crushing, shaking, life-smashing pain and it was all I could do to hold myself together for him.

He smelled like cheap beer, Old Spice, and my dad. I squished my eyes closed and imprisoned every rogue tear.

"I'm here now," I told him. "Wouldn't miss it."

He kissed my head again, not calling me on the lie. He knew I would miss this if I could. That I had missed plenty of invitations for supper with my parents. He knew I would rather be a hundred different places because so would he.

"It's ready," my mom declared.

Dad and I moved apart. He ambled over to his seat while I pulled water glasses down and filled them. My mom and I added ham balls—which sounded gross, but were, in fact, amazing—rice pilaf and lettuce salad to the table. Once we were all seated, we began passing the food around.

"Well, Molly Monster, let's hear it. Tell us all about your life," my dad demanded with his rich, warm voice. "Who are the boys that are chasing after you?"

Just like that I was transported to my twelve-year-old body that had no idea what to do with boobs or how to get my knees to stop being so knobby. "There aren't any boys," I answered honestly. "I've decided to focus on cats instead."

I always assumed my mom was uninterested in this conversation or at the very least rebelliously uncooperative. But tonight, she surprised me by asking, "I thought you had a date with someone last week?"

"No, not in months. I've given up going on dates forever and ever amen for now. I always end up with refreshed disappointment with the human race as a whole," I corrected. "I hung out with Wyatt and Vann last week. Is that what you're thinking of?"

"Now what's wrong with Vann?" Dad asked. This wasn't the first time or the hundredth time he'd tried to convince me to go after Vann. Since I was a kid, dad had constantly been pushing me toward him. "He's a nice boy. And he won't disappoint you like the rest of them poor bastards."

I smiled patiently at my dad. "Vann and I are never going to happen, daddy. We're friends. Nothing more."

My mother's left eyebrow rose. "What about the other one?"

"Wyatt? He's a friend too."

"All these friends," my mother tsked. "You say they're good guys, but you're never interested in them. Maybe you're too picky for your own good, Molly Nichole."

I was definitely that. "Is it so bad to be picky?"

"Of course not," my dad assured me.

My mom's voice hardened and she threw surreptitious glares at my dad from across the table. "Of course, be picky. You're not in a hurry. Just make sure they do what they're saying to do. Don't just listen to the words they say or believe them at their word. Most of the time those mean nothing. Find a hard worker, Molly. Find someone that's going to work hard all his life."

"Patty," my dad growled, picking up on the dig. "Is that really necessary?"

My mom's unrelenting stare jerked to him. "I just want her to be careful, Tom. Decisions have consequences. Or have you forgotten?"

My dad's teeth clicked together and he gritted out, "Oh, I'm perfectly versed in *consequences*. My entire life is built on a house of *consequences*."

"So maybe you should stop encouraging her to go out on these dates. We don't want her to marry the first guy that asks and get stuck with someone that can't carry their share of the burden."

"I got a new project!" I announced as cheerfully as any human was capable of. "There might be a promotion of sorts at the end of it!" And by promotion, I loosely hoped people would start noticing me.

So like a social promotion.

"That's nice, kitten," my dad mumbled.

"You already told me about it," my mom muttered.

I pushed my ham ball around, my appetite disintegrating. "Well, it's a big deal."

"Is this about work, Patty?" my dad demanded. He jabbed his fork down in a ham ball so it stood up straight on his plate. "You're still pissed off that I got canned? If I've told you once, I've told you a hundred times, the company couldn't support four salesmen! There's only room for two or three and the jobs go to the guys that have been there the longest."

My mother leaned forward, a dark storm cloud brewing over her head. "It's not about this job, Tom. It's not about this one! It's about all of them!"

"Oh, for crying out loud!" My dad shoved back from the table, his plate rocking precariously in protest. "I am so sick of your holier than thou attitude about this, Patty."

"You're sick of me?" my mom railed. "Of me?!"

And on and on it went. I felt sick to my stomach, but I forced myself to eat, knowing it would be worse if I didn't. I tuned out the familiar fight and focused on counting my bites of food, and sipping my water as slowly as possible. I drew little pictures in the sweet sauce that went over the ham balls with the tip of my fork. I didn't engage. And I didn't speak. I simply listened and endured and waited for the moment I could slip away unnoticed.

Eventually my mom stood up from the table and started clearing the dishes, and my dad stomped back to the bedroom with a few more beers in hand. Mom would spend the rest of the night regretting every minute of her life up until now while she furiously cleaned the kitchen. And dad would drink until he passed out in a blissful heap of unconsciousness. They would go to bed, not really recognizing their dysfunction. Or at least not caring enough to do anything about it. And then tomorrow it would start all over again.

I was the one that would carry this with me when I left, that would wrestle with it all night and tomorrow, and on and on, forever. I would tuck it into the imaginary backpack I'd carried since I was a child and add it to all the other memories like this one that have never left me.

Tomorrow, I would go to work and I would bust my ass to do the very best I could at every single element of my job. I would make a conscious effort not to end up like my dad who didn't value a steady job or a bright future. And I would vow to never to turn into my mother who never let my dad hear the end of it, who didn't care about whatever ailment he had that wouldn't let him work or kept him from being successful. I would swear to myself that I would never be a nag or cruel for the purpose of being cruel.

I would love my parents always, but I would never let myself become them.

As for tonight? I would paint.

I all but crawled back to my apartment after I left my parents. I thought about a bottle of wine, but then I remembered my dad carrying half a six pack back to his room and couldn't stomach the idea of drowning my own sorrows in alcohol too.

So instead, I settled for my favorite playlist, a Diet Coke, and my paints. Despite work in the morning and an irresponsible agreement to meet Vera at the gym even earlier than that, I didn't leave my canvas until after eleven.

And when I had finally finished purging my emotions and frustrations, and expelling everything I didn't say or think or want anyone to know, I stumbled back from my easel and sucked in a steadying breath.

For once, it wasn't a version of Ezra staring back at me. I hadn't focused on minute details of eyes or lashes or lips. I hadn't bothered to make anything lifelike, eye-catching, or pretty.

Instead, it was all slashes of bright paint. Red, blue, and yellow. Splotches of orange, green, and black.

And then just black, and black, and black.

And red on top of that.

And so much color in places it hurt my eyes and then so much more color everything turned black and I wanted to weep.

I left my brushes without washing them and my palette without cleaning it. I turned my back on the room, not having the energy to deal with it tonight.

The mess would wait for me until morning, just like this room and all of the paintings that remained in it.

I leaned against the doorframe for a long minute, examining the room with tired, frustrated eyes. Part of me wanted to walk away from painting forever. For a hobby, it was a painful one. It demanded too much of my soul, forced me to admit too much of myself. And then it put all of those pieces and parts of me I tried so desperately to keep hidden on display for everyone to see.

On the other hand, yes it was a hobby, but it also felt like so much more. It felt deeper and more stable than anything else in my life. But most of all, it felt like the lifeline back to sanity I needed so desperately.

When I finally fell asleep it was with tears in my eyes, but if you would have asked me why I was crying, I wouldn't have been able to tell you.

Maybe it was for my parents that couldn't even be decent to each other.

Maybe it was for myself and my perpetual state of singlehood, the inability to find a decent guy, and the very real prospect that I was going to be alone for the rest of my life.

Or maybe it was for the art that meant so much to me, the creative outlet I relied so heavily upon to heal the broken pieces of my spirit.

Maybe it was because I knew I didn't have the ability to fix any of the things that haunted me. I couldn't mend my parents' marriage or make them respect each other. I couldn't make Mr. Right suddenly show up in my life and sweep me off my feet. I couldn't make Mr. Tucker give me lead on a good account. I couldn't make my coworkers respect me and take my ideas seriously.

From where I sat everything felt impossible. Everything except painting.

Chapter Eleven

*M*onday morning the office drummed with the beat of a funeral dirge. Any other day of the week, people moved around with a spark in their step, hurried with the drive to get the job done, overwhelmed with all they needed to do before lunch.

But not on Mondays.

Instead of the insistent, purposeful buzzing of the rest of the week, people stumbled from their desk to printers, guzzling coffee as they went. Their expressions were droopy and insincere, and their eyes slowly blinked with the memories of a beloved weekend that had died very suddenly the night before.

Usually, I enjoyed the amusement of Monday morning. Emily and I would play Guess Who's Hungover over our second, third and fourth cups of coffee and laugh at our Monday-oppressed coworkers.

But this morning, after a fitful night's sleep and a stressful weekend, I was the worst of the worst. I didn't have a case of the Mondays, I had the bubonic plague of the Mondays.

This was how the zombie apocalypse would start. I was person zero.

"You look like the Grim Reaper's undead bride." Emily sympathized as I plopped into my chair across the aisle from her.

I waved her off. "Stop with the compliments already. You're making me blush."

She pushed her chair over to my desk, her four-inch stilettos clicking across the bamboo floor. "Seriously, Molly, are you sick? Hungover? Did something happen to Chris Pratt?"

Giving her a look that reminded her not to joke about Chris Pratt, I took a shaky sip of my coffee and said simply, "I'm tired."

Emily's eyes bugged. "This is more than tired. Girlfriend, you look like eight miles of hard road."

I mustered a laugh, even though I really wanted to slither off to the bathroom and cry. "I just need coffee." Tipping my to-go triple espresso latte at her, I added, "This is my first cup."

"Well, drink it quickly," she warned. "Rumor has it there is a very important potential client here to see you."

Perking up at her announcement, I rolled my neck and tried to will energy into my limp appendages. "Black Soul?"

She shook her head. "No, someone new."

My coffee hit my stomach with a weird gurgle and I abruptly felt nauseous. "You didn't get a name?"

Her eyebrows danced over her very expressive eyes. "Only that he asked for you specifically."

"He who?"

Emily shook her head, her lavender hair bouncing around her shoulders. "Molly, I have no idea." She leaned forward pressing the back of her hand to my clammy forehead. "Are you sure you're okay? You look white as a ghost all of sudden."

My desk phone rang and I made a squealy noise and flailed in my chair. Ignoring Emily's deeper expression of concern, I reached for my phone and answered as confidently as I could. "Th-this is Molly Maverick."

"Hi, Molly," Mr. Tucker's secretary greeted pleasantly. "Mr. Tucker would like you to join him in his office. There is a client here to see you."

"Oh." I silently fretted and worried my bottom lip as I tried to think of an excuse to leave for the day. Or maybe I would just quit. A sinking feeling of intuition had snaked through my gut, warning me that going to Tucker's office would be a giant mistake. "I'll be right there."

I hung up the phone and gripped my travel mug with two hands, bringing it to my lips for a steadying gulp of lukewarm coffee. "Is it too late to call in sick?"

Emily glanced down the aisle and then back at me. "What is going on, Molly? You're making me nervous."

"I'm fine." I lied. "I'll be fine." Another lie.

The heat kicked on over my head, sending a puff of stifling air all around me. Beads of sweat popped up around my hairline and I desperately wanted to start shedding layers. I immediately regretted the rose pink blazer I wore over my white blouse. I couldn't take it off because I'd stupidly worn a paisley print bra that my thin shirt would be helpless to hide.

Why did I make such bad decisions before coffee?

With one last long sip, I stood up from my desk, grabbed my notebook, thick planner and a Tic-Tac. I stuck a pen in the base of my high bun and waved goodbye to Emily. She stayed at my desk to watch me walk away, a look of worried consternation on her pretty face. Shooting her a confident smile, I had to admit that I was acting a bit crazy—even by my standards.

Mr. Tucker's secretary, Teresa, waved me through to his office where my worst nightmare came true. I tried not to make a face even though I mentally admitted to myself that I should have seen this coming.

I should have known he wouldn't take no for an answer.

I should have realized that as a general rule, STS would be thrilled to land a high-profile client like him.

Ezra Baptiste.

He sat across from Mr. Tucker looking way too suave for his own good. His long legs were crossed casually showcasing his tailored charcoal dress pants. His hands rested in his lap, an expensive watch blinking from his wrist. His strong torso leaned back in the chair, clothed in a layered black sweater that molded perfectly to his too-toned body, a white dress shirt poking out at his wrists and collar. His hair had been styled, laying in expert waves that begged fingers to run through it or brush it back or grab it and pull it and...

I licked dry lips and met his concentrated gaze. He stood up as I entered the room, acknowledging me with all his somber intensity. Mr. Tucker reluctantly stood too, and I was thankful for an excuse to look anywhere but at Ezra.

"Hi, Molly." Mr. Tucker's eyebrows rose subtly with surprise. He hadn't been expecting me. I had a feeling he only knew my name because Ezra had asked for me specifically. I imagined Mr. Tucker waiting impatiently to find out which one was Molly. Now he knew.

Next week he was going to make us start wearing name tags. I could feel it.

"Hello, Mr. Tucker," I returned professionally, unruffled, completely and utterly in my element.

Or at least pretending to be.

"Have a seat." He gestured at the chair next to Ezra. "This is Ezra Baptiste," Mr. Tucker went on. "He and his company EFB Enterprises are interested in our marketing services and he's requested your assistance. Seems he's aware of your outstanding reputation."

Mr. Tucker smiled proudly at me as if he was also aware of my outstanding reputation. The outstanding reputation that didn't exist. And even if it did it would not be important enough information for Mr. Tucker to familiarize himself with.

Ezra didn't jump in to corroborate the claim, so there was a heavy minute of awkward silence in which I refused to speak and Mr. Tucker didn't know what else to say.

Finally, unable to withstand the tense pressure, I crossed my legs, looked at my boss and said, "Thank you."

That also left Mr. Tucker scrambling for the appropriate response since he wasn't sure if I was thanking him or Ezra for the compliment or for the job.

Finally, Mr. Tucker cleared his throat and nodded. "You're welcome." We fell into silence again.

If this had happened to anyone else, I would have found the entire meeting entertaining. Instead, as the victim in this situation, I tried to discreetly scope out the underside of Mr. Tucker's desk in the probable chance I decided to crawl under it and rock myself back and forth until everyone left for the day.

Mr. Tucker scratched the underside of his chin and glanced desperately back and forth between Ezra and me. He wanted so badly for one of us to take over the conversation. Poor, naïve, Mr. Tucker.

"You're in the restaurant business, isn't that right?" Mr. Tucker asked Ezra.

"That's right," Ezra agreed, *finally* speaking up. "I own four fine-dining restaurants around Durham, but my logo and website are dated. I'm interested in working with Miss Maverick to revamp my image, give the corporation a fresh look. I'm also interested in hearing her thoughts on a better social media approach, running a few commercials for the different restaurants and whatever else you have to offer. I want the whole package."

Mr. Tucker smiled and I could swear dollar signs started floating in his eyeballs. I resisted the urge to kick Ezra in the shins.

Was this even a real conversation? Did he honestly want all of those things from STS? From me?

If he had been anyone else, I would have understood his motivation. I was awesome at my job. Especially if he wanted a big social media package. I would kick serious internet ass for him. But this was Ezra we were talking about.

110

Just this weekend he'd called me *green*. And tried to dictate my style by telling me which colors to avoid *in an email for the love of all things holy*. The man wasn't capable of letting me do my thing without dipping his fingers into every single thing.

So maybe this was something else? Maybe he was picking on me or punishing me for daring to stand up to him Friday night. Maybe he was just trying to make my life complicated.

Because he was doing that. He was so doing that.

There had been an email from him in my inbox this morning, but I hadn't had a chance to read it. Or there was a possibility I hadn't read it out of spite. Now I wished I hadn't left my cell phone at my desk.

Besides, STS was most known for their stellar design team. We rocked the local area with our logos, graphics and print ads. I was doing my best to help with social media strategy, but STS as a whole wasn't as savvy when it came to competing on the different social outlets and what worked. I was fighting an uphill battle, although if Ezra really wanted those things at least he'd picked the right person.

But commercials? Maybe he hadn't done his research after all.

While we offered a media package, it was nothing to boast about. We charged an exorbitant amount of money, but in my honest opinion, couldn't deliver the quality and finesse Ezra would be looking for.

Mr. Tucker congratulated Ezra on having good taste and then launched into a schmoozy-pitch about how much more we could offer him. I zoned out in favor of staring a hole into the side of Ezra's head.

He glanced at me, doing a double-take when he caught me staring. With a second turn of his head, the corner of his mouth kicked up in a half smile and he cut Mr. Tucker off mid-sentence to say, "I trust you, Molly."

My heart skipped, or rather, tripped over itself at those precious few words that meant more to me than I wanted them to. *He trusted me? Why?* I hadn't done anything worthy of gaining his trust. I hadn't even earned the trust of my bosses yet. Or coworkers. Or parents!

I opened my mouth to argue with him when the office door creaked open and Henry Tucker walked in uninvited. If I hadn't understood that there was nothing in my power to get rid of Ezra, I would have screamed with frustration. Not only was Henry being incredibly rude and intrusive, he was jeopardizing my standing with a potential client. Henry had no idea I had history with Ezra. He had no idea what he was walking in on.

"Henry, my boy!" Mr. Tucker grinned that cat eating the canary smile. "I'm so glad you stopped by. This is Ezra Baptiste, head of EFB Enterprises. He's interested in a full workup. With Molly of all people."

Henry stepped up behind me, dropping his hand to rest on my shoulder. I felt his body heat through my blazer, too warm, too slippery, too wrong. I wanted to cringe and I wanted to shake him off, but most of all I wanted to die from embarrassment because Ezra's shrewd, always alert gaze dropped right to where Henry's hand had covered my collarbone.

"Of course he is," Henry said through a stretching smile. He squeezed my shoulder and I wanted to stop, drop and roll the hell out of here. "She's our very best."

Lie.

I wasn't the very best. I wasn't even close to it. His hand stayed perched on my shoulder longer and longer, elongating the awkwardness until the hairs on my neck stood up. It was all I could do not to wince. His fingers pressed below my collar bone too familiarly and then his thumb, his unwelcomed, uninvited thumb drew a slow path along the nape of my neck where it buried itself in my hair. A sickly feeling slithered beneath my skin while my brain tried to convince my instinct that this was an accident or that Henry was overly touchy but not threatening. And that's when my body decided to ignore them both by making a complete fool out of myself.

Dropping my shoulder and sliding out of my chair, I practically jumped to standing startling half the room. Without having a game plan I thrust out my hand to Ezra. "I'm looking forward to working with you," I heard myself say.

Damn it! That was not at all what I meant to do. My flight reaction got in the way of common sense.

Ezra blinked up at me, clearly not expecting me to walk into this arrangement so easily. He glanced back at Junior before he stood to his full height, crowding me, towering over me, eating up every inch of space that his tall frame needed and then some. His hand wrapped around mine, warm and firm and dry—such a contrast to the hand I'd just run away from. "As am I," he said coolly.

Mr. Tucker slammed his hands on the desk excitedly, no doubt already preparing Ezra's invoice. He started to say something congratulatory but all I wanted to do was get out of this office.

"I can take you to our conference room," I blurted to Ezra, my hand still wrapped in his. "We can go over details while you acquaint me with your company and give me a better vision of what you're hoping to accomplish with STS." I let out a slow, steady breath, hoping the beads of sweat along my hairline weren't obvious.

"That's a great idea," Ezra replied. "Lead the way, Miss Maverick."

112

I turned and smiled bravely at Mr. Tucker without meeting his eyes and shot another nod of confidence somewhere in the vicinity of Junior's feet. Then I escaped quickly to a conference room, Ezra close on my heels.

Pushing the door open with one arm, I gestured for Ezra to enter. "Right in here." I followed after him just as soon as I'd glanced back to make sure Senior and Junior hadn't bothered to follow me.

"I had been prepared to negotiate," Ezra began talking. "I should probably apologize…"

Nervous energy buzzed through me, but I blamed it on Ezra's sudden appearance. Although I could still feel the phantom brushing of Henry's thumb over my neck. I shuddered, wishing I could erase the memory altogether as I walked to the wall of windows in the conference room.

I should say something to Henry, I decided. That was too much. Too intimate. And on top of every terrible thing, super inappropriate. He was my boss and in general he gave me the creeps. *If he gets close again, I'll say something. I'll ask him to stop. He'll listen. He's a professional. I'm a professional. It will be fine.*

"Molly?"

Ezra stood up and walked over to me. Belatedly, I realized I had been staring out the window at downtown Durham, completely lost in thought and he'd been talking since the door closed behind us. Actually, now that I thought about it, I thought maybe he'd been apologizing, but I hadn't heard a single word of it.

"Sorry," I told him, reverting to my familiar tactic of always being the one that had to make the other person comfortable. "It's been a weird day."

His eyebrows scrunched together over his eyes. "Are you okay?"

"Fine," I told him with a smile that lied. "Perfectly fine. I just wasn't expecting…" I met his dark gaze again, braving the concentrated gaze I knew would be waiting for me. "You."

He let out a slow breath, seeming to gather his thoughts. "I told you on Friday that I wanted to work with you."

"I didn't realize you would go above my head to do it," I snapped, dropping the happy façade I didn't feel.

"You're angry," he concluded.

"I'm pissed," I countered.

He looked away and I swore it was to hide a smile, further feeding the furious dragon-woman living inside me. "Aren't they the same thing?"

Aren't they the same thing? Somebody hold my earrings!

"Is this really what you want, Ezra? You could hire anybody. Anybody! But you really want me?"

113

His entire body swiveled to face me again, tension pulling him taut, straightening his shoulders and widening his stance. His face was all cut marble, stone, granite, *something* that symbolized immovable strength and conviction. He was too intimidating, too beautiful. Too *him*.

"No one tells me the truth anymore, Molly. Not even the people I pay to do that. The current website is dated and dysfunctional and yet I paid my last web designer excessive amounts of money and all he did was give me exactly what I wanted." I decided not to argue with him about why his last web designer was doing what he was paid to do. He went on, "I want someone who is going to ignore my personal taste and instead make something that has market appeal. I want someone who is going to stand up to me and fight me when I'm wrong. I believe that person is you. It's true, I don't like your taste. You're too modern. Your designs are too simplistic and I hate your color schemes. And that is why I need you on my team."

I glared at him even while I tried to convince my mind to stop plotting his murder. He wanted to hire me because he hated everything about my style?

"Despite what you think, Ezra Baptiste, I don't get paid to fight with my clients. Nor do I want to spend my valuable time standing up to a pigheaded, outdated, stubborn old man. So here is how this is going to go, since I'm clearly trapped in this project that you're forcing me into. You're going to listen to my advice and you're going to take it. You're going to approve my designs and social media strategy and then you're going to hire more people to implement every single thing I tell you to do. And lastly, but this is probably my most important point, you're going to go somewhere else for your on-screen advertising because so help me God if I do all of this work for you and then you mess it up by letting STS do your commercials..."

His head cocked back in surprise. He blinked once, twice, then his mouth broke open in a victorious smile. "This is exactly why I hired you."

I resisted, barely, the urge to roll my eyes. "I'm confident you're getting more than what you asked for."

His eyes darkened with promise, his smile turning sly and secretive. "That's what I'm counting on."

A shiver skittered down my spine, pulling goose bumps from my arms. It was the exact opposite reaction of how jittery I felt toward Henry. Fine, I was still jumpy and frustratingly nervous, but I was also too hot and too dizzy and something else entirely.

Ezra Baptiste had some kind of magic juju that lured confident, professional women in and turned them into melting piles of goo. This was why nobody could be honest with the man. This was why everybody told him what they thought he wanted to hear. Because frankly, they lose their damn minds around him.

I refused to be that girl. I refused to be hypnotized by his good looks and entranced by his secret charm. I refused to find his dark eyes mesmerizing and his smile adorably boyish. I refused to like this man that was heavy-handed and bossy and so ridiculously confident.

Do you hear that, libido? This is a sexy man boycott!

And I was definitely going to have to reopen my eHarmony account. Tonight.

Maybe over my lunch break.

I needed a date STAT.

"I have a worksheet," I blurted, hating how I was starting to soften and lose my hard edge. "It will help me better understand everything you need." He glanced at his watch and I took the opportunity to step back far enough that I couldn't smell him anymore. "I just need to grab my tablet."

His expression flattened with his familiar frown. "I hate to do this to you, but I am late for another meeting. Can you email it to me?"

I nodded to cover my inability to form coherent sentences. "Y-yes. That's fine. Is it just for Lilou? I can tweak it to your specifications if I know which website I'm working with."

"All of them," he said casually, like it wasn't about to cost him thousands and thousands of dollars. "The four restaurants and the EFB master website. Do you need links? My assistant can email them later today."

"I'll find them," I assured him. "That's part of my process. I need to evaluate how easy it is to search your sites and use them."

"Well, you're already familiar with Lilou." His words had a playful bite to them and his eyes danced with that same surprising mischief. "You'll want to find your way to the social sites as well?"

I nodded. "Yes."

"I'll look for your email later today."

"Sounds good."

He stuck out his hand once more and I tentatively reached for it. "Thank you for agreeing to work with me, Molly."

Holding his steady gaze, I felt the first authentic burst of confidence bloom inside me. "I hope you know what you're getting yourself into, Ezra. I'm not going to go easy on you."

He leaned in, surrounding me with his delicious scent. "That is exactly why I want you."

My mouth went dry at his words, dropping open with surprise. Thankfully, Ezra had already turned around and headed for the door. Tucker Junior just happened to be there.

Henry held the door open for Ezra. They chatted in the doorway and I overheard Henry offer to show Ezra out. For some reason, I was relieved when Ezra declined.

It wasn't that I thought Ezra would take his business elsewhere should Junior decide to get handsy in the elevator, but everything about Henry made me prickly and I found myself wanting to spare Ezra from all that potential awkwardness.

"Look at you, superstar," Henry crooned when Ezra finally walked away. "Two major clients this month. Someone's on her way to the top."

He'd blocked me in, resting his hip against the table Ezra and I had never sat down at. "Coincidence," I told him.

"Maybe it's hard work," he countered, giving me a look that made me feel sweaty. "Or maybe your boss just likes to look at you." This time he winked.

I laughed nervously, trying to play it off. "Speaking of hard work…" I shuffled closer to the wall. "I should get back to it."

His expression turned predatory. My shoulder brushed the wall as I tried to skirt around the room, officially nervous around Henry. "That's a good girl," he murmured as I walked by him.

Just after I'd passed him, he stood up. There was a moment when we were too close and something brushed over my butt. My heart started pounding and adrenaline kicked in. I walked quickly back to my desk, not breathing the entire time. But it wasn't until I was at my desk that I finally let myself admit that he'd touched my butt.

Henry had patted me on the butt.

The space where we were had been small though. It could have been an accident.

I stared blankly at my computer screen for the next twenty minutes trying to decide what to do. But that didn't lead to any answers. I had no precedent for this, no prior experience with an inappropriate boss or coworker.

I didn't see Henry again for the rest of the day. He stayed in his office, and I stayed at my desk or escaped to the bathroom whenever I spotted him walking around.

By the end of the day, I'd convinced myself that I was making more of this than it was. I was uncomfortable around Henry, but he hadn't really done anything overt. He'd put his hand on my shoulder. And maybe, accidentally bumped my butt. He was always polite. Always nice. He'd

116

picked me to be on Black Soul out of an office of more experienced designers.

I would just work harder to keep my distance. I wouldn't get caught in conference rooms with him or put myself in potentially compromising positions. And I would make my intentions clear. I didn't want him touching me. I would definitely tell him that next time.

Definitely.

And in the meantime, I would throw all of my energy into Black Soul and EFB Enterprises. I would be the best damn social media strategist in the city. Nay, the state! And I would design the crap out of my logos and promo pics.

Ezra Baptiste would be grateful he hired me, but that would be it. I could finish his project and then finally be done with him. Plus, his company would look amazing in my portfolio. Okay, it wasn't ideal to work for Vera's fiancé's best friend. But, I would turn this into a positive opportunity.

Black Soul would be great too. Sure, my part was much smaller in that project, but I would still be able to put all the final work in my portfolio and use it to build the foundation of a stable, lifelong career.

This was all going to work out. It would be fine.

I would be fine.

And starting next month, I would stop lying to myself.

Chapter Twelve

*M*y phone buzzed with an incoming email and I resisted the urge to check it during the middle of spin class. I could wait to open it. I didn't need to know what it said just this second.

Really, it would be fine.

It could wait.

I could wait.

The sender could wait until after I'd sweated off the three pounds of pasta I'd gained this week from my favorite Italian takeout spot to hear back from me.

I couldn't help the small smile of anticipation that lifted the corners of my mouth though or the way I suddenly didn't notice the pain from pushing up the hill climb at 5:45 a.m. Resisting the urge to pick up my phone, I opted for my water bottle instead. But even after a big, refreshing gulp, I still didn't manage to lose the smile.

"Why do you look happy?" Vera panted next to me, her legs moving approximately one thousand miles per hour. "You should be miserable right now. At the very least you should be contemplating puking. No smiling."

"I think I see Jesus," I ~~wheezed~~ said serenely. "I've pedaled myself to death. He's coming to get me."

Vann chuckled on my other side. "This is only the warm up."

"Stop showing off, Vann." My smile disappeared. "We get it. You're a super cyclist. The bike seat up your ass isn't bothering you at all. Stop bragging." To Vera, I said, "Why did you invite him again?"

"Hey!" Vann protested.

She rolled her eyes. "I didn't invite him. I tried very hard to keep this a secret from him. But when he heard we were doing something bicycle related, he invited himself."

"I'm here to motivate you," he said seriously. "This is good for you girls. You both are in serious need of some cardio."

"Your face is in serious need of some cardio," Vera snarled back. At my look of not-the-best-insult-you've-ever-come-up-with, she shrugged. "My brain is still sleepy."

Vann leaned forward on his bike, lifting his bum off the seat and adjusting his bike to make it harder for himself. Because he was crazy and liked weird things- like exercise. ~~This was the end of our friendship forever. I officially hated him.~~ His overachieving did nothing to motivate me to work harder. This was it. This was as hard as I spinned. Spun? My brain was sleepy too.

My phone buzzed again in the holder thingy next to my handlebars. I realized I was the irritating person that brought her phone to class with me, but juggling two major clients wasn't as easy as it sounded. Especially because of the two clients I had to juggle.

Black Soul wasn't terrible. Our big meeting with them was still a ways off so Henry was the only one that dealt with them directly so far. Meanwhile, Ethan and I had been coordinating on kick ass campaigns that were bound to blow their socks off.

On the other hand, we also had to work with Henry. And he was ~~a giant pain in my ass~~ more difficult. He made things doubly more complicated. No, it was worse than that. Triply. Quadruply?

He was always up in my business. *Always*. And not just with his work ethic and slave driver tendencies. He was hands everywhere, body everywhere, coffee breath everywhere all day every day.

I was over him and how uncomfortable he made me. His bad jokes, his creepy stares, the way he always, no matter what I was wearing or how vigilantly I tried to disguise my boobs, stared at my chest, were out of control. I avoided him the best I could, but since we were on the same project, it was impossible to completely evade him.

The worst part was that he was probably going to get me fired in the end. Yes, *he* was the creep, but I was about one more unwelcomed back rub away from punching him in his throat.

120

And then on the other side of things, I had to work with Ezra. The man was completely insufferable. He emailed at all hours of the day or night because apparently he never slept. And who could blame him when there was so much work to do?

Just kidding. I could blame him. I could totally blame him.

We were different in this way. Where he was a complete and utter workaholic, I was a very strong proponent of beauty sleep. I had lost count of the number of emails I had sent him encouraging him to get those eight hours or hey, even six hours. But he was stubborn and determined to drive me crazy.

He also never seemed to get tired of emailing. No matter when I sent mine, he always responded within a half hour. I got that he was spending money on this project and he really wanted it done well, but the amount of attention he wanted was silly. We sent at least a couple a day and sometimes he sent multiples in a row before I got the chance to get back to him.

They would always start very early in the morning with a simple hello and have you made any progress? Then they evolved from there into back and forth verbal duels. We didn't just email, we sparred, we went head to head and refused to let the other person win.

For instance, two weeks ago, I'd emailed this:

Ezra Franklin Baptist
Ezra Festivus Baptist
EFreakingB
Ezra,
How comfortable are you with selfies?
MM.

He'd written back,

Molly,
I'm not.
~EFB
P.S. When are we going to meet again? As your most important client, I feel neglected.

I'd rolled my eyes at the screen and then proceeded to send him thirty emails and seventeen text messages the rest of the day just to make sure he felt important.

That night he'd replied with:

All right! You win. You've exhausted me.
~E
P.S. How about next time you let me take you to lunch so we can avoid
the spam.

Apparently, I'd exhausted him so thoroughly he could only sign his
name E.
I'd replied:

Ezra,
I just wanted you to know, as my most important client, that you were
well taken care of.
MM.
How about next time you bring me frites from Lilou so I can work
through lunch.

The next day, a runner had shown up with steak and frites from Lilou.
My entire office had been jealous. I'd sent him an email thanking him for
lunch, but he hadn't responded to that one.

Molly,
Not a big fan of the color scheme. How many pictures do you want me
to post a day? You can't be serious. Also, it's still a hard no on the selfies.
~Ezra
P.S. Do you mind if I pass your name along to a friend? He's apparently
impressed with my recent social game and wants to know what my secret
is. I told him that I'm being innovative and he laughed in my face. He
wants my secret.
He's sixty by the way. He just became a grandfather. He also owns a
bakery.

I had been flattered that Ezra's acquaintance had noticed all the work I
had been doing to bring Ezra's business into modern day. The man had
zero talent for the internet. I had no doubt that he was a business genius
and knew his way around the industry, but getting him to post a picture of
tonight's special or a behind the scenes look at one of his kitchens was
like pulling teeth.

Ezra,

*I'll rework the graphic tones if you promise to try for at least two
pictures a day. Three would be better. You have to trust me a little bit, but
I think you'll be happy with the results.*

*As far as selfies, I'm going to need you to get over that asap. You
should practice. Send them to me and I'll give you pointers. Use filters.
Avoid pouty lips.*

*Once you get that down, we can move on to stories. If you think selfies
are bad, just wait.*

MM.

*Feel free to pass along my name! It doesn't bother me that he's a
grandpa. I can work with any demographic. I'm versatile like that.*

I'd gotten a reply approximately three minutes after I'd pressed send.

Molly,
*I just didn't want you to think I was trying to set you up. I know you
hate that.*
~E

I might have had a glass of wine before I responded. I also might have
felt like poking the bear ~~as usual~~ again.

Ezra,
*I'm into grandpas. I want you to set us up. Also I'm really into baked
goods. So, I might just use him for his pastry connections.*
MM.

He'd emailed back immediately.

Molly,
Duly noted.
~Ezra.

I had been irrationally disappointed with his email, expecting more
from him. But then the next day he'd sent a box from one of the coolest
French bakeries in town filled with macaroons, chocolate croissants, fruit
tartlets, and several different flavors of eclairs.

The note that accompanied the box said, *I have connections too, ~Ezra.*

I'd ~~grudgingly~~ shared with the people around me and tucked the note
away in my desk. And then spent the rest of the day trying not to
overanalyze pastries.

Last Saturday, he'd sent a work-related email that required thought and effort, and a whole gamut of skills that I pretended I didn't have during the weekend.

I'd shot back a quick email that had said:

~~Ezra,~~
Dear Mr. Workaholic,
I know you have heart palpitations when I don't let you work, but it's the weekend! Take a break. You deserve it. More importantly, I deserve it.
XOXO
MM.

He'd written back almost immediately.

Molly,
There is no rest for the wicked. The weekend is when I make the majority of my money.
~Ezra
But you do deserve a break. I'll talk to you on Monday. Unless you wanted to stop by Bianca tonight so I can stay in business. I'll save a table for you.

I hadn't stopped by Bianca because I didn't think it was a real offer, even though my insides had gone squishy and I'd been unable to stop smiling for the rest of the weekend. Plus, I knew it was almost as popular as Lilou, so walking in the door without a reservation was not even an option. I probably would have been assassinated by vengeful foodies up in arms that I cut the waitlist. They would have poison-darted me from the bushes.

It was now Monday. And when did Ezra email me? At 5:45 in the morning! He was crazy. And obnoxiously adorable. And apparently had no life outside of work.

I had always found that an annoying quality when I'd been setup before. I didn't understand why men always seemed able to commit to their jobs, but not a woman. Wasn't a loyal life partner better than paperwork or promotions or prestige? Wouldn't they prefer to get laid rather than meet deadlines? Wouldn't they rather have a family than a corner office?

And yet, with Ezra, I found it endearing. He'd built this empire out of blood, sweat, and a hell of a lot of work. So for him to pour himself into his different businesses was admirable.

124

It didn't mean that I was changing my opinion on workaholics. But he always seemed to be the exception and not the rule. It was ~~annoying~~ frustrating.

In one of his emails, he'd mentioned wanting to hire his sister. I mean, right? How could you not find that completely swoon-worthy?

Not that he was swoon-worthy in general. But maybe he wasn't a totally intolerable person. And maybe there was a possibility that he knew what he was doing in business.

He for sure still needed my guidance.

But he wasn't totally helpless.

Spin class ended with a groan from me and an enthusiastic fist pump from Vann.

"Vera, do something about your brother," I huffed. "His energy is getting on my nerves."

Vann grinned at us, hopping off his stationary bike like he had no issue with taking the next class or moving or standing in general. Meanwhile, Vera and I weren't going to be able to walk for two days, just in time to drag our carb-loving asses back here and torture ourselves all over again.

"Listen, brother of mine, this class is for people that hate exercise, hate losing weight and in general, hate themselves. And if you can't respect that, we're going to have to ask you to leave."

He blinked at us. "This class is for experts. This is an advanced level class."

Vera waved at some other spinners and tipped her water bottle in salute. "I want to look good in my wedding dress," she murmured more to herself than anyone else. "I want to look good on my honeymoon."

"Why are *you* here?" Vann asked me bluntly.

I shrugged. "Team spirit? Also, I live off of take-out and Hot Pockets, and sit at a desk all day. I have to do something to counterbalance my lifestyle."

"Thanks for the great class," Vera called to the instructor as we walked into the hallway.

I didn't feel the pressure to suck up to our evil instructor like Vera did. She was all about being nice to him because of the theory that he would be nice to her in return. I was all about googling how to make a voodoo doll that gave him temporary paralysis of the legs.

But in a nice way. And only in the early morning.

We ~~waddled~~ walked out of the room as a trio, Vann perfectly fine, Vera and I dying on the inside. And outside. And all the sides.

"We need protein shakes," Vann announced.

Vera's face scrunched in disgust and she shook her head back and forth quickly. "Don't make me. Molly, make the bad man go away."

"Let's make a run for it, Vere. We won't stop until we're safely inside the girl's locker room. On my signal…"

Vann let out an exasperated sound. "There's something seriously wrong with you two. I don't know how you have any friends."

"Well, for starters, we don't force them to drink protein shakes," Vera countered.

Vann's head tilted, considering. "I'm doing you a favor. They speed up your metabolism. Also, they don't taste gross. They make them with peanut butter and chocolate."

Vera and I shared a look. "It couldn't hurt to try them," she said.

"I mean… we might as well see what the fuss is about."

Vann turned around and led us to the café, muttering the entire way. I pulled out my phone and finally checked my email, careful not to trip over rogue weights, random jump ropes, or air.

Molly,
Call me when you get into the office. We can discuss the email you ignored over the weekend.
~Ezra
P.S. I went to brunch with Dillon on Sunday and then we caught a movie. I can take breaks. I'm the best at taking breaks. What did you do?

"You're smiling at your phone again," Vera pointed out.

I cleared my throat and wiped the goofy look off my face. "Am I?"

"What is going on with you?" she demanded.

"Nothing."

"Don't play coy with me, Molly Maverick. If there's a man in your life, I should be the first one to know about him. Maybe even before you do!"

I rolled my eyes and looked at Vann for support, but he was as curious as his sister. We stepped up in line at the café that was teaming with protein-shake drinking crazies.

"It's a work email," I told them. "It's just from Ezra."

Vann's eyebrows shot up. "Ezra Baptiste?"

"He hired me to do some work for his company. It's not a big deal."

"You're smiling again!" Vera pointed out. "Vann, she's smiling about work!"

"So?" I shrugged. "I like working for him. I'm the only one on his project so I get to do whatever I want. It's nice."

Vera's eyes narrowed. "I thought you were afraid of him."

126

I felt my cheeks heat from their unwanted attention. I didn't need the third degree from these two this early in the morning. Mostly because I hadn't had coffee yet and I didn't think I'd be able to deflect their accusations with the kind of expert ninja skill I usually had. "He's not so scary once you get to know him."

"I thought you were working for him," Vann pressed. "Why are you getting to know him?"

"Oh, my gosh. I'm getting to know him because I'm working for him."

The siblings shared a look. "I've known him as long as you have," Vera argued. "I haven't gotten to know him. Not really."

"Stop," I begged them. "It's nothing. Just work stuff."

Vera attempted to hold back a smile. And failed. "I said the same thing about Killian."

Vann smiled now too. "He's cool, Molly. You could do a lot worse." He thought about it for a second. "You *have* done a lot worse."

"Thanks for your approval, guys, but seriously, we're just working together. That's it."

I didn't even have to lie to them. That was the truth. Ezra had hired STS to help him with marketing. And I was the designer that he'd handpicked happened to get picked for the project. Hardly a romantic fairy tale.

Vann stepped up to the counter to order for us while Vera continued to smile at me, her head practically exploding with unsaid well wishes. "He's just so perfect for you."

Laughing at her disproportionate reaction to a few simple emails, I threw her a bone. "He's at least not as horrible as I thought he was. He's... nice."

"And hot," she added.

"So hot," I agreed, finally giving into the gushing that had been building since I read his email. "How is it even fair that he's that hot?"

"It's because he's also nice. Looks are one thing, but when they're good people too, that's like a whole other level of hot."

"And funny," I added without thinking about it. "He's surprisingly funny. And thoughtful in an unexpected way. And he sends me things, Vera. Like pastries and lunch. I don't know what to think about him."

Her smile softened and her expression warmed. "It sounds like you guys work really well together."

I ignored her innuendo. "I'm just realizing that maybe I don't hate him as much as I thought I did."

She nudged me with her elbow. "I remember those days. I was so young, so naïve, so... in denial."

We laughed together because she really had been in denial about Killian. "This isn't the same thing," I told her. "You and Killian had all that chemistry right off the bat. Plus, you have so much in common it just makes sense for you guys to be in love. Ezra and I are… completely different. We have nothing in common except this work project. I'm just happy I can walk down the aisle with him at your wedding without wanting to stab him."

"I'm happy for that too," she said sincerely. Vann turned around with our shakes and she dropped her voice to a whisper. "If we drink this fast enough, we'll still have time to swing through McDonald's before you have to be at work."

"This is why I love you." Well, giving up her code of chef ethics to sneak in a breakfast burrito was just one of the reasons I loved her. Laughing over chalky protein shakes that lied about tasting like chocolate and peanut butter was another. And knowing I could trust her to keep me grounded when it came to Ezra was also topping the list lately.

She was the biggest cheerleader for my happiness and in her current blissful state of mind, of course she would see potential where there wasn't anything. Now if only I could remember that too. And stop looking forward to my first work phone call of the morning.

Chapter Thirteen

To: mollythemaverick@gmail.com
From: ezra.baptiste@yahoo.com
Date: March 31, 2017 16:46:29 EST
Subject: Tonight
Molly,
I have some thoughts on what you've sent me. I want to go over them
with you. Bring your laptop to Killian and Vera's dinner thing.
   ~Ezra

   I stared at Ezra's command. Then I looked at the clock. Exactly one
minute ago, I had been excited for Friday night and the opportunity to
leave work behind for a solid two days. I didn't want a lot in life, but the
possibility of a free weekend was non-negotiable.

   And now Ezra had managed to ruin the most exciting thing about my
weekend. Vera and Killian had invited a small group of people to their
house for supper tonight. I hadn't known Ezra was one of them though.
After spending more than a month working for him, I was pretty sure the
only thing the man did was work. Which was fine. He was free to spend
his life however he wanted. If he wanted to miss out on friends and family
and weekends and the plethora of wonders Netflix had to offer, that was
up to him.

   Only now he wanted to make me work that much too.

I glared at Ezra's email. "No," I told the computer. Then I tapped out a quick reply.

To: ezra.baptiste@yahoo.com
From mollythemaverick@gmail.com
Date: March 31, 2017 16:54:12 EST
Subject: Re: Tonight
No.
MM.

With only six minutes until ~~freedom~~ five, I started to gather my things and the work I actually did need to glance at over the weekend. It just didn't need to happen tonight. Or without wine. But with two major projects in hand, there just weren't enough hours during the work week to get it all done.

Ezra replied back before I shut down my laptop. Although, to be fair, I had left it open just in case he got right back to me.

What do you mean no?
~Ezra

I found myself smiling at the short email. I pictured him groomed, tailored and completely baffled.

I mean NO, Ezra. Killian and Vera are slaving away to make us one of the most perfect meals we'll ever eat. We're not going to ruin it by working all night. Plus, don't you want to relax a little? This is one of those rare moments you could have some fun. You're currently at risk of becoming a curmudgeon.
MM.

This time I didn't wait for Ezra to answer me. I threw my laptop in my messenger bag and all but ran from the building. I had gotten really good at slinking around the office unseen, blending into walls and hiding behind corners. Also, I was getting better at finding excuses not to meet Junior in his office whenever he had a good idea about the Black Soul account.

Henry was running out of patience for my ducking and dodging, but it turned out that Ezra was good for something. Especially with so much of Mother Tucker's support behind Ezra's account. I often used EFB Enterprise's project as an excuse to get out of menial Black Soul tasks.

To be fair, there were some setbacks with this plan. Like it was doing the opposite for my career that I wanted it too. I was supposed to be schmoozing Junior with my sweet social media skills, convincing him I needed more lead designer projects and building the reputation that would sustain the career I wanted.

Unfortunately, he was more interested in staring at my chest and accidentally bumping into me. He could care less about my portfolio or what I could offer the company he was set to inherit. I'd gone from highly optimistic that Black Soul was the project that would set me up for lifelong success to the dismal realization that I was just eye candy for Henry to ogle while he was forced to work.

I was less disappointed with that realization than I expected to be. Not that I loved being mentally undressed all day long by one of the skeeziest people I had ever met, but maybe the expectations I'd put on myself to climb this company ladder and make a name for myself had been somewhat contrived. Maybe. Possibly... Consider me still undecided.

The weather had shifted now that we'd made it to the end of March. I could smell spring in the air, feel it in the fragrant breeze, although there was still a chill, and the temperature always dropped when it started to get dark. But the days were gradually getting longer. It felt so good to leave work at five o'clock and walk out into early twilight instead of black night. The sun was warming and brightening and the trees had started blooming.

My phone buzzed in my purse. I reached for it, struggling to pull it free while also carrying an empty coffee thermos and my office parking pass.

To: mollythemaverick@gmail.com
From: ezra.baptiste@yahoo.com
Date: March 31, 2017 17:11:38 EST
Subject: Re: Re: Tonight
We'll ride together. We can talk website on the way. I'll pick you up at 6:45.
Ezra
P.S. Curmudgeon? I thought you had more moxie than that, Molly the Maverick.

Something fluttered low in my belly, making me decidedly hot and also cold and also queasy. I slid onto the driver's seat of my two-year-old Volkswagen Jetta that I had named Joan—Joan Jetta—and allowed myself one, brief, necessary smile. Depositing my things on the passenger's seat,

131

I tapped the screen of my phone with nails that needed a manicure badly and decided my next move. I had moxie. I had moxie in spades.

To: ezra.baptiste@yahoo.com
From: mollythemaverick@gmail.com
Date: March 31, 2017 17:18:06 EST
Subject: Re: Re: Tonight
I'm a professional, Mr. Baptiste. It's not my style to insult clients. Or accept rides from them to dinner parties.
  MM.

There. That settled it. That would put an end to this email string and his ridiculous notion of working tonight.

I pulled out of the parking garage and headed home slowly, smashed between the rest of downtown traffic anxious to get to their Friday night plans. My phone buzzed in my cup holder, but I waited three entire stoplights before I let myself check it.

To: mollythemaverick@gmail.com
From: ezra.baptiste@yahoo.com
Date: March 31, 2017 17:29:27 EST
Subject: Re: Re: Tonight
Excellent. Since you, the consummate professional, don't want to insult me, the curmudgeon client, I'm happy to hear you'll accept my offer to drive you this evening during our mobile meeting. I'll pick you up at 6:45, Miss Maverick. Bring your notes.
  Ezra
  P.S. This is fun. Does that count?

I blinked at my phone trying to distinguish between the bubbly feeling in my belly and the irritated tension settling on the back of my neck. Of all the high-handed, bossy bosses, Ezra Baptiste was the worst.

The. Worst.

Which was why I ignored the email totally. And why I practically ran inside my apartment building and then smashed my floor button convinced that I could make the elevator move faster. It was why I threw all my things on the kitchen counter in a messy pile and stripped on the way to the bathroom so I could take the world's fastest shower. It was also the reason I picked out a subtly slutty outfit—my most flattering skinny jeans that made my butt look banging, my favorite and only pair of Jimmy Choo heels, and a cream, long-sleeved, wrap blouse that tied at the nape of my neck and was mostly backless. I would have to get creative with the bra situation but it was worth it.

I had just finished applying my last layer of lip gloss when my phone buzzed. A text this time. From a number I didn't have programmed into my phone yet, although we'd shared texts for work for the last two weeks so I had it memorized.

If you buzz me in, I'll be a gentleman and come get you.

The clock read 6:39. He was early. And ~~sexy as hell~~ chivalrous. And confusing because I knew he was up to something, but I didn't know what.

I stared at the phone for another minute, deciding what to do with him. There was a lot I had *thought* about doing with him. Quitting the EFB Enterprises account just to teach him a lesson, or driving myself tonight just to spite him, or throwing myself at him and sucking his face like the sex-starved hermit I was were just a few ideas I'd tossed around.

In the end, I chickened out completely and didn't even text him back. I grabbed my purse, locked up my apartment and managed to get downstairs all on my own.

He was standing next to the lobby door when I stepped off the elevator. There was a narrow hallway that led to glass doors so I could see his profile perfectly as he stared at the buzzer waiting for me to let him inside.

I bit my cheek to keep from smiling, blushing, or reacting in any way. He'd dressed subtly sexy too. But I doubted he'd done it on purpose. His jeans were casual and strange after seeing him so often in suits and tailored pants. He wore a heather gray sweater that clung to firm, corded muscles. And he'd styled his hair in a more casual way than usual. Or maybe he hadn't styled it at all and that was the problem. The stupid, delicious, irresistible problem.

The ends still looked damp from a shower and it was disheveled in a way that made me want to run my fingers through it.

My movement must have caught his attention because he turned to face me fully and my heart kicked once, twice... three times. A patient smile broke free, and his eyes squinted with disapproval.

"I'm an independent woman," I told him before he could say anything. "Which means I know how to take an elevator all the way to the ground floor without help."

"Yet, you still can't remember to wear a coat," he said pointedly.

I looked up at him, annoyed with how much taller he was than me. It made me feel too small, too delicate. Too vulnerable. "You're not wearing one either."

133

His head dipped and he hummed his agreement. "You're a bad influence."

My mouth dried out and for one senseless second, I imagined leaning forward, closing the distance between us and kissing him.

That would be crazy, right? He was bossy. And irritating. And my client now. Maybe the Black Soul project hadn't panned out like I'd wanted it to, but EFB Enterprises could. And with a client like Ezra Baptiste in my portfolio, I could avoid working with Henry Tucker ever again and grab creative director spots instead.

Clearly, I was losing sight of what was important. My mom's warnings clanged through my head. *Don't mess this up*, I scolded myself. *Focus.*

I patted my purse and took a step back. "I have my notes," I told him. "So if you want to go over them in the car, I guess we can."

He straightened, pulling back like he'd been trapped in the same spell surrounding us as me. Even though I knew that wasn't right. Ezra Baptiste didn't kiss girls like me. As in normal, common, boring girls. Ezra Baptiste, CEO of EFB Enterprises dated exotic women named Lilou, Bianca, and Sarita. They were as wild and passionate and dysfunctional as you could imagine. And when they left him, he named high-end restaurants after them that garnered Michelin stars and boasted James Beard winners for executive chefs.

He was a wealthy, successful CEO with wine cellars worth more than my entire apartment and everything in it.

I was a twenty-something graphics designer considering buying a cat or two for companionship.

This man was not thinking about kissing me. I probably had something in my teeth.

I ran my tongue over them just to be safe and started toward his car in case he decided to say something about it and accidentally murder me with embarrassment.

"Thank you for indulging me," he said to my back. "I've liked all of your mockups so far. I think the sooner the changes to the website go live the better."

"Because your restaurants are struggling?" I asked only half kidding.

He stepped in front of me and opened the door to his car that he'd parked illegally in front of the building. "Not struggling, but they could always make more money. You should never turn down an opportunity for more money, Molly."

He was teasing me, but I wondered if he really believed what he said. "It's hard to make *more* money when you're booked solid months out. I think you've hit the limit on your money-making capacity."

134

I slid onto the passenger's seat and he shut the door without answering. While he walked around the car, I flipped the visor down and checked out my teeth quickly. Nothing there. Whew.

When he was seated next to me, he paused with his hand hovering over the push button ignition. "Lilou is booked out thanks to Killian. Well, Wyatt now. But Killian was the one that originally built the reputation. Sarita does all right, although she has room to grow. But she's also my newest venture. Bianca could drown us all."

"Did Vera say you have a bad chef?"

"Had a bad chef," Ezra clarified while he pulled out on the main roads. "And he wasn't bad in that he couldn't cook. He was bad in that he terrorized his staff and the diners. He was a hazard that I gave too much leniency for much too long. Now Bianca is without a leader and none of the current staff are brave enough to step up. It has to be an outside hire, but I can't find anyone with the right caliber that is also willing to resuscitate a damaged reputation."

"You can't find a chef that wants to take over Bianca? I find that hard to believe."

"I offered her to Vera. Did you know that? She turned me down. Every chef I've taken her to has turned me down. Excluding Vera, most of the chefs I've met would rather walk into a sure thing than gamble a flailing liability. They don't want to tarnish their reputations and I'm not willing to bet on someone straight out of school. I need experience and wisdom. I need someone with grit." He turned his head, meeting my gaze for a brief, sincere second before he turned back to the road. "It's much harder to find someone like that than you'd think."

I didn't know what to say or how to respond. So I blurted the first thing that popped into my head. "I can't believe Vera turned you down. She's wanted something like Bianca forever."

"Yeah, well that was before she met Killian. Her dream changed. I don't fault her for it. Actually, I respect the hell out of her. Any woman that can tame Killian deserves sainthood or something. At the very least, her own restaurant."

"She tames him and he pushes her to get outside of her box and face her fears. They're so perfect for each other it's kind of nauseating."

His mouth kicked up on one side. "I didn't peg you for a cynic, Molly."

"Well, a growing number of bad blind dates will do that to you. True love is for the very few and the very, very lucky."

He glanced at me out of the side of his eye. I thought he was going to call me on my true love dig, but instead he asked, "Why do you keep agreeing to blind dates if so many of them have been bad?"

135

Good question. Why did I keep saying yes? "Hope, I guess. Maybe I'm a cynic, but not by choice. I'm holding out for that one blind date that isn't so bad. Or a guy that's also a man." I felt like slapping my hand over my mouth. I couldn't believe I just said that! Or that I kept talking, apparently unable to shut up before I made a fool of myself. "I'm just tired of boys that don't know what they're looking for in a woman or in life. And I'm really tired of late night dick pics after just a couple dates. For real, it's like your entire species doesn't understand that not everyone is as obsessed with your penis as you are."

"Hey, now! Not all of us enjoy taking genital selfies." Ezra looked truly offended.

"Apologies then. Maybe there are a few of you out there with some self-restraint."

He nodded thoughtfully. "So Molly Maverick's dating criteria include men of a certain age with steady jobs and no dick pics?"

Smiling at his profile, I wondered what he thought of me and my broken filter. "Is it really asking so much?"

He tapped the steering wheel while his car vroomed through traffic, taking on the road with firm decisiveness and lightning quick speed—the same way I imagined Ezra did everything in life. His shrug was the same way, a simple lift and drop of his broad shoulders.

The car slowed to a stop at a red light. He turned his head again, the glow of the streetlights casting his face in gold and red, backdropped by the neon lights of buildings and the glitter of the pavement. "I agree with you. Molly the Maverick, you deserve a man."

Having expected him to elaborate more on what kind of man I deserved, a surprised laugh escaped me. "Just any old man?"

He shot me an impatient glare. "A man, Molly. Not a boy. Not a pervert. Not a blind date that doesn't know the difference between the incredibly smart, uncommonly beautiful woman sitting in front of him and a casual hookup."

His words soothed some mysterious ache inside me. They were like balm on a wound I didn't know I had.

This was it. The crux of it. What I'd been so worried about. The source of my frustrating jealousy for Vera.

I *wanted* a man. Not in like the heterosexual obvious way. But like Ezra had said. *I wanted a man.* Not a boy pretending to be a man. Not an overly sexualized, horny douchebag that only wanted one-night stands. Not a guy afraid to call me on the phone, or ask for my number, or pick up the dinner tab because it wasn't PC anymore.

I wanted a man that still believed in chivalry. I wanted a strong, capable counterpart that would protect me, shelter me, and always, always do what was best for me.

Maybe that made me old-fashioned or outdated or whatever, but it was the truth. I was tired of playing games that got me nowhere. I was exhausted with dating apps and possibilities that fizzled to nothing. I was worn out with meeting Mr. Wrong, after Mr. Wrong, after Mr. Wrong.

I saw what Vera had now. I'd witnessed how special it could be. Killian cherished her. He thought about her needs first and bent over backward to make her happy. Of course they still fought and they were learning to live together, which was not an easy transition according to her. But he respected her and loved her and made her feel loved.

That was what I wanted. It wasn't that I was jealous that Vera had Killian. I was jealous of what Vera and Killian had because I so badly wanted it for myself.

Before them, I hadn't held a whole lot of hope for relationships. My parents hated each other. Vera's dad had spent his entire life in a kind of grieving misery over his dead wife. I had never had a stellar example of real love until Vera and Killian. Seeing the real deal had awoken some kind of love-hungry beast inside me.

I could no longer be satisfied with casual dating or meaningless hookups. I could no longer wait out my twenties or my thirties or the rest of my single life because it didn't matter.

It did matter.

I mattered.

And I deserved a relationship with someone that believed that too.

But I couldn't tell Ezra any of that. So I said, "You barely know me."

Turning down a quiet, tree-lined street, he pulled into Killian's driveway and idled for a minute before he said, "Killian's been my friend since we were kids. I've known him longer than I've known my sister. Ask him if he's ever ridden in my car." He paused and then added, "I might not know you yet, but I want to. I want to know all of you."

Then he got out of the car, walked around to my side and opened the door for me.

Skeptical meet chivalrous.

There wasn't a whole lot left for me to do except follow him. And internally analyze what that meant for the rest of ~~my entire life~~ the night.

Chapter Fourteen

Vera met us at the door, swinging it open before we could knock. "You guys made it! And at the same time. I'm impressed, Molly. You're on time for once in your life!" She laughed at her own joke. "But where did you park?"

Ezra squeezed by her and threw out a casual, "We rode together."

Vera's eyes bugged. "You did what?"

"It's true," I told her in a softer voice. "He picked me up so we could work on his website on the way."

"Wh-what?"

I pulled her onto the porch, as far away from Ezra as I could without making a scene. "He wanted to work on stuff tonight at your house, but I told him I wouldn't do that. So he said he'd pick me up and we could work on the way here."

Her nose wrinkled. "Is that what you did?"

My cheeks flamed. "Er, no. We didn't actually get around to it."

"What does that mean?" she whisper-shouted.

Having no idea what kind of perverted thoughts were running rampant in her head, I quickly assured her. "We just talked. That's all. It was kind of... nice."

"You just talked?" she asked and I nodded. "I would have been less surprised if you told me you gave him a blow job on the way over."

I slapped her arm. "Oh my god!"

She made a "duh" face. "Molly, you rode in a car with Ezra Baptiste and talked to him the entire time! I mean, are you serious?"

"It's not that big of a deal. Stop making it weird."

"I'm not making it weird. It *is* weird. It just is. I mean, what did you talk about if you didn't talk about graphic design stuff? I didn't even know Ezra was capable of having a conversation that revolved around anything besides work."

"Let's go inside, nosey. I think I smell something burning."

Vera perked up, jumping into action. "My Brussels sprouts!"

I followed her inside and shut the door behind me. Vera raced toward the kitchen while I moved at a much slower pace. Killian had owned the bungalow he shared with Vera before they met, but since she had lived with her dad until recently, it had made sense that she move in with him.

The house was still mostly all Killian, but Vera was slowly making her mark. Framed pictures of the two of them were scattered on bookcases and end tables. Vera had ordered decorative pillows for Killian's leather couch and chairs. Wedding odds and ends were strewn about, boxes of invitations that hadn't been sent out yet and swatches of colors piled sporadically. This wasn't my first time hanging out here, but every time I came over it felt more and more familiar, more and more like Vera.

Everybody had gathered in the kitchen. While Killian and Vera moved around, testing sauces and braising things or doing whatever it was that they did, Ezra had joined Vann by a cheese platter. The two men stood with beers in their hand picking at lavosh crackers and salami.

After Vera verbally assaulted me outside, I felt awkward and out of place. These were my people, well, except for Ezra. I should feel totally at home here. Vann was basically my brother. And over the past few months, I'd gotten to know Killian and fallen in platonic love with him. And of course Vera, who was my soul sister, my kindred spirit, my ride or die best bitch.

But now the atmosphere was tense, strained with uncertainty. It would be perfectly normal for me to become friends with Ezra. It would be weird if we weren't friends. But I didn't know how to do that.

I want to know all of you.

Was that what friends said to each other? I shivered. No, no it was not.

I glanced over at him and found him already looking at me. The corner of his mouth lifted in a secretive smile and my heart jumped into my throat and stayed there. His gaze warmed and softened and did all kinds of magical things that weren't humanly possible in thirty seconds.

"So, Molly, what's the Alfa like?" Killian asked.

It's at this point I would like to amend my earlier statement in which I claimed Killian and I had gotten close. Okay, we had in a way. But he was still one of the hottest chefs in the country, and therefore, super intimidating. Not just because of his success, but also because he was scary as shit when he wanted to be.

"The what?" I asked because I had no idea what he was talking about.

"The car," he clarified with a mean look at Ezra. "The one not even his sister is allowed to ride in."

"Oh, stop," Ezra ordered. "It's not that she's *not allowed* to ride in it. It's just that I don't trust her not to spill something all over it. She's messy."

Killian tugged on his long beard. "Okay, but I'm not messy."

Ezra reached for another cracker. "You also don't want a ride. You want to drive it. And that's not happening."

Killian snorted. "I'd settle for a ride. You've never even offered."

I shared a look with Vera and swallowed a laugh. "Killian, are you jealous?"

He turned and focused his glare at me. "Do you know how much shit I put up with from this guy? I don't even work for him anymore and I still have to deal with his bullshit. And then he buys a sweet ass car and won't even let me sit in it. Explain to me how that's fair, Molly."

"It's not fair, Killian. I definitely think he owes you a test drive." I plopped my chin in one hand and reached for a grape from the cheeseboard with the other. "At the very least you should be allowed to take it on a road trip. I mean, if it were my car, I would let you."

Ezra glared at me. "That's enough out of you." I smiled innocently and grabbed another grape.

"What kind of car is it?" Vann asked, amused with the entire conversation.

When we all looked at Ezra, his gaze moved to the ceiling before he admitted, "Alfa Romeo. The Coupe."

Vann's eyes widened. "The 4C?"

"Since when do you know anything about cars?" Vera asked her brother. "I thought they were the arch nemesis of Mother Nature? The slow poison humanity is addicted to?"

Vann barked out a laugh. "I've never said that."

"It's the mantra of your granola loving brethren," Vera challenged.

Vann waved her off. "That's not just any car, Vere. That's a sweet ass car."

I half expected the guys to start high-fiving each other. They didn't. But you could tell they wanted to.

141

"It *is* pretty cool. The seats are super comfortable." I confirmed, which only made Killian curse creatively.

"I'll give you a ride right now," Ezra told Killian. "Let's go."

Killian looked around the kitchen, his shoulders sinking with defeat. "But dinner's ready."

"Really?" Ezra sympathized, not sounding disappointed at all. "Oh, well."

"Selfish bastard," Killian grumbled.

"Whiny baby," Ezra countered.

"Okay, everybody, go sit down," Vera said in an extra chipper voice. "We'll bring it out to you."

"What can I carry?" I asked as I moved to standing again.

Vera handed me a basket of rolls and an uncorked bottle of wine. "We're probably going to need more of that."

I contemplated drinking straight from it. "Yes, we are."

She turned back to the stove and I headed for the dining room. Ezra and Vann had already taken their seats, Vann at the head of the table and Ezra on one side. I took my time setting the rolls in the middle of the table and filling up wine glasses and passing them out.

It shouldn't be this troublesome to pick a chair, but I couldn't decide where to go. Finally, Killian and Vera came in carrying the most amazing smelling dishes with them. I grabbed the other seat at the head of the table. Killian could fight me for it.

"We're eating family style tonight," Killian smiled, steam wafting in front of his face. "This is the best rib roast you will ever eat. You can all thank me later."

Vera set her dishes down and added, "To accompany, we have Brussels sprouts braised with bacon and cranberries with some shredded Pecorino to finish. And then we've got a lobster mac and cheese that honestly is probably better than Killian's prime rib. But don't tell him that. He gets sulky when I outcook him." She shot him a saucy smile. He just shook his head at her.

"Don't get any ideas, Ezra," Killian warned his friend. "If this pops up on Lilou's menu next week, I'll find out."

"Oh, you're one to talk!" Vera laughed.

"Hey, when I did it, it was flirting," Killian defended himself.

Vera turned to me. "I had not realized until just now that he was flirting with me when he stole my recipes and served them at Lilou. This is breaking news."

I snorted. "Only to you, my friend. Pretty sure the rest of us knew exactly what was going on."

142

Vann and Ezra agreed with me causing Vera to protest loudly, officially launching us into more comfortable territory. Killian continued to give Ezra a hard time about the car while Vera and I discussed wedding details. Vann jumped back and forth between conversations never really landing, although he didn't seem to mind.

By the second glass of wine, I'd started regretting my decision to wear skinny jeans. I should have picked an outfit with more room. Like sweatpants. Or a muumuu.

"Don't get too full!" Vera warned. "There's still dessert."

The rest of us groaned. Having dinner at Killian and Vera's was basically like eating Thanksgiving supper, only the dishes were the kind that shaped modern American cuisine and there was no watery Jell-O salad.

"Molly, I haven't had a chance to thank you for the painting," Killian said, nodding toward a canvas I'd painted at Vera's request. It was a smaller version of the Foodie logo I'd hand-painted on her Airstream turned food truck. Since Foodie had relaunched her culinary career and led her to Killian, she'd wanted something for their house. I'd painted Foodie the same way I'd done on the side of her truck, but added the top half of a silver Airstream in the right corner and Lilou's simple silhouette in the top left corner. "It looks awesome. You did a really great job."

I pushed a leftover Brussels sprout around my plate. "Oh, thanks. It wasn't a big deal."

"Vera and I were talking and we'd love for you to create some originals for the restaurant."

Vera grinned at me, but all I could do was shake my head at her. She was always pushing me to paint more, make it public, sell pieces. I knew it was hard for her to understand why I didn't want to. She was all about following your dreams and going hard after the things you loved most in life.

But that was because she had turned her dream into a career.

There wasn't a stable future in painting. Painting was way harder to make lucrative than cooking. Plus, Vera was an exceptional chef. She wasn't just good at what she did, she was the best. And now with Killian by her side, they were totally unstoppable.

It wasn't the same for me. I wasn't interested in turning the thing I loved most into a job. It was my escape from reality. It was my therapy and sanity and hope all wrapped up in one, selfish activity. I didn't want to give that away to everyone. I didn't want to cheapen what I loved so very much by putting a price tag on it.

"What are you thinking?" I asked Killian just to be polite. I would talk to Vera about her overstepping later. Much later. When we weren't surrounded by three super successful men that would have no idea how to relate to my non-ambitions.

"Maybe six originals? Four? You can look at the space and decide for yourself what we need." Killian suggested. "They can be all different sizes. We'd like a longer one above the bar and a really big one along the back wall."

Immediately, ideas started popping into my head. It wasn't that I had tried to feel inspired or intended to conceptualize a series. It just happened. Creativity was like that. She wasn't careful or well-timed or convenient. She was a selfish hag that withheld her muse when you had time and made you drunk with inspiration the second you couldn't do anything about it. "Portraits? Abstracts? Do you have a feeling or color scheme in mind?"

"Er, abstracts with meaning?" Killian answered. "We don't want straight portraits, but we also want something that captures what we're all about."

"You mean food?" I asked with a straight face.

Killian looked at Vera, reaching over to grab her hand. "And love. And passion for both of those things. We just want like this really cool, urban feel. More gallery than hotel art if you know what I mean."

"Killian, she's not going to paint hotel art," Vera groaned. "That's so rude."

Killian's attention snapped back to me. "I'm sorry, I didn't mean for it to—"

I waved him off. "You didn't. I get what you meant."

"So, what do you think?" he asked, his eyebrows raised expectantly.

I glanced at Vera again, hating that she'd put me in this spot and hating even more that Killian had brought it up in front of so many people. Fine, it wasn't exactly a secret that I liked to paint. But I wasn't worthy of an offer like this.

If they wanted original pieces, they should hire a professional. I didn't have the chops for this kind of job.

But instead of telling them that, I said, "I'll think about it."

Killian settled back in his chair, more relaxed. "When you decide, we can give you a better idea of what we're looking for."

"What's the timeline?" I asked, abruptly nervous over paintings that hadn't even been fully decided on yet.

"By the wedding this fall," Vera answered. "We're going to have it at the restaurant before the grand opening. So we'd like everything setup by then."

"I can't believe you're considering this," Vann huffed. "I asked you for two pieces for my shop and you flat-out refused."

I shook my head at him, embarrassed that he was bringing that up now. "I haven't agreed yet. I'm just thinking about it."

"We'll pay you!" Vera added.

I raised one eyebrow, focusing on Vann just so I wouldn't break out into a sweat. "Are you going to pay me?"

"Obviously. At least twenty bucks a pop."

Laughing, I shook my head at him. "Wow, Vann, I had no idea I was worth so much."

He winked at me. "Plus, I'll give your bike a free tune up whenever you need it."

"I don't own a bike."

He shrugged one shoulder. "Well, hey, I can help you out there too."

I contemplated reminding him how our cycling class had ruined me for bike riding from here until forever and ever amen. But I didn't want to totally crush him.

So instead, I shifted the conversation. "You know I have a real job too, right? And some of my clients are really high maintenance." I nodded toward Ezra who was staring at my Foodie painting that was the focal point of the room. It hung centered in the middle of the wall above a trendy buffet table made with different shades of wood and looked like it weighed approximately three thousand pounds.

"You're a brave man, Ezra," Vann laughed. "Hasn't she driven you crazy yet?"

Ezra seemed to blink back into focus, but he never lost the thoughtful look in his eyes. "Absolutely," he answered Vann. "More than once."

"Hey!"

"But I have to admit," Ezra went on, "she knows what she's talking about. She's only accused me of being elderly once a day since we started and dismisses all of my brilliant ideas, but I think I'm starting to trust that she's not going to tank my entire company and everything I've worked so hard for." He paused thoughtfully, then said, "At least as far as her design goes. She might still try just for fun."

My cheeks heated while the room burst into laughter at my expense. It wasn't that I was offended, but I hated all the attention so focused on me. I had been trying to deflect it onto Ezra, but he somehow managed to bounce it right back at me. "Careful," I warned him. "Hell hath no fury like a woman insulted."

He pushed his plate to the side and leaned his forearms on the table. "I believe that from you."

Only I wasn't insulted. Not even a little bit. Somehow Ezra's backward declarations felt very much like compliments. It was unnerving to remember his success, all his accomplishments. And he was trusting me with them—well, at least as much as his control freak self would let him. He had asked specifically for me. He had gone out of his way to get me.

"Who's ready for dessert?" Vera asked, breaking the staring spell that had come over Ezra and me again.

I turned away from him and tried to protest, but Vera had made coconut sorbet and dark chocolate brownies from scratch, so to be fair, I didn't try very hard. We spent the rest of the night finishing off another two bottles of wine and laughing until my stomach hurt.

We talked about Killian and Vera's plan for their restaurant and the progress they were making. They were living off savings and a business loan, so things were tight for them. And on top of that, they were also planning a wedding. They were very stressed, but also very much in love. They laughed at a lot of their problems, having to eat cheaper and buy less wine. It was so interesting for me to watch a couple struggle financially without ripping each other's heads off.

Vann filled us in on his cycle shop and his dysfunctional dating life. At Vera's suggestion, he'd started trying to date women that weren't the nice, good girls he usually went for. This had led to a series of high-maintenance crazies that he was positive were now stalking him.

Ezra shared his struggle to find a chef for Bianca. He and Killian spoke in depth about who he could reach out to and who would be right for the job. They also talked about Ezra's sister Dillon and how she was doing in her final year of culinary school. Apparently, she'd been flakey for the first part of her twenties thanks to a large inheritance from their dad. But now she was serious about growing up and had decided that she wanted to be a chef.

"She knows I'll give her a job," Ezra sighed. "That's why she's doing it."

"Seems like a lot of work just to get a steady paycheck," Vann laughed.

Ezra's eyebrows scrunched over his nose. "Good point. She knows I won't fire her then."

"That's probably more accurate," Killian agreed. "How's she doing, though? Is there any talent there?"

Ezra shrugged. "She really isn't bad. She needs some experience, but she's well-traveled so her palate is mature. And she's brave."

146

"Put her in Wyatt's kitchen," Killian suggested. "He'll whip her into shape."

"You're sure you don't want to take her on?" Ezra asked. "She knows you. I'm sure she'd be more comfortable in your kitchen."

"She wouldn't make it two days with me," Killian admitted candidly. "I don't have patience for green. I'd traumatize her."

"He would," Vera agreed. "He regularly traumatizes *me* in the kitchen."

"And in the bedroom," I added.

We'd had enough wine that my joke was hilarious. Which probably meant it was time to go. I didn't want to spend two Saturdays in a row hungover.

Ezra seemed to read my mind. "Are you about ready?"

I pushed away from the table and stood up, the three glasses of wine rushing to my head. "Yep. But are you okay to drive?"

"I've stuck to water," he explained.

"Thanks for a fabulous dinner," I told Vera and Killian. "Next time I'll cook for all of you, then you can really be impressed with yourselves."

Vera cackled at my offer. "No thanks, Molls! I'd rather not die of food poisoning just months before my wedding. But any time you want a decent meal, you're welcome here."

My heart warmed knowing she was serious. There had been so many secrets between Vera and me while she was with Derrek, that I had often wondered if things would ever be totally honest between us again. I knew she was convinced she was a good liar, but those closest to her saw the truth. She had lived in fear for a long time. She had been oppressed and hurt and broken.

And she'd kept it all bottled up inside her, afraid that we would be carried away in the riptide of her crisis.

When she'd finally left Derrek, she'd run away to Europe. She'd claimed it was for cooking, to hone her skills and expand her palate. But I had been her best friend since childhood. I saw right through her. She'd been terrified to face us, to tell us the truth. She'd been afraid of the consequences for a failed relationship that was not her fault.

Our relationship had taken some serious work to rebuild, even after she finally came back to Durham. She hadn't been ready to trust for a long time, not even me or Vann or her dad. She'd still carried the weight of Derrek's abuse on her shoulders like a hiking backpack filled with boulders.

Slowly, bit by bit, we'd pieced our relationship back together. And slowly, bit by bit, she'd picked up the shattered remnants of her career, life and spirit. But nothing really clicked until Killian came into the picture.

147

Things were finally back to normal. There was no more reason to worry about her or wonder if she'd ever truly heal. She was damaged by Derrek, but not destroyed. She had been hurt by tragedy, but not defeated.

She was an inspiration to me. I saw what she'd been through and what she'd overcome and secretly longed to have those same victories. Our struggles were widely different, but she inspired hope that things wouldn't always be this hard, this confusing, that maybe my backpack wouldn't always be this heavy. She had this gorgeous happy ending that I couldn't help but want to mimic.

She was the fairy tale that I aspired to be.

Killian and Vera walked us to the door while Vann ordered an Uber for himself from his phone. Vera pulled me into a hug on her porch, the chilly night air nibbling on our skin. It went straight up my spine thanks to my backless shirt and I wiggled into her, clinging for warmth.

"Make sure you *work* the whole time you're in the car with him. Then call me in the morning and tell me all about how *productive* you two were."

I chose to ignore her innuendos. "I will call you tomorrow," I told her. "And you'll be so impressed with everything. It's going to blow your mind!"

She giggled and said, "Who's mind is it going to blow?"

I stepped away from her. "Oh, my gosh, you are a pervert."

"See how the tables have turned?" She swirled her finger back and forth between us. "Not so fun on the other side now, is it?"

"No," I agreed. "I much prefer being the depraved sidekick."

"What are you two talking about?" Killian asked.

"Nothing!" we said together.

Ezra jerked his head toward his super exclusive car that nobody was allowed to ride in or touch or look at. "Ready, Molly?"

"Yep." Vera and I said our final goodbyes, I thanked our hosts again for a lovely dinner and got into Ezra's car for the third time more conscious than ever about not messing something up.

When we were back on the road and headed toward my apartment building, I decided I needed to prove Vera wrong. So, ignoring the warm tipsy feeling from the wine, I reached into my purse and pulled out my work notebook and phone.

The night was chilly, but Ezra's car was the opposite. The heated seat warmed my back, making me cozy and sleepy. The city zipped by us in late-night silence. Mumford and Sons drifted softly from the stereo in the background.

It's in the eyes. I can tell, you will always be danger.

I shivered at the truth in those lyrics. Ezra noticed and reached over to adjust the heat settings.

Feeling raw and exposed for no reason at all, I hugged my notebook to my chest and asked, "What did you want to go over?"

He looked at me briefly, his dark eyes giving nothing away. "I want to hire you."

Cocking my head to the side, I resisted the urge to smile. "You already hired me."

"To paint," he clarified. "I have an idea for Bianca that I—"

"No." He couldn't be serious. "Absolutely not."

"You haven't even heard my proposal."

My expression flattened. "This feels familiar. Are you getting déjà vu?"

"Molly, I'm serious." His voice roughened, deepened, and became that commanding tone I was oh, so familiar with.

"But you can't be. You haven't seen any of my work. You don't even know if I'm any good or not."

"The portrait at Killian's was incredible. You perfectly captured them. It wasn't just in the colors and images, but the feel of the painting. If it had been anywhere else, it would have captured my attention without trying."

"Uh, thank you." I swallowed around the fist-sized lump in my throat. "But you're missing the point—"

"And if Killian is willing to hire you and Vann wants to hire you, I know there is more to your talent than just that one painting."

"Okay, but what I'm saying is that you have no idea if what I do is right for you."

He slowed the car to a stop and turned that too-intense gaze to look at me. "You're wrong. I know exactly what is right for me, Molly." The light turned green but he didn't move. "You. You're right for me."

I licked dry lips and tried to focus on the conversation and not my wildly beating heart.

He turned back to the road. "Five thousand dollars."

"Wh-what?"

"Ten." He countered an argument I hadn't made.

"Are you kidding?"

"Name your price," he demanded. "I'll pay it."

"Ezra, stop," I pleaded breathlessly. "You can't just throw money at me. You've only seen one of my paintings and I don't even know if I can do what you're asking me to do. I'm not a painter. I'm not an artist. I have a hobby, that's it. I've only taken a handful of classes and I'm way underqualified to make anywhere near that kind of money."

He seemed to consider my words. His head tipped to the side thoughtfully, but he was like a dog with a bone. There was no getting this man to back off once he'd decided he wanted something. "There's this wall at Bianca. It's always felt awkward to me, because of how smooth and uninterrupted it is. We've tried to dress it up and decorate it, but nothing has ever fit quite right. I want a mural or whatever you call it. Something emotional. I want every person that leaves my restaurant to remember it."

My lungs stopped working. Like straight up quit on me. I couldn't breathe. "That's a lot to ask of someone who is one step above paint-by-numbers."

He pulled up in front of my apartment building, idling on the curb. He turned again, leaning toward me so that I inhaled him, cologne and the coconut sorbet and something that was achingly him. "Name your price, Molly. Whatever you want is yours."

The wine and perfect evening muddled my thoughts. I couldn't think straight with him this close. I couldn't remember all of my intelligent reasons for telling him no.

"You give me complete control of your EFB account." I heard myself name my price, but I still didn't believe I'd been the one to speak. That was a bold demand. Especially from an overbearing dictator like Ezra. And I wasn't bold. I was meek and mild mannered. I didn't demand things from anybody, especially not super successful business tycoons like him.

"Excuse me?" His lips pressed into a frown.

I patted my tipsy self on the back. There, I'd found the one price he wasn't willing to pay. That would teach him to ask ridiculous things of me late at night. This was a bad habit I needed to break asap.

"You back off the website and social strategy and all of it. I want complete control."

"You can't be serious."

"Oh, I am." Gaining confidence, I laid out my reasoning. "You're impossible to work with, Ezra. I can't make any progress with your fingers in every single aspect. I spend most of my time convincing you to let me do what I know is best, which leaves very little time to actually work on the project. If you want me to paint this mural, then you have to back off the graphic design side and give me complete autonomy."

His jaw ticked. He couldn't do it. "Anything else?"

"And you can't interfere with the painting project either. If you hover over my shoulder the entire time, I'll be too nervous to get anything done. I'm not a professional and I don't want to be treated like one. If you really want me to paint something for you, you have to trust my process. Which is isolated. I work alone. You can't come anywhere near it until I'm finished."

"And how much do you want to get paid?"

Was he seriously considering this? My stomach filled with angry butterflies, flapping poison tipped wings. I hadn't believed he would take me seriously, but now that I was in the middle of negotiations I wasn't sure I could back out. Not if I got Ezra to concede to leave me and his account completely alone.

I waved off the idea of getting paid. "I have no idea," I admitted honestly. "I've never done anything like this before. I'm sure there is a standard rate or whatever, but I'll have to look it up."

He raised one eyebrow. "You'll let me know if it's over ten thousand?"

I rolled my eyes, finding the entire idea ludicrous. "Yes, Ezra, if I plan to charge you more than ten thousand dollars, I'll warn you. Right before I commit myself. Don't be crazy."

His full lips twitched with the smile he held back. "I'm starting to think it's too late, Molly Maverick. There is just something about you that makes my common sense completely disappear."

That shouldn't have felt like a compliment. But it did. It so did. "Thanks for the ride, Ezra. Don't worry about not getting any work done tonight. I'm on it."

This time he did smile and it was perfect. Confident, genuine and so, so stunning. "Will you at least give me updates?"

"You mean before I upload everything to all your sites and totally revolutionize your business and way of life as you know it?"

His smile widened and my heart tried to jump out of my body altogether. "Yeah, before all of that."

"Let's just say, good behavior will go a long way. We could come up with a reward system? A gold star chart?"

"I think all this power is going to your head," he murmured, his voice pitching low and smooth.

I sucked in my bottom lip and suppressed a victorious smile. "That doesn't sound like me at all."

His eyes glittered when he laughed. "From everything I know about you, it sounds exactly like you."

His words hit me in some secret, hidden part. Was that true? Did he somehow see something in me that I didn't know existed?

But to be fair, I acted differently around him than the rest of the people in my life. I was assertive and antagonistic and... outspoken. I didn't hold back my thoughts or my words. I argued with him. I even picked fights with him on purpose.

151

But that was because of him, not me. He pulled that strong personality out of me with his boorish, overbearing behavior.

It was his fault I was like this.

Except I found that I didn't want to give him all of the credit. I didn't mind this side of me. Maybe I was even proud of it. I wanted to keep some of the credit for myself. I wanted to believe that I was capable of this all on my own.

"Thanks for the ride, Ezra. You can email me the details of your mural whenever you get a chance." My hand found the door handle and I forced myself to leave the warmth and strange intimacy of his car.

"I'll walk you inside," he offered.

"No, that's—" But he'd already jumped out of his side and was headed around to mine. I scrambled out of the passenger's side door before he could do something drastic that ruined every other man for me for the rest of my life—like open my door again.

We walked in silence the short distance to the door of my lobby. He'd left his car idling unmanned and I was irrationally nervous that someone was going to run up to it, jump inside, and drive off.

"If someone steals your car because of me, I'm going to have to sell a kidney to pay you back."

The corner of his mouth lifted, amused. "It's just a thing, Molly. Not worth a kidney."

"Don't tell Killian that," I warned. "Pretty sure he thinks it's a bigger deal than most internal organs."

He leaned in, bringing our faces close together, our bodies following suit. My gaze dropped to his lips for just a second. Okay, maybe five seconds. Possibly a good ten seconds.

"We'll keep that just between you and me." His head dipped down and he pressed a slow-burning, heart-stopping, over-too-quick kiss on my lips. "Goodnight, Molly the Maverick."

Then he stepped back and jogged the distance to his car while I was left internally flailing as I fell and fell and fell down an endless well of uncharted territory.

I stepped inside my building and went straight up to my studio. If ever there had been a reason to paint, a gentle kiss by a man like Ezra Baptiste was it.

So, paint I did. Until I couldn't keep my eyes open. Until my fingers were stiff and my back ached. Until, without any of the details or specs, I had the perfect idea for Ezra's mural.

Chapter Fifteen

Sunday did not go anything like I wanted it to. I hadn't realized how much work I had agreed to until I started to plan out all of my different projects for the week.

As promised, Ezra had emailed the details of his mural along with dimensions and pictures of the space. I could see what he meant about the wall being awkward in his otherwise trendy restaurant. The artwork he'd picked nagged at my creative eye, demanding more of something. But that something was hard to put my finger on. Despite the sizes of the various pieces, they looked small in the big space.

He'd included another picture of a design he'd tried in the past that had featured more artwork in an effort to fill the space, but that had only made it look cluttered and overly decorated.

To his credit, a mural would be perfect. It would fill the wall without making it feel chaotic or overused. He wanted something attention grabbing and eye catching without trying too hard to be those things. I had the perfect idea. Well... if I could get it just right.

I spent the majority of the afternoon sketching ideas, still disbelieving that I'd actually agreed to do it. Especially considering the time I would have to spend at Bianca before and after hours.

Ezra wanted the project done as quickly as possible, understanding my limitations both with my real job and his dining hours. We would set up screens until it was finished, but they weren't ideal.

We'd planned a time to meet this week so I could scout out the space in person. But knowing it would take weeks to finish, he wanted me to start next weekend.

When I'd told Vera what Ezra asked of me, she hadn't been fazed at all. "Obviously, he hired you," she'd said. "Why wouldn't he?"

"It's weird though, right?" I'd pressed. "He's stalking my professions."

"You're the best, Molls. He recognizes that. He wants it for his businesses. You should feel flattered."

She was right. And I did feel flattered. But I also felt too hot and breathless with nerves and maybe like I was going to puke at any given moment.

Working for Ezra Baptiste was this strange dichotomy of receiving major opportunities, but also getting gigantic chances to screw everything up in the biggest way possible on the biggest stage possible in front of the biggest audience possible.

I still couldn't believe I'd demanded he butt out of his EFB account. What had I been thinking? Was I really planning on handling that entire account all on my own?

My computer made a sound, alerting me that I had a new email. I jumped at the sound, afraid it was Ezra firing me already. He'd come to his senses.

Only it wasn't Ezra, it was the little Tucker. He wanted to schedule a meeting first thing in the morning. We had things to go over. He needed updates on where I was with the Black Soul account. We were meeting with them face-to-face for the first time this week, and we had to prepare strategically.

Realizing, I wasn't nearly where I should be with that project, I took a minute to panic. Shooting back an email full of false bravado, I agreed to the meeting. Then, I abandoned Ezra's mural and dove into my real job.

Black Soul was the project that would change things for me, I reminded myself. This was the one that would be the foundation of a lifelong career. This was the one that should be getting all of my attention.

I played around with graphics and fonts and the exact measurements for every single detail. It was tedious and precise and I drove myself crazy with over-the-top perfectionism. But the wrong font could mean the difference between a wild success and utter failure. Same with the right placement. Even the slightest degree one way or the other could mean a graphic I had slaved over, poured myself into and placed all my hopes and dreams in could totally bomb.

The key to graphic design wasn't natural talent. It was the patience to be totally, completely, obnoxiously anal with every minute detail. It wasn't just the devil that lived in the details. Designers had real estate there too.

My graphics were as perfect as humanly possible because I didn't leave room for error. I would spend hours fussing over moving elements one degree at a time or finding just the right shade of a specific color.

Painting was the same way. I couldn't just slop something on canvas. I mixed paints until they were the exact shade I'd imagined. I meticulously added details and color and with slow, painstaking care breathed life into what was once flat, white space.

I took nothing and created something.

When my eyes started to cross, I decided it was time for a break. I stood up, stretching my hunched shoulders and worried over the hump I knew I was growing.

This was why I would be single for the rest of my life. Give me another five years and I was going to be a living, breathing cosplay of the Hunchback of Notre Dame. Another Disney reference? You're welcome.

I walked over to my kitchen and grabbed a bottle of water from my fridge. I rummaged around for something to eat, but there wasn't anything except Greek yogurt and carrot sticks.

The rumors were true, I was a terrible cook. It wasn't that I had never been interested in learning how, but the kitchen was my mom's space and she didn't often invite visitors. The few times I had been allowed to help out, she'd been so obsessed with the mess and my mistakes that I'd been too afraid to try. Eventually, I gave up.

In recent years, I'd asked Vera for help, but even she had been daunted by the amount of work it would take to teach me simple tasks. I couldn't bring myself to take interest now. It had been ruined for me.

Plus, I was really good at ordering takeout. Not to brag, but it was one of my top life skills.

Opening my junk drawer, I rifled through the different menus that delivered in a reasonable amount of time, but nothing sounded good. What I really wanted was breakfast because that was what Sunday night needed. I didn't want dishes or anything heavy. I just wanted... cereal.

But the cupboards were bare. Also the milk was expired. I would have to leave the house. Which was a travesty.

Stopping by the bathroom, I threw my wilder-than-usual hair into a messy bun on the very top of my head, not bothering with the specifics of making it look nice. I'd been working all day, so my outfit was straight from the I've-given-up-on-life-completely collection. Paint-stained yoga pants, and an off the shoulder sweatshirt I'd stolen from my dad and cut the collar off. Basically, I looked homeless.

I grabbed my keys and my wallet and headed for the small market a couple of blocks away. The sun sat low in the sky, hidden by the tall buildings rising up on every side of me. I wrinkled my cold nose and hurried along quiet streets that had been abandoned for the evening.

The market was quiet when I stepped inside. I shivered in the fresh warmth and inhaled the delicious smells coming from the deli. My stomach rumbled and I remembered why I was here.

I snagged a basket next to the door and headed for the produce. Clementines were a staple in my kitchen, but mainly because I was irrationally terrified of scurvy. I could admit that I didn't have the best diet, something Vann liked to remind me of constantly. But I'd be damned if I got scurvy because I didn't get enough Vitamin C.

I rounded the corner to the dairy section, wishing I'd grabbed a cart instead of a basket now that I had to tote around milk and oranges. And coffee creamer. Oh, and bagels. Also cream cheese. And some new yogurt I'd never tried before.

Maybe I should go grocery shopping more often...

"Molly?"

Looking up, I came face to face with the prettiest blonde. She was dressed similarly to me because it was Sunday evening after all, only she looked less like she'd just gotten over the ten-day flu and more like she was modeling athleisure. Her hair was pulled over her shoulder in a braid and the yoga pants and long sleeve tee she wore were not stained or ill-fitting.

She was the yin to my very badly dressed yang.

"Hi," I smiled at her, hoping I didn't smell bad too.

"Dillon." She pointed at herself. "I don't know if you remember me or not, but we met at Killian and Vera's engagement party. I'm Ezra's sister."

I nodded along, feeling weird that she was explaining herself to me. I felt like out of the two of us, I was the forgettable one. She made a very strong impression.

"I remember," I assured her. "So did you have a good time?"

Her eyebrows drew down, reminding me of her brother. "Where?"

"Er, at the engagement party?"

"Oh, right! Yes, I did." Her expression relaxed and her smile widened. "I always have a good time at parties. They're like, my thing. If I could do them professionally, I would. Although Ezra's head would probably explode."

156

We laughed together and then I realized this was a really good opportunity to covertly pry into Ezra's life uninvited. Hey if he could stalk me at my jobs, a little secret spying on my end wasn't going to hurt anybody.

"He's super intense about work, isn't he?" I prompted.

"For sure. He's always been like that. Our dad was a workaholic too. I would swear it's genetic except I'm the total opposite."

"You're in culinary school though, right? Killian mentioned it Friday night when we hung out."

She nodded, patting the basket hooked over her forearm. "I'm almost finished actually. I just have this semester left."

"Where are you going?"

"Charlotte. CAI."

"Oh, my friend Vera went there. She loved it."

Dillon grinned. "Vera is basically my hero. I love her."

I smiled back, immediately endeared to anybody that loved the same people I did. "Me too." I set my basket on the ground when it got too heavy to hold and resumed my snooping. "So, are you going to get Bianca after you graduate? I hear Ezra is having trouble finding an executive chef."

She glanced at the ceiling, again reminding me of her exasperated brother. "I wish. But there's no way Ezra would trust me with executive chef. Or even sous chef. Honestly, I'll be lucky if he lets me be a dishwasher in one of the three witches."

"The three witches?"

"His restaurants," she clarified. "It's what I call them because he named them after three of the worst hags that I have ever met."

I felt my eyes bug, but there was little I could do to hide my surprise. "Are you serious?"

"You have no idea. They were horrible women. They only cared about his money."

Swallowing a laugh, I admitted, "I always pictured these great, passionate love stories. I mean, he named famous restaurants after them! And the names are so... exotic."

She rolled her eyes. "Please, Ezra is not that exciting. He works too much to have erotic affairs. Really, they were just money hungry party girls that wouldn't know a good man if he bit them in their lipo'd asses."

Dillon was this perfect mixture of stuck-up socialite blended with sass and genuine charm. I really liked her. "If they were so awful, why did he name restaurants after them?"

She shrugged. "Revenge? To remind him of all the mistakes he's made along the way? I honestly have no idea. He's weird."

"I agree with that. He is weird."

Her smile wobbled. "But you like him, don't you? I mean, you're friends?"

~~Not in the slightest.~~

"Er, maybe? I don't really know what we are, but *friends* doesn't seem to fit us."

Her eyes brightened and she nodded enthusiastically. "You're friends," she decided. "He talks so highly of you. He's always like, Molly this and Molly that and you should see what Molly did to the website. Honestly, I feel like we're already friends because I've heard so much about you." She wiggled her finger back and forth between us.

I laughed nervously, not knowing what to make of any of that. "Can I ask you a question?"

She dropped her heavy basket next to mine. It was full of ingredients I would have no idea what to do with. "Sure."

"He has this weird thing with me wearing a coat. What's that about?"

"What do you mean?"

"Because it's cold out. He always wants me to wear a coat. He's like obsessed with it."

She rolled her eyes, but her expression was warm with sisterly affection. "He's used to taking care of people. It's how he shows love. Trust me, I know how annoying it can be, but it's better to just let him have his way. Besides, he can't help it. His mom was really sick when he was a kid and he had to take care of her until she died. And then he didn't really have anyone, so he learned from a very young age to take care of himself. Then he took care of our dad when he was dying. Although our dad, the selfish bastard, didn't deserve it. And now he takes care of me. I probably don't deserve it either to be honest." She looked down at her shoes and smiled warmly. "And thank God, you know? Could you imagine me on my own? I would be so lost without him."

Something warm and bubbly sprung up in my chest. It felt like melted chocolate and fuzzy slippers and understanding for a man that was always such a mystery. The feeling shocked my entire system, surprising me with its permanency. I tried to reason it away. This was the heavy-handed maniac that had basically demanded I ride with him the other night. No gentle please. No thoughtful consideration. Just bullying me into whatever he decided was right. I shouldn't feel sympathy or compassion or anything hot and fizzy and comfortable. "I guess that explains why he's always so... responsible."

158

"Oh shit!" she gasped. "Is that really the time? I'm so late! I'm sorry, but I have to go."

"No worries!"

She stepped forward, pulling me into a surprising hug. "It was so good to chat with you. We should go to dinner or something sometime. I'll get your number from Ezra."

"Oh, uh, okay." I cleared my throat, feeling awkward in her prolonged hug. "Sounds fun."

Dillon pulled back and gave me her thousand watt smile. "Yay! K, see you soon!"

Then she was gone, taking all her excitable energy with her. I stared after her for a minute, marveling at how different she and Ezra were. She was all in your face with her enthusiasm and big smile. Ezra was dark ambiguity that slipped in and out of social situations, preferring to be unseen. She came in like a hurricane. Ezra was the silent night sky.

Or storm clouds before they released their rain.

But then again, Ezra was different than anyone I knew. Different and alluring, and totally unexpected.

I finished up my shopping, adding cereal, ice cream and Skittles to the basket. Fact: I should know better than to shop on an empty stomach. Second Fact: I said that every time I bought ice cream.

When I left the market the sky had darkened, bringing twilight. I hurried home, my hunger urging me to move faster.

I put my groceries away and turned on the news over dinner, which consisted of two bowls of Golden Grahams and an orange. Yep, that's right. Molly Maverick, twenty-seven-year-old independent woman, graphic designer, closet toddler.

Grabbing my phone, I pulled up Vera's number and texted her. **I just had kid cereal for supper. I give up on life. Maybe I should let you teach me to cook?**

Vere: No way. You're a lost cause.

Me: It could be fun!

Vere: It could be dangerous!

Me: Do you want me to starve? Man cannot live on sugar and carbs alone.

Vere: YOU'VE been living off sugar and carbs for your entire life.

She had a point.

An email notification popped up and I abandoned all hope that Vera was going to rescue me from my life sentence of terrible cooking.

Maybe I could convince myself that I liked burned food. Maybe it could become my thing. Like I would start asking for restaurants to purposefully scorch my steak and char my chicken.

With that disgusting thought in my head, I opened my email to see a new one from Ezra. I'd sent over notes on his website earlier today, although since it was Sunday, I hadn't expected a reply until tomorrow. Even Ezra carved out a little time on Sunday to have a nap. Or maybe not a nap, that didn't really seem like his style, but a few hours away from work.

Immediately, I felt restless. I thought about walking away from my phone completely. I wanted to paint. I wanted to grab a bowl of ice cream. I wanted to go to spin class and drive out my confusing frustration by torturing my butt and legs.

That's how desperate I was.

In the end, I settled for pulling my legs beneath me and braving the email.

To: mollythemaverick@gmail.com
From: ezra.baptiste@yahoo.com
Date: April 2, 2017 19:12:51 EST
Subject: Re: Questions
Molly,
Do you really think we need new photos of all the restaurants? Do you have a photographer in house? Or is that someone I'll need to hire?
I've never considered a newsletter signup before. It's hard to believe that newsletters are the wave of the future. But, if you think it would be beneficial by all means, go for it.
Why do you ask about cooking classes?
We should meet next week about the mural.
~Ezra
P.S. You were right about Friday night. I had fun. We should do it again sometime.

I blinked at the email. What did that mean?

I reread it three more times. *We should do it again sometime.* As in eat supper at Vera's? Have Killian cook for us? Ride a short distance together in his car?

What should we do again sometime, Ezra?!

Setting my phone down, I muted the TV so I could think. When that didn't work, I went after the ice cream, attempting to freeze the frenzied butterflies flapping around inside me.

160

As I considered bowl number two, I decided it was better to be brave and face ~~my problems~~ Ezra than gain two pounds by stress eating.

To: ezra.baptiste@yahoo.com
From: mollythemaverick@gmail.com
Date: April 2, 2017 19:23:40 EST
Subject: Re: Answers
Ezra,
I can recommend a photographer that we often use. The new pictures are up to you though. I won't move forward until you decide, but take your time thinking it over. I know it's just one more expense.
Yes, to the newsletter. You don't have to send one out every week, but by offering the signup, you create a database of clientele that you can reach at any time. Valentine's Day dinners, reminders for Christmas gift cards, upcoming cooking classes, etc.
Which leads me to my next point, have you considered offering high-end classes for a fee? I was just thinking that you have all of these incredible chefs. What if you offered specialized classes that your customers could take as couples? Charge them a couple hundred dollars, teach them a skill and offer a meal. Like a wine-pairing night or pasta-making class. As I was doing research, I saw that CAI offers these classes to the community. I found a few things like this in Durham, but nothing from a restaurant of your caliber. Advertise through your newsletter and social sites and keep it small, intimate. I think it would only further build your reputation around the city and you'd be utilizing all those award-winning chefs you pay so highly.
MM.
P.S. I'm always right.

I jumped up from the couch, abandoning my phone on a cushion. There were loose ends I needed to tie up for my meeting tomorrow morning. I wasn't totally satisfied with my social media package for Black Soul. I had another piece to add, I just hadn't figured out what it was yet.

But I didn't have the mind for work right now. I escaped to my studio, pulling out paints and brushes and palette. I propped up a fresh canvas and perched on my stool.

Squeezing a generous line of white, black and cerulean blue, I started blending colors and shades, looking for the shade that matched the grays that I felt all the way to my bones.

I couldn't get the image of a thunderstorm out of my head. I pictured the comparison I'd made to Ezra earlier. He was the dark sky before the

161

rain fell. The flash of distant lightning. The roll of thunder, low and rumbling. He was big, billowy clouds stretching from one horizon to the other.

The portrait flowed from my vigorous fingers as I brushed paint in flicks and swoops, blending everything together in a kind of ominous harmony. My grays were dark at first, profound and foreboding. Clouds swirled in warning, pregnant with the threat of downpour. I added the blue, softening the yawning charcoals, but deepening at the same time. They weren't less dangerous, just now also beautiful. Treacherous and lovely and worrisome all at once.

I streaked lightning through the heavy clouds. Crooked fingers of thin light breaking through the sky, splitting it in two, then three. My hands moved swiftly around the canvas, adding, blending, detailing more and more and more.

The whole time I worked, I kept making it darker, scarier, more and more menacing. And yet when at last I sat back to examine my work, I wasn't satisfied with it. There was something missing.

This was how I felt about Ezra, how I imagined him. He was everything I didn't understand about men. He was the unattainable, the too successful, the tempting mystery that I would never get to explore. Except he wasn't any of those things now that I knew him better.

"Son of a bitch," I whispered.

I reached for a clean brush and jabbed at the white, quickly mixing it with yellow, and then orange, and a tiny bit of blue. At the top of the canvas, above the black, thunderous clouds, I added light—bright, pure and striking.

The sun stretched over the dark clouds, mostly hidden from those who would stand beneath the storm. But those with hope would believe the light existed behind the rainy curtain. Those that dared to believe that the clouds were only one small part of the vast sky would know how bright the sun shined.

I set my brush down with shaking fingers, finally coming to terms with the fact that maybe, possibly, I didn't quite hate Ezra as much as I wanted to believe.

Not even a little bit.

When I checked my phone before bed, Ezra had sent one final, simple email that said:

Come see me tomorrow night. At Bianca. I'll show you the wall.

Chapter Sixteen

I tried really hard to be on time to the meeting. Really hard. But being punctual just wasn't in the cards Monday morning. The past two hours had been a comedy of errors. I'd had one problem after another. Starting with stupid spin class. My foot had slipped off the pedal at an ungodly, inhuman pace and I'd managed to knee myself in the chin. Which took a bit of talent and unexpected flexibility. But it had resulted in an instant headache.

To cure said headache, I'd stopped for coffee. Except they'd given me the wrong order. I'd asked for the flavor of the day with cream and sugar. They'd given me the flavor of the day without cream and sugar making it completely undrinkable because everybody knew that coffee without creamer was *just the worst*. Basically, I'd declared war with their Twitter account. *Hasta la vista, Daily Grind, @mollythemav is coming for you!*

To rectify the caffeine situation, I'd been forced to stop at a gas station to pick up a new to-go coffee. In step with the rest of the morning, they had only had one working cash register and a new girl behind the counter. I'd stood in line for fifteen minutes sipping cheap, sickly sweet sludge that barely took the edge off.

Now I was exactly seventeen minutes late to the Black Soul strategy meeting and I was only seventy-five percent prepared.

Holy bad Mondays, Batman.

"You better have a damn good excuse for making us wait," Henry growled when I attempted to slip quietly into his office.

"The printer jammed," I mumbled lamely, quickly passing out the hard copies of my graphics. I avoided his glare and plopped down next to Ethan. "Sorry, I didn't realize how late it had gotten."

Ethan handed me a stapled packet of papers. His logo was front and center, revealing an entirely new brand identity. He'd done an excellent job. Together with my graphics package, Black Soul was getting the hottest makeover ever. I also had an idea for a social media push that I hoped Henry would listen to.

The missing piece. I'd thought of it late last night while I was trying to fall asleep without success.

Henry glided into his chair, rolling it forward so he could rest his elbows on his mammoth desk and steeple his fingers in front of him. "Now that we can finally get started, let's begin with you, Ethan."

Ethan dove into his presentation, giving the specs of the logo and how it would appeal to the widest audience. He then talked about the brand, how we could help Black Soul expand with the right social media package.

When it was my turn, I walked them through the graphics and how I wanted them to be used on each platform. Henry had a lot of questions about the different sizes of banners and pictures and why they had to be altered according to the different sites. I patiently explained the clarity and resolution of each platform and the ability of that site to display high res graphics on all devices.

Henry had no idea what I was talking about. But his cluelessness didn't stop him from asking inane questions. About halfway through my presentation, his eyes started to glaze over. I got it. The specifics of my work weren't interesting to anybody, not even me. But they were important.

Unfortunately, Henry didn't get it even a little bit. By the time I suggested my major giveaway idea using hashtags and the current signed bands from Black Soul, he was totally lost.

"It's simple," I explained. "We'll blast Black Soul and their current talent by having their followers post hashtags of the shows they can't wait to go to. The grand prize will be a season pass to Black Soul's summer concert series. Second place can pick three concerts of their choice or something and third place can pick one. Their followers will post about the bands they love and use hashtags that promote Black Soul so it's a win-win for everybody. We can also require that to enter they must follow Black Soul and the bands they want to see on all of their socials on top of using the hashtag we pick."

"Who would host the giveaway?" Henry asked.

"Nobody is hosting it," I explained. "We'll use hashtags as a search tool. As long as they use the hashtag-black-soul-summer-fun or whatever we pick, we'll be able to add them to the pool of contestants."

I could tell he still didn't understand, but I'd been over it enough times that I had lost patience with him.

"It's an interesting idea, Molly, but I don't think we want to bring up a giveaway during our first meeting. I can't ask them to give away a season pass at the same time I hand them the bill for our services."

"No, I get that it will cost them money to do this giveaway, but it will also bring them money in the end when their listenership is expanded."

He nodded along as if he understood, even though I knew he didn't. And maybe it was the hashtags that were tripping him up. Or maybe he just didn't want to understand, maybe he didn't see the value in a strong social media game. Either way, the end result was the same—disappointing.

"I'm not sure you're considering the best interest of the client, sweetheart. We'll table this for now and see how our initial meeting goes before we discuss it further."

I bit my tongue, swallowing bitterness at being scolded for having a brilliant idea. The meeting went on. We—and by we, I mean the Little Tucker—decided that Ethan and I could be present for the meeting, but as creative director, he would take lead. Which was fine, except he hadn't actually done any work. He was going to pitch our ideas and take all the glory while Ethan and I cheered him on from the invisible background.

By the time we wrapped up, I was stewing with silent fury. I gathered my things with the poise of an angry bull while Ethan hurried out of the office like his desk was on fire.

"Molly, can I talk to you for a minute?" Henry asked in a much gentler voice than he'd used during the meeting.

I looked up at him, hating that I hadn't been as quick as Ethan. Somehow, I managed to sound polite when I said, "Yes?"

"Look, I know I came down hard on you today, but I want you to have the right perspective going into the meeting on Thursday. You're innovative, Molly. And light years ahead of your peers. It's why you've done so well here. It's also why I put you on this project. But what you need to understand is that not everyone speaks your techy language." He got up from behind his desk and walked around to put a hand on my shoulder. "The most important piece of advice I've ever gotten at this job was to know the temperature of the room. You can have the greatest marketing plan in the world, but if you don't know who you're pitching to, the message will never make it to the audience."

I breathed in deeply through my nose, hating that he made a good point. It was an intuitive idea to feel out Black Soul before I pitched a giant giveaway. It physically hurt me to admit, "You're right. It's smart to hold back for now."

His hand moved over my bicep, brushing up and down in a slow caress that grabbed my attention. Abruptly, my priorities shifted from the Black Soul project to Henry's inappropriate touching. Was this the right time to say something?

He stepped closer, smiling serenely at me. "I'm so glad you see it my way." His hand squeezed my bicep but didn't let go. "How are your other projects going? Specifically, I'm interested in the EFB Enterprises account. It's not too big for you, is it? I'm happy to step in and help out where I can."

"That one is going great." My voice shook with nerves, so I pasted on a plastic smile to hide how uncomfortable I was. "I have a meeting with him later today." Er, tonight... "He's very open to my ideas."

"And why wouldn't he be?" Henry asked, but his words were facetious and patronizing.

He had single-handedly made me feel like a child playing pretend at the grown-up job where she didn't belong. I took a step to the side, desperately trying to shake Henry's hand off me.

It worked. But it worked too well.

To my utter horror, as Henry's hand disengaged with my arm it passed over my boob, resting there for a second too long. His whole palm flattened against my breast before he pulled it away.

"Oh my god," I gasped, feeling dirty, molested and small. So, so small.

"What?" Henry asked, totally unfazed.

I stared at his shoes, my voice shaking as I choked out a horrified whisper. "D-did you just grab my b-boob?"

His voice flattened, turning sharp as a knife. "Excuse me?"

I was only marginally more confident when I asked the question for a second time. "D-did you just grab my boob?"

"What? Are you serious? Of course not!"

His outrage soothed some of my worst fears. "It-it felt like you did."

He laughed, but it was bitter and accusatory. "Do you mean just now?" His voice dropped low in a snarl, "I didn't grab your boob, Molly. For god's sake. You moved and my hand accidentally bumped into you. I didn't realize it was your breast until you accused me of assaulting you." He pumped his hands. "You need to settle down."

166

My spine started to crack and crumble beneath the weight of his defensiveness. "Henry, your hand rested on my breast."

"Miss Maverick, that was a complete and total accident. If you'd like to drag my name through unnecessary mud, you're welcome to complain about me to HR. But good luck getting the charge to stick *when it was an accident*. Do you really think I'm in the habit of fondling my employees during the middle of the morning? On a Monday for fuck's sake?"

The hysterical part of my brain wondered why it made any difference that it was Monday? Was he just not usually up for fondling on Mondays? Did he prefer to fondle closer to the weekend? Was there a specific day of the week that was best for fondling?

Regardless, he was adamant that he'd touched me on accident. And while it didn't feel like an accident to me, in fact, it felt very, very on purpose, right now it was his word against mine. I wanted to call him out on his bullshit. I wanted to go straight to HR like he'd suggested and file a formal complaint. But there was no proof that he'd done it on purpose. I couldn't even be sure myself. So what good would it do to complain about the son of the founder of the company I was working for?

Nobody would believe me.

And while I felt icky from the inside out, an accidental brush of my boob wasn't the end of the world.

It wasn't, I told myself again. And then once more with feeling.

I took another step back, debating. He *was* handsy. He'd made me feel uncomfortable on several occasions. But if I drew the line now, then maybe it would stop him from reaching out and grabbing my boob whenever he felt like it.

I could end his inappropriate behavior without escalating this into something that could really damage his standing in this company.

"Please don't touch me again," I told him, barely meeting his eyes. *God, this was awkward. And awful. And I needed it to be over STAT.*

"I told you it was an accident," he huffed. "I'd appreciate it if you would be more careful in the future."

~~And I'd appreciate it if you'd keep your filthy hands to yourself.~~

I shook off the lingering scummy feelings and stepped farther away from him. "Then it's settled. You won't touch me again on accident or otherwise and I won't unintentionally put my boob in your hand."

"That's all I ask." He gave me a tight-lipped glare before he turned back to his desk, effectively dismissing me.

He didn't have to tell me to leave; I was more than ready to escape. I all but ran back to my desk, needing to get away from Henry as quickly as possible. God, I felt like such an idiot! I hated that had happened. And I hated even more that I couldn't decide how to feel about it.

Two parts mortified, two parts furious, all I wanted to do was burst into tears. And take a hot shower. A hot, scalding shower was definitely in order.

It wasn't like I was this giant prude, but I had never been touched inappropriately before without my consent. Maybe it had been an accident, but instinct burned through me, whispering that it hadn't been. But what was there to do about it?

I pushed my laptop out of the way and contemplated banging my head against the desk. See? This was the problem with confrontation. I'd been afraid to talk to Henry for weeks about his inappropriate touching and yet the second I was forced into it, I wanted to give up or puke or move to Tahiti. *Real smooth, Molly. Real fucking smooth.*

"Are you okay?" Emily asked when she returned from the break room with a fresh cup of coffee. "How did the meeting go?"

"Fine," I told her quickly. "Terrible. I don't know. Ask me later."

"What happened?"

The words were there, on the tip of my tongue. I wanted to tell her. *Henry grabbed my boob.* But it sounded ridiculous in my head. Would she laugh about it and make a joke?

It wasn't funny to me. Because it wasn't a joke.

And yet if I told her, then I would have to make a formal complaint. I loved Emily, but she wasn't going to keep something like that a secret. It would get around the whole office. Without a formal complaint I would look like a liar or like I wanted to ruin him out of spite.

"He hated my giveaway idea." I heard myself say the words, but I felt detached from the conversation, like I was outside of my body watching myself cover up for someone I couldn't stand. My mind spun and spun and spun with the memory of what had happened, trying to remember every single detail so I could make sense of it.

So I could figure out the unbiased truth of it.

"That sucks." Emily frowned in sympathy. "But are you surprised? He's not exactly on the cutting edge of trends."

"Y-you're right. I shouldn't be surprised. I guess I'm more disappointed."

She reached out to pat my hand, but I pulled it back quickly. My personal bubble had just tripled in size and I wasn't ready to touch another human yet. Even if it was one of my friends.

Her head cocked back. "Are you sure you're okay, Molly?"

168

"I have a headache," I told her. "I think it's becoming a migraine." Truth. "And it's just been a really rough morning." Noticing my hands had started to shake I balled them into fists and tucked them beneath my desk.

"Can I get you something? Coffee? Water?"

~~Whiskey. Neat.~~ "W-water would be great. Thank you."

Her expression stayed concerned, but she got up and headed for the kitchen. I took a shaky breath and tried to convince myself that it wasn't the end of the world. I was just jostled. I hadn't been expecting to face this today. Or any day. Or ever.

I closed my eyes and his hand was on my breast again. His fingers had stretched around the full circumference, his palm pressed firmly against my nipple.

Okay, so maybe I didn't want to relive every second of that altercation.

A shudder slithered over me and I felt abruptly nauseous. Nervous energy rushed through me and before I totally grasped what I was doing, I had started a casual lap around the office. I probably wasn't going to talk to HR, but it wouldn't hurt to check out who was here today.

Nobody it turned out.

Doris ran the entire department by herself and she was nowhere to be found. Her desk looked untouched. Apparently, she had the day off.

Spinning around, I cased Mr. Tucker's desk. It was across the office, but because of the open floor plan, I could see it from here. The only thing standing in my way was basically every single one of my coworkers, a brick pillar and my own doubt and fear.

"How's the account?"

I jerked, surprised by the person standing to my left. "Oh my God. Catherine, you scared me."

As the top female designer at STS, Catherine Dawes was everything I aspired to be. She was at least five years older than me and light years cooler. Starting with her perfectly smooth, expertly tamed platinum blonde hair to her houndstooth wrap dress, she embodied poise and professionalism.

Today, I looked like a cracked-out hipster with hair that wouldn't lay nicely or do what I asked it to do. I couldn't blame the hair on Henry though. That was one hundred percent me.

The Maverick curse.

"What account?" I asked stupidly.

"The Black Soul account. Didn't Henry handpick you for that project?"

"Uh..." I didn't know what to say. Her gaze probed mine, looking for something I couldn't identify. Was she jealous? Did she want the project?

She could have it. I was over Black Soul and working with Henry Tucker. "I guess."

"What's it like working with him?"

I folded my arms over my chest, feeling distinctly singled out. Catherine never spoke to me. Not even when we'd been paired on projects together. In general, she always kept to herself.

So I didn't understand where this was coming from. Had Henry asked her to say something? Feel me out? In the proverbial sense, anyway. We already knew that if he was going to do it literally, he would do it himself.

"It's fine." I wished I wouldn't have walked all the way over here for Doris who couldn't even bother to show up for her job.

I must have glanced at Doris's desk because Catherine's gaze moved in the same direction. "Are you looking for Doris?"

"I was," I admitted. "But it's not a big deal. I can just talk to her when she gets back."

"She won't be back for another ten days," Catherine supplied. "She's on a cruise."

Well, shit. "Are you serious?"

"Is it important? We got a memo about this last week. We're supposed to go to Henry if we need something HR related. He's covering while she's out of the office."

Of course he is.

"It's seriously not a big deal." I started to move away from Catherine toward my desk. "I'll catch her some other time."

"Molly," she called after me. I only stopped because I was so surprised she knew my name. "If there's something you want to talk about or if... something happened that you feel should be shared, I'm here for you."

I licked dry lips and determined to forget about what had happened and move on with my life and this project. "Okay. Uh, thanks."

Catherine's bizarre proposal stayed with me for the rest of the day while I pretended to work. I wanted to tell someone. I would even tell Emily if it meant getting it off my chest. But I couldn't seem to get the words past my lips.

It wasn't until she started packing up for the day that I finally found the courage to confess.

She turned and asked, "Happy hour?"

I blinked at her and said, "Henry grabbed my boob this morning," in a rushed, whispered explanation.

Her response boomed through the office. "He did what?"

Glancing around, I dropped my voice and repeated, "Henry grabbed my boob, Em. After the meeting this morning. He started by putting his

170

hand on my shoulder and when I tried to move away, *he grabbed my boob.*"

She dropped her purse and laptop on the floor and shoved her rolling chair over by me. "Like full on?"

"Like a grab, Emily! Like you grab something. Like you intentionally try to grab something. That's what he did. To my boob." *And if I'm forced to say boob one more time today, I might scream.*

"Holy shit! What are you going to do?"

"I tried to talk to HR earlier, but Doris is on a cruise for the next ten days. The Little Tucker is filling in for her."

"Yeah, well the Little Fucker can go to hell." Her outrage soothed some of my own. "Did you say something?"

I took a steadying breath. "I told him not to touch me again. But since I shouldn't have had to say that to begin with, who knows if he'll listen."

"He better listen!"

"I know."

"Molly, what are you going to do?" she asked for a second time.

"Do you have any ideas? Seriously, I'm open. At this point my only other option is to go to his dad. But Henry is adamant that it was an accident. It's his word against mine."

"And mine," she added. "I'm happy to speak up for you."

"Except you weren't there," I reminded her. "You're only hearing my side of the story."

She rolled her eyes. "Because your side of the story is the only one that matters."

We fell silent, neither one of us having the right answer.

Eventually I decided, "I'll wait till Doris comes back and then I'll tell her what happened. She'll do something. It's her job to do something."

Emily nodded. "And in the meantime, I'll protect you from Junior. He's not going to be able to get within fifty feet of you on my watch."

The pressure in my chest eased up even though I knew she wouldn't be able to keep her promise. Henry and I were in the middle of an important project together. There was no way I would be able to avoid him forever. But maybe for ten days? I could make it until Doris got back. Then I could decide what to do.

Emily walked me to my car and I appreciated her kindness. I didn't want to need help right now, but I did need it. Mostly, I just wanted to crawl back to my apartment and forget this day ever happened. But since I couldn't do that, it was nice to have a friend like Emily to walk alongside me.

And it was nice to have the meeting with Ezra to look forward to, to give me something else to think about. Maybe it would be less awful than the rest of my day. A girl could hope anyway.

Chapter Seventeen

Bianca was alive with dinner activity when I walked through the doors. Placed on the outskirts of downtown in a recently redeveloped art district, the restaurant was tucked between an old house that had been turned into an antique shop and a French bakery (*the* French bakery) that was currently closed.

The restaurant itself was almost hidden behind vines of ivy twining over her brick front. A wrought iron fence outlined a cute patio just to the side of the main doors. A menu board stood at the entrance so people walking by could stop and check out what the special was.

I walked inside, nervous and uptight from a long day, but Bianca's enchantment slowly began to chip away at the icy armor I'd been wearing for hours.

Immediately, my eyes fell on the focal point of the space, which was an oval bar in the center of the dining room. A huge chandelier hung above it, shaped like a flower with dripping crystals glittering in the golden light. The flower theme continued around the room. Over every table was a hanging white pot with overflowing white flowers, dripping down the sides. The artwork was all white flowers, white shapes and buildings. White everything.

Since Ezra had forced me to work with him, I'd been doing my research with each of his restaurants. Bianca meant white. So it was only appropriate that he'd painted his entire restaurant in it.

Even his hostesses were dressed in white. Unlike Lilou, where everyone wore black.

I would have to visit Sarita next. Just to see what color scheme he'd gone with.

Red I would guess.

The uninspired wall caught my attention. Two of the four walls of the restaurant had windows letting in light. The back wall hid the kitchen and was broken up by in and out doors and the space for the bathrooms. But the fourth wall, the one to the right of the bar, was windowless and in desperate need of *something*. It was even more obvious how badly it stuck out standing in the restaurant. Pictures didn't do the tragic space justice.

My idea bloomed into something more substantial with the dimensions in front of me. Bianca was modern, yet whimsical. Simple, yet completely charming.

"Are you meeting someone?" the hostess asked.

"Ezra," I told her, finding I didn't have much strength for many words.

Her eyes widened with surprise. "Ezra Baptiste?"

"Yes."

"Is he expecting you?"

"Yes."

She puckered her lips and looked toward the bar. "I think he's in the kitchen tonight, but I'm not totally sure. I'll go check."

When she walked off to hunt down her boss, I picked up a menu. Bianca was considerably smaller than Lilou, but just as fancy. I barely recognized any of the dishes on the simple menu and the descriptions were even worse. Even the cocktails seemed written in a different language.

I needed Vera to interpret the menu for me. From my research, I knew Bianca served modern French cuisine, but that meant nothing to someone who knew zero about high-end food.

My stomach growled anyway. Apparently it didn't care what they served, just that they had food. And to be honest, after watching several plates being delivered to nearby tables, I couldn't blame it. Whatever these people were eating looked incredible.

A few minutes passed before Ezra emerged from the kitchen. To my surprise he sported a white chef's coat. He pulled off a short, floppy chef's hat on his way over to me, a serious look on his usually serious face.

"Molly," he greeted in his typical way. "Sorry to keep you waiting."

I stared at him, my mouth going dry with wonder at this new version of him. He always looked so put together in his suits and dress clothes. And the few times I'd seen him clad more casually had been heart stopping. But this? The white coat hugged his toned arms and muscular chest. He still wore navy blue trousers instead of the usual pants I knew chefs wore. And his shoes were shiny, expensive and out of place in the kitchen. He was... disheveled, and mismatching, and completely gorgeous. "Are you a chef?"

He cleared his throat, glancing away from me. "Not formally. But I know my way around a kitchen, regardless of what Killian's told you."

"He hasn't told me anything," I assured him. "I'm just surprised to see you back there."

His eyes still refused to meet mine and if it were any other person I would have guessed that he was nervous. But this was Ezra after all. The man didn't get nervous. Or uncomfortable. Or anything but cocky and self-assured. "There was an issue with dinner service. I stepped in to help."

"That was nice of you."

His smile was self-deprecating and humble, proving all of my theories about him wrong. "No, it wasn't. It was completely selfish. I don't want my restaurant to fail."

I couldn't help but laugh. "Okay, you're right. It was completely selfish of you to save the day. How dare you take care of your business."

His lips split in a warm grin, but he changed the subject. "You're here to see the wall?"

"Is that all right? I don't want to be a nuisance."

He waved me off. "It's fine. We'll save the painting part for after hours, but take whatever measurements you need."

"Lead the way," I prompted him.

He did just that, taking me around the edge of the room until I was face to face with my future project. Staring at this giant white space which was basically the biggest canvas I'd ever been given, finally released the tension that had been bottling up inside me all day.

I released a happy sigh of anticipation and reached out to press my hand on a blank section of white paint. "This is going to be fun," I whispered.

Ezra turned to me. "Hmm?"

"Nothing." I walked around Ezra to check out more of the wall. "I was just talking to myself."

"You look happy," he commented. "Did you have a good day?"

Without looking at him, I admitted, "I had a terrible day." I ran my finger down the side of a black picture frame. "But this makes it better."

175

I heard the smile in his voice without looking at him. "I was just thinking that."

Those butterflies came back full force, jumping and flapping and causing all kinds of chaos inside me. Spinning toward him, I met his gaze bravely. "Do you want to hear my idea?"

He stared at me. "Do you want to tell me your idea?"

I shook my head, half mesmerized by the mysterious look in his eyes. It was warm and tender and familiar all at once. "Not really."

He lifted one shoulder in a slow shrug. "Then I'll wait for the big reveal."

His answer made me doubt his sincerity. "You're kidding, right?"

"Why would I be kidding?"

Because you're a ~~completely adorable~~ control freak. "You really trust me that much? I'm painting an entire wall, Ezra."

"In matters like these, Molly, I'm beginning to think I trust you more than anyone else I know."

What was I supposed to do with that? Besides memorize it and the way he looked right now and the way his words made me feel safe, and important, and *seen*. I wanted to bottle this moment and keep it with me forever so I could pull it out every time I felt insecure or less than. So I could remind myself of what it was like to feel respected.

Because I did feel respected. For whatever reason, this super successful restaurateur had decided that I was a peer. Where my entire office failed to put any faith in me, he had risked his entire empire on me and my taste. He trusted me. When my boss shot down my ideas and dismissed my vision and groped me, this man had asked me to help him, put his full trust in me.

And he'd given me complete autonomy to do what I thought was best.

Ezra had no idea how much that meant to me, how much he had changed every single thing I believed about the world and being a grown-up and having a job.

"What do you need from me?" he asked when I hadn't said anything after a while.

"Nothing right now," I told him. "Will it be okay to put up the screens? I'm hoping to get a good start Saturday, but I don't want to be too intrusive."

"You'll be fine," he promised. "Let me know what I can supply you with and I'll have it here for you."

"Thank you."

"Are you hungry?"

"What?"

176

He'd somehow managed to close the space between us. "Are you hungry? Have you eaten?"

"Uh, no."

"Do you want to join me for a quick bite?"

My heartbeat tripled. "Like right now?"

One half of his mouth lifted in a smile. "Yes, like right now." The smile disappeared. "Unless you have somewhere else to be."

An irrational need to see his smile reappear prompted me to say, "No, I don't have anywhere to be. So sure, dinner sounds good."

"Okay, great. Have a seat over… here." He walked me to a two-person table near the kitchen. "I have to go check on the kitchen before I sit down, but I'll have Sienna bring you a menu."

He pulled the chair out for me with a swift tug of his arm and suddenly I was beyond nervous. What was this exactly? An obligation? A working dinner?

"Thank you," I rasped, barely getting words out of my dry mouth.

He motioned for Sienna the hostess to come over with an elegant flick of his wrist. She hopped into action, scurrying through the restaurant to see what he needed. Either she had a high school crush on him or he was a terrifying boss that she was petrified of pissing off.

Or a mixture of the two.

Not that I knew anything about that.

"Can you bring Molly a menu," he asked her. "And a glass of water." He looked at me. "Do you want anything else? A cocktail? Wine?"

I cleared my throat, hoping to magically get better at speaking. "I'll just start with water. Thank you."

"I'll be right back," Sienna promised.

Ezra smiled down at me when she'd disappeared. "I will be too. I just have to make sure everything's running smoothly. Flag Sienna down if you need anything, or any of the wait staff if you can't find her. This is my usual table so they'll check on you."

"Okay."

He started to walk away, but paused halfway between me and the kitchen in door. "You'll wait for me?"

His uncertainty made something hum inside me. "I'll wait for you," I confirmed.

That rare smile appeared, transforming his entire aura into relaxed happiness. It was amazing how he could switch it on and off. He went from intimidating dictator one second to blindingly beautiful in the next.

Not that he'd been much of a dictator tonight. In fact, he'd been really kind and thoughtful and attentive. Surely that would change. When he came back we'd find something to argue about. There weren't two people that were more different than us. It was only a matter of time before we slipped back into our old habits.

He'd order me to do something. I would obviously refuse. He'd argue with me. I would win the argument this time. Then he'd have me escorted from the premises.

Which would be the perfect ending to my already stellar Monday.

But for some reason, I was looking forward to sparring with him.

Instead of dwelling on my work day, I pulled out my phone and started discreetly googling the ingredients to the French dishes he wanted me to pick from. They weren't any help. I thought about grabbing Sienna to see if she could help make sense of the menu, but I chickened out when she refilled my water.

After a few minutes of waiting, Ezra returned to the table sans chef's coat. He ran a hand through his hair several times on the way to the table as if trying to get it to obey again after it had been held captive beneath his chef's hat. That alone should have kept my attention for the next five ~~years~~ seconds, but there was so much more to him than just the hair.

He was wearing a t-shirt. A t-shirt!

I had never seen him in a t-shirt before. And to be honest, I had never once, not one single time, thought a t-shirt could be revolutionary. But on Ezra it somehow was.

He looked younger and more relaxed. His arms were on display for the first time ever and they did not disappoint. Muscular and defined just like I knew they would be. He instantly made me recommit to five-thirty in the morning spin class.

His smile was big and genuine, gentle in a way that was so unexpected from him. He sat down across from me and I thought that maybe this was the moment I fell in love with him. Or okay, not love, but definitely lust.

So much lust.

He leaned forward, relaxing his elbows on the table. "Did you decide what you're going to eat?"

I cleared my throat and forced my gaze to the menu so I wouldn't be tempted to stare at him. "It all looks so good." Okay, moment of honesty, I had no idea what any of this was, but I was positive it would be good. So that counted, right? "I'm just not sure which one to pick. What are your, um, favorites?"

"The coq au vin is spectacular," he answered casually. "Also our duck confit was saved when I fired Marcel. I'm happy with how the kitchen has been preparing it lately."

178

Yes, my best friend was a chef, but that didn't mean I'd paid attention to anything she'd ever said about cooking before. Just like she couldn't pick up a paintbrush and do anything useful with it just because she was friends with me. To be honest, when she started talking about food, I usually tuned out the Charlie Brown teacher voice that made zero sense.

But hindsight was twenty-twenty, and what I wouldn't give to remember at least a few of her helpful tidbits! Like what the heck was coq au vin? Was that a meat? Or a wine? And duck might be okay, but was the confit part of it something weird? Like the intestines or something? One thing I knew about chefs was that they were willing to eat anything. And most of the time the weirder the food got, the better the acclaim. Like beef hearts and tongue, and thousand year eggs.

I didn't think I was up for the strange parts of a duck tonight.

When I didn't respond, Ezra added, "Or is there something you'd rather have that's not on the menu? I can have them make you whatever you want. Just name what you're hungry for."

My cheeks heated at his generous offer. "Actually, I just can't decide. Sorry. Usually Vera orders for me when we go out. Everything looks amazing. I don't know what to get."

"Ah." He tugged on the menu and I easily gave it up. "Do you mind if I order for us then? Would you like to try a few things and we could share them?"

I let out a deep breath of relief. "I would love that."

"How do you feel about mussels?"

"Go for it. Whatever you think is best." And if I didn't like any of it, I could always stop at Taco Bell on the way home. Just sayin'.

He motioned his wait staff over and a server popped up right away. "I'm going to put in an order, David."

"Yes, sir," David replied.

Ezra began rattling off a long list of dishes including the mussels, coq au vin and duck confit. Then he added words I recognized—cordon bleu and steak frites. He looked at me, a subtle smile hidden in his beautiful mouth. "Wine?"

I shrugged. "Sure."

"And we'll do a bottle of the Chateau-Grillet."

David disappeared and I realized I was alone with Ezra Baptiste. In one of his restaurants. At one of his tables.

I didn't even know how to feel about it. Or what to think! Just a couple months ago, I had been unbearably nervous around the man. I had hated him because that seemed like the safest emotion to feel.

179

He was Vera's famous acquaintance. He was Killian's successful friend. He was Wyatt's boss.

But he was nothing to me.

And I was nothing to him. Just a person he would recognize in a police lineup should I rob a liquor store while he happened to be in it.

Except lately it didn't feel like we were such strangers. And hating him didn't feel safe anymore either. In fact none of the emotions I felt for Ezra felt safe.

But they didn't necessarily feel wrong either.

Dangerous for sure. But not wrong or safe or comfortable.

"So, be honest, am I asking too much with the mural?"

I tipped my head back and laughed at his question. Was he asking too much? He was always asking too much. "Are you serious?"

He scrunched his guilty face. "I was inspired by that painting you did at Killian's. I might have come on a little strong."

Shaking my head at him, I ran my finger through the condensation on my water glass. "You came on strong for the engagement party. Then you came on really strong when you hired me at STS. By the time we got to the mural, I would have been more surprised if you'd have said please and let me say no."

It was his turn to chuckle. "I'm not used to hearing no."

"So I've noticed."

"Well, to be honest, that doesn't paint the whole picture. I have heard no. I've heard it so many times that I'm tired of hearing it. Now I do whatever it takes to get a yes."

His eyes were sincere, lost in memories I could only guess at. Some of his enigmatic energy had settled, gentled. My icy walls continued to melt. The harsh words that always sat on the tip of my tongue when he was around dissolved. I wanted to hear more about him. I wanted to know more. See more.

I want to know all of you.

Maybe he wasn't alone in that pursuit.

"With your restaurants?" I asked, probing.

He tilted his head back and forth. "Yes, absolutely. Lilou was a massive learning experience for me. Even after my first venture." He paused and then added, "My ex-wife and I own a restaurant together. Quince. Have you heard of it?"

Ezra seemed calm, but I was suddenly buzzing with nervous energy. I had always remembered that he owned a fourth restaurant, but it was harder for me to remember that he had an ex-wife.

"Yes," I told him. "I've heard of it. Although I haven't ever been."

180

He made a face. "It's fine. It suits Elena and stays profitable. Nothing I would consider groundbreaking."

"Elena is your ex-wife?"

He nodded once, but didn't elaborate. So I should have let it drop and moved onto something else. With anybody else, I would have been too meek to ask direct questions. But with Ezra it was almost like I couldn't help myself. I wanted to know what had happened. I wanted to know everything, not just about his marriage, but about his entire life. I wanted to pry and poke and pester until he confessed it all.

Until I knew everything.

Until I knew him.

"But you still own the restaurant with her?" There, that was ~~nosey as hell~~ subtle.

His expression hardened, thunderclouds rolling in, lightning flashing, tornado sirens wailing. "When I met Elena she was in the process of developing the idea. She was passionate and fiery. She wanted to bring good Mexican food to Durham, but she wanted to do it with old world style. I fell in love with the idea immediately and almost just as quickly with her. We were married six months after we met and once she'd secured my last name and my money, we opened the restaurant together. A year after Quince opened, we divorced."

The deep sadness in his eyes stabbed at my heart, breaking my chest open for this man and his past so it had room to hemorrhage for him. "It was too hard to run a business together?"

He looked up at me, hitting me with the entire force of his past grief. My breath caught in my throat when he said, "She had an affair with our head chef. They're married now." He looked away, thoughtful, subdued. "They have three kids together."

"Oh my god, Ezra."

His chin jerked to the side. "Don't feel sorry for me. I'm just as much to blame. I'm hard to put up with. Especially back then. I... I can be closed off, hyper focused on work and you know, all those things that send women running to other men. She... we... I am better because of what happened. Thanks to Elena, I found my love for restaurants. I found a life I am passionate about and a pursuit that I am happy to spend my time chasing. I was angry for a while, but out of that dark time Lilou was born. I asked Killian to take the helm and the rest is history. That was ten years ago. Since then I've moved on and now with the three independent restaurants doing so well, it's hard to be bitter at a time that pressed out so much good."

"So, Elena still runs Quince?"

181

"She's part owner, but she has little to do with the business side of things. She manages the restaurant and I've let her keep her menu choices and style. But I'm the reason it makes money."

There was no arrogance to his tone. It was simple truth.

Our food appeared, carried over by an army of waiters. We moved apart, straightening in our seats and moving cutlery and glasses out of the way to accommodate all the food.

David, the same waiter that had taken our order, explained all of the dishes for my benefit and poured wine. We spent the next ten minutes tasting food, and sipping wine, and having our minds basically blown.

Or at least mine was blown. The food was just as good as when I'd shared that incredible meal with Vera at Lilou, or the extensive menu Wyatt had prepared for the engagement party, or any of the meals Vera had made for me to taste.

"This is incredible," I moaned with a bite of medium rare steak and thin French fry doused in delicious sauce at the end of my fork. "I know you're having chef problems, but I'm very sure your kitchen is not suffering."

He smiled at his plate. When he looked up at me, his eyes were darkened and secretive again. "These are old recipes," he explained. "The kitchen can serve these with one hand tied behind their back. But I haven't had a menu change in months. I need someone to step in and take the reins. I need leadership. I need inspiration. I can only do so much."

Now I understood. "What are you going to do?"

He held my gaze, his confidence never wavering. "I'm going to update my website, develop a kickass social media strategy and paint a fucking gorgeous mural on that wall." He pointed at said wall. "I'm going to make Bianca irresistible."

A piece of duck got lodged in my throat and for a second I was positive I was going to need the Heimlich. Which of course would have been too humiliating in front of Ezra and his dining room full of posh customers. The only alternative to having Ezra beat a hunk of poultry out of my windpipe was to just die.

So that's how my life was going currently.

I reached for my water glass and made a total fool out of myself did what I could to save the situation from complete mortification.

It didn't totally work. "Are you okay?"

I held up a finger to let him know I needed a minute and continued to gulp the life-saving liquid. It wasn't my most graceful moment and I might have needed to wipe my mouth with a napkin as soon as it was over, but I survived.

I was a survivor.

"Fine," I squeaked. "I just didn't realize... that... I didn't know that was what I was doing for you."

He raised an eyebrow. "If you'd known would that have changed anything?"

Did he mean, would I have still demanded that he get out of my way? Obviously. I could only handle so many micromanaging men in my life. Instead, I decided sarcasm was the best policy. "Well, I probably would have tried harder."

Half his mouth lifted, amused. "Is that so?"

"It is so. Oh, well, I guess we'll just have to make do with what we have. Which is a not that great to be honest."

"You're so full of shit, Maverick."

Good thing my mouth was empty. His cavalier teasing would have for sure made me choke again. "Yeah, but you like it, Baptiste. You need someone to give you hell lest you continue thinking you're so special."

He leaned forward again, his arm reaching to the center of the table. "Oh, so that's what you're doing? Driving me crazy to keep me humble?"

I found myself leaning forward too. "Obviously. Is it working?"

"Well, you're definitely driving me crazy. I'll get back to you on the humble part."

"Maybe I need to try harder."

His expression darkened, his voice dropped, and he became all things irresistible man. "Yes, please."

Oh my god. *Please.* One simple, commonplace word, but oh, the power it had over my quivering libido. I might have accidentally orgasmed.

I pulled back, afraid I would start drooling all over the coq au vin. "You're trouble, Ezra. So much trouble."

He sat back too, diving his fork into the pot of mussels. "You're one to talk, Molly the Maverick. You've been a hell-raiser since the moment I met you. I'm just trying to keep up."

His accusation made me pause. That couldn't be true. I mean, yes we'd fought the first time we met and most of the times we'd been forced to interact since then. But nobody had ever called me a hell-raiser before. Ever.

My senior class had voted me Most Likely to be a Kindergarten Teacher. In college, one of the guys I'd dated had broken up with me because we didn't fight enough. He'd said I was boring.

183

I wasn't a hell-raiser or trouble or difficult in any way. I was nice and easy to get along with. I was shy. I was a pushover.

I was the definition of the friend zone.

"Should we do dessert?" Ezra asked even though we hadn't made it through half of the food he'd ordered.

"I want to," I told him honestly. "But I have a ton of work to get to tonight."

He glanced away and I couldn't tell if he was disappointed or just thoughtful. "Me too actually."

"Thanks for dinner," I told him sincerely. "This was so much better than the Hot Pocket I had been planning on."

He laughed because he thought I had told a joke.

I hadn't.

"Well, anytime, Molly. I'm happy to save you from Hot Pockets anytime."

My cheeks hurt from smiling so much. "I'll be back here Saturday morning to start. Does nine work?"

"Of course. I'll be here to let you in. Email me anything you need in the meantime."

For someone that never spoke her mind, I'm not exactly sure what came over me. But I found myself reaching out for his hand and saying. "She's an idiot." His gaze snapped to mine, a question bright in his eyes. "Elena," I clarified. "I know you're in this way better place and your experience with her opened up all of your restaurant opportunities. But honestly, she's an idiot. You're difficult, but not impossible. And you're definitely a workaholic, but you're also thoughtful, and caring, and one of the most respectable people I have ever met. You didn't send her to another man's arms, Ezra. She settled for a cheaper version because she wasn't strong enough to see the amazing man standing right in front of her."

He was quiet for so long that I worried I'd offended him. Abruptly, he stood up and held out his hand to me. I took it.

Of course I took it.

"I'm going to walk you to your car."

"O-okay."

We left the table with our discarded meal and cluttered plates and empty wine glasses and he led me outside. I wasn't sure he knew what kind of car I drove, but it turned out he wasn't really interested in my safety or sending me home.

We stepped outside Bianca and he pulled me into the empty patio area that was still closed down from winter. The ivy didn't have leaves

184

yet. The brick beneath our feet was uneven. There was still a chill in the air. None of it mattered.

He stepped into me, bringing his body heat with him. The night sky framed his outline, stars twinkling overhead. A nervous tingle spread through my body, starting at my toes and working its way upward until I was nothing but nerves and anticipation and hope.

"I tried to save you from this, Molly." Ezra's voice was gentle, roughened. "I'm tired of failing."

Before I could ask any questions, his lips were on mine. His touch jolted through me, surprising me with the feel of his mouth, the press of his body, the realization that Ezra Baptiste was kissing me. I probably should have been expecting this, but honestly there was not any way to prepare for this kiss.

This kiss that was everything I had never felt or experienced before, or had the chance to enjoy. If all of my blind dates that turned into bad dates, and ~~really~~ bad dates had been with boys pretending to be men, then this single experience was enough to erase them all from my memory forever. Because Ezra wasn't a boy or pretending to be a grown up or anything but a sexy, irresistible, virile male.

His mouth moved over mine with skill. Caressing, nibbling, sucking until I kissed him back in the same way. His hunger was subtle at first, growing with intensity the longer we stood there. His hands found my waist, tugging me against his hard body. My hands belatedly fluttered to his chest where I clutched his t-shirt with two fists and held on for my life.

He kissed me in a way I had never been kissed before. In a way I knew, *I just knew*, I would never be kissed again, not by any other man. Nobody could replicate this moment. Nobody could compare. I was totally lost to the sensation of his tongue tangling with mine and the rumbly sound he made in the back of his throat when I caught his lower lip in my teeth.

He wasn't shy or reserved. His mouth moved with mine until we fell into an intimate dance of lips and tongue, and a ton of heat. So much heat. He stoked the fire with his talented hands, moving them up and down my sides, drawing me closer, teasing, tempting... seducing.

When he trailed kisses along my jawline and down the column of my neck, I gasped for breath in an effort to calm my racing heart. He didn't let me take much of a break before his mouth came right back to mine as greedy for me as I was for him.

Time passed, but I was lost to it—lost to this man. This man that was not cocky, but confident and successful. This man that was not inconsiderate and rude, but loyal to those that he cared about, wounded from past hurt, and so unbelievably thoughtful.

This man that was so completely different than I'd assumed.

His kisses eventually slowed and he reluctantly pulled back, but he didn't go too far. He kept his head bent low, touching his forehead to mine. His hands stayed spread over my ribs, holding me close, reminding me of how intimate we had just been.

He let out a shaky breath. "Finally."

I let out a surprised laugh. "Finally?"

Straightening, he gazed down at me. "I'm not sure I can remember a time when I didn't want to kiss you."

My already pounding heart jumped excitedly in my fluttering chest. My insides were a mess of adrenaline and endorphins, and way too much feeling. "You haven't known me for that long," I reminded him.

He took another step back, his hands grabbing mine. "True. But you of all people know I'm not known for my patience."

I shook my head at him, feeling some of my spine return. "Did you get it out of your system?"

He always responded differently than I thought he would. For instance, I expected hurt or anger, or even mild irritation at the very least after a snarky comment like that. Instead, that one side of his mouth lifted in an affectionate half-smile and he said, "Not even a little bit."

I gulped making a straight-up audible sound that reminded me of a cartoon. "I have work to do."

"Get to it then," he ordered. "I'll see you Saturday."

Not sure what to think of him or that kiss, I disentangled my hands from his and said, "Okay." That was my genius response. After one of the best meals of my life, one of the most interesting conversations of my life and by far the best kiss of my life, I ended the night with a dorky, "Okay."

Ugh.

This was Ezra's fault somehow. I blamed the sexy restaurateur that had effectively turned my mind and my resolve to hate him to mush.

I left Ezra and practically ran to my car in an attempt to escape. Keeping my fingers pressed to my lips the entire drive home, I tried to hold on to the feeling of him kissing me for as long as possible. Just in case it never happened again, just in case Ezra came to his senses and wanted nothing to do with me ever again.

When I got home, I didn't paint all night like I wanted to. I didn't even dwell on Ezra's kiss and relive every single second of it like I *really* wanted to.

No, I worked.

And I hated every second of it.

It was only when I went to bed three hours later that I let myself check my email and finally, *finally* gave into the butterflies and gooey feelings, and the uncertainty of what all of this meant.

To: mollythemaverick@gmail.com
From: ezra.baptiste@yahoo.com
Date: April 3, 2017 23:18:45 EST
Subject: Thanks for dinner.
And that kiss.
Looking forward to Saturday.
~Ezra

Chapter Eighteen

~~T~~he week passed like a snail—slow and slimy. Even the Black Soul meeting had been ~~a waste of my time~~ anticlimactic. I had been looking forward to representing edgy artists with our branding push, excited about all the possibilities our marketing team had to offer. Instead, I'd gotten stuffy suits that were more interested in dollar signs than original content.

Considering the client, Henry was perfect as acting creative director. He pitched to their level, offering overused, dated tactics that wouldn't do anything for their image, reach or business. Even Ethan's super cool new logos were debated over, deciding at long last that they would take the logo options to a focus group and see how they tested.

My social media package went about as well as you can imagine—in that it ~~was a train wreck~~ didn't go well at all. There were vague compliments regarding my graphics, but the majority of the meeting was spent debating the ROI of social media ads and trying to explain that seventy-one percent of digital minutes were spent on smartphones—not desktops. Clearly making it pointless, or at least less relevant, to target desktops alone.

And yet all of my golden nuggets fell on deaf ears.

When we got back to the office, Henry had made us congregate in the conference room for a brand-new strategy meeting. He wanted to start from scratch. We wouldn't have to throw out all of our graphics, just one hundred percent of our innovative ideas.

The Black Soul project, the project that was supposed to launch me into office-wide notoriety, had been about as successful as my previous projects for the Baptist church and the mowing company. It had done nothing to further my career or cement my standing at STS. I was stuck on the same rung of the corporate ladder I'd started on.

And I hated it. I was no longer satisfied with anonymous background jobs and being the sucker Henry got to sexually harass.

However, there was still work to be done for Black Soul, and maybe not all was lost. We had been told at the meeting that two of their marketing experts were in California for the week. The rumor was that the missing execs were better in tune with what was on trend.

I had to keep trying, right? It wasn't in me to quit anyway. If my mother had taught me anything in this life it was that you never, ever, no matter how awful or wretched or dangerous, you never quit anything. Or so help me, God.

Other arguments included: *Do you want to end up like your father? Where would the world be today if everyone just gave up and quit? Oh my god, you're turning into your father.* And my personal favorite: *Quitters quit, Molly. Do you want to be a quitter? Well, do you?*

Ahem. Needless to say, I couldn't actually imagine a scenario in which I walked away from this project. I didn't want to be a quitter after all. And I really didn't want to end up like my dad. Or my mom for that matter.

I would continue to come up with original ideas that would blow their socks off and make them jump feet first into this wonderful new technical age. I would continue to pour myself into this project even though it had lost all its luster and made me feel sad for the bands that signed with such a backward-thinking studio. And I would continue to put up with Henry and his silent staring and not so silent accidental touching. Although if his hand landed anywhere near my boob again, my knee was definitely going to find its way to his balls. Chuck Norris style.

It all seemed pointless. I realized it was too late to pass the account off to someone else, but I dreamed about doing that every single day. I had been so looking forward to this account. I'd placed so many hopes and dreams and future shopping purchases on it, but when it had come down to it, this was the account that would end up ruining the façade that I loved what I was doing.

Because I didn't.

This was nothing like painting. I couldn't lie to myself for a second longer. Graphic design was the antithesis of having the freedom to create.

Because there was no choice in this. There was no open-minded thinking or wide space to invent and process and make. It was all rigid lines and somebody else's visions. It was people pleasing, mindless *yes sirs*, and the corporate world disguised in a cool office with a loose dress code. I couldn't *for the life of me* remember why I'd wanted to move up in the company so badly. There was no end game to this madness. Only the constant crazy cycle of pleasing stubborn clients and perverted bosses.

When I finally walked into Bianca Saturday morning to work on the mural, I took a deep breath and it felt like the first one all week. Ezra had met me at the front door all easy smiles and sleepy eyes. It wasn't fair how attracted I was to him. Not even a little bit.

"Molly," he'd greeted instead of a regular good morning.

"Ezra," I'd returned, wondering if he was going to kiss me again.

He'd taken my awkward canvas tote that contained all the paint and supplies I'd brought with me. The bag was overpacked with brushes and more brushes— every kind, size and shape in my arsenal. I'd brought them all. Even though I was pretty loyal to my pouncing brush and it was the best choice for what I had in mind. But the truth was I'd never painted an entire mural before so I didn't really know what I needed. Better safe than sorry.

After he'd placed my things on a cloth-covered table set aside just for me, he started digging around in my tote. "There are so many brushes." He looked up at me. "I had no idea there were so many to choose from."

I shrugged, basking in the excitement I felt because he was interested. "They all serve different purposes."

He looked doubtful. "If you say so."

"How many different kinds of forks are there? Or spoons? How many serving spoons or spatulas, different kinds of whisks, pans, dishes? Knives?" I pointed at my brushes. "Same concept."

His smile stretched wide. "You've explained this before."

"Once or twice. I can provide the same comparison using bike gears, aerodynamic wheels, and tools if you'd like."

Taking a step toward me, his hand slipped around my waist. "No need."

I looked up at him, amazed that he had initiated physical contact. We'd exchanged work emails and fun texts during the week, but there was nothing said that indicated whether our kiss was a blooper or a prologue.

I'd tried to focus on work instead of ~~obsess~~ think about what this was with Ezra, but let's be real. Obviously, I was only human. And obviously, Ezra was more than human. Although I couldn't tell you exactly what he was yet, I was positive it was along the lines of a Greek god or superhero, or maybe even a sparkly vampire. It didn't really matter, because I was none of those things and it was hard to believe that our kiss had meant anything to him.

He probably had epic kisses all the time. Like he was so sick of being kissed until the point of orgasm that he was like, *Yuck, stop kissing me all you beautiful women!*

Me on the other hand? The last time I had been kissed so thoroughly that my eyes crossed and my toes tingled was... well... Okay, fine, I couldn't remember ever being kissed like that. And now I had to live with the very real possibility that I might never be kissed like that again. Ever. Which was a giant, ugly, bitter tasting pill to swallow.

Just when I'd decided I couldn't stand being this psychotic over one minor makeout, his expression flattened abruptly and he asked, "When you said bike gears, was that in reference to Vera's brother?"

"Mmmhmmm. Vann."

He rocked back on his heels, but his hand didn't leave my hip. "Should I have made sure you were single before I kissed you?"

"Do you mean Vann?" I couldn't help the small laugh that escaped. "No, no, no. No. I'm sorry, but no. We're just friends. He's like my big brother. I've known him all my life."

He didn't seem convinced. "There's nothing between you?"

"Would you date Dillon?"

His face scrunched up reflexively. "No. Never. But she really is my sister. Half. By blood."

"Maybe Vann and I don't share DNA, but he's my brother in every sense of the word. He's overprotective and annoying and wonderful all at once. There will never, ever, ever be anything between us. Ever."

He thought over my answer and then upped the ante. "What about Wyatt? Is there something going on between you two?"

My pulse pounded at my wrists, nervous and uneasy. "Maybe you should just ask what you want to ask."

"Are you seeing anyone, Molly? Interested in anyone?"

My heart kicked and my thoughts jumbled together all at once. He wanted to know if I was interested in anyone? I suddenly felt like we were back in fifth grade and I was being forced to face my crush during a tragic game of spin the bottle.

"You," I said tentatively, with my heart in my throat and my contingency plan to move to Mexico in place in my head in case he shot me down. Head's up, step one of the plan is me crashing through one of Bianca's windows and stealing ~~Ezra's Alfa~~ a car. "Ezra there's no one else."

His entire body relaxed, melting into me as he swooped down to capture my mouth in an immediate kiss. I sucked in a sharp breath of surprise, giving him all the incentive he needed to tangle my tongue fully with his. His lips pressed against mine, not gently, not tenderly, but with hunger, purpose and wicked heat.

We picked up right where we'd left off. Our mouths moved together with familiarity, learning each other's curves and tastes and needs. I clutched his polo with two fists, desperate to have more of this man that had driven me crazy for months and was currently driving me crazy in an entirely better new way.

But all good things must stupidly come to an end. Our kiss was sensual and sexy, and way too short. When a chef walked out of the kitchen, spotted us and then walked right back into the kitchen, Ezra pulled back, ending the bliss we'd only just begun to explore. Although, he didn't go too far.

"Sorry," he murmured with an annoyed glance over his shoulder. When he turned back to me, he said, "I've been wanting to do that all week."

That made me grin like an idiot. I rested my cheek on his chest to hide my red cheeks and silly smile, listening to his sprinting heart and feeling satisfaction at how quickly it beat. Because I was the reason it pounded so frantically. "So there's no one else for you either? Girlfriends? Friends with benefits? Escorts you need to settle your bill with?"

His chuckle vibrated through his entire body, rumbling against my cheek. I closed my eyes and savored the sensation.

"There's no one else, Molly. Not even a casual hookup. I've been single for over a year. Maybe longer. You've had a string of bad dates, but I've had a very long string of very bad relationships. I haven't been interested in getting involved with a woman since... after Sarita opened."

I needed to see the truth in his eyes, so I tipped my head back and let my gaze meet his. "Really?"

"What can I say? It took a feisty graphic designer biting my head off in my own, very successful restaurant to catch my eye."

"You're lying," I accused him because I was terrified that he wasn't. "You have not been interested in me for that long."

"Intrigued," he amended. "Absolutely. From the second I met you, I was intrigued. Although I kept my distance out of respect for Killian and Vera. I wasn't interested in anything serious and I didn't know you well enough to feel you out. I couldn't hurt you and then expect everything to stay chill with Killian. I've been attracted to you since the second I met you, but it wasn't till later that I was willing to risk pissing him off to chase you."

Chase me. Had he been chasing me? I closed my eyes briefly and imagined his car rides and emails and hiring me for every possible thing in his life. *Oh, my god, Ezra Baptiste had been chasing me!* And I had been ~~completely dense~~ totally oblivious! Could I get a life do-over to go back and savor that time??? "When did that change?"

He lifted one shoulder and stepped closer. "I don't know. I can't pinpoint one exact moment, only that my interest marinated slowly until I saw you in the kitchen with Wyatt before the engagement party. I hated myself for letting other people's potential opinions get in the way. I hated Wyatt for making you smile and laugh, and for inviting you into my space. I hated you for not seeming to notice me or be able to tolerate me. From that moment, it was my mission to get your attention, to get you to notice me." He smiled that gentle, unassuming smile again, the one that made me all melty inside. "Although I'm not sure how well it worked. I used Meg to try to impress you, but you had the party handled without her. I tried to wow you with my wine cellar. You weren't interested. I showed you my car. Again, you didn't care. I've about exhausted my resources, Maverick. And I think you've given me a complex."

Well, I just died. I was dead. This had to be death. Because Ezra could not have said what he just did. "I was already impressed by you! That's why I didn't react to anything else. Did you not notice I was a basket case around you? And I assumed you were just showing off to be a douche!"

The high planes of his cheeks heated and his smile was both embarrassed and adorable. "That does not bode well for my reputation."

I laughed, and maybe it was a little hysterical, but he was talking crazy and my rational mind could not wrap around the words that he was speaking. "It worked," I promised him. "Whatever you did, worked."

Something clattered in the kitchen, jolting us with the violence of it. He groaned and dropped his forehead to mine. "That sounded expensive. I should probably go check on it."

Holding back a smile, I told him, "Go. But don't terrorize them too much."

Standing up to his full height he asked, "Do you have everything you need? Can I get you something?"

A curling fear of dread interrupted the most exciting forty-five minutes of my dating life and I nearly winced from the sharpness of it. "Was hiring me to do this mural part of your seduction?"

He shook his head—it looked like he was trying to recover from my conversational whiplash. "What?"

194

"Did you only hire me to do this job because you want to get in my pants?"

A slow, promising smirk lifted one corner of his mouth. If I hadn't been so panicked, I would have spontaneously combusted from it.

"Is getting in your pants an option?" he asked.

"That absolutely depends on your answer," I countered. "And I'll be able to tell if you're lying." He raised one eyebrow. "You're very transparent," I explained. Which wasn't at all true, but it was better to let him think I had the upper hand. Maybe then he would believe it.

"The mural had nothing to do with us," he answered sincerely. "And everything to do with your talent. I'm definitely interested in you, Molly, but I'm also a businessman. I wouldn't have hired you to change the entire interior of my struggling restaurant if I didn't think you would be able to make a seriously positive change."

My fears abated and I sucked in a steadying breath. "Sorry, I freaked out at you. I just didn't want this to be a pity painting."

His lips twitched at my description. "It's anything but. I'm anxious to see what you come up with."

"What about the marketing account?" I demanded, half hoping he would tell me that was just a ploy to spend more time with me and that I sucked at design. Because then I would have a reason to quit STS and start over. I could pursue painting or basket weaving or beekeeping. Anything would be better than working with Henry at this point.

My argument was foolproof. Foolproof-ish.

"Again, Molly, I'm worried you don't see how talented you are. Since I've hired you, I've learned more about the ins and outs of advertising than the last firm taught me in the entire three years I employed them. You know your stuff. I'm truly lucky to have you working for the restaurants."

That was not the answer I was looking for, because it was leagues better. Those weren't the kind of criticisms that ended careers, those were the kinds of compliments that reignited the deep and abiding love for my job.

I hated the politics of STS and my bosses, and okay, fine, my clients too. But I loved the design part of it. I loved that creating graphics was the opposite of painting, and that was okay, because I enjoyed the details and the hours of perfecting a meaningful project. I hated the company I worked for, but damn I loved the grind.

Which probably made me ~~insane~~ different than the rest of the world.

"Fine," I groaned. "You win. I like you. A lot."

He chuckled again, and the sound was rich and chocolatey. I felt it all the way to my toes. He kissed my forehead. "That does make me a winner." He stepped back for real this time. "Holler if you need anything."

"Sure thing."

I watched him walk into the kitchen without moving. This was crazy. Right?

And if it wasn't crazy, what was it? What were *we*?

We hadn't even been on a date yet. We'd done nothing but kiss and confess feelings. I hadn't even had time to process this long enough to decide what I wanted from Ezra.

Besides more kisses obviously.

So maybe I didn't need to put a label on us yet. Or any kind of pressure to figure it out. I wasn't going to obsess over him or us or this. I was just going to let it happen. Because it was anybody's guess right now where we'd end up.

I was just Molly, remember? And he was Ezra F-something Baptiste.

I was just a girl trying to figure out what the hell I was doing with my life. And he was everything smooth and successful. He'd already figured out life. He'd already accomplished what he'd set out to do.

Oh my god. We were too different. This would never work.

It couldn't.

I was in so far over my head, I was already drowning and we'd only just put our feet in the water.

Spinning around to face the white wall, I tried to stay the panic rising up inside me like a tidal wave. My chest hurt as I struggled to even out my breathing. My hands started shaking and I reflexively reached for a paintbrush.

There, that feels better.

When my heartbeat didn't slow, I grabbed my palette too. I'd asked Ezra to repaint this wall before I started my mural, so a fresh coat of white gleamed back at me, like a lighthouse in the middle of a storm. A beacon calling me to safer waters.

I couldn't analyze Ezra right now without freaking out. I couldn't wrap my head around our conversation or his kisses or anything that had to do with him having feelings for me.

I pushed my rampant thoughts out of my head and turned them into an endless flow of inspiration instead. His dark hair, those endless eyes, his mysterious smile that made my soul move in a way that nothing else ever had turned into a relentless vision that I couldn't wait to chase.

After I'd sketched a rough outline with pencil, I returned to my palette. Reaching for the acrylics I'd bought just for this project, I spread them out

196

on my palette and began mixing the right shades. When I finally reached for my paintbrush, something significant settled inside me, lessening my fears and strengthening my spirit.

Painting became the protective cocoon that rescued me from the trembling fear I only just kept at bay. Ezra stopped by later to ask if I wanted to eat lunch with him, but I couldn't give up painting. I told him I was in the zone, but I would take a raincheck.

The truth was I'd only bought myself time. I had no idea if I would take a raincheck. I had no idea what I was doing at all with my life. Except for this mural, my life suddenly felt very much like it was careening out of control.

I needed to do something about that. Later. When I could think and obsess and freak out in private.

For now, I was going to paint.

Chapter Nineteen

We need to talk."

Instantly I was angry. Just like that I was bubbling with silent rage, my teeth dripping with venom, my claws growing and curling and preparing, ready for war. It was the voice. And the person. And every single thing about him.

I slowly lifted my glare to find the Little Tucker hovering over me. I had been in the middle of a graphic and he'd interrupted just as I was trying to place the emblem in the exact spot to look life changing. But his voice had startled me enough that my hand had jerked, dragging it to the upper left corner, far away from my target. He'd ruined thirty minutes of work.

I contemplated ignoring him as I gripped the mouse with refreshed determination. Earlier in the week I'd sent an email to Doris from HR, explaining what had happened with Henry and how I felt harassed by him on an almost daily basis. I hadn't expected an immediate return email since she was still on her cruise, but two hours later she'd responded. By telling me that it sounded like a colossal misunderstanding and that I should respectfully bring up the matter with him if I ever felt uncomfortable again. She was confident we could work things out without her. She was positive Henry would never do it again. ~~She wanted me to leave her the hell alone so she could get back to sun tanning on the lido deck.~~

199

"About what?" I asked as I went back to staring at the computer screen. Graphic development was ten percent skill, twenty percent taste, thirty percent ability to keep your hand steady and three hundred percent mentally willing everything into place.

The numbers work. Don't ask questions.

"I haven't gotten your Black Soul updates, sweet cheeks," he snarled. "I needed them three hours ago and they're nowhere to be seen."

A nervous feeling ticked inside me. I had ignored an email from Henry this morning in favor of working on Ezra's stuff all day. I was starting to make headway with his websites so I was feeling extra inspired to do something that I could show him.

Since I'd been avoiding Ezra since Saturday, I was still fuzzy on when that would be. Sometime in the very distant, very ambiguous future, whenever I worked up the courage to see him again, he was going to be so impressed.

To be fair, he hadn't made a huge effort to reach out to me either, so I felt vindicated. In like a really depressing way.

Victory! As I cried into my ice cream every night.

~~Not kidding.~~ Just kidding.

Instead of dwelling on my ability to ruin every good thing, I'd thrown myself entirely into his project so I could impress him with my design genius. I would then proceed to ignore him from now until the end of time.

Fine, I had been the one to retreat Saturday, slinking out of Bianca without saying goodbye. And fine, I hadn't made any effort to reach out to him or email him or text him or try to have any contact with him whatsoever since then. But it was Wednesday. Wednesday! He'd said he liked me and then let this go until Wednesday without even a work email!

Also, I hated being this girl.

I wanted the record to show, I loathed being this undecided, fickle, ~~crazy person~~ terrified female that didn't know what she wanted or who she wanted or when she wanted it.

But I couldn't seem to talk myself down from this ~~psychotic~~ ledge.

I couldn't even paint my way out of these feelings. And believe me... I'd tried.

I barely spared Henry a look when I explained, "I've been really busy with the EFB Enterprises account. Sorry. I'll get to the updates in a bit."

"I need them now," Henry gritted through clenched teeth.

The second meeting with Black Soul wasn't until next week and all I had to do was change the color scheme they didn't like. And no, for those interested, I hadn't used gray and yellow.

200

I'd used black and white with some striking reds. It had a vintage Guns and Roses vibe to it. The suits wanted something subtler with softer colors. Basically, I should have gone with gray and yellow to begin with.

It would be a pain to go back through everything and re-shade, but I didn't have to create anything new. I just needed a few focused hours to get it done.

Giving up on the graphic in front of me until Henry had slithered off, I pushed away from my desk and bit back a growl. "I don't have them ready for you right now. But if they're that important I can walk away from what I'm working on and start them."

Henry's expression turned sour, reminding me of a petulant child. "I had a feeling two major projects were going to be too much for you. You're not ready for a lead role yet, baby. I told my dad that he should have let me run the EFB account. "

I resisted, barely, the urge to punch him in the throat. Was he seriously attacking my work ethic? If I had slacked on anything it was the Black Soul project and that was all his fault. And I would be more than happy to have a conversation with *his dad* about why I wasn't totally enthusiastic about working with his deviant of a son.

But to Henry, I remained professional, poised, and only mildly bitchy. "They're not too much," I said coolly. "I've carved out plenty of time for each, but I was planning on starting the Black Soul touchups later in the week since my EFB account is on a tighter timeline. Why do you need them right now?"

Ignoring my question and my explanation and my entire A-plus work history, he tapped his fingers on the chest high partition and said, "I want those updates before you leave for the day. Got it?"

Clenching my teeth together to keep from ~~choking him~~ saying something I would regret, I nodded once. "Fine."

"Good girl." He smirked.

Expecting him to leave, I was surprised when he stayed. He stood there for another minute staring directly at my chest. He didn't even try to hide it. I'd taken to wearing the most modest, dowdy clothing I owned to work. The chambray button-up paired with the Aztec printed maxi skirt I was wearing were hardly revealing, and yet Henry salivated all over my cubicle like he was front and center at a strip club.

"Do you mind?" I asked bluntly.

He reluctantly lifted his lascivious gaze and winked at me, then *finally* walked away.

That's when I threw up all over my computer. Okay, maybe not all over my computer, but at least a little bit in my mouth. *God, he was such an asshole!*

A gross, disgusting, asshole.

After he disappeared, I contemplated running to HR again and demanding that they file a report for his employee record. I wasn't imagining his gross behavior.

He was out of line.

At least, to my personal standards, he felt very, very out of line. Maybe Doris hadn't understood before. Maybe she hadn't realized how out of control he was. I knew she wanted to protect her own job and felt that writing up a formal complaint about the boss's son maybe wasn't the best way to do that. But she couldn't ignore his behavior anymore. He was a liability. And pissing me off!

I stood up and walked over to her desk, but she still wasn't there and writing a handwritten complaint wasn't going to get me anywhere if she still wouldn't be back for several days. Spinning around, I observed the whole office, trying to decide what to do. I spotted Mr. Tucker's office and wondered about going directly to him. What would he say? What would he do? Was I prepared to accuse his son of sexual harassment directly to his face?

No, no I was not.

When I got back to my desk I opened all of my Black Soul files. But I just wasn't mentally ready to start working on them yet. The last thing I wanted to do was give Henry what he wanted. He'd interrupted my entire day. Plus, now my planner was all out of order. He was the absolute worst!

Out of spite, I picked up my cell phone.

Henry would get the updates when I was finished with them. Which might be today. Or maybe tomorrow. Or maybe I wouldn't do them after all and he could make the adjustments himself.

Wasn't that a crazy thought?

Vera answered on the third ring. "What up, Molls? Are you at work?"

She was in a kitchen somewhere if the sound of clanking dishes, pots and pans was any indication. Immediately, I felt better, more relaxed. When everything felt crazy, jumbled and out of my control, she was the pillar that kept me anchored to sanity.

"Yes. Remind me why though?" I begged her, hoping to keep the real emotion out of my voice. "I vaguely remember winning the lottery. Tell me it was real."

"First, stop buying scratch tickets. They never solve your problems. Second, you love health insurance. That's why you're at work." Her voice gentled. "Have you had a bad day?"

"Super bad," I admitted. "Unless those scratch tickets end up paying off."

"They won't," she laughed. "Sorry to burst your bubble."

I groaned. "Pretty sure my bubble was already popped."

"Well, hey, I have news that might perk you up."

"Give it to me," I sighed. "Give me the will to work again."

Vera's laugh indicated that she was super excited to share her information with me. My curiosity was instantly piqued.

I heard a door open and close as she moved to a quieter space. Her voice dropped low and she said, "I overheard Killian on the phone with Ezra. Apparently, he wants to take you on a legit date. He wanted Killian's advice on how not to screw this up with you."

"Oh, no," I whispered. "Oh, no!"

Of course Vera knew everything about Ezra and me. Because I'd told her everything. There was nothing else to do after my worst-case scenario reaction on Saturday than invite my BFF over, ply her with wine and ice cream, and confess all of the kissing, flirting, and running away like a giant chicken I did. Afterward, she'd graciously analyzed every single nuance with me until she was convinced we were going to have a double wedding—our childhood dream—and I confirmed she was insane.

She had reacted exactly like I'd expected her to—with massive congratulations and a wedding lecture like I had never heard before.

She had so many opinions on flowers and dresses and groom's cakes. But after that, I had shared all of my fears and concerns. She had sympathized like I knew she would and together we'd decided that I should calm down and take this one day at a time.

I didn't have to have all of the answers with Ezra right this second. I didn't have to know how every single thing would play out or what would happen to us or if we would get past the first date. I just needed to make the best of today.

It was wise advice that I immediately took to heart.

I had been ~~failing miserably~~ doing that until just now.

"Molly, you can't hide from him forever." Her voice dropped to a whisper indicating that her fiancé was in listening distance. "From what I heard Killian say to him, I'm not even sure Ezra realizes you're hiding from him. I think he's just been so focused on work that he might think this is normal. No offense! Things at Bianca are tense."

"Son of a bitch," I growled. It wasn't that I wanted to make this great big I'm-avoiding-you statement. It just complicated my feelings for him. I'd wrongly assumed he was avoiding me on purpose, because of some flaw or miscommunication. But if he'd been swamped with work and I'd turned this into something that it was not, then the stupid softening of my heart and anticipatory sighing of my girly bits could be a problem.

I had already decided that we couldn't date. I didn't even want to date him. Okay, fine, that was a dirty, filthy lie. But I only wanted to date him in theory. I couldn't actually date him. Not if I enjoyed an intact heart and not having to hear about a fabulous new EFB Enterprises restaurant named Molly.

Vera made an impatient sound in the back of her throat. "Are you really that worried about going on one date with the man? I mean, Molly, he's freaking gorgeous. And he's a really good guy. He's dependable and loyal and secretly nice. At least get a free meal and solid make out from him. You're too uptight these days. You need a good lay."

"Oh, my god. Vera May Delane! Don't be gross!"

She laughed on her end of the phone. "Come on, be honest. When's the last time you got some good, mind-blowing action."

Wrinkling my nose, I confessed, "Um, college? No, it was before then. Er, that guy I dated from senior chemistry? What was his name... Josh?"

"Jed?" Vera guessed too. "Jake!"

"Jake Begley. Good lord, he was hot."

"And dumb. Remember how he thought the periodic table was an actual table. He kept looking for it in the chem lab all year."

I snorted. "That's not true."

"Mmm, pretty sure it's true."

"Well, the dummy could kiss. That's all I cared about."

"Do you hear yourself? Your last good kiss was in high school, Molly! That's like a crime against your adult self! You deserve a hot date with expensive food and good drinks and a sexy, sexy man."

"Who's a sexy man?" I heard Killian ask in the background.

Embarrassed that he'd heard so much of Vera's side of the conversation, I lay my forehead on the edge of my desk and talked to my shoes. "I don't want to lead him on." Or me.

"He's a big boy," she argued. "He'll be okay. Or not. The disappointment of not wooing the most incredible woman he's ever met might be his undoing. But either way, you can't blame yourself. If you're not into him, you're not into him and so be it. But you should at least let yourself try."

That wasn't it at all. I *was* into Ezra—too into him. So into him I knew I was headed for epic disappointment and the utter annihilation of my heart. "Vera, I'm scared."

She was silent for a few moments, then finally she said, "Cook for him."

"Uh, what?"

"Cook for him," she ordered.

"Vera, I said I wanted to keep my distance, not commit accidental homicide. I'm just not ready to go on a real date."

"So cook for him," she repeated. "Then you won't feel the whole date-induced pressure because you're at some super fancy restaurant and he'll have to face the cold, hard truth that you hate food. That might be enough of a deal breaker for him to back off all by himself."

"Hey!" I protested.

"At the very least, it will buy you time before you have to speak to him again."

"Okay, maybe that's not a terrible idea."

"It's a genius idea!" she gloated. "You're welcome. As payment, Killian and I will accept the reservations at whatever exclusive restaurant Ezra was planning on taking you to. I think that is only fair."

"Oh, you don't think he would have just made a reservation at one of his own?"

She barked out a laugh. "Because that's romantic? No, Molly. He wasn't going to take you to one of the restaurants he owns named after one of his ex-girlfriends. He's not that tacky. It would have been someplace good though. For sure."

"If he asks, and that's a big if, I'll see what I can do about the reservation."

"You're the best!"

"I know. You're also the best." I felt instantly lighter after talking to Vera. Lighter, but also heavier. I was no closer to having this whole Ezra thing figured out than before the phone call, but I had a friend that always had my back and was willing to listen to every single one of my freak outs. It was okay to suck at relationships as long as I was good at this one. "Thanks, Vere."

"Let me know what happens." She told someone she would be right there. "I gotta go."

"Me too."

We hung up and I ~~kind of~~ tried to focus on work. It wasn't easy. In fact, it was the hardest thing I did all day. By five o'clock, I was exhausted from staring at shades of gray and trying to figure out which one would appeal to the widest audience.

Ugh.

"You leaving?" I asked Emily as she gathered her things.

She wrinkled her nose. "Oh, yes. Want to walk out with me?"

"Yes, please!" I quickly clicked the right buttons, sending Henry the updated, but not final, versions of the graphics and shut down my desk. Emily waited for me to put my computer in my bag and sling it over my shoulder before she started walking toward the elevator bank.

"How's the Black Soul project?" she asked when we were in an elevator heading down to the parking garage.

"Terrible," I groaned. "It's not at all what I thought it was going to be."

"That sucks," she sympathized. Her expression shifted and she waggled her eyebrows at me. "But at least you're getting some action, right? Henry's such a gentle lover."

My entire body shuddered at her joke. "Oh my god, that's so gross. That man is a lawsuit waiting to happen."

She turned serious again. "Wait, he hasn't tried to—"

I quickly shook my head. I didn't know why I was so worried about her thinking the wrong thing. If he'd tried anything again with me, it would be his fault not mine. So why was I so worried about people thinking the wrong thing? I was the innocent person in this whole debacle. He was the assailant. I shouldn't even want to stick up for him. Still, I said, "No, he hasn't tried to touch me again, since I emailed Doris. But he's always undressing me with his eyes and staring at my chest. He might not be touching me, but whatever he is doing is just as bad."

"I can't believe this hasn't gotten back to his dad. Mr. Tucker would shut that shit down so fast."

"You think?" For some reason, I wasn't so sure.

"For the sake of his business," Emily nodded as she went on. "He doesn't want a lawsuit or a bad reputation just because his son is a pervert."

That was true. Even if Mr. Tucker didn't believe everything I had to say, surely he would step in just to avoid legal action. Sexual harassment wasn't a small thing and Henry was set up to take over the entire company in a few years. Maybe I should revisit going over HR's head.

My phone dinged when we got off the elevator, so I pulled it out of my purse on my way to my car. "See you tomorrow, Em."

"Later, babe," she called back.

I threw my laptop in the back and settled into the driver's seat with my phone in hand. An email had popped up and I almost didn't check it because I was sure that it was Henry giving me shit for the work I'd just uploaded.

It wasn't Henry though. It was Ezra. And the subject read: Hey.

Not able to contain my curiosity, I opened the email against my better judgment.

Call me when you get a minute.
~Ezra

I drove home first, not wanting to seem super available. Plus, the parking garage got terrible reception. Plus, plus, I had to talk myself into it and work myself up and find some courage in my terrified little soul to push the buttons.

When I got home, I changed into leggings and settled on my couch with a salad I picked up on the way home. Then I called Ezra.

For a second I didn't think he was going to answer. The phone rang just long enough that I prepared myself to hang up before it asked for a message.

But then he answered, his voice clear, deep and tender. "Molly."

God, why couldn't he just say hello like a normal person? It would be so much easier on my flailing heart. "Hi, Ezra."

"I didn't want to interrupt you at work."

"I just got home."

"Are you coming in to paint tonight?" There was something in his voice that sounded like hope and it did damaging things to my resolve to keep my distance.

"I am not," I told him trying not to sound disappointed. "I didn't want to interrupt your dinner service."

"Oh, well, when do you think you'll be in again?"

Was this all he wanted to talk about? When I would be back to paint his mural? I was less nervous now. "Saturday morning, I think."

"Well, damn. I have a thing Saturday so I won't be there."

I hadn't realized he needed to be there. "Is it okay that I still come in if you're not there?"

"It's fine," he assured me, that smooth, rich voice of his chasing me through the phone. "Bianca is yours for as long as you need her. Come in whenever you'd like. I just haven't seen you all week."

His disappointment came out of nowhere, kicking me right in the butterflies. "Oh."

"So I think we should fix that," he continued. "Are you free Sunday night?"

"Um, to paint?" I slammed my eyes shut at my effort to play cool. What was wrong with me?

His chuckle was genuine and rumbly, and *God, why did I want to avoid this man again*? "No, not to paint. To go on a date. With me."

I couldn't think of the right thing to say so I sat there silent for way too long. Clearing my throat I went for totally smooth. "Uh, s-sure. That sounds great." I stared at my freezer. Forget the salad. I needed to go straight to the ice cream tonight.

He was unruffled by my inability to be as cool as him. "Can I pick you up?"

Vera's plan blared through my head and I sat up with more confidence. "How about I cook for you and we stay in?"

I expected him to argue with me, sure that he'd heard the rumors of my tragic cooking and would do whatever it took to escape a meal that could end in death—or possibly serious food poisoning.

Instead, he let out a sigh of relief and said, "Actually, that sounds amazing. I'd love that."

Softening, I smiled and opened up all at once, I relaxed into a feeling that this was right, that this would be good. Something like anticipation and hope and feelings of rightness. "How about six?"

"Do you need me to bring anything?"

"Wine," I told him. "Bring lots of wine." Because when we couldn't eat anything, we would at least be able to drink.

"See you Sunday, Molly."

"Okay, Ezra."

I painted that night. Cloudy skies with sun crowned horizons. Eyes that were deep and mysterious and soft. A delicate hand cradled in a strong, masculine one. All things that would have previously made me roll my eyes and embitter my cold, cruel, cynical heart.

Now I was halfway to infatuated and my painting was evidence that I'd lost my mind completely.

And maybe, possibly... my heart.

Chapter Twenty

*S*unday night came too quickly. One second I'd been dodging Henry at work and spending all of Saturday working on Bianca's mural. The next, I had done my hair like whoa, spent thirty minutes picking out the right lip stain, and dressed in my new distressed skinny jeans and sheer, lacy black tunic with strappy cami underneath.

My outfit sounded casual, but it had taken me the entire week to pick it out. Ugh. Why wasn't the not-showered-ratty-pajama look in?

Society was the worst.

Feminists unite!

Also, lazy people.

I would also take homebodies.

Now I stood at my stove, slaving away over spaghetti and meatballs and panicking because Ezra was going to be here any minute. And I knew I had gotten myself into this mess, that it had been my stupid idea, but now that the time was almost here to push Ezra away with my terrible cooking, I found that I didn't want him to know I couldn't handle myself in the kitchen.

Like at all.

I'd even tried tonight!

Spaghetti and meatballs was something I could usually throw together. I mean, how hard was it to boil water and pour a jar of sauce into a pan? Not hard. Not hard at all.

But I'd taken so long to get ready that I'd gotten a late start on the meatballs. In order to cook them quicker so they could have time to marinate in the marinara I'd bought, I had turned the heat up too high and burned the shit out of them. The onions I'd tried to sauté with them looked like slimy black slugs. I had been under the impression that if I kept cooking the onions they would caramelize. But that theory had been so very wrong.

I was pretty sure they were going to taste like an old cigarette. But I didn't have time to start over.

They were currently simmering in marinara sauce while I prayed that the tomatoes would hide how blackened and unappetizing they were. Not to mention the ~~charcoal lumps~~ meatballs. They were in no better shape. I'd slammed a lid on the pan so I didn't have to look at it. Also, to protect my outfit from the spitting red sauce.

It was probably poisonous by now anyway.

Or nuclear.

To add to the chaos, my noodles stuck to the bottom of their pot and I'd over-dressed the salad. The giant bowl I'd grabbed at the store earlier was approximately one-fourth of the way filled with soggy spring mix.

"I can fix this," I told my colander, setting it in the sink and preparing it for the noodles I needed to drain in approximately two minutes. I started to hunt for more lettuce in an effort to give the salad volume when a knock sounded on my door.

Ezra. *Damn it!* Of all the nights to be on time.

I'd texted him earlier today with my apartment number and door code to get in the building. Because apparently, he terrified me in a relationship sense, but I trusted him enough that I didn't think he was a serial killer.

I spun around, pressing a hand to my forehead and wishing I could make this all just disappear. Was it too much to tell him I had been vandalized? That this was the work of a vindictive neighbor? *Don't start sweating. Don't start sweating. Whatever you do don't start sweating!*

Oh my god, I'm a disaster.

Finally, I faced the door, still contemplating shutting off all the lights and pretending nobody was home.

My feet betrayed me by walking toward the entryway. My hands joined the mutiny and somehow, despite what my brain was telling them to do, unlocked the deadbolt and opened the door for Ezra.

He stood there waiting patiently in casual, dark wash jeans and a navy-blue oxford with the sleeves rolled to his forearms. There was a bottle of wine in his hand and a half smile on his handsome face.

Be still my heart.

It had only been a little over a week since we'd been together, but the sight of him here, at my apartment, looking like he always did, made my breath catch.

"Hi," he said.

Hi.

He'd said hi. Not Molly. Not just my name. But hi.

The way he said my name always did funny things to my insides—like turn them into warm honey. But this simple hi was shockingly intimate. It wasn't bold, familiar or demanding. It was gentle. And tentative. And sexy as hell.

God, *this man*.

"Hi," I managed to return breathlessly. "Come on inside?"

He stepped in my apartment and set the wine down on the side table. The door clicked shut behind him, then his mouth found mine without hesitation. I wasn't even sure how it had happened or when he'd pulled me against him or how I'd gotten pushed against the wall. But there we were, kissing hello in my hallway.

It started slowly as we explored each other again, relearning the touch and taste of each other. He tasted like mint and smelled so very good. I couldn't get enough of him or this kiss. I wanted more. Needed more.

Apparently, so did he. Our innocent hello kiss quickly turned into a building appetite for each other. His mouth was addicting, and the way it moved against mine made my toes curl and my belly heat. My hands landed on his broad shoulders while his wrapped around my waist, pulling me against him. I willingly went, letting my chest press against his, enjoying every inch of his hard, toned body and the way he bent down to meet my mouth.

His tongue brushed over my bottom lip and I opened my mouth, letting him deepen the kiss. My teeth grazed his bottom lip, knowing it would drive him crazy. I was inordinately pleased when it did. He groaned in the back of his throat, making a sound that I felt all the way to my core.

His hands splayed over my ribs, his thumbs resting just beneath my bra. He moved his kisses to the line of my jaw, trailing down my throat. I lost the ability to think when he kissed me like this...to remember all the reasons I had been afraid of seeing him again. We were nothing but lips and tongues and teeth. And as his hands got braver and braver, I thought I would explode with anticipation.

"It's a good thing we decided to have dinner here," he murmured against my skin.

Reality crashed over me like ice cold water, releasing me from the spell his mouth had cast. "Dinner!" I pushed him away and sprinted to the

211

kitchen, readying myself for the horror that awaited me. "Oh no!" My noodles bubbled over, splashing big drops of water all over the burner. The sauce hissed angrily and I realized I had forgotten to turn it down. "Oh no!" I repeated when I remembered the garlic bread in the oven. Not wasting time with pot holders, I dove for it, retrieving a dark brown, oblong rock instead of bread.

I juggled it back and forth before eventually tossing the inedible hunk of carbs in the sink.

Staring at my burned meatballs, charred bread, overly-cooked noodles and limp lettuce made me seriously reevaluate what I was doing with my life.

"Awesome," I snarled at the unused colander.

"Is everything okay?" Ezra asked carefully from behind me.

A hysterical laugh bubbled out of me. No. Everything was not okay. But I didn't even know where to start or how to explain. I mean, the evidence spoke for itself. But what was I going to do now?

I made an exasperated sound.

Ezra peered over my shoulder into the sink. "Was that for dinner?"

Dropping my head into my hands, I tried to think of a solution, some way out of this mess, but nothing came. I had zero ideas except this would be a fantastic time for a zombie apocalypse to breakout.

The worst part was now I didn't have a best friend because I was going to have to kill Vera for even suggesting that I cook for Ezra. This was her fault. What had she been thinking?

What had I been thinking listening to her?

"I ruined it," I admitted to my hands. "It's totally ruined."

He made a sound that could have been a laugh or possibly a wince. Maybe it was the sound he made before he ran away. "It can't be that bad."

I moved out of the way so he could look for himself. Crossing my arms over my chest, I waited for him, in all his restaurant owning glory, to determine time of death on this solid but failed effort.

He poked at the bread. "Oh," he said. Then he moved over to the noodles. They had been soaking in the pot since I'd given up the idea of draining and serving them. "Huh." Passing by the salad, he sniffed at it. "I don't... I'm not sure what to say." He reached over and flicked off the burner that had still been heating the meatballs. "Do I want to know what's under there?"

I lifted my head and met his amused gaze. "I'm fine if we want to leave that one a mystery."

He chuckled, surveying the messy, ruined scene once again. "Molly, I... You... What went wrong?"

My eyes widened as the full weight of my bad choices were realized. I had invited Ezra Baptiste to my apartment knowing I couldn't cook. The man owned four of the most successful restaurants in Durham. He sometimes filled in at Bianca because he "knew his way around a kitchen." He had probably eaten five star meals every day for the last decade of his life. At the very least, multiple times a week.

This was the man I had invited over to scare away with my cooking. Mission accomplished.

"I-I don't even know where to begin," I told him. God, this was humiliating. My entire face flamed red, spreading a splotchy blush from the roots of my hair to the tips of my toes. I pressed my hand to my mouth and wrapped my other arm around my waist. I needed someone to console me. Apparently, that someone was myself.

Would it be totally out of line to make him leave? It seemed like a better option than having him witness this total humiliation.

Finally, when the silence had stretched to uncomfortable and neither of us had any idea what to say to make this better, I blurted, "It's your fault! You started kissing me and... and then this happened!"

Our gazes clashed across the small space between us and something shifted inside him, something widening and deepening and spreading wings that were bigger than my entire apartment.

He smiled, prompting me to say, "Everything was time sensitive and you... distracted me."

"Don't move." He walked back to the entryway and returned with the bottle of wine he'd brought with him. "We should open this." He looked around for a second, then asked. "Do you have a cork screw?"

Silently, I walked over and retrieved the bottle opener from a drawer. I handed it to him. He took it from me and held it up to examine it.

"This is a nice one," he commented.

I blinked at him. Was he really moving on this quickly? We were surrounded by terrible food! And messy dishes. Wasn't his professional integrity insulted?

"I can't cook," I confessed. "But I take my wine very seriously."

He stayed focused on the task of uncorking the bottle he'd brought, but his mouth widened into a smile. "I thought it was my fault that this happened."

Nerves hit my stomach and I felt like doubling over to stop the sensation. "It is." I pulled two glasses down from the cupboard and set them on the countertop next to him. "But more accurately, I'm terrible in

the kitchen. I can't even do simple things like toast, or cookies, or...
spaghetti."

He lifted that so intense gaze again, searching my face and my eyes
and my soul. "Then why did you offer to make dinner tonight? We could
have gone anywhere. You didn't have to stress out over this."

I bit down hard on my lip, trying to figure out how to spin my decisions
so I didn't sound crazy. "I underestimated my propensity for disaster."

Ezra laughed again. "I think I did too."

"Sorry," I whispered to him. "You don't have to stay if you don't
want—"

He cut me off before I could finish my thought. "I'm going to stop you
right there. Dinner was only an excuse to see you again, Molly. You could
have served goldfish and I would have pretended to love it. I'm not here
because I want you to impress me with your cooking. You already impress
me because of who you are. You impress me with your knack for business.
You impress me with your painting, and design style and mural making.
You impress me with your kindness, your sense of humor and the way you
nibble on your bottom lip when you're deciding what you want. Molly, if I
wanted a chef to make me a good meal, I would have stayed at work. I'm
here because I want to spend the evening with you. And no other
reason."

I suddenly found it difficult to breathe. "Oh."

He stopped fiddling with the wine bottle and stepped over to me,
pulling my hands into his. "I hope you didn't feel pressured to cook for
me. I would hate to know I'm the reason..." He paused to look around at
the mess in the sink and on the stove and all over the counters. "Your
kitchen exploded."

A trembling sigh of relief moved through me. I'd wanted to scare him
away with my bad cooking, but I'd ended up falling harder and faster and
deeper for him. Did he even know what he'd done? Did he know how
important his words were?

"I don't know what I was thinking," I told him honestly. Because it was
true. It had been a terribly stupid idea. Not just because it hadn't worked,
but because I didn't want to push this man away. I had great big fears
when it came to him, to us. I was filled with debilitating uncertainty. I
didn't know if I trusted whatever this was between us to last. But I did
know I enjoyed spending time with him. I liked the way he made me feel
when we were together. And I liked the way he looked at me, and
touched me and kissed me. I liked Ezra Baptiste way more than I knew
what to do with.

And I wanted to see where this thing between us was going to go.

I wanted to know him.

He stepped away to pour a glass of wine for me. "It's impressive though," he chuckled. "I've never seen so many things go wrong at once."

"I know it's hard to believe, but I was born this way. It's all natural talent." I took a sip of my wine and then another sip. I tried to talk myself out of gulping the entire glass, but it was too good to stop.

Half his mouth lifted in that crooked smile that made my belly quiver. "How about we clean this up and I cook us something instead."

"You can't do that."

"I can," he argued. "I promise not to burn the bread." He looked at the salad again like it was the most offensive thing of all. "Or turn the lettuce into soup."

I snorted on a surprised laugh. "I meant, you literally can't make us dinner. I have nothing but cereal and yogurt and maybe some cheese."

"That can't be true." He turned around and walked straight to my refrigerator. Yanking open the door, he leaned inside and moved the milk around. "What is the opposite of lactose intolerant?"

"Lactose tolerant?"

He shot me a look over his shoulder. "What I'm saying is, I've never seen so much dairy in one refrigerator. You literally only have dairy."

"I also have oranges," I told him. "And I think some grapes."

Ezra stood up and opened my freezer. He pulled out the Mint Chocolate Chip I'd been saving for a rainy day. "Oh, look. More dairy."

"Hey! That's a different variation at least. I should get credit for that."

He moved over to my pantry, rummaging around until he came out empty handed. "You weren't kidding. I can't even make eggs."

"Sorry, I don't do the whole big shopping thing. I prefer to make several intrusive, bothersome trips a week. This time, I only got enough ingredients to ruin them all."

"How do you survive like this, Molly?" He looked genuinely concerned, but I didn't know what to tell him. I had a system that worked for me.

Sure, it would have been beneficial to introduce more vegetables to my diet and maybe some fiber, but let's review what happened with the spaghetti. It was safer for everybody if I just stuck to microwaveable meals.

And the dairy of course.

"I'm really good at ordering Chinese," I told him.

His eyebrows furrowed. "How about this. I'll start on the dishes and you order the Chinese."

My chest warmed, my heart expanding to accommodate a flurry of new emotions. "What do you want?"

215

"You pick," he ordered. "Show me just how good you really are."

I shook my head at him, but did as he asked. When I came back to the kitchen he had already thrown away all of the food and started on the dishes. I stepped up next to him and reached for the noodle pot to dry.

"You don't have to do this," I told him.

He stared intently at the salad bowl he was scrubbing. "I know."

"But you're going to do it anyway?"

"We all have our domestic talents, Molly. Washing dishes is mine."

I laughed, thinking he was joking. "Why don't I believe you?"

He turned his head, giving me the full force of all his broody intensity. "It's true," he insisted. "Killian always had to be the one to help make dinner. That left me on cleanup duty."

The heaviness in his statement surprised me. "I forget that you guys grew up together."

He turned back to the bowl. "Yep."

I hadn't meant to kill the conversation, but I was also curious to know more about his childhood. I knew he came from foster care. I knew his mom had died. I knew his dad had died later. But those were random facts anyone could Google. I wanted to know the details, the specifics. I wanted to know so much more than the highlights.

But I didn't know how to ask those questions, so instead, I said, "It's cool you guys are still friends. Vera and I grew up together too. I can't even imagine what my life would look like without her."

"Yeah, I'm not sure I feel the same way about Killian."

I laughed because I hoped he was making a joke. He didn't. We fell silent again. Realizing he wasn't going to offer any information about his childhood, I decided to pry. "So what was it like growing up with Killian? Was he as scary back then as he is now?"

"Worse," Ezra grunted. "He's always been a cocky bastard, but back then he was always picking fights and causing trouble. He hated everything and everyone. Even me. Maybe especially me."

"Why you?"

He shut off the water and dried his hands on my kitchen towel. Settling back against the counter after he set the towel down, he crossed his arms over his chest and dropped his voice reverently. "Because I had known my mom. He hated that I'd gotten to live so much of my life with a parent. But he had no idea. I still think he's clueless. He lost his parents, but he didn't lose them, you know? Not like I did."

"What do you mean?"

216

My chest pinched at the desolate look in his expression. I immediately wanted to throw my arms around him and tell him it was going to be okay.

"My mom and I were close," Ezra explained. "Losing her... losing her was like losing everything." His gaze met mine. He tapped his chest with a flattened palm. "It still hurts. After all these years, I still feel it here as sharply as I did the day it happened."

I licked dry lips and tried to swallow past the lump in my chest. "How did she die?"

"Breast cancer."

"I'm sorry, Ezra. I'm so sorry."

He reached out and linked our hands. I hadn't been expecting him to need comfort, but I wished I'd given it to him before he asked. His grief was so palpable, so real and heavy that I had been momentarily paralyzed by it, lost in the swirling emotions he didn't try to hide.

I squeezed his hands. "What was she like?"

"Kind," he answered with a tender smile. "She was kind and thoughtful. We were very poor and when she got sick, things only got worse. But she always managed to take care of the people in our life that had less than we did. She always remembered birthdays and holidays, and she reached out when people had a need. She had this beauty that everyone was attracted to. Not just outwardly, but her soul drew people in. And funny. She had the best sense of humor. Even at the end."

"Your dad wasn't around at all?"

Something harsh and unforgiving flashed in his expression, making me regret the question. "No, my dad didn't show up until years later. Which I will always be grateful for." There was a weighted pause and then he said so softly I almost didn't hear him, "He didn't deserve her." He blinked, breaking out of a memory. "What about you? What are your parents like?"

It was all I could do not to pull my hands from his and curl into myself. There were only a few topics I liked less than my parents. But he had been so open and honest with me, it was only fair to return the favor. "They're... difficult," I admitted. "And really different."

"What do you mean?"

Avoiding his probing gaze, I confessed, "My mom is a crazy workaholic that thinks everyone in the world should work at least as hard as her. And my dad is... the opposite." I didn't want to bring up my dad's lack of job yet. Whenever I told people that my dad was out of work, they immediately started placing all of their judgments on him. "He's laid back," I finally said.

217

"What do they do?"

Apparently, I wasn't going to be able to skirt around the conversation after all. "My mom runs an elementary school lunchroom. She's in charge of the kitchen. And my dad is currently unemployed. He was recently let go."

Ezra made a face. "Oh that's hard. I'm sorry. What's his field?"

"Uh, sales, mostly."

"What does he sell?"

"Everything."

He laughed, thinking I'd made a joke. "What?"

"He sells everything. Or he's sold everything. At least once. This has been somewhat of a theme my whole life. He sells something. He gets fired. He tries to sell something else. Eventually he gets fired. He's... I don't know how to explain him. He just, he's not a very good worker."

"Your parents are still married?"

I exhaled a long sigh. "Yeah. They hate each other, but they're still married."

Nodding in empathy, he said. "At least they're trying."

"I don't know if that's true," I told him. "It's hard to tell with them."

Ezra let out a slow breath. "You know, when my mom was dying, I didn't know who my dad was. My mom never told me. So the whole time she was sick I believed very strongly that if my dad had been around, she would have been able to survive. I just knew that if he'd been there to take care of her instead of me, she would have been fine. Which is a heavy burden to carry as a kid. But then I met him, and I realized I'd been wrong. He wasn't the kind of father that would have shouldered burdens and made things better. He was a taker. He wasn't just sick physically, there was something wrong with him on the inside. But there was nothing I could do about it. By that point, he was going to die no matter what. I either had to accept him as he was and be thankful I had finally gotten to meet him and know him or I was going to have to live with never getting to know my dad. I made the right choice. Our parents aren't perfect people. They're as human and flawed as we are. Which means they're as likely to mess us up as they are to not."

I felt myself smile at his truth. "Wise advice."

He lifted one shoulder. "You still turned out fine, Molly Maverick. I've been very impressed with everything you've done for the websites. I think your social media strategy is really going to make a difference. I already have some people on it. And the cooking classes were a genius idea. Wyatt is really excited about that."

That lifted my spirits. "Yay!"

His lips kicked up in a teasing smile. "If you're ever ready to leave STS just give me a call. I'll have a job waiting for you."

"Oh, really? How's your health care?"

His grin widened. "Excellent."

The door buzzed. The food was here. Ezra paid for it, even though I offered more than once since I'd been the one to ruin dinner, but he wouldn't hear of it.

We spent the rest of the night laughing over Kung Pao chicken and Mongolian beef, fighting over the last crab Rangoon, and talking about every other single thing.

He made me think and listen, and I was surprised with how open he was. We'd ended up on the couch flirting and teasing and becoming something more than friends... something more than a casual kiss.

Not that we didn't kiss.

Because we did.

When we'd gotten tangled in each other's limbs and our words had run out, he'd kissed me on my couch like he'd been looking forward to it all night... all week. And then he'd kept kissing me. He'd kissed me long and thoroughly until I'd been greedy for more of him, more of his touch.

Until he'd somehow made tonight the best first date I'd ever had. Even though I'd started the night by destroying supper.

He'd finally pulled away sometime after midnight when it was impossible to keep our bodies and hands and minds from trying to push us past kissing.

I'd walked him to the door where he'd kissed me again and promised another night like this.

"Come see me at Bianca this week," he'd demanded. "Thursday night. Give me something to look forward to."

At this point I'd been drunk on him and his sinful mouth and the best conversation so I'd nodded. "Okay. Thursday."

"Goodnight, Molly."

"Goodnight, Ezra."

Then he'd walked away leaving me bursting with hope and possibility. My poor cynical heart grew two sizes in anticipation of the next time I would see a man that only hours ago I'd tried to scare off.

I'd texted Vera even though it was late. **It didn't work. He wasn't scared off.**

She'd texted back almost immediately—**Duh.**

That's when I realized she'd tricked me. I hated her.

And loved her.

And couldn't wait to thank her in person.

219

Chapter Twenty-One

It was after nine by the time I parked at Bianca Wednesday night. It had been two weeks since the spaghetti mishap. Two weeks of new-relationship bliss and constant smiles and getting to know the most amazing man I had ever met.

Ezra had asked me to stop by to work on the mural. He'd hired a photographer to take new website pictures, but the mural needed to be finished first.

Nervous energy buzzed through me. I hadn't seen him since last Sunday when I'd spent the day at Bianca painting. And we hadn't been on a second date since we had Chinese food at my apartment.

We did email. We always emailed. Sometimes they were work related, sometimes I found myself grinning like a fool at the computer screen and trying not to audibly sigh. But it wasn't just emails anymore either. We'd added talking on the phone and texting to our constant stream of conversation.

Ezra was... amazing. And thoughtful. And funny—which was the most surprising thing of all. He had become the thing I looked forward to all day long, the reason I pounced on my phone every time it made a dinging noise, the reason I constantly refreshed my email.

He'd single-handedly softened my cynical defenses and turned me into one of those obnoxious girls that believed in relationships.

It was wonderful.

And terrifying.

I was enjoying every second of getting to know Ezra, but I also couldn't shake the paranoid feeling that eventually the other shoe was going to drop. All good things came to an end at some point. And Ezra was too good to be an exception.

Also, the more I got to know him, the more the differences between us were highlighted...and underlined. He was a savvy businessman with an empire to run. He didn't have free time or hobbies or shows that he'd dedicated entire weeks to binging. He spent every hour of his day working on his restaurants until eventually his body gave out and he was forced to sleep. He had confessed that he set aside an hour in the very early morning to work out, but that was it. Every other minute was dedicated to work.

From meetings to menus, to all the logistical pieces that went into running three restaurants and working around Elena at Quince, the man was busy. But he also loved what he did. No matter what I'd thought of him before, he was not motivated by money. His drive for success was fueled by his total and complete devotion to his craft.

His restaurants meant more to him than establishments that made money or successful restaurants shaping American food as a whole. These were his babies, pieces of his soul that felt pain and victory and worry along with him. As he revealed his struggles with Bianca while she didn't have a chef, he shared his fears that she would fail or that he couldn't be enough for her to succeed. He shared his very real anxiety over finding the perfect executive chef to champion her going forward.

But at the same time, even while so much of him was wrapped up in his restaurants, there was more to know, to learn... to fall for. He was like a never ending well of only good things.

And that's how I knew we would never last. He was reshaping every idea I'd ever had of men. He was showing me that they could be invested in one female, that they could work hard all day long and still be patient, interested and attentive even when they were exhausted.

He showed me what it was like to live with passion and build your life into a work of art. Not just pieces or parts, but every single day without giving up, without becoming complacent. Because it wasn't just about trying every once in awhile, or not hating what you do. This was about going all in, throwing caution completely to the wind and betting all you had on turning your profession into a lasting tapestry of deeds well done.

Ezra didn't live to be happy. He strove to be satisfied and proud of what he accomplished. He didn't just tick tasks off his to do list, he mastered and conquered and handled it. Handled everything.

He taught me to hope for more than happy. Happiness was fleeting and fickle. I could be happy watching Netflix for fifteen hours straight. I could be happy at STS if the Little Tucker would leave me alone.

But at the end of my life would I be satisfied with those things? Or would I realize I had missed a giant chunk of my purpose?

I had no idea to be honest, but Ezra had inspired me to start thinking about it seriously.

Most of all, our conversations and deep talks highlighted how very different we were. Where he was ambitious and focused, I was questioning my life choices. Where he was savvy in business, I struggled to remember to pay my electric bill on time. Where he was cool, unruffled by anything life threw at him and always considerate, I was weird and spastic. And selfish.

He was always professional.

I was always putting out fires I'd accidentally started.

He was obnoxiously punctual.

I was *never* on time.

There was this huge chasm between us and it had nothing to do with our eight-year age gap. Although I couldn't help but be anxious about that as well.

We were nothing alike. We had nothing in common. I was always amazed when I got off the phone with him and we'd managed to fill every single space with something to say or laugh about. And with every phone call, text, or flirty email, I felt myself slipping further and further into this thing we were creating together, this... relationship.

I was falling hard for this man that was completely opposite than I'd originally thought. I'd asked for a man instead of a boy and I'd gotten one. But now I didn't know what to do with him or how to stop my heart from giving itself over to him so completely.

When he finally ended things with me, I would never recover from this. I would never find another relationship that was so completely everything I'd ever wanted.

If I was picky before, then Ezra was ruining me totally for any other man.

Spinster life was my real future.

I'd live out the rest of my years with my twenty cats, dreaming about the gorgeous businessman that had once swept me off my feet and tricked me into believing that maybe I had a chance at happily ever after.

Bianca was nearing the end of dinner service when I walked in. Ezra's hostess nodded hello, but I'd been in the restaurant enough times that she knew I was there to see him.

223

Ezra had suggested a late dinner and then I could work for an hour or two while the restaurant shut down for the night. It would be a late night for me, but spending it with Ezra made it a no brainer.

I found him at his usual table, a tablet in front of him as he tapped out an email to someone. Something low in my belly heated at the memory of his emails to me.

He looked up as I approached, sliding to his feet so he could pull me against him and drop a sweet kiss on my lips. "Molly," he whispered against my mouth.

I made a humming sound and let him have his wicked way with me.

The kiss was too short and too demure and all I wanted was more of him and that talented mouth and for everyone in his restaurant to leave now, please. Thank you.

He gestured at the table. "I ordered for us, I hope that's okay."

"Since the menu makes zero sense to me, I appreciate it."

His mouth curled in that crooked smile I found irresistible. "It's in French," he said obviously, like that was the reason I didn't know what was on it.

"No, it's in food," I countered. "Which is so much worse than French."

He stared at me for a long moment. "You should let me help you. I'll teach you the basics so you don't have to be so afraid of a kitchen."

My heartbeat quickened. My best friend wouldn't even teach me how to cook. "You're so busy," I reminded him, not wanting him to promise something that he didn't really want to follow through on. "I'm a commitment that you don't have time for."

"Are you in a hurry?" His hand moved over my back, soothing both my physical body and emotional mind. "I mean, we have time, don't we?"

His gaze was achingly sincere and maybe he hadn't meant time as in the rest of eternity, but there was a deep, hidden part of me that relaxed. Let's be real, I didn't need him to mean the rest of eternity. I wasn't sure I wanted the rest of eternity. But I wanted his immediate future. And I hoped he wanted mine too.

Of course, I needed to not vomit these thoughts all over him, so I deferred to sarcasm. "So you're saying hold back on my application for *Chopped*?"

He wrinkled his nose and made a disapproving sound. "Reality shows are what's wrong with America."

"Whoa, whoa, whoa, Mr. Judgmental. Let's not throw insults around like they're candy."

His lips twitched. "I'm afraid to ask which shows you like."

"*Real Housewives*."

"You're kidding."

"Have you ever watched an episode?"

"Not an entire episode but I've seen—"

I put my fingers over his lips stopping his next words. "Okay, so your argument is null and void. Don't worry, I'll introduce you to the *Real* ladies. It will be fun."

His smile finally broke free. "You're going to introduce me to the *Real* ladies?"

"We'll make a night of it. Netflix and chill."

"Relationship goals?"

I laughed. I couldn't help it. "Was that a pop culture reference?"

He shrugged, looking embarrassed, adorable and enamored all at once. "This gorgeous girl I know is teaching me all about hashtags. I can't help it."

"Wow, she sounds amazing."

Ezra's head dipped toward mine. "Oh, she is."

We kissed again. Nothing more than a PG, end of a Disney movie lip-lock, but it was perfect and meaningful, and my skeptical heart grew three whole sizes.

A waiter appeared with food for supper, which ended up being tonight's special—crispy frog legs with lemon aioli, and sausage and pork belly cassoulet. We were like the romantic version of *Fear Factor*, only everything was incredibly delicious and I would never be able to go back to eating Hot Pockets and cereal for supper again.

Ezra had ruined me for all other men *and* food that wasn't five stars.

Great. I was wasn't setting myself up for a lifetime of regret and disappointment. Not at all.

After dinner, Ezra disappeared into the kitchen or his office to get more work done and I meandered over to my wall where my vision was beginning to take shape.

I ran my fingers over an unpainted section of white and smiled at what I knew it would become. I had heard once that art wasn't supposed to be beautiful, it was supposed to make you feel, make you think make you step outside of your own life and view the world with a bigger perspective.

Personally, I thought art could be both. Beautiful and emotive. I liked beautiful things. I liked drawing, painting, and creating them. But my definition of beauty was also broader than the societal norm. I didn't pay attention to the flat beauty of a pretty face or perfect body.

Beauty was found in the things that caught my eye, that made emotions flow. It was deeper than the skin, buried in the spirit, in the

225

soul, in eyes that sparkled, or a mouth that twisted in an interesting way. It was at that one moment of life when you knew everything would be different, when you were finally forced to wake-up and pay attention, or change something about yourself, or even let go of something you loved. Beauty was not just an opinion, it was a way of life. Something I aspired to capture every time I picked up a brush.

I spread a generous amount of black and white on my palette and added a spot where I could mix the two colors to blend a neutral gray. Then I got to work.

Chapter Twenty-Two

My pouncing brush danced over the wall, twisting together smoke from one end with smoke from the other. I added dark lines of black to give it depth and quick flicks of white to give it light. I intertwined wisps and tendrils until the entire wall from floor to ceiling was covered in smoke. There were large sections where white was the predominant color, and others where I'd went heavier with the black. But the overall story was smoke.

Stepping back, I surveyed my work. It wasn't finished. I had places to touch up and rough edges to smooth, but it was getting there. Looking around the restaurant, I noticed for the first time that everyone had left. Even the kitchen was dark and quiet.

I spun around, disbelieving that I'd painted my way through closing. Ezra sat at his usual table, his long legs stretched out and crossed at the ankles, his arms crossed over his chest. There was a laptop and papers spread out in front of him, but he was staring at me, lost in thought.

"Don't let me interrupt you," he said quietly, his voice rough and deeper than usual.

My mouth lifted in an embarrassed smile. "I didn't realize it was so late. I must have been in the zone. Sorry, you probably want to go home for the night."

He gazed at me, but his eyes were unreadable from this distance. "Go back to it," he said. "I have more work to do anyway."

227

"Are you sure?"

He ducked his chin in a succinct nod. "Absolutely."

My progress had inspired me to do more and I was anxious to start a new section, so I turned back to the wall. Keeping the colors I'd been using, I talked to Ezra over my shoulder.

"So, tell me about Bianca?" I asked, my voice only barely trembling with nerves.

"What do you mean?"

"The woman," I clarified. "Not the restaurant."

He did not sound willing to release details when he demanded, "Why?"

"I'm about to paint her soul," I told him. "I need to know what kind of woman she is."

He remained silent for a while, thinking. Tension rolled through the room as his mood shifted and changed. I couldn't turn around to look at him. I stared at the curls of smoke in front of me, adding details in an effort to distract my skipping heart.

I heard him exhale in a long forced rush, like he'd been holding his breath and couldn't keep it in any longer. "Cold," he finally said. "Calculating. She never smiled."

Staring at my shoes I tried to imagine Ezra with a woman that never smiled. A few months ago, it would have made sense to my uninformed mind. I would have pictured him with a woman just like that. The two of them arm in arm, never smiling, never laughing, never talking about anything important.

But now? I couldn't reconcile Ezra without laughter, without deep, late night conversations or secret smiles. He was the opposite of cold and calculating. Careful maybe. Shrewd for sure. But not distant, not deliberately cruel.

"She didn't like Dillon," he added, not as an afterthought, but the crux of his entire point.

My rounded arc became a harsh slash. I swiped the paintbrush through my palette and transformed the pair of eyes I was working on from exotic and mysterious to angry, bitter... tired.

Without looking at Ezra, I asked, "How long did you date?"

He loosed another long exhale. "A year."

I had been afraid to look at him until now, afraid that he would see the insecurities floating so close to the surface. But I wasn't expecting a year, and had to turn to see his face.

For someone that couldn't make it past the first date, let alone secure a long-term boyfriend, a year felt like forever. A year felt almost permanent. A year felt messy.

"You dated her for an entire year?" I didn't mean to sound accusing or disappointed, but I felt both.

His gaze met mine across the restaurant. "Are you judging me?"

I lifted one eyebrow to let him know that I was and pointed my paintbrush at him. "She didn't like your sister. That's pretty unacceptable."

"We weren't as serious as you think," he argued. "We dated for a year, but we barely knew each other. Barely even saw each other."

"You named a restaurant after her."

He leaned forward in his chair, dropping his elbows on his knees. "I named a restaurant after a pretty name that for a long time reminded me not to get distracted by pretty things."

I laughed because... honestly. "So, Bianca, Sarita, and Lilou are all cautionary tales? Past mistakes that you're unwilling to make again?"

"Kind of pathetic it took three of them, right?"

I shook my head at him, slowly moving it back and forth. He was unbelievable. "I can't decide if you're sugarcoating or not."

"I lost my mom when I was twelve." His voice grated with deep grief that sounded surprisingly fresh. "She was my entire world. Even when she was sick. And then one day, she was gone. Not just her, but my whole life was over. I lost my home and my friends, my school, my neighborhood, but most of all I lost the one person that loved me. I spent the next four years in and out of foster homes until I finally met Jo, the one woman on the planet who wouldn't put up with my shit. She was brutal sometimes— so heartless I questioned if she wasn't a robot. She whipped my ass into shape and I will always be grateful for my time with her, but she did not come into my life and love me. She didn't replace the missing piece that I lost when my mom passed. And I'm okay with that now. Jo is a hard woman that has her own grief to contend with. But for a long time, I thought that not having someone in my life that loved me was a character flaw that belonged to me. I took the weight of that burden and carried it around for years. And as people came into my life offering something that looked like love, I couldn't help but be attracted to it. Even when it turned out to be false or broken... or attached to strings."

My hands trembled as he opened up to me. I hadn't been expecting him to say or admit these things. I didn't expect him to feel these things. His raw truth scraped at my chest, clawing its way to the heart of me,

229

desperate to make me feel something so much deeper than what I was ready for. "Ezra."

He gave me a helpless look and a deprecating half smile. "Tragic, right?"

"You're not," I promised him.

He turned his head and it felt like he had torn his gaze away from me, like I'd been clinging to it, grasping it with two fists and he'd ripped it away from me. I was left with aching fingers and a hollow feeling carved out in the center of my chest.

"After Elena, I should have known better."

"There are certain women out there that—"

He jerked his chin, interrupting me. "It's a certain kind of person. They don't have to be female. My dad was the same way. They're users. They see something they want and they do whatever they have to, become whatever they need to in order to get it."

"How long did you know your dad?"

"Two years. By the time he found me, his disease was very advanced. I'd thought... I'd been young enough to believe he'd gone out of his way, used his resources, etcetera, because of me, because he'd found out he had a son and wanted to do right by him. I was wrong. He didn't want a son, he wanted an heir. He wanted someone to pass his legacy to, someone that would keep it in his name. He wanted a caretaker." He swallowed. His Adam's apple moved up and down with the effort. "I got his estate and he died knowing we were even." His voice dropped again. "I did get Dillon, though. Maybe I won after all."

Only he and his father weren't even. I tried to picture Ezra as a child, as an orphan. I tried to picture him happy with the mother he loved so much, or happy that he was found again by a father he hadn't known to hope for. I tried to picture him giving Jo hell or meeting Dillon for the first time.

Until this moment, it would have been impossible. He had always been so confident, so utterly without fault. He had been this intimidating, larger than life, fictional creature that I had been terrified of. But now... Now, he was worse.

He was human. He was real—vulnerable in a way that was surprising but also bewitching. My insides felt fizzy, and electrified, and unsure all at once. I couldn't catch a breath at the same time I felt like I'd just taken the first big breath of my entire life. I couldn't make sense of my muddled thoughts, and at the same time my mind had never been clearer.

But most of all, I couldn't stand the distance between us, the look on his face... the grief strangling the oxygen in the room.

Tossing my palette and paintbrush on the sheet-covered table next to me, I walked over to him.

My movement captured his attention again, and with his full focus on me I questioned every step I took. My heart divided in two, half convinced I should run away and half desperate to run to him.

He had more baggage than I knew what to do with. He had been hurt and betrayed, and still he'd always risen above it, always marched forward with his head held high and his dignity intact.

I wanted to cry for him, but at the same time I wouldn't do him the dishonor. He was... everything a man should be.

Everything a person should be.

And I couldn't believe I'd tried to stay away from him.

He watched me move toward him with a look on his face I couldn't define. I didn't know what it meant, but I knew how it made me feel.

Fluttery and trembling and... beautiful.

"You're the most amazing man I've ever met," I told him. "Those people... your dad, Elena, the rest of the three witches... they did not deserve you. They didn't even deserve pieces of you."

He didn't respond verbally, but his entire body responded, changing his expression and infusing the atmosphere with gratitude, and pride. and something deeper, something lasting.

Meeting me in the middle of the dining room, his lips met mine before my arms could wrap fully around his neck. We were fireworks exploding, and cars crashing, and worlds colliding.

The kiss was hungry at the same time it was healing. He wasn't gentle. He wasn't sweet. This kiss was no longer exploratory.

With the restaurant completely to ourselves, we finished saying with our bodies everything we couldn't verbalize.

He kissed my mouth and moved to my jaw, down the line of my throat, the tops of my breasts walking me backward the entire time. I smoothed my hands over his crisp shirt making it wrinkly and disheveled, putting my mark on him.

My back hit the wall, crashing into the dried section of my mural. I grasped at the freshly painted surface, desperate for balance as his teeth nipped at my throat. I made a sound I had never made before, gasping for breath and begging him to touch me.

He took my mouth again, deepening an already soul-altering kiss. His hand moved over my hips, trailing a hot path over my ribs and then finally to the crest of my breast. His thumb rubbed over my nipple and I made another one of those mewls that would have embarrassed me with any other man. But I was so past that with Ezra. I was done overthinking, analyzing and finding fault. I was done pushing him away because I was afraid of getting hurt, or being rejected, or feeling unwanted.

He pinched my nipple between his skilled fingers and I decided that the clothes we were wearing were frustratingly in the way. I pulled back, but barely as he already had me pressed against the wall, his long leg cleverly positioned between mine. Tugging at the hem of my shirt, he saw what I wanted and didn't hesitate to deliver.

My shirt disappeared, and then my bra followed quickly after. Before I could take a full second to feel self-conscious, his mouth descended on my nipple, making my skin tingle and my entire body flush with desire.

"Fucking beautiful," he murmured against my skin as he tasted and nibbled and drove me out of my mind.

I struggled to get his buttons undone while he made me wild with seductive kisses and talented hands. He finally gave me mercy, reaching back to rip his shirt over his head before I'd fully unbuttoned it. There was a funny moment where his sleeves got caught on his wrists, but with some necessary teamwork, we finally got the damn shirt off. His undershirt went into the pile of our clothes with little fanfare.

His lips found mine again, his heated, muscular chest pressed against my softer, fuller, female one.

He was much taller than me, but it was like we had been designed for each other. His body towered over mine, conforming all of my curves to his. He felt like heaven pressing in on all of my sensitive spots, driving my body wild with sensation and seduction and his wonderfully sinful mouth.

"More," I pleaded. "Ezra."

His kisses slowed, not lessening, but somehow becoming more… hotter… needier. His hand moved over my hip, finding the front of my jeans until his fingers disappeared inside. I gasped again, nearly exploding the second he touched me.

It had been so long since I'd been intimate with someone and I had never felt the way I did about Ezra. Which was what? I couldn't even put words to it. Something that burrowed into my soul and became a permanent, treasured thing. Something that would never let me walk away from this man again.

I wouldn't be his father that used him for needs Ezra shouldn't have had to meet. I wouldn't be Elena that didn't understand his drive to be successful, or the relentless push inside him to carve out an empire. I wouldn't be Lilou, or Sarita. Or Bianca, or any other girl that only wanted to use him for what he had to offer: his money, his connections, his… business know-how.

I would be me—a broken, lost, terrified woman that didn't know if she could tolerate her job for a second longer, or if she would ever be able to check her oil or change a tire, or cook. I would be honest with him and let him decide.

It was the only thing I knew how to do.

His fingers moved inside me and mine curled into his shoulders, desperately holding on for strength, needing him to anchor me to this place. To him. To us.

His free arm braced his body over my head as our mouths pushed and pulled in a kiss that was achingly tender. His fingers moved in, out, deeper, slower until I was gasping for breath, hovering at the brink of internal combustion.

My leg wrapped around his hip, giving him better access to the hidden, secret parts of me. He pulled his head back and gazed down at me, studying, watching... worshiping.

"Do you know how beautiful you are, Molly? God, I could watch you all night."

I was too close to the edge to respond coherently, my eyes shut as I chased that delicious surrender. My head dropped, my forehead landing on his chin. So close...

"You're unexpected and lovely, and something that very much feels like salvation," he murmured against my hairline, his scruff-shadowed jaw scratching my overly sensitive skin.

His last, whispered words were my ruin. I fell apart in his arms, his capable fingers doing something magical inside me. I dropped my defenses and let go with a man I realized I completely trusted, respected. With his hard, beautiful body pressed against mine in a restaurant he had named after a woman that had hurt him, I came undone.

And I knew, *I just knew*, it was because I felt something for this man that I had never felt in my life.

He kissed me again, slowly and tenderly... reverently. "Don't stop," I pleaded. "I don't want you to stop."

A wolfish grin flashed, greedy with the promise of more. Tugging me off the wall, he laid me down on the sheets covering his floor and hovered over me. My heart kicked in my chest. His skin was perfect, muscular, smooth and so enticing. I wanted to taste every inch of him and return his most recent favor.

But I knew I wasn't alone with those feelings as his dark, rich chocolate eyes moved over my own topless body, drinking in the sight of me. I was drowsy with desire, my body limp with experienced pleasure and pooling heat. But fear curled too, whispering truth and realization and the very real possibility that this man could destroy my heart.

I was too far gone for him.

"Please don't name a restaurant after me," I whispered as his hot skin touched mine.

He must have seen the terror in my eyes, because his gaze softened and he bent down to nip at the swell of my breast. Lifting his head for only a second, just long enough for me to catch the raw plea, he countered. "If you left Molly, one restaurant would never be enough. They would all be you."

It shouldn't have been a compliment. I shouldn't have felt cherished at that moment, adored. But I did.

And because of that, my fears disintegrated and I found him again hovering above me. He had been waiting patiently for me to give into it, to him. He had been watching as I decided that I wouldn't hurt him, that I couldn't walk away.

Whatever had started between us as a seedling of angst, had blossomed into a tree with roots and stretching branches. I wouldn't leave him.

I couldn't.

This was what my mom had meant all those times she'd told me not to quit. It wasn't the job that was the most important thing in my life, or the life I'd imagined myself. It was this. Ezra.

It was the thing building between us that I wasn't quite ready to name.

Which was amazing when you considered how different we were, how unalike. He was successful and confident and maybe a little tragic. I was floundering and boring. Not to mention insecure. He had a complicated past with women landmarking the way. I hadn't been in a serious relationship since college, and my only booty call option was spin class. He had known he was interested in me the second he saw me and I'd waited this long to realize I should not let him go.

I should hold on to him for the rest of my forever and trust that he would do the same to me.

So that's what I did. Or at least for tonight. I clung to him as we explored each other's bodies. We kissed and touched, finding creative ways to lose ourselves in each other. Beneath my mural, on his restaurant floor, we found new, exciting ways to push and pull. And when at last we collapsed next to each other satisfied and yet savoring every second of it, I knew I had lost myself completely in Ezra Baptiste.

And I wasn't scared of that at all.

Chapter Twenty-Three

I closed another email from Henry and resisted the urge to scream at my computer. The important thing was that I was able to keep all of my rage and fury and bitterness bottled up. Everybody knew keeping the angry feelings inside was the best way to handle tough situations.

Although, apparently I needed to practice because Emily immediately lifted her head and gave me a funny look. "You okay, Slugger?"

Stacking loose papers with the grace of a charging hippopotamus, I glared at her. "You are so lucky you didn't call me something gross. Like doll face or hot stuff. I might have reflexively punched you in the junk on accident."

She pursed her lips like a fish. "You could have tried." Then more seriously, with her nose wrinkled she asked, "What does the little Tucker want now?"

I rolled my eyes. "For me to work late tonight. Because even though Black Soul has rejected all of my interesting ideas to ensure they become the most boring record label on the planet, Henry wants to go over my graphics. Again. He wants me to plan on a late night."

"Weren't you in there yesterday doing the same thing?"

I nodded. "And every day this week. He has a serious control freak problem. Also, a massive touching problem."

Her eyebrows shot up to her hair line. "Is he still being inappropriate?"

My head dropped back and I stared at the ceiling. "He's awful. I hate him."

"Molly, what are you going to do?"

Her voice was a concerned whisper. She wanted me to go to HR again. But I'd already been twice and both times Doris had shrugged me off. I didn't think a third time would matter. I didn't think three thousand times would matter.

Doris was protecting her job and by proxy Henry. As long as he didn't cross the line to full on sexual assault, she was going to let all the small things slide.

Only they didn't feel like small things to me. They didn't feel petty or forgetful or insignificant. They felt horrible.

I hated being the object of Henry's unwanted attention. I loathed the way he would casually bump into me, pressing his body against mine for way longer than was appropriate. I hated that his eyes were always on my boobs, talking to them, staring at them, following them around wherever they went. I wanted to scream every time he made an inappropriate joke or called me a gross pet name.

He was out of line, and he behaved as though he was exempt from real world consequences. Maybe Doris wasn't going to do anything about it, but I wasn't going to take it either.

Fine, it had taken me this long to find the courage to truly stand up to him, but I had finally arrived. Watch out world.

I blamed Ezra. Ever since our conversation and intimate night at Bianca a little over a week ago, I hadn't been able to shake the feeling that I was finally comfortable in my adult life, in my own skin. There was something suddenly so right about my apartment, my car, and my boyfriend, that I could almost overlook just how not right my job was.

Okay, the job was a big part of being a grown-up. But it was also something I'd let go of too. It didn't need to be the absolute defining feature in my life. I'd released some of my mother's voice and the expectations she'd placed on me to always be successful—at the cost of every other happiness.

She meant well, but that didn't make her right. Ezra had helped me see that. Maybe I couldn't totally believe it just yet. There was still lingering doubt, and years and years of performing and pleasing and pacifying. It would take a lot of work to get me in a healthier head space about who I was supposed to be and what I was supposed to be doing with my life. I'd decided to borrow Ezra's confidence and freedom until they felt like mine.

He said he'd learned that from his dad and their relationship. His dad had been very successful in business, but lonely in life. He hadn't even known Ezra's mom had gotten pregnant. She was a fling that Ezra's dad, Immanuel, had met through mutual friends. It wasn't until those friends revealed her secret years later, that Immanuel had started the tedious, frustrating process of finding Ezra. And when he found him it had been too late to rescue him from some of the hardest challenges any child should face.

His dad had brought Ezra to his house and given him a job, sent him to college and introduced him to his soon-to-be-beloved, little sister. And then he'd died, leaving Ezra almost everything. For as heartless as his dad seemed, he had a true knack for business.

Which Ezra obviously inherited.

We'd spent the last week sharing more and more about our lives, getting to know each other, learning the ins and outs of each other's past, present and imagined future. And we'd been spending a fair amount of time kissing.

There had been a lot of kissing. And to be honest, a whole lot more than just kissing. The man drove me crazy. He was stubborn and impossible and so irresistible I wanted to scream.

Or maybe, I did scream. But like in a hotter, more consensual context.

"Hey, if you see Ethan can you send him to the office?" I asked Emily as I got ready to head to Henry's lair.

She frowned, glancing around. "I think he's out today. One of his kids is sick or something."

"Argh," I growled. "Kids are so annoying." At her giggle, I added. "Just kidding. Only Ethan's kids are annoying." That garnered me a few dirty looks from surrounding coworkers. But I didn't see any of them spending a whole lot of time with Henry alone in his office, so they could just save their judgment for someone else. "Are you heading out soon?" I asked her.

She nodded. "I am. I have a hair appointment tonight."

"That's exciting," I told her, jealous that she got to go do something fun and relaxing while I had to sit with Henry Tucker all evening and dissect all the work I'd done that he wanted to take credit for. "Are you going lavender again?"

She pulled her hair over her shoulder, examining the faded ends of it. "Maybe. I haven't decided yet."

"I think you should go full mermaid. You would look amazing. And I would have epic hair envy."

Her grin turned into a laugh. "Well, then it's worth it."

"Glad you see things my way." I stood up, clutching my various necessities to my chest. "Okay, I'll see you tomorrow."

"Hey, Molly." Her serious tone made me pause. "Be careful, okay?"

"You mean with Henry?"

She nodded once. "Yeah. It worries me that he hasn't gotten the hint to back off yet. Make sure you're... I don't know... on your guard."

My mouth dried out at her concern. It was one thing to tell myself these things, but hearing them from a trusted friend escalated all of my wariness. "Thanks, Em. I appreciate you looking out for me."

She waved me off. "You'd do the same for me."

"Hey, that's what friends are for."

"It's true," she smiled again. "We drink together, we survive boring meetings together, but most of all we save each other from perverted bosses that try to feel us up next to the copier."

I couldn't even force a laugh, it was too close to the truth to be funny. "Gross."

"Text me later," she hollered at my back.

"Will do!"

Even though I took the long way around the office, I still made it to Henry's office in no time. He sat at his computer, staring thoughtfully at paperwork. My nose wrinkled with disgust automatically. I would rather be so many other places than his office right now. Like getting a root canal. Or a Brazilian wax. Or renewing my license at the DMV. Anything would be better than stepping into this office alone with this man.

I plastered on a professional, but blank expression and knocked on the half-opened door. "You wanted to see me?"

He looked up at me and smiled, his gaze traveling down the length of me before settling on my boobs. "Come in, Molly. Have a seat."

With one last helpless glance around as my coworkers filtered out for the night, I finally gave up on escaping and did as he asked. He watched me sit down and cross my legs before he stood up and joined me in the chair usually reserved for Ethan.

Turning to me, he leaned forward and plucked the pen I'd been nervously clicking out of my hands. "That's annoying," he said casually.

"Sorry." I cleared my throat, hating that I apologized so reflexively. "Nervous habit."

"What is there to be nervous about?" he asked. "I'm not scary."

~~You're terrifying.~~ "I don't even notice I'm doing it."

"Well, relax. It's all good things today."

"About the Black Soul account?" I asked, mostly as a way to keep him on task. "Have you heard back about the new mock-ups?"

His smile stretched. "Yes, I have. Molly, they're very impressed with your work. They wanted me to pass on the word that everything is coming along perfectly."

It should have felt amazing to receive praise from a high-profile client. This was what I'd set out to do. I'd wanted this account for the sole purpose of impressing them. And yet... it fell flat.

I'd given up every one of my original designs and interesting ideas to cater to their style and lackluster vision. They were the client, so of course it made sense. But realizing all of the concessions I had made to please them lessened any pride I felt in the project.

I wasn't really the mastermind behind a widely successful social media account—they were. I was the grunt that simply did their bidding.

That was obviously my job. They were paying me to bring their vision to life, not my own. My entire profession revolved around pleasing business owners and giving them what they wanted.

But for some reason, at this level, I had been expecting more. More freedom. More creative control. More room to be innovative, and take risks, and try new things. The reality was that I had less of everything. I had more of a leash than ever.

I was more dissatisfied than ever.

To Henry, I managed a weak smile. "That's great."

"It is," he agreed, missing my lack of enthusiasm completely. "I took a risk on you, sweetheart. I can't tell you how pleased I am to know it paid off." His hand patted my knee and then stayed there.

I crossed my legs the other way, knocking his hand free. My shoulders pushed back and I sat up straighter, instantly on the defensive. "Glad to know it paid off for you."

"I could have gone with anyone," he added. "But I knew there was something special about you. Something I just couldn't resist."

My tongue was like a stone in my mouth, heavy and gritty, unwilling to show him gratitude. "Did you have more to say about the account, Henry?"

He looked over my shoulder at the now empty office. "You know, the client isn't the only one impressed by what you did. I really enjoyed working with you. I think we made a great team."

"Ethan helped," I added slightly hysterical. I hated how he kept grouping us together, as if he could take credit for my job well done or worse, as if it meant something more than what it did. "Ethan is the reason either of us could do our job well."

He ignored me, choosing instead to move his appreciative gaze over my fully clothed body as if I were sitting there buck naked. His hand

239

landed on my thigh this time—flat, wide, and grossly heavy. "There are a lot of pretty girls out there, Molly. But I have to tell you, you are definitely one of the sexiest in this office."

My goodwill dried up immediately. That wasn't a nice thing to say. At best, it was a backhanded compliment. In reality, it was offensively out of line, and unwelcome. But the little Tucker had his head too far up his own ass to realize that. "Henry, if you don't have anything else to say about the account, I'm going to leave."

His eyelids hooded and his smile softened to only mildly condescending. "We make a good team, honey. I think we should try out our talents in other areas."

Jumping to my feet, I moved as far away from Henry as possible. Unfortunately, I ended up cornering myself against the wall furthest from the door. My heart raced and my blood rushed with adrenaline. This was not happening. "I'm not comfortable with you talking to me like that," I said firmly, sounding braver than I was.

He stood up too, pushing my chair to the side so he could walk straight to me. "Come on now, Molly. I gave you the biggest opportunity you've had yet. I went to bat for you. I included you on a project with a big fat commission. Don't you think you should return the favor?"

My sense of professional pride took a serious hit. "I'm good at what I do," I argued for some stupid reason. "You picked me because I was best suited for the job."

He rolled his eyes even while he moved closer to me, crowding me against a filing cabinet. "I picked Ethan because he was best suited for the job. I picked you because you have the nicest rack in the office. You should feel flattered." He leaned forward, pushing into my space. His hand reached out to touch me, but I swatted it away before he made contact. He looked mildly annoyed. "You should be grateful."

I didn't feel flattered. I sure as hell did not feel grateful. I felt disgusted. "You're a pig," I snarled. "And maybe HR is afraid of you, but I'm not. Back off, Henry. Tomorrow your dad can hear all about how you talk to women around the office. I've tried to be professional about this. I've tried to go through the right channels. But I'm done putting up with this misogynistic bullshit from you. You're out of your goddamn mind if you think I'll let you touch me."

His smile disappeared and his face soured, speckling red with fury. "Why don't you shut your fucking mouth and let those tits get you a promotion."

My hand processed his words before my brain fully comprehended how awful they were. My palm hitting his cheek resounded with a loud

240

smack, making him grunt at the impact. His head turned to the side as he brought his hand up to cradle his face.

Mine tingled as it settled back against my side in a fist. My entire body shook with rage and humiliation and unshed tears. "Keep your promotion," I growled, venom dripping from every word. "And your help. I don't want any of it. Stay away from me."

His head snapped back to mine as he repositioned his body quickly to keep me from fleeing. "Relax, Molly, we're just having some fun." He slid his finger down the front of my blouse. I knocked it away, but he wasn't deterred. "You owe me this. You fucking owe me this."

I had never felt as sickened by someone's words or humiliated. Fury vibrated through me, chased quickly by panic and frustration. I wanted to cry, but mostly I wanted to knee this asshole in the balls so hard he would choke on them, then run away.

Instead, I pushed him away and scrambled past him. "You're a disgusting bastard," I bit out, grabbing my things off the chair and rushing to the exit. "And everyone's going to know it."

He slumped against the edge of his desk, running a hand through his greasy hair. His smug smile reappeared, confidence twinkling in his narrowed eyes. "Nobody's going to believe you, doll. You messed up. This is my company, my house. You're done."

I paused at the door, finally speaking the words I had wanted to say for weeks. "Fuck you."

His grin widened. "That's what I was trying to do!"

Oh my god, what an asshole. I fled the office, rushing past a desk that I would be happy to never return to. I grabbed my purse, but abandoned my laptop. It was the company's anyway and I wanted nothing to do with anything that belonged to STS.

Not unless they fired Henry Tucker.

I didn't take a breath until I was safely in my car and out of the parking garage. My hands trembled aggressively as I tried to see through frustrated tears. My stomach roiled as I fought the urge to puke. My mind spun and spun and spun with the entire spectrum of emotions I couldn't land on.

I was angry. Furious. Outraged. Anything and everything mad. But I was also shocked in a way that made me feel completely detached from what had happened. Had he really come on to me? Had he really said those awful things? Offered a promotion for sleeping with him?

The whole thing felt violently strange. Should I go to the police? Had he committed a crime? Or was this something the office had to handle.

241

I loathed the idea of making a scene about this, of drawing attention to myself over his horrific behavior. I hated the idea of having to talk to his dad, confessing Henry's intentions and sharing the disgusting words he'd said. I knew I had to. I knew that I was right. But that didn't negate the embarrassment and humiliation on my part. I would have to face both things—doing what was right and owning up to the rumors, reputation and reality of what had happened.

More tears surfaced. I was probably more frustrated than anything. I hated conflict, and I also hated being the center of attention on me, and now I would have to face both. Not because of anything I did, but because of the grotesque actions of someone else.

"It's not fair," I hiccupped uselessly in the car. Which, of course, it wasn't. But what a ridiculous thing to say. Especially in light of everything that had happened. Especially acknowledging all that did not happen, all that I avoided by running away.

Rationally, I knew that it could have been worse. I realized that Henry had held back. He hadn't physically assaulted me. He hadn't raped me. He hadn't hurt me. But that didn't make his actions more right or less wrong. He still had behaved in the worst possible way. There were just certain things I needed to be grateful for.

I sniffled, blindly grabbing for a tissue from my purse. Wiping my eyes, I tried to decide on my next plan of action, but I couldn't make sense of my thoughts.

I had likely just lost my job. Henry had his dad's ear. He was set to take over in the next couple years. He was future CEO, and my boss, and an integral part of SixTwentySix. I was nobody. And before Black Soul, the project Henry had given me, I had worked on the lowest of all the projects.

It was his word against mine.

Which meant I better update my resume.

And even if I didn't get fired for this, did I really want to go back? What if Henry didn't take over his dad's job? What if he only stayed on as an employee? It was no longer a place I could see a future at or even contemplate finishing out the week.

I pulled into the parking lot without knowing where I was heading. I couldn't remember consciously deciding to drive here.

The wall of ivy was blooming vibrantly green, and the tree in the courtyard had budded with dainty white flowers. The building looked bewitching framed by the golden, setting sun. Bianca was the safe haven I needed.

I didn't overthink my choice to find Ezra. I didn't even think far enough ahead to worry if he would be here or not. I just needed him to tell me everything was okay when everything felt decidedly not okay. I needed his calm stability to sooth the fiery nerves exploding beneath my skin. I needed his strong arms wrapped around me, reminding me that there were good, decent men in this world.

And beyond what I wasn't able to think through and rationalize, I just needed him. It was as simple and as complicated as that.

Chapter Twenty-Four

I bypassed the hostess, the floor manager, an army of waiters, and headed straight into Bianca's kitchen. Unlike at Lilou where Ezra's office was separate from the main kitchen, in Bianca, his workplace was tucked in the back of the expansive kitchen area.

The kitchen was abuzz with activity as cooks hurried around in their professional attire—toques bobbing between stations. Another difference between Lilou and Bianca was the way service ran. At Lilou, with Wyatt in charge, everything flowed directly from him. Maybe it wasn't always smooth or easy-going, but Wyatt was the source and the kitchen moved in a kind of synchronized chaos around him. Like the mouth of a mighty river.

Bianca wasn't a steady-pathed stream. Or even a turbulent current. At least not tonight. She was the ocean in the middle of a hurricane. Chefs were shouting demands back and forth at each other, cursing furiously. The air was tight with tension and panic. Dishes clanked on messy surfaces and orders were bellowed from one side of the room to the other. I related in a way I never thought I would.

Several of the kitchen and wait staff paused in their frantic activity to watch me as I slinked along the edges, trying not to draw attention. Too late.

"I'm just here for Ezra," I muttered, doubting any of them heard me anyway.

I had only been back here once and it was not during dinner service. It was on one of the Saturday mornings I had painted. Ezra had given me a little tour and then we'd made out in the cooler.

There hadn't been anyone here then. The kitchen had seemed huge and empty and void of life. Now it was the opposite. Crammed with people running in every direction, the space no longer appeared big enough to accommodate all of Ezra's staff. It was all madness and mayhem and delicious food, and I loved it.

I loved every part of it.

Any other day I would have grabbed my phone and taken video of the flurry of activity to post online. I would have captioned it #workvibes and watched social media go crazy over the interesting aspects of how a five-star plate of food is made.

Not that it mattered now. My future at STS looked grim. Instead of one-minute videos and interesting hashtags, I was going to be busking portraits on a busy street corner instead. *Excuse me, ma'am, can I interest you in a caricature? I promise to make your boobs and head look ginormous.*

That was my life now, a big-boob drawing chalk artist. #lifegoals.

Thankfully, Ezra was in his office when I finally scuttled back there. Nerves assaulted my already weak heart as I realized I should have texted or called first, or at least let him meet me out front. He wasn't expecting me. He probably wasn't ready to see me…

"Molly." He looked up at me from behind his desk, his tie tugged loose and his fingers poised on a keyboard mid-email. His mouth split open in a warm smile and I exhaled a breath I hadn't realized I had been holding. "I was just sending a note to ask if you wanted to do dinner."

Seeing him there, behind his desk, tired from a long day but happy to see me, did something permanent to my shaky spirit. My chin trembled and I pressed my lips together in a valiant effort to hold back hot tears.

He noticed my emotional state, pushed back in his chair and leaped to standing. "Are you okay?"

I shook my head, unable to speak for fear of sobbing again.

"Come here," he demanded.

This time I didn't have a single problem doing what he asked. I threw my body into his and let his arms tighten around me, holding me to him. I didn't wail, sob, or scream like I thought I would, but I couldn't help the few rogue tears that slipped out.

I crushed my body against his, relishing the warmth and safety of his arms. As far as hugs went, this one was an *A-plus*, perfect in every way. He held me tightly against him without asking me for details. He simply held me, giving me the sanctuary and healing I needed so badly.

And I gratefully clung to him, soaking up every second of this man that had come to mean so much to me over the last few months.

"Do you want to talk about it?" he asked, his voice low and soft, but edgy too—prepared to fight. For me, I hoped. I didn't have it in me to fight with him tonight.

My arms tightened around him. "I was at work..." I sniffled, feeling pathetic all over again. "My boss... We were working on a project and he came onto me."

Ezra's entire body stiffened, tightened, and readied for battle. "He did what?"

"But not in a nice way," I hiccupped. I pulled back, drying my eyes with the back of my hand and getting a grip on my wild emotions. I bravely met Ezra's hard glare and confessed what happened. "He's been harassing me for a while. Always saying inappropriate things or accidentally touching me. But he's the CEO's son. When I complained to HR, they accused me of making something out of nothing. They made it seem like I was a drama queen. And before maybe it wasn't anything... I wasn't afraid of Henry at that point, he was more obnoxious than dangerous. He irritated me and disgusted me, but he didn't scare me. Then this afternoon, he called me into his office to discuss the client we're working together on, and that's when he took things too far."

I told Ezra everything, the horrible things he'd said to me, how he felt entitled to me because of the project, how he threatened to fire me. Ezra listened attentively, his body coiling with his reaction the longer my story went on. His jaw ticked with every mention of Henry, and he never once let go of me. Not once.

"I don't know what to do," I told him. "I don't know how to go back into that office and deal with those people... with Henry."

"You're not going to do it alone," he growled. "I'll go with you in the morning."

"You don't have to—"

"Enough, Molly. You are not an inconvenience to me. This is not something I'm going to make you do alone. I am going with you because I'm going to let those assholes in your office have it, and it's going to be my privilege to stand up for you." He reached for his phone. "I'm going to call my lawyer, Brent. He should go with us." His gaze snapped back to mine. "You will be suing, won't you? Brent is the best in the city. He'll know exactly what to do."

247

"I-I haven't thought that far ahead. I'm just really still trying to get through today."

His expression softened and he tossed his phone back on his desk, forgetting about it. "I'm sorry," he murmured sincerely. "My default is action. Especially when I feel helpless. We'll get through today and you can think about what you want to do."

I tilted my head at him, staring up at this gorgeous man that cared so deeply for me. It still seemed crazy. "Why do you feel helpless?" He wasn't the one that had been attacked. He wasn't the vulnerable female fleeing her own job.

He gently pressed the back of his hand against my cheek, rubbing a slow, sweet path. "Do you really not know? Molly, I want to murder the asshole that touched you... talked to you that way. I want to kill him for making you feel this way, for expecting you to give him whatever his depraved mind came up with. He's a scumbag and he tried to *touch* you. How can I feel anything but helpless? This asshole deserves my fist in his fucking face, and I'm going to have to settle for destroying him legally. It's killing me."

I shivered. Nobody had ever stuck up for me like this. Nobody had ever needed to. I had spent twenty-seven years of my life blending in.

But I wasn't invisible with Ezra. *He saw me.* And I was enough for him.

I couldn't speak or reply or even think straight. Words sat on the tip of my tongue that I didn't think I was ready to say yet. I felt them. I felt them all the way to my bones. Ezra had been this life-changing event that had shaken up everything I'd convinced myself that I knew about the world, dating, and men.

He didn't come into my life gradually or delicately. He swept in like a wildfire, consuming every single thought and word and thing until there was only him and me and it was like we were always supposed to be this way.

"Thank you," I told him. Those simple words containing so much raw emotion that I could barely even whisper them.

He brushed his thumb over my bottom lip as he stared at my face, looking for the words I couldn't or wouldn't say. "I'm taking you back to my place," he said gruffly. "Yeah?"

I nodded. "Yes."

"I just need to grab some things."

"Okay."

Before he let go of me, he bent down and kissed my forehead. His lips were warm and soft, and so perfectly gentle that tears flooded my eyes again. "It's going to be okay, Molly. You're going to be okay."

248

He let go of me for just a minute to gather his computer and phone, and I was left reeling with wonder that I believed him. I had no idea what I was going to do tomorrow or the next day, or if I even still had a job. Or if I wanted that job. But I had Ezra and this new sense of inner strength that I couldn't seem to scare away.

I was still shy. I was still meek in some instances. But I had this deep sense of worth too. My life plans could change, maybe I really would have to resort to busking portraits to pay the rent, but I was still me. I still had all the things that made me Molly.

And I had Ezra too. Despite how I felt about us before, about past relationships in general, or *anything else*, I realized I wasn't going to lose this man easily. He wasn't going anywhere, and I wasn't in any hurry to make him leave.

"Ride with me?" he asked as we walked out the back door of Bianca, not really waiting for an answer. His Alfa Romeo glistened in the twilight, looking pretty in the golden light. A spring breeze danced over my skin, and the air smelled like budding flowers and freshly cut glass.

I had just had to face one of the ugliest moments of my adult life. Yet, holding Ezra's hand in the employee parking lot of Bianca made today feel oddly like one of the most profoundly beautiful days of that same life. It was a strange dichotomy that I had trouble reconciling. I had to admit it had everything to do with this man next to me.

There were so many bad people in the world, so many people that would rather hurt and harm and crush. But the good people were the ones that made life worth living, that made searching for them worth every bad relationship and heartache, worth the pain, suffering and potential heartache of finding them. I would never want to relive any of the bad dates or guys or lonely nights that I had been through before Ezra. But I also wouldn't give them up either. They led me to him. And that was all that mattered.

He held the door open for me and I climbed into his fancy sports car feeling more at home than anywhere else in my life. We listened to good music and talked carefully about things that weren't important. He held my hand whenever he didn't need it to shift.

By the time we reached his apartment building, my chest felt less pinched and my eyes were completely dry. He parked in an adjacent lot and then led me into a renovated turn of the century industrial building.

I had been expecting sleek and modern, simple lines and smooth surfaces. Instead, his fourth-floor apartment was all exposed brick walls and insanely high ceilings. The only thing that screamed modern was the kitchen with its cement countertops and floating shelves. The appliances were all shiny stainless steel and state of the art.

But the rest of the apartment? Surprisingly warm and masculine, but not overly so. His bedroom was an elevated loft with a cedar and iron staircase. The rest of the main floor was a mixture of different living spaces. A giant TV hung on the wall surrounded by rich, chocolate brown leather couches. A desk and computer were tucked in another corner. I was surprised with his large dining table, a massive statement piece of iron and wood that matched his staircase.

"Big enough table?" I set my purse down on it and smoothed a hand over the top.

"It's a good table," he answered. "I like to have people over."

In the time that I had known him, he had never had me over or that I was aware of, anyone else. I faced him again, raising my eyebrows expectantly. "Really?"

Half his mouth lifted in a smile. "You know, when I have time."

"Oh, so never."

He didn't take my bait. Instead, he jerked his chin and beckoned me over to him. "Come here."

I did.

His arms wrapped around me again and his forehead dropped to mine. "I'm sorry for what happened to you today. You deserve so much more than to be treated like that. You deserve so much more than assholes, bad dates and crappy jobs. Molly, you're brilliant. The most brilliant person I've ever met. You don't need that job. And not just because of that dickhead that molested you. But because they never recognized your fucking genius."

I chuckled at his devotion to me. "There are other good designers there. I'm not the only talent."

"You'll never get me to believe that," he said without laughing. "I checked out the company, remember? Even if I hadn't been trying to get in your pants, I would have picked you. For the sake of my business. You're good at what you do, Molly the Maverick. The best."

Wait. What? He hired me because he was what? "I need you to start from the beginning," I told him.

He smiled. It was devastating and relaxed and everything I had never even known to hope for. "Did you really not know?"

"That you hired me because you wanted to sleep with me? No. No, I did not know that. Also, so far it's backfired because there has been no sleeping or other bed-related activities."

250

His hands slid down my back, coming to rest possessively on my butt. With a firm tug, he pulled me flush against his body, hard and muscled and unbelievably tempting. "Don't be fooled by the long game. When you're serious about a girl, you can't make your move too quickly. You get her to care about you first, fall for you. Then you take her to bed and show her she can't live without you."

He was saying so many words that I was struggling to comprehend. My fists curled into his shirt, wrinkling the smooth material. "The long game?"

"Molly, you have to realize how much I care about you, yeah?" I shook my head. His milk chocolate eyes deepened with heat and grew more serious all at once. "I've been careful with you, with us. I've been terrified of scaring you off or starting something you weren't willing to finish. But I have to be honest with you, I have waited a very long time to find someone like you. And I've made a lot of mistakes trying to make people fit this role that you glided into effortlessly. You demanded my attention the second I met you, and then you claimed my respect and admiration, and now you're stealing my heart. This is real for me. This is serious. I'm sorry if that scares you, but I need you in my life as much as I want you there. Here."

I licked dry lips and willed my heart to stay inside my chest. "I'm falling for you too," I confessed. "I... I did try to stop this from happening. You terrify me." His lips kicked up in an affectionate smile as if that was the most adorable thing anyone had ever said. "I'm serious. You're gorgeous and surprisingly funny, loyal, and this crazy, successful restaurateur. And I'm weird and flighty, late all the time, and I'm pretty sure I'm unemployed. I'm a mess, Ezra. We're so different."

"Thank God," he murmured. "I don't want to date myself. You make me smile when I've had the worst day. And you make me see the world in brighter colors and unique angles. You've opened my mind to my business, but also to my friends. I would be so boring without you. We are different, but in the best possible ways. And maybe that means we'll fight more than other people, or disagree or whatever, but we'll also makeup more because of it. And laugh and talk more, and feel more. Molly, I've waited my entire life to find the person that didn't just want something from me, but wanted me. All of me. Now that I've found you, I can't let you go."

I couldn't stand the distance between us any longer. With my hands grasping his shirt I yanked him to me, our mouths meeting in the middle. We were all passion and desperation, and greedy hunger that could not be sated. This kiss was explosive, and all things bright and beautiful.

251

His lips moved over mine with a new sense of urgency, savoring and tasting as if for the first time. His tongue slid over my bottom lip, and when I opened my mouth, he deepened the kiss making my toes curl with anticipation. His hands dipped into the waistband of my skinny jeans, one sliding around to the front to flick open the button.

I fumbled at his shirt buttons, clumsily grasping each one. He moved me toward the staircase as we shed our shoes and pants, tripping up each step, refusing to take a break from this kiss.

God, this man was everything I didn't know I wanted. Everything I didn't know I needed. His words resonated in every secret chamber of my soul. I had been waiting for him too. Maybe I hadn't realized it. Maybe it wasn't a concerted effort on my part to find him. But I had been waiting. With every bad first date that I refused to revisit, and every pretend grown-up that I refused to call back, and every single attribute added to my picky list of qualifiers, I was shaping my desire for a man like Ezra. Hoping that he was real and that I could find him, and knowing that I would never, ever settle for anything less.

Now that I've found him? He was so much better than anything I could have imagined.

He was so much more than anything I could have dreamed up.

Best of all, he was real and really mine. Maybe he was right. Maybe we would fight, and bicker, and disagree. But every second together was infinitely better than apart. I would rather take his bossy, heavy-handed and stubbornly opinionated self than live one minute without him.

He laid me down on the bed, slowing our frantic kisses as he moved over my body. My blouse was left somewhere near the foot of the bed, and I was almost completely exposed to him in my bra and panties.

It didn't occur to me to be self-conscious. I was too wrapped up in the sensation of his lips moving over my skin, his teeth scraping across my nipple, his fingers disappearing inside me, bringing me closer to an edge that I was restless to find.

His mouth hovered over my breast and I made a sound I had never made before, half-mad with need for this man. His tongue moved slowly over my nipple, before he closed his lips around it and sucked it into his mouth. My fingers clutched the sheets to keep me anchored to the bed, the planet. His fingers did something wicked inside me, heightening pleasure until my back bowed off the bed and I lost my breath with need.

He looked up at me, his gaze so hot I felt it blaze across my skin. He held me there, halfway to bliss and irrevocably forever feelings. "Perfect, Molly. You're so fucking perfect."

"Ezra." I didn't have adequate words to reply with. I felt too much, wanted to say too much. There were a thousand thoughts racing through my head, at the same time my body hummed with desire for more of him, more of this, more of every single thing. Finally, I settled on a brave confession, something I didn't know I had the courage to say.

I placed my hand on his pounding heart and whispered, "This is forever for me. You are my forever. I don't care about your money or your job, or anything but you. I want you and that's it. I want you forever."

He struggled to swallow, gazing down at me with those words still reflected in his eyes, he could barely move his throat. And then, as if suddenly remembering what we were in the middle of doing, he snatched a condom out of the nightstand and got back to business.

He slid inside me and everything was right with the world. His hands braced his spectacular body over me while my legs wrapped around his waist. We wound together in a sweaty, desperate tangle of soul-deep emotions and fiery desire.

I had never experienced anything so satisfying or achingly lovely. He held onto me, whispering sweet, sexy things in my ear as his body moved over mine. I lost myself in his words, and touch. This man meant everything to me.

When we were both sated, limp with exhaustion and love, he pulled me against his body and wrapped his strong, safe arms around me.

"So I've been thinking," he murmured over my racing heart. "Now that you're jobless, I think I have a position that might interest you."

"Oh my god," I groaned. "Are you seriously talking about work *now*?"

He chuckled and his whole body vibrated with the relaxed sound. "You should know by now, I always talk work."

"You're a maniac."

"Social media specialist for EFB Enterprises. It comes with a pay raise."

"You don't even know what I make!"

"Then you should tell me, so I can guarantee a pay raise."

I turned in his arms, laying my head on his chest and tangling our legs together. The moment was absolutely perfection. The kind of moment all other moments would be compared to for the rest of my life. "What does the F stand for?"

He sounded sleepy when he murmured, "Hmm?"

"EFB. Ezra... what?"

"Felix. Ezra Felix Baptiste."

Raising up on one arm, my hair fell in a curtain around his face. "I'm not going to work for you, Ezra Felix Baptiste. But I will let you make me something to eat."

His sleepy eyes blinked. "I'll change your mind," he decided. "I always do."

I didn't respond, because I was afraid he was right.

That was the last we mentioned business that night. He threw on pajama pants and gave me a t-shirt, which meant all other over-sized t-shirts in my collection would hereby need to be burned. I was basically the Cinderella of boyfriend t's and I'd finally found the right fit.

We walked back downstairs to his kitchen where he made me eggs and toast, bacon and hollandaise sauce from scratch. We laughed and talked for hours, getting to know all the simple things about each other that would never get boring. And then he took me back to his bedroom where he made love to me again and then again.

I woke up the next morning wrapped in his arms and his blankets, with the crazy beautiful realization that I'd found my very own happily ever after.

Chapter Twenty-Five

$\mathcal{A}$ month later, on a hot June Saturday morning, I walked into Bianca like I owned the place. I didn't, obviously, but dating the owner had its perks. Bianca and Lilou, even Sarita and Quince, were all completely familiar to me. I still didn't always know what I was eating at them, but they were the places I spent the most time these days.

This morning, I had some finishing touches to make on the wall mural. It was finally finished.

Nobody greeted me as I slipped quietly into the restaurant and headed straight for the transformative piece that had taken me so long to accomplish.

Smoke danced from one side of the wall to the next—wispy, and dark, and emotive. I was proud of the way I'd shaded all of the different tendrils, giving it depth, making it come alive with hidden meaning. On the left, a pair of female eyes sat half-hidden under the cloak of gray and black. Cold and calculating, sad with unspoken grief. They were clearly feminine, but they were also mostly faded, barely visible in the rest of the scene.

In another two feet were another pair of eyes—they were hungry, desperate to fit in and be seen. In another couple feet a third pair, and then another pair after that. Each telling a tragic story that evoked sorrow and longing, leaving you with the feeling of something missing as real pieces of them had been left unpainted. Two more pairs of eyes could be seen on the far right, closer together than any of the others. Finally, there was hope. Finally, completion. They were brighter than the rest, meant to be there and connected by some unseen force. And all around the smoke swirled and billowed, becoming the most entrancing part of the mural.

Ezra had been a bit shocked to see that I'd painted his dating history on the wall of his restaurant. And embarrassed. But I assured him that only he knew the secrets of the painting, to everyone else it was only art.

In the end, he'd admitted that he couldn't stop looking at it. The mural had done exactly what he wanted it to do, which was fill the awkward space of his restaurant and give it a memorable quality.

And not only that, but I was finally happy with how his eyes had turned out, finally pleased with how I'd painted him.

They were deep and mysterious, but warm too, and kind. The eyebrows were exactly right and the lashes were thick and defining. They were eyes that you could fall in love with if you stared at them too often.

Eyes I did fall in love with.

I prepared my paints and readied my brush to add a few brushstrokes here and there. Ezra walked out from the kitchen, murmuring about asshole chefs.

"Any luck?" I asked him, already knowing what was on his mind.

"He's a fucking narcissist. He'll take the job as long as his film crew can come in and restructure the entire building for when they need to tape. Fucking reality shows," he growled. He held his thumb and forefinger an inch apart. "I'm this close to putting out a Craigslist ad."

I tried not to laugh or even smile. But his indignation was adorable. "Patience, babe. You'll find the right fit soon."

His attention turned to the mural. "It's stunning, Molly. Every time I walk out here, I'm blown away all over again. Hiring you was such a good decision on my part."

Of course he would take all the credit. "You're so smart," I deadpanned. "You're such a genius."

He flashed me a devilish grin. "Thank you."

Wrapping his arm around my shoulder, he pulled me against his chest. We stayed like that for a long moment, hugging, holding onto each other... holding each other.

We'd been nearly inseparable for the last month. It had been the most beautiful, blissful challenge of my life. He was a difficult man and it turned out I was obviously a kind of a difficult female. But we needed each other. Our push and pull was what made me keep falling for him more and more and more. Because apparently there was no end to how deep my feelings for this man could go.

256

The morning after I'd slept over at his apartment, he'd marched me into SixTwentySix and raised hell like he promised. I didn't need him to fight my battles for me, but dang was it nice to have him on my side.

His lawyer had joined us.

We went straight to the Mother Tucker's office and let him have it. It turned out Henry Junior had done exactly what I'd expected him to. He'd run to Daddy and they'd decided to fire me. Not deal with Junior's sexual deviance in any way. But fire *me*.

So, I quit.

And even though Henry had subsequently been put on probation and sent away for training and rehabilitation in sexual misconduct, Brent was still gathering a case. It included my testimony of course. And Catherine Dawes, who had come forward after I made such a scene and stormed out of the building with my dignity intact. There were three other women from the office who were also contributing to the case. They had been shut down by HR and Mr. Tucker just like I had.

I didn't know what would happen to STS because of the suit. But I had trouble caring. I was sad of course that so many people might be out of a job, but if they were smart, they would jump ship before worse came to worst.

Like Emily. Who had left STS the same day I did. We'd decided to open up a social media strategy consulting firm together. Thankfully, we knew some wealthy investors who were very interested in our services.

Obviously, Ezra. But Killian and Vera also wanted in. They were dying for our help as they got closer to the opening of Salt. Plus, Vann wanted to hire us as well. For being only a couple of weeks old, our client list was bomb.

Our friends were also extremely happy for us. After I officially quit STS, we'd met Vera and Killian for lunch. Our first double date. And it had been everything.

Vera was the biggest cheerleader for our relationship, although I still blamed her pending marital bliss for her over-the-top reaction.

But nobody had been as thrilled for us as Wyatt. Which might have sounded nice of him, but his felicitations were totally selfishly motivated. Apparently, Ezra in a committed relationship was a much easier man to work for.

I liked to take all of the credit for that. *You're welcome, chefs of Durham.*

"Jo wants us to come over for dinner tonight," Ezra said into my hair. "She says she wants to see this for herself."

"See what for herself?" I asked on a laugh. I had met Jo a couple times through Vera before, but not in this context with Ezra.

"You and me," he explained. "She doesn't believe me."

"My parents want to have us over tomorrow night," I countered. "They're having trouble believing this is real too."

Ezra pulled back, his hands holding my body like I was the most precious thing in the world and I could float away at any second. I loved the way he held me... held onto me. "What don't they believe?"

"That you're real. My mom, especially. She definitely thought I was going to marry a homeless man."

"I like your mom," he said on a smile. "She's terrifying."

He had to be lying. Nobody liked my mom. Not even Vera. Of course, Ezra would be the one person on the planet to appreciate her scariness. "She likes you for the same reason."

Leaning forward, he murmured, "I like your dad too. And I'm pretty sure he thinks I'm awesome."

"He doesn't." He totally did.

He smiled down at me. "I better win him over with his favorite six-pack then."

"That would definitely help your case," I told him. "What doesn't Jo believe?"

"That I'm in love," he answered easily like it wasn't the most profound thing he'd ever said. "She doesn't think I'm capable."

My heart hammered against my chest and my fingers went numb. Did he not realize he had never said that before?! That this was the first time ever I was hearing that crazy, beautiful, soul-changing admission. "I'm sorry, wh-what?" I gasped.

"She doesn't believe that I fell in love."

I blinked at him, vaguely aware that my mouth was unhinged. "Ezra," I pleaded.

"Oh, have I not told you that before?" His grin was wide, and cocky, and achingly real. "I've been thinking it for a while. It's hard to believe I haven't said it. Are you sure I haven't?"

"Don't torture me," I pleaded.

His expression softened and his hands began the slow, steady caress of a man that felt every ounce of truth in his words. "I love you, Molly Maverick." His lips dropped to mine, kissing as if sealing his confession in me. "I love you."

Unbidden tears pricked at the corners of my eyes. "I love you too, Ezra Felix Baptiste."

He let out an impatient sigh. "I keep telling you not to use my whole name."

I smiled, because I knew it drove him bananas. "I like it. No, wait. I love it."

His head cocked back. "Are you making fun of me for telling you I love you."

"No, I wouldn't do that." I tried to keep a straight face. "That doesn't sound like me at all."

"Unbelievable," he groaned. "You're completely unbelievable."

"But you love me anyway. I know because you just told me."

He didn't know whether to glare or laugh, so instead of either, he threw me over his shoulder and stomped back to his office. I laughed hysterically when he smacked my butt.

"Ezra Felix!" I shouted since we were the only ones in the restaurant.

"I'm going to make you pay for that, woman," he threatened.

And he did. In his office, with the door locked. With laughter that never left us and whispered I love yous that we absolutely meant. With kisses that I could never get enough of, and promises of a future together that would never get boring, never lose our push and pull, and never, ever end.

It didn't matter how different we were or how different we would always be, Ezra was now the driving force in my life that made everything else make sense. He was my anchor when I felt like I was lost and floating away. He was my common sense and reason, and also my relentless drive. And I was his reality check when work became his life and he forgot about everything else. I was the fun and meaningful purpose for why he strove so hard.

Yes, we were different, but only in the way two puzzle pieces are made to fit together exactly right. He was made for me and I was made for him. And we would spend the rest of our lives discovering all the ways we blended together.

Thinking back to when I met Ezra, I couldn't believe how wrong I'd gotten him. I'd expected arrogance and snobbery and aloof cruelty. Intsead, I'd found a man that was humble and devoted and so full of love I knew I would never get to the end of him. He swept me off my feet and changed my life forever. He'd closed the space between us and showed me just how perfect love can be.

Our story was a complex piece of art that we worked on every day. It wasn't always beautiful in the traditional sense, but it was captivating, and worthy and endless.

Our happily ever after was so different than what I'd pictured, but it was right. And it was ours.

Thank you for reading The Difference Between Us! I hope you enjoyed reading Ezra and Molly's story and fell in love with them as hard as I did! The third book in the Opposites Attract Series, The Problem with Him, is coming this November. Each book is a standalone romance following a different couple! Keep reading to find out more about Kaya Swift and Wyatt Shaw.

The Problem with Him coming November, 2017!

I'm over men.

I'm done with them.

Or at least the ones that work in my kitchen. Fine, one man in particular. Wyatt Shaw is cocky and condescending and so far out of his element that he doesn't know which way is up. Or how to run his brand new kitchen all by himself.

That's where I come in. Sous chef extraordinaire. Second in command. Bane of his existence. I am the reason Wyatt's doing so well as the new executive chef of one of our city's most prestigious restaurants. He has me to thank for his glowing accolades and five-star write-ups. Only if you were to ask him, he'd say I'm his biggest problem.

Despite his discouragement and bullish behavior, I've set two goals for myself.

The first? I'm going to fight my way to the top of this male-dominated industry and claim my own award-winning kitchen.

The second? I'm going to do whatever it takes to ignore Wyatt and his rare smiles and the thickening tension that's started to simmer between us.

Wyatt Shaw might be Durham's new shining star. He might be up for a James Beard Award. He might be my new boss and key to my future success, but he's also in my way.

So he can keep his smoldering looks and secret kisses. And he can be the one that figures out how to make it through service without getting distracted by me.

I'm not the problem.

The problem is him.

Acknowledgments

To God, who restores my soul, who sustains me, who gifted me these words and this book and every other thing. This is Your miracle. Thank You for letting me write it.

To Zach, thank you for your patience with dirty laundry and takeout for every meal and all the things I failed at this time around. You are my rock when I am falling apart and my anchor when I am overwhelmed. I couldn't do this life or this job or really anything without you. I love you.

To Stella, Scarlett, Stryker, Solo and Saxon. Thank you for being patient with me as I worked sleepless nights and forgot playdates and birthday parties and fed you pizza more than any mom ever should. Thank you for cheering me on and missing me and loving me through all of my flaws. I love you more than the sun and the moon and the stars. You're each my favorite.

To my mom, for all of those sleepovers and days that let me work. Thank you for being a Nana that my kids love and trust and want to spend time with. Thank you for swooping in to save the day just like you have all my life.

To Katie, thank you for being together when I am perpetually falling apart. Thank you for caring about my mess and my kids and my deadlines, even though none of it is yours. You are a doer of deeds, my friend. And this book couldn't have happened without your graciousness.

To Katie, Tiffany and Sarah Jo, thank you for being the friends I've waited for all my adult life. Thank you for your laughter and your prayers and stepping in as social media gurus when I disappeared into the writing cave. I'm a better human because I know you girls. #communelife

To Georgia, Shelly, Amy and Samantha, thank you for always being there for me, for always listening when I freak out and for always supporting me through everything. I could never survive this job without you. Your wisdom, your sane advice and your laughter saves me on a daily basis. I'm working on an island for us.

To Lenore, who is basically one of my favorite humans ever. Also, my favorite beta reader ever! Thank you for understanding who I am and how I function. Thank you for always being willing to squeeze my books in and cheer them on. I would not be the writer I am without your thoughtful notes and insightful eye. Oh, you're also my favorite Canadian!!!

To Amy Donnelly from Alchemy and Words. Let me just say that when life threw up all over me, you are the one that kept me sane! Thank you so much for encouraging me daily. Thank you for promising that we would get this done and that everything would be okay and for being right. Thank you for being the most flexible editor on the planet- you have no idea how much that means to me. But most of all, thank you for caring about my characters and plots and words as much as I do and for making them the very best that they can be.

To Caedus Design Co, thank you for your fantastic attention to detail and for making this cover smoking hot. Also, thank you for stepping in to make dinners all those times I forgot.

To the Rebel Panel. You ladies have supported me for so long now, I can't imagine releasing a book without you behind it! Thank you for putting up with my flakiness, for wanting ARCs even when they're last minute and for loving my characters as much as I do.

To the bloggers and reviewers, thank you so much for taking the time to read my words. I can't tell you how honored I am that you would choose this book in a sea of other amazing works. Your time, your thoughts and your support mean everything to me. The Difference Between Us is successful because of you all. I am so grateful for your help.

To the reader, whether you started with The Opposite of You or dove straight into the Difference Between Us. Whether you've been with me from the beginning or this is your first read of mine or you found me somewhere in the middle. Thank you for taking a chance on me and this book and these characters. You are the reason I get to keep writing and I am so grateful that you would spend your time with one of my stories.

About the Author

Rachel Higginson was born and raised in Nebraska, but spent her college years traveling the world. She fell in love with Eastern Europe, Paris, Indian Food and the beautiful beaches of Sri Lanka, but came back home to marry her high school sweetheart. Now she spends her days raising their growing family. She is obsessed with reruns of *The Office* and Cherry Coke.

Look for The Problem with Him coming November, 2017!

Other Books Out Now by Rachel Higginson:

Love and Decay, Season One
Volume One
Volume Two
Love and Decay, Season Two
Volume Three
Volume Four
Volume Five
Love and Decay, Season Three
Volume Six
Volume Seven
Volume Eight
Love and Decay: Revolution, Season One
Volume One
Volume Two

The Star-Crossed Series
Reckless Magic (The Star-Crossed Series, Book 1)
Hopeless Magic (The Star-Crossed Series, Book 2)
Fearless Magic (The Star-Crossed Series, Book 3)
Endless Magic (The Star-Crossed Series, Book 4)
The Reluctant King (The Star-Crossed Series, Book 5)
The Relentless Warrior (The Star-Crossed Series, Book 6)
Breathless Magic (The Star-Crossed Series, Book 6.5)
Fateful Magic (The Star-Crossed Series, Book 6.75)
The Redeemable Prince (The Star-Crossed Series, Book 7)

The Starbright Series

Heir of Skies (The Starbright Series, Book 1)
Heir of Darkness (The Starbright Series, Book 2)
Heir of Secrets (The Starbright Series, Book 3)

The Siren Series
The Rush (The Siren Series, Book 1)
The Fall (The Siren Series, Book 2)
The Heart (The Siren Series, Book 3)

Bet on Love Series
Bet on Us (An NA Contemporary Romance)
Bet on Me (An NA Contemporary Romance)

Every Wrong Reason

The Five Stages of Falling in Love

The Opposite of You

Connect with Rachel on her blog at:
http://www.rachelhigginson.com/

Or on Twitter:
@mywritesdntbite

Or on her Facebook page:
Rachel Higginson

Keep reading for an excerpt from Rachel's second chance romance,
The Five Stages of Falling in Love.

Prologue

"Hey, there she is," Grady looked up at me from his bed, his eyes smiling even while his mouth barely mimicked the emotion.

"Hey, you," I called back. The lights had been dimmed after the last nurse checked his vitals and the TV was on, but muted. "Where are the kiddos? I was only in the cafeteria for ten minutes."

Grady winked at me playfully, "My mother took them." I melted a little at his roguish expression. It was the same look that made me agree to a date with him our junior year of college, it was the same look that made me fall in love with him- the same one that made me agree to have our second baby boy when I would have been just fine to stop after Blake, Abby and Lucy.

"Oh, yeah?" I walked over to the hospital bed and sat down next to him. He immediately reached for me, pulling me against him with weak arms. I snuggled back into his chest, so that my head rested on his thin shoulder and our bodies fit side by side on the narrow bed. One of my legs didn't make it and hung off awkwardly. But I didn't mind. It was just perfect to lie next to the love of my life, my husband.

"Oh, yeah," he growled suggestively. "You know what that means?" He walked his free hand up my arm and gave my breast a wicked squeeze. "When the kids are away, the grownups get to play..."

"You are so bad," I swatted him- or at least made the motion of swatting at him, since I was too afraid to hurt him.

"God, I don't remember the last time I got laid," he groaned next to me and I felt the rumble of his words against my side.

"Tell me about it, sport," I sighed. "I could use a nice, hard-"

"Elizabeth Carlson," he cut in on a surprised laugh. "When did you get such a dirty mouth?"

"I think you've known about my dirty mouth for quite some time, Grady," I flirted back. We'd been serious for so long it was nice to flirt with him, to remember that we didn't just love each other, but we liked each other too.

He grunted in satisfaction. "That I have. I think your dirty mouth had something to do with Lucy's conception."

I blushed. Even after all these years, he knew exactly what to say to me. "Maybe," I conceded.

"Probably," he chuckled, his breath hot on my ear.

We lay there in silence for a while, enjoying the feel of each other, watching the silent TV screen flicker in front of our eyes. It was perfect- or as close to perfect as we had felt in a long time.

"Dance with me, Lizzy," Grady whispered after a while. I'd thought maybe he fell asleep; the drugs were so hard on his system that he was usually in and out of consciousness. This was actually the most coherent he'd been in a month.

"Okay," I agreed. "It's the first thing we'll do when you get out. We'll have your mom come over and babysit, you can take me to dinner at Pazio's and we'll go dancing after."

"Mmm, that sounds nice," he agreed. "You love Pazio's. That's a guaranteed get-lucky night for me."

"Baby," I crooned. "As soon as I get you back home, you're going to have guaranteed get-lucky nights for at least a month, maybe two."

"I don't want to wait. I'm tired of waiting. Dance with me now, Lizzy," Grady pressed, this time sounding serious.

"Babe, after your treatment this morning, you can barely stand up right now. Honestly, how are you going to put all those sweet moves on me?" I wondered where this sudden urge to dance, of all things, was coming from.

"Lizzy, I am a sick man. I haven't slept in my own bed in four months, I haven't seen my wife naked in just as long, and I am tired of lying in this bed. I want to dance with you. Will you please, pretty please, dance with me?"

I nodded at first because I was incapable of speech. He was right. I hated that he was right, but I hated that he was sick even more.

"Alright, Grady, I'll dance with you," I finally whispered.

"I knew I'd get my way," he croaked smugly.

I slipped off the bed and turned around to face my husband and help him to his feet. His once full head of auburn hair was now bald, reflecting the pallid color of his skin. His face was haggard showing dark black circles under his eyes, chapped lips and pale cheeks. He was still as tall as he'd ever been, but instead of the toned muscles and thick frame he once boasted, he was depressingly skinny and weak, his shoulders perpetually slumped.

The only thing that remained the same were his eyes; they were the same dark green eyes I'd fallen in love with ten years ago. They were still full of life, still full of mischief even when his body wasn't. They held life while the rest of him drowned in exhaustion from fighting this stupid sickness.

"You always get your way," I grumbled while I helped him up from the bed.

"Only with you," he shot back on a pant after successfully standing. "And only because you love me."

"That I do," I agreed. Grady's hands slipped around my waist and he clutched my sides in an effort to stay standing.

I wrapped my arms around his neck, but didn't allow any weight to press down on him. We maneuvered our bodies around his IV and monitors. It was awkward, but we managed.

"What should we listen to?" I asked, while I pulled out my cell phone and turned it to my iTunes app.

"You know what song. There is no other song when we're dancing," he reminded me on a faint smile.

"You must be horny," I laughed. "You're getting awfully romantic."

"Just trying to keep this fire alive, Babe," he pulled me closer and I held back the flood of tears that threatened to spill over.

I turned on *The Way You Look Tonight*- the Frank Sinatra version- and we swayed slowly back and forth. Frank sang the soft, beautiful lyrics with the help of a full band, while the music drifted around us over the constant beeping and whirring of medical machines. This was the song we thought of as ours, the first song we'd danced to at our wedding, the song he still made the band at Pazio's play on our anniversary each year.

"This fire is very much alive," I informed him sternly. I lay my forehead against his shoulder and inhaled him. He didn't smell like himself anymore, he was full of chemo drugs and smelled like hospital soap and detergent, but he was still Grady. And even though he barely resembled the man I had fallen so irrevocably in love with, he still *felt* like Grady.

He was still *my* Grady.

271

"It is, isn't it?" He whispered. I could feel how weak he was growing, how tired this was making him, but still he clung to me and held me close. When my favorite verse came on, he leaned his head down and whispered in a broken voice along with Frank, "There is nothing for me, but to love you. And the way you look tonight."

Silent tears streamed down my face with truths I wasn't ready to admit to myself and fears that were too horrifying to even think. This was the man I loved with every fiber of my being- the only man I'd ever loved. The only man I'd *ever love*.

He'd made me fall in love with him before I was old enough to drink legally, then he'd convinced me to marry him before I even graduated from college. He knocked me up a year later, and didn't stop until we had four wild rug rats that all had his red hair and his emerald green eyes. He'd encouraged me to finish my undergrad degree, and then to continue on to grad school while I was pregnant, nursing and then pregnant again. He went to bed every night with socks on and then took them off sometime in the middle of the night, leaving them obnoxiously tucked in between our sheets. He could never find his wallet, or his keys, and when there was hair to grow he always forgot to shave.

And he drove me crazy most of the time.

But he was mine.

He was my husband.

And now he was sick.

"I do love you, Lizzy," he murmured against my hair. "I'll always love you, even when I'm dead and gone."

"Which won't be for at least fifty more years," I reminded him on a sob.

He ignored me, "You love me back, don't you?"

"Yes, I love you back," I whispered with so much emotion the words stuck in my throat. "But you already knew that."

"Maybe," he conceded gently. "But I will never, ever get tired of hearing it."

I sniffled against him, staining his hospital gown with my mascara and eye liner. "That's a good thing, because you're going to be hearing it for a very long time."

He didn't respond, just kept swaying with me back and forth until the song ended. He asked me to play it again and I did, three more times. By the end of the fourth, he was too tired to stand. I laid him back in bed and helped him adjust the IV and monitor again so that it didn't bother him, then pulled the sheet over his cold toes.

His eyes were closed and I thought he'd fallen asleep, so I bent down to kiss his forehead. He stirred at my touch and reached out to cup my face with his un-needled arm. I looked down into his depthless green eyes and fell in love with him all over again.

It was as simple as that.

It had always been that simple for him to get me to fall in love with him.

"You are the most beautiful thing that ever happened to me, Lizzy." His voice was broken and scratchy and a tear slid out from the corner of each of his eyes.

My chin trembled at his words because I knew what he was doing and I hated it, I hated every part of it. I shook my head, trying to get him to stop but he held my gaze and just kept going.

"You are. And you have made my life good, and worth living. You have made me love more than any man has ever known how to love. I didn't know this kind of happiness existed in real life, Liz, and you're the one that gave it to me. I couldn't be more thankful for the life we've shared together. I couldn't be more thankful for you."

"Oh, Grady, please-"

"Lizzy," he said in his sternest voice that he only used when I'd maxed out a credit card. "Whatever happens, whatever happens to me, I want you to keep giving this gift to other people." I opened my mouth to vehemently object to everything he was saying but he silenced me with a cold finger on my lips. "I didn't say go marry the first man you find. Hell, I'm not even talking about another man. But I don't want this light to die with me. I don't want you to forget how happy you make other people just because you might not feel happy. Even if I don't, Lizzy, I want you to go on living. Promise me that."

But I shook my head, "No." I wasn't going to promise him that. I couldn't make myself. And it was unfair of him to ask me that.

"Please, Sweetheart, for me?" His deep, green eyes glossed over with emotion and I could physically feel how painful this was for him to ask me. He didn't want this anymore than I did.

I found myself nodding, while I sniffled back a stream of tears. "Okay," I whispered. "I promise."

He broke out into a genuine smile then, his thumb rubbing back and forth along my jaw. "Now tell me you love me, one more time."

"I love you, Grady," I murmured, leaning into his touch and savoring this moment with him.

"And I will always, always love you, Lizzy."

273

His eyes finally fluttered shut and his hand dropped from my face. His vitals remained the same, so I knew he was just sleeping. I crawled into bed with him, gently shifting him so that I could lie on my side, in the nook of his arm and lay my hand on his chest. I did this often; I liked to feel the beat of his heart underneath my hand. It had stopped too many times before, for me to trust its reliability. My husband was a very sick man, and had been for a while now.

Tonight was different though. Tonight, Grady was lucid and coherent, he'd found enough energy to stand up and dance with me, to tell me he loved me. Tonight could have been a turn for the better.

But it wasn't- because only a few hours later, Grady's heart stopped for the third time during his adult life, and this time it never restarted.

Stage One: Denial

*N*ot every story has a happy ending. Some only hold a happy beginning.

This is my story. I'd already met my soul mate, fallen in love with him and lived our happily ever after.

This story is not about me falling in love.

This story is about me learning to live again after love left my life.

Research shows there are five stages of grief. I don't know what this means for me, as I was stuck, nice and hard, in step one.

Denial.

I knew, acutely, that I was still in stage one.

I knew this because every time I walked in the house, I wandered around aimlessly looking for Grady. I still picked up my phone to check if he texted or called throughout the day. I looked for him in a crowded room, got the urge to call him from the grocery store just to make sure I had everything he needed, and reached for him in the middle of the night.

Acceptance- the last stage of grief- was firmly and forever out of my reach, and I often looked forward to it with longing. Why? Because Denial was a *son of a bitch* and it hurt more than *anything* when I realized he wasn't in the house, wouldn't be calling me, wasn't where I wanted him to be, didn't need anything from the store and would never lie next to me in bed again. The grief, fresh and suffocating, would cascade over me and

I was forced to suffer through the unbearable pain of losing my husband all over again.

Denial *sucked*.

But it was where I was right now. I was living in Denial.

Chapter One
Six Months after Grady died.

9 snuggled back into the cradle of his body while his arms wrapped around me tightly. He buried his scruffy face against the nape of my neck and I sighed contentedly. We fit perfectly together, but then again we always had- his big spoon nestled up against my little spoon.

"It's your turn," he rumbled against my skin with that deep morning voice I would always drink in.

"No," I argued half-heartedly. "It's always my turn."

"But you're so good at it," he teased.

I giggled, "It's one of my many talents, pouring cereal into bowls, making juice cups. I might just take this show on the road."

He laughed behind me and his chest shook with the movement. I pushed back into him, loving the feel of his hard, firm chest against my back. He was so hot first thing in the morning, his whole body radiated warmth.

His hand splayed out across my belly possessively and he pressed a kiss just below my ear. I could feel his lips through my tangle of hair and the tickle of his breath which wasn't all that pleasant first thing in the morning, but it was Grady and it was familiar.

"It's probably time we had another one, don't you think?" His hand rubbed a circle around my stomach and I could feel him vibrating happily with the thought.

"Grady, we already have three," I reminded him on a laugh. *"If we have another one, people are going to start thinking we're weird."*

"No, they won't," he soothed. *"They might get an idea of how fertile you are, but they won't think we're weird."*

I snorted a laugh. *"They already think we're weird."*

"Then we don't want to disappoint them," he murmured. His hand slid up my chest and cupped my breast, giving it a gentle squeeze.

"You are obsessed with those things," I grinned.

"Definitely," he agreed quickly, while continuing to fondle me. *"What do you think, Lizzy? Will you give me another baby?"*

I was getting wrapped up in the way he was touching me, the way he was caressing me with so much love I thought I would burst. *"I'll think about it,"* I finally conceded, knowing he would get his way- knowing I always let him have his way.

"While you're mulling it over, we should probably practice. I mean, we want to get this right when the time comes." Grady trailed kisses down the column of my throat and I moaned my consent.

I rolled over to kiss him on the mouth.

But he wasn't there.

My arm swung wide and hit cold, empty mattress.

I opened my eyes and stared at the slow moving ceiling fan over my head. The early morning light streamed in through cracks in my closed blinds and I let the silent tears fall.

I hated waking up like this; thinking he was there, next to me, still able to support me, love me and hold me. And unfortunately it happened more often than it didn't.

The fresh pain clawed and cut at my heart and I thought I would die just from sheer heartbreak. My chin quivered and I sniffled, trying desperately to wrestle my emotions under control. But the pain was too much, too consuming.

"Mom!" Blake called from the kitchen, ripping me away from my peaceful grief. "Moooooom!"

That was a distressed cry, and I was up out of my bed and racing downstairs immediately. I grabbed my silk robe on the way and threw it over my black cami and plaid pajama bottoms. When the kids were younger I wouldn't have bothered, but Blake was eight now and he'd been traumatized enough in life. I wasn't going to add to that by walking around bra-less first thing in the morning.

He continued to yell at me, while I barreled into the kitchen still wiping at the fresh tears. I found him at the bay windows, staring out in horror.

"Mom, Abby went swimming," he explained in a rush of words.

A sick feeling knotted my stomach and I looked around wild-eyed at what his words could possibly mean. "What do you mean, Abby *went swimming?*" I gasped, a little out of breath.

"There," he pointed to the neighbor's backyard with a shaky finger.

I followed the direction of his outstretched hand and from the elevated vantage point of our kitchen I could see that the neighbor's pool was filled with water, and my six-year-old daughter was swimming morning laps like she was on a regulated workout routine.

"What the f-" I started and then stopped, shooting a glance down at Blake who looked up at me with more exaggerated shock than he'd given his sister.

I watched her for point one more second and sprinted for the front door. "Keep an eye on the other ones," I shouted at Blake as I pushed open our heavy red door.

It was just early fall in rural Connecticut. The grass was still green; the mornings were foggy but mostly still warm. The house next to us had been empty for almost a year. The owner had been asking too much for it in this economy, but I understood why. It was beautiful, clean-lined and modern with cream stucco siding and black decorative shutters. Big oak trees offered shade and character in the sprawling front yard and in the back, an in-ground pool was the drool-worthy envy of my children.

I raced down my yard and into my new neighbor's. I hadn't noticed the house had sold, but that didn't surprise me. I wasn't the most observant person these days. Vaguely I noted a moving truck parked in the long drive.

The backyard gate must have been left open. Even though Abby had taught herself how to swim at the age of four- the end result gave me several gray hairs- there was no way she could reach the flip lock at the top of the tall, white fence.

I rounded the corner and hopped/ran to the edge of the pool, the gravel of the patio cutting into my bare feet. I took a steadying breath and focused my panic-flooded mind long enough to assess whether Abby was still breathing or not.

She was, and happily swimming in circles *in the deep end.*

Fear and dread quickly turned to blinding anger and I took a step closer to the edge of the pool while I threw my silk robe on the ground.

"Abigail Elizabeth, you get out of there right this minute!" I shouted loud enough to wake up the entire neighborhood.

She popped her head up out of the water, acknowledged me by sticking out her tongue, and promptly went back to swimming. *That little brat.*

"Abigail, I am *not* joking. Get out of the pool. *Now!*" I hollered again. And was ignored- again. "Abby, if I have to come in there and get you, you will rue the day you were born!"

She poked her head back up out of the water, shooting me a confused look. Her light brown eyebrows drew together, just like her father's used to, and her little freckled nose wrinkled at something I said. I was smart enough or experienced enough to know that she was not on the verge of obeying, just because I'd threatened her.

"Mommy?" she asked, somehow making her little body tread water in a red polka dot bikini my sister picked up from Gap last summer. It was too small, which for some reason infuriated me even more. "What does *rue* mean?"

"It means you're grounded from the iPad, your Leapster and the Wii for the next two years of your life," I threatened. "Now get out of that pool right now before I come in there and get you myself."

She giggled in reply, not believing me for one second, and resumed her play.

"Damn it, Abigail," I growled under my breath but was not surprised by her behavior. She was naturally an adventurous child. Since she could walk, she'd been climbing to the highest point of anything she could, swinging precariously from branches, light fixtures and tall displays at the grocery store. She was a daredevil and there were moments when I absolutely adored her "the world is my playground" attitude about life. But then there were moments like this, when every mom instinct in me screamed she was in danger and her little, rotten life flashed before my eyes.

Those moments happened more and more often. She tested me, pushing every limit and boundary I'd set. She had been reckless before Grady died, now she was just wild. And I didn't know what to do about it.

I didn't know how to tame my uncontrollable child or how to be both parents to a little girl who desperately missed her daddy.

I focused on my outrage, pushing those tragic thoughts down, into the abyss of my soul. I was pissed; I didn't have time for this first thing in the morning and no doubt we were going to be late for school- again.

I slipped off my pajama pants, hoping whomever had moved into the house, if they were watching, would be more concerned with the little girl on the verge of drowning than me flashing my black, bikini briefs at them over morning coffee. I said a few more choice curses and dove into the barely warm water after my second born.

I surfaced, sputtering water and shivering from the cool morning air pebbling my skin. "Abigail, when I get you out of this pool, you are going to be in *so* much trouble."

"Okay," she agreed happily. "But first you have to catch me."

She proceeded to swim around in circles while I reached out helplessly for her. First thing I would do when I got out of this pool was throw away every electronic device in our house just to teach her a lesson. Then I was going to sign her up for a swim team because the little hellion was too fast for her own good.

We struggled like this for a few more minutes. Well, I struggled. She splashed at me and laughed at my efforts to wrangle her.

I was aware of a presence hovering by the edge of the pool, but I was equally too embarrassed and too preoccupied to acknowledge it. Images of walking my children into school late *again*, kept looping through my head and I cringed at the dirty looks I was bound to get from teachers and other parents alike.

"You look hungry," a deep masculine voice announced from above me.

I whipped my head around to find an incredibly tall man standing by my discarded pajama pants holding two beach towels and a box of Pop-Tarts in one arm, while he munched casually on said Pop-Tarts with the other.

"I look hungry?" I screeched in hysterical anger.

His eyes flickered down at me for just a second, "No, you look mad." He pointed at Abby, who had come to a stop next to me, treading water again with her short child-sized limbs waving wildly in the water. "*She* looks hungry." With a mouth full of food he grinned at me, and looked back at Abby. "Want a Pop-Tart? They're brown sugar."

Abby nodded excitedly and swam to the edge of the pool. Not even using the ladder, she heaved herself out of the water and ran over to the stranger holding out his breakfast to her. He handed her a towel and she hastily draped it around her shoulders and took the offered Pop-Tart.

A million warnings about taking food from strangers ran through my head, but in the end I decided getting us out of his pool was probably more important to him than offering his brand new neighbors poisoned Pop-Tarts.

With a defeated sigh, I swam over to the ladder closest to my pants and robe, and pulled myself up. I was a dripping, limp mess and frozen to the bone after my body adjusted to the temperature of the water.

Abby took her Pop-Tart and plopped down on one of the loungers that were still stacked on top of two others and wrapped in plastic. She began munching on it happily, grinning at me like she'd just won the lottery.

She was in *so* much trouble.

I walked over to the stranger, eying him skeptically. He held out his remaining beach towel to me and after realizing I stood before him in only a soaking wet tank top and bikini briefs, I took it quickly and wrapped it around my body. I shivered violently with my dark blonde hair dripping down my face and back. But I didn't dare adjust the towel, afraid I'd give him more of a show than he'd paid for.

"Good morning," he laughed at me.

"Good morning," I replied slowly, carefully.

Up close, he wasn't the giant I'd originally thought. Now that we were both ground level, I could see that while he was tall, at least six inches taller than me, he wasn't freakishly tall, which relieved some of my concerns. He still wore his pajamas: blue cotton pants and a white t-shirt that had been stretched out from sleep. His almost black hair appeared still mussed and disheveled, but swept over to the side in what could be a trendy style if he brushed it. He seemed to be a few years older than me, if I had to guess thirty-five or thirty-six, and he had dark, intelligent eyes that crinkled in the corners with amusement. He was tanned, and muscular, and imposing. And I hated that he was laughing at me.

"Sorry about the gate," he shrugged. "I didn't realize there were kids around."

"You moved into a neighborhood," I pointed out dryly. "There're bound to be kids around."

His eyes narrowed at the insult, but he swallowed his Pop-Tart and agreed, "Fair enough. I'll keep it locked from now on."

I wasn't finished with berating him though. His pool caused all kinds of problems for me this morning and since I could only take out so much anger on my six-year-old, I had to vent the rest somewhere. "Who fills their pool the first week of September anyway? You've been to New England in the winter, haven't you?"

He cleared his throat and the last laugh lines around his eyes disappeared. "My real estate agent," he explained. "It was kind of like a 'thank you' present for buying the house. He thought he was doing something nice for me."

I snorted at that, thinking how my little girl could have… No, I couldn't go there; I was not emotionally capable of thinking that thought through.

"I really am sorry," he offered genuinely, his dark eyes flashing with true emotion. "I got in late last night, and passed out on the couch. I didn't even know the pool was full or the gate was open until I heard you screaming out here."

Guilt settled in my stomach like acid, and I regretted my harsh tone with him. This wasn't his fault. I just wanted to blame someone besides myself.

"Look, I'm sorry I was snappish about the pool. I just... I was just worried about Abby. I took it out on you," I relented, but wouldn't look him in the eye. I'd always been terrible at apologies. When Grady and I would fight, I could never bring myself to tell him I felt sorry. Eventually, he'd just look at me and say, "I forgive you, Lizzy. Now come here and make it up to me." With anyone else my pride would have refused to let me give in, but with Grady, the way he smoothed over my stubbornness and let me get away with keeping my dignity worked every single time.

"It's alright, I can understand that," my new neighbor agreed.

We stood there awkwardly for a few more moments, before I swooped down to pick up my plaid pants and discarded robe. "Alright, well I need to go get the kids ready for school. Thanks for convincing her to get out. Who knows how long we would have been stuck there playing *Finding Nemo*."

He chuckled but his eyes were confused. "Is that like Marco Polo?"

I shot him a questioning glance, wondering if he was serious or not. "No kids?" I asked.

He laughed again. "Nope, life-long bachelor." He waved the box of Pop-Tarts and realization dawned on me. He hadn't really seemed like a father before now, but in my world- my four kids, soccer mom, neighborhood watch secretary, active member of the PTO world- it was almost unfathomable to me that someone his age could not have kids.

I cleared my throat, "It's uh, a little kid movie. Disney," I explained and understanding lit his expression. "Um, thanks again." I turned to Abby who was finishing up her breakfast, "Let's go, Abs, you're making us late for school."

"I'm Ben by the way," he called out to my back. "Ben Tyler."

I snorted to myself at the two first names; it somehow seemed appropriate for the handsome life-long bachelor, but ridiculous all the same.

"Liz Carlson," I called over my shoulder. "Welcome to the neighborhood."

"Uh, the towels?" he shouted after me when we'd reached the gate.

I turned around with a dropped mouth, thinking a hundred different vile things about my new neighbor. "Can't we... I..." I glanced down helplessly at my bare legs poking out of the bottom of the towel he'd just lent me.

"Liz," he laughed familiarly, and I tried not to resent him. "I'm just teasing. Bring them back whenever."

I growled something unintelligible that I hope sounded like "thank you" and spun on my heel, shooing Abby onto the lawn between our houses.

"Nice to meet you, neighbor," he called out over the fence.

"You too," I mumbled, not even turning my head to look back at him.

Obviously he was single and unattached. He was way too smug for his own good. I just hoped he would keep his gate locked and loud parties few and far between. He seemed like the type to throw frat party-like keggers and hire strippers for the weekend. I had a family to raise, a family that was quickly falling apart while I floundered to hold us together with tired arms and a broken spirit. I didn't need a nosy neighbor handing out Pop-Tarts and sarcasm interfering with my life.

Made in the USA
Middletown, DE
19 May 2018